PHILI

In 1997 Philip Roth won th
American Pastoral. In 1998 he received the
National Medal of Arts at the White House,
and in 2002 the highest award of the American
Academy of Arts and Letters, the Gold Medal in
Fiction, previously awarded to John Dos Passos,
William Faulkner and Saul Bellow, among others.
He has twice won the National Book Award
and the National Book Critics Circle Award. He
has won the PEN/Faulkner Award three times.
In 2005 *The Plot Against America* received the
Society of American Historians' Prize for 'the
outstanding historical novel on an American
theme for 2003–2004'.

Recently Roth received PEN's two most prestigious
prizes: in 2006 the PEN/Nabokov Award 'for
a body of work . . . of enduring originality and
consummate craftsmanship' and in 2007 the
PEN/Saul Bellow Award for Achievement in
American Fiction, given to a writer whose 'scale
of achievement over a sustained career . . . places
him or her in the highest rank of American
literature'. In 2011 Roth won the International
Man Booker Prize.

Roth is the only living American writer to have
his work published in a comprehensive, definitive

ALSO BY PHILIP ROTH

Zuckerman Books

The Ghost Writer
Zuckerman Unbound
The Anatomy Lesson
The Prague Orgy

The Counterlife

American Pastoral
I Married a Communist
The Human Stain

Exit Ghost

Roth Books

The Facts
Deception • Patrimony
The Plot Against America

Kepesh Books

The Breast
The Professor of Desire
The Dying Animal

Nemeses: Short Novels

Everyman • Indignation
The Humbling • Nemesis

Miscellany

Reading Myself and Others
Shop Talk

Other Books

Goodbye, Columbus • Letting Go
When She Was Good • Portnoy's Complaint • Our Gang
The Great American Novel • My Life as a Man
Sabbath's Theater

PHILIP ROTH

Operation Shylock

A Confession

VINTAGE

20

Vintage,
20 Vauxhall Bridge Road,
London SW1V 2SA

Vintage is part of the Penguin Random House group of companies
whose addresses can be found at global.penguinrandomhouse.com

 Penguin
Random House
UK

This edition reissued in Vintage in 2016
First published by Vintage in 1994
First published in Great Britain in 1993 by Jonathan Cape

penguin.co.uk/vintage

A CIP catalogue record for this book is
available from the British Library

ISBN 9780099307914

Printed and bound in Great Britain by Clays Ltd,Elcograf S.p.A.

Penguin Random House is committed to a sustainable future
for our business, our readers and our planet. This book is made
from Forest Stewardship Council® certified paper.

FOR CLAIRE

Contents

PREFACE, 13

I

1 · Pipik Appears, 17
2 · A Life Not My Own, 49
3 · We, 70
4 · Jewish Mischief, 103
5 · I Am Pipik, 138

II

6 · His Story, 175
7 · Her Story, 215
8 · The Uncontrollability of Real Things, 239
9 · Forgery, Paranoia, Disinformation, Lies, 282
10 · You Shall Not Hate Your Brother in Your Heart, 321

EPILOGUE:
Words Generally Only Spoil Things, 355

NOTE TO THE READER, 399

וַיִּוָּתֵר יַעֲקֹב לְבַדּוֹ וַיֵּאָבֵק
אִישׁ עִמּוֹ עַד עֲלוֹת הַשָּׁחַר

So Jacob was left alone, and a man wrestled with him until daybreak.

—GENESIS 32:24

The whole content of my being shrieks in contradiction against itself.

Existence is surely a debate . . .

—KIERKEGAARD

Operation Shylock

Preface

For legal reasons, I have had to alter a number of facts in this book. These are minor changes that mainly involve details of identification and locale and are of little significance to the overall story and its verisimilitude. Any name that has been changed is marked with a small circle the first time it appears.

I've drawn *Operation Shylock* from notebook journals. The book is as accurate an account as I am able to give of actual occurrences that I lived through during my middle fifties and that culminated, early in 1988, in my agreeing to undertake an intelligence-gathering operation for Israel's foreign intelligence service, the Mossad.

The commentary on the Demjanjuk case reflects accurately and candidly what I was thinking in January 1988, nearly five years before Soviet evidence introduced on appeal by the defense led the Israeli Supreme Court to consider vacating the death sentence handed down in 1988 by the Jerusalem District Court, whose sessions I attended and describe here. On the basis of Soviet interrogations dating from 1944 to 1960 that came fully to light only after the demise of

the Soviet Union—and in which twenty-one former Red Army soldiers who volunteered to become SS auxiliaries and whom the Soviet
authorities later executed established the surname of Treblinka's Ivan
the Terrible to have been Marchenko and not Demjanjuk—the defense contended that it was impossible for the prosecution to prove
beyond a shadow of a doubt that the Cleveland autoworker John Ivan
Demjanjuk and the notorious gas-chamber operator were the same
"Ivan." The prosecution's rebuttal claimed not only that the records
from the old Soviet Union were riddled with inconsistencies and
contradictions but that, even more importantly, because the evidence
had been taken under unascertainable circumstances from guards no
longer available for cross-examination, it was inadmissible hearsay. In
addition the prosecution argued that newly discovered documentation from German federal archives now proved conclusively that
Demjanjuk had perjured himself repeatedly in denying that he had
also been a guard at the Trawniki training camp, the Flossenburg
concentration camp, and the Sobibor death camp.

As of this date, the Supreme Court is still deliberating the appeal.

P.R.

December 1, 1992

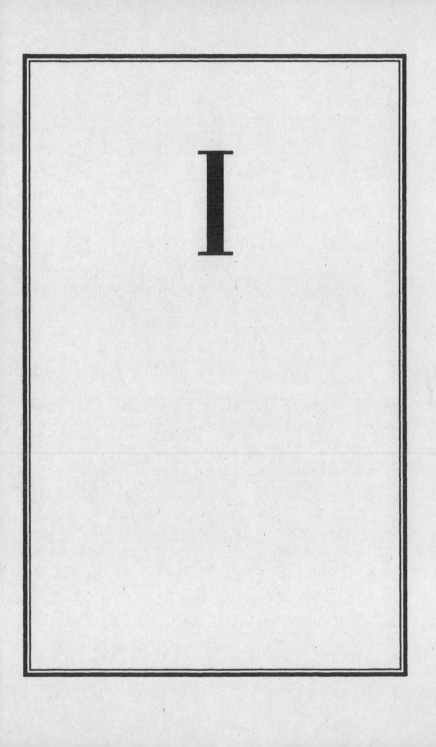

I

1

Pipik
Appears

I learned about the other Philip Roth in January 1988, a few days
after the New Year, when my cousin Apter° telephoned me in New
York to say that Israeli radio had reported that I was in Jerusalem
attending the trial of John Demjanjuk, the man alleged to be Ivan the
Terrible of Treblinka. Apter told me that the Demjanjuk trial was
being broadcast, in its entirety, every day, on radio and TV. According
to his landlady, I had momentarily appeared on the TV screen the day
before, identified by the commentator as one of the courtroom spectators, and then this very morning he had himself heard the corroborating news item on the radio. Apter was calling to check on my
whereabouts because he had understood from my last letter that I
wasn't to be in Jerusalem until the end of the month, when I planned
to interview the novelist Aharon Appelfeld. He told his landlady that
if I were in Jerusalem I would already have contacted him, which was
indeed the case—during the four visits I had made while I was working up the Israel sections of *The Counterlife,* I'd routinely taken Apter
to lunch a day or two after my arrival.

This cousin Apter—twice removed on my mother's side—is an unborn adult, in 1988 a fifty-four-year-old who had evolved into manhood without evolving, an under-life-size, dollish-looking man with the terrifyingly blank little face of an aging juvenile actor. There is imprinted on Apter's face absolutely nothing of the mayhem of Jewish life in the twentieth century, even though in 1943 his entire family had been consumed by the German mania for murdering Jews. He had been saved by a German officer who'd kidnapped him at the Polish transport site and sold him to a male brothel in Munich. This was a profitable sideline the officer had. Apter was nine. He remains chained to his childishness to this day, someone who still, in late middle age, cries as easily as he blushes and who can barely meet one's level gaze with his own chronically imploring eyes, someone whose whole life lies in the hands of the past. For that reason, I didn't believe any of what he said to me on the phone about another Philip Roth, who had showed up in Jerusalem without letting him know. His hunger is unappeasable for those who are not here.

But four days later I received a second call in New York about my presence in Jerusalem, this one from Aharon Appelfeld. Aharon had been a close friend since we'd met at a reception given for him by Israel's London cultural attaché in the early eighties, when I was still living most of each year in London. The American publication of his newly translated novel, *The Immortal Bartfuss,* was to be the occasion for the conversation I'd arranged to conduct with him for *The New York Times Book Review.* Aharon phoned to tell me that at the Jerusalem café where he went to write every day, he'd picked up the previous weekend's edition of *The Jerusalem Post* and, on the page-long listing of the coming week's cultural events, under Sunday, come on a notice he thought I should know about. Had he seen it a few days earlier, Aharon said, he would have attended the event as my silent emissary.

"Diasporism: The Only Solution to the Jewish Problem." A lecture by Philip Roth; discussion to follow. 6:00 P.M. Suite 511, King David Hotel. Refreshments.

I spent all that evening wondering what to do about Aharon's confirmation of Apter's news. Finally, having convinced myself during a largely sleepless night that some fluky series of errors had resulted in a mix-up of identities that it was in my best interest to disregard, I got out of bed early the next morning and, before I had even washed my face, telephoned suite 511 of Jerusalem's King David Hotel. I asked the woman who answered—and who answered speaking American English—if a Mr. Roth was there. I heard her call out to someone, "Hon—you." Then a man came on the line. I asked if this was Philip Roth. "It is," he replied, "and who is this, please?"

———

The calls from Israel had reached me at the two-room Manhattan hotel suite where my wife and I had been living for nearly five months, as though aground on the dividing line between past and future. The impersonality of big-city hotel life was most uncongenial to the domestic instinct so strong in both of us, yet ill-equipped though we were to be displaced and to be living together in this uprooted, unfamiliar way, it was preferable for the time being to our returning to the Connecticut farmhouse where, during the previous spring and early summer, while Claire stood helplessly by, fearing the worst, I had barely made it through the most harrowing exigency of my life. Half a mile from the nearest neighbor's dwelling and encompassed by woods and open fields at the end of a long dirt road, that large, secluded old house whose setting had for over fifteen years furnished just the isolation my concentration required had become the eerie backdrop for a bizarre emotional collapse; that cozy clapboard sanctuary, with its wide chestnut floorboards and worn easy chairs, a place where books were piled everywhere and a log fire burned high in the hearth most every night, had suddenly become a hideous asylum confining side by side one abominable lunatic and one bewildered keeper. A place I loved had come to fill me with dread, and I found myself reluctant to resume our residence there even after we'd mislaid these five months as hotel refugees and my familiar industrious personality had drifted back to take the reins and set me again to trotting reliably enough along the good old rut of my life. (Drifted back tentatively at the start, by no means convinced that things were as secure as they had seemed before; drifted back rather the way the work force standing out in the street drifts back into an office building that has been temporarily cleared because of a bomb scare.)

What had happened was this:

In the aftermath of minor knee surgery, my pain, instead of diminishing as the weeks passed, got worse and worse, far exceeding the prolonged discomfort that had prompted me to decide on surgery in the first place. When I went to see my young surgeon about the worsening condition, he merely said, "This happens sometimes," and, claiming to have warned me beforehand that the operation might not work, dismissed me as his patient. I was left with only some pills to mitigate my astonishment and manage the pain. Such a surprising outcome from a brief outpatient procedure might have made anyone angry and despondent; what happened in my case was worse.

My mind began to disintegrate. The word DISINTEGRATION seemed itself to be the matter out of which my brain was constituted, and it began spontaneously coming apart. The fourteen letters, big, chunky, irregularly sized components of my brain, elaborately intertwined, tore jaggedly loose from one another, sometimes a fragment of a letter at a time, but usually in painfully unpronounceable nonsyllabic segments of two or three, their edges roughly serrated. This mental coming apart was as distinctly physical a reality as a tooth being pulled, and the agony of it was excruciating.

Hallucinations like these and worse stampeded through me day and night, a herd of wild animals I could do nothing to stop. I couldn't stop anything, my will blotted out by the magnitude of the tiniest, most idiotic thought. Two, three, four times a day, without provocation or warning, I'd begin to cry. It didn't matter if I was alone in my studio, turning the page of yet another book that I couldn't read, or at dinner with Claire, looking hopelessly at the food she'd prepared that I couldn't find any reason to eat—I cried. I cried before friends, before strangers; even sitting alone on the toilet I would dissolve, wring myself dry with tears, an outpouring of tears that left me feeling absolutely raw—shorn by tears of five decades of living, my inmost being lay revealed to everyone in all its sickly puniness.

I could not forget my shirtsleeves for two minutes at a time. I couldn't seem to prevent myself from feverishly rolling up my shirtsleeves and then rolling them down just as feverishly and meticulously buttoning the cuff, only immediately to unbutton the cuff and begin the meaningless procedure once more, as though its meaning went, in fact, to the core of my existence. I couldn't stop flinging open the windows and then, when my claustrophobic fit had given way to chills, banging them shut as though it were not I but someone else who had flung them all open. My pulse rate would shoot up to 120 beats a minute even while I sat, brain-dead, in front of the nightly TV news, a corpse but for a violently thumping heart that had taken to keeping time to a clock ticking twice as fast as any on earth. That was another manifestation of the panic that I could do nothing to control: panic sporadically throughout the day and then without letup, titanically, at night.

I dreaded the hours of darkness. Climbing the obstacle course of stairs to our bedroom one painful step at a time—bending the good leg, dragging the bad leg—I felt myself on the way to a torture session that this time I couldn't survive. My only chance of getting through to daylight without having my mind come completely apart was to hook hold of a talismanic image out of my most innocent past and try to ride out the menace of the long night lashed to the mast of that recollection. One that I worked hysterically hard, in a kind of convulsion of yearning, to summon forth to save me was of my older brother guiding me along our street of rooming houses and summer cottages to the boardwalk and down the flight of wooden steps to the beach at the Jersey shore town where our family rented a room for a month each summer. *Take me, Sandy, please.* When I thought (oftentimes mistakenly) that Claire was asleep, I would chant this incantation aloud, four childish words that I had not uttered so passionately, if ever at all, since 1938, when I was five and my attentive, protective brother was ten.

I wouldn't let Claire draw the shades at night, because I had to
know the sun was rising the very second that sunrise began; but each
morning, when the panes began to lighten in the east-facing windows
just to the side of where I lay, whatever relief I felt from my terror of
the night that had just ended was copiously displaced by my terror
of the day about to begin. Night was interminable and unbearable,
day was interminable and unbearable, and when I reached into my
pillbox for the capsule that was supposed to carve a little hole where
I could hide for a few hours from all the pain that was stalking me, I
couldn't believe (though I had no choice but to believe) that the
fingers trembling in the pillbox were mine. "Where's Philip?" I said
hollowly to Claire while I stood gripping her hand at the edge of the
pool. For summers on end I had swum regularly in this pool for thirty
minutes at the end of each day; now I was fearful of even putting in a
toe, overwhelmed by the pretty, summery surface sheen of those
thousands of gallons of water in which I was sure to be sucked under
for good. "Where is Philip Roth?" I asked aloud. "Where did he go?"
I was not speaking histrionically. I asked because I wanted to know.

This and more like it lasted one hundred days and one hundred
nights. If anyone had telephoned then to say that Philip Roth had
been spotted at a war-crimes trial in Jerusalem or was advertised in
the Jerusalem paper as lecturing at the King David Hotel on the
only solution to the Jewish problem, I can't imagine what I would
have done. As thoroughly enveloped as I was in the disaster of self-
abandonment, it might have furnished corroboratory evidence just
unhinging enough to convince me to go ahead and commit suicide.
Because I thought about killing myself all the time. Usually I thought
of drowning: in the little pond across the road from the house . . . if I
weren't so horrified of the water snakes there nibbling at my corpse;
in the picturesque big lake only a few miles away . . . if I weren't so
frightened of driving out there alone. When we came to New York
that May for me to receive an honorary degree from Columbia, I
opened the window of our fourteenth-floor hotel room after Claire
had momentarily gone downstairs to the drugstore and, leaning as far
out over the interior courtyard as I could while still holding tight to

the sill, I told myself, "Do it. No snakes to stop you now." But there was my father to stop me now; he was coming from New Jersey the next day to see me get my degree. Jokingly on the phone he'd taken to calling me "Doctor," just as he'd done on the previous occasions when I was about to receive one of these things. I'd wait to jump until after he went home.

At Columbia, facing from the platform the several thousand people gathered festively together in the big sunny library plaza to watch the commencement exercises, I was convinced that I couldn't make it through the afternoon-long ceremony without beginning either to scream aloud or to sob uncontrollably. I'll never know how I got through that day or through the dinner welcoming the honorary-degree candidates the evening before without letting on to every-body who saw me that I was a man who was finished and about to prove it. Nor will I ever know what I might have gone ahead to do halfway out the hotel window that morning or even on the platform the next day, had I not been able to interpose between my denuded self and its clamorous longing for obliteration the devotion linking me to an eighty-six-year-old father whose life my death by suicide would smash to smithereens.

After the ceremony at Columbia, my father came back to the hotel with us for a cup of coffee. He'd surmised weeks before that some-thing was critically wrong even though I insisted, when we saw each other or spoke on the phone, that it was only the persistence of the physical pain that was getting me down. "You look drained," he said, "you look awful." How I looked had made his own face go ashen— and he was as yet suffering from no fatal disease, as far as anyone knew. "Knee," I replied. "Hurts." And said no more. "This isn't like you, Phil, you take everything in your stride." I smiled. "I do?" "Here," he said, "open it when you get home," and he handed me a package that I could tell he had encased himself in its bulky brown-paper wrapping. He said, "To go with your new degree, Doctor."

What he gave me was a framed five-by-seven portrait photo taken by a Metropolitan Life photographer some forty-five years earlier, on the occasion of my father's Newark district's winning one of the

company's coveted sales awards. There, as I could barely remember
him now, was the striving, undeflectable insurance man out of my
early grade school years, conventionally stolid-looking in the American style of the Depression era: neatly knotted conservative tie;
double-breasted business suit; thinning hair closely cut; level, steady
gaze; congenial, sober, restrained smile—the man that the boss wants
on his team and that the customer can believe is a balanced person,
a card-carrying member of the everyday world. "Trust me," the face
in the portrait proclaimed. "Work me. Promote me. You will not be
let down."

When I telephoned from Connecticut the next morning, planning
to tell him all too truthfully how the gift of that old picture had
buoyed me, my father suddenly heard his fifty-four-year-old son sobbing as he hadn't sobbed since his infancy. I was astonished by how
unalarmed his reaction was to what must have sounded like nothing
short of a complete collapse. "Go ahead," he said, as though he knew
everything I'd been hiding from him and, just because he knew everything, had decided, seemingly out of the blue, to give me that photograph picturing him at his most steadfast and determined. "Let it all
out," he said very softly, "whatever it is, let it all come out. . . ."

I'm told that all the misery I've just described was caused by the
sleeping pill that I was taking every night, the benzodiazepine triazolam marketed as Halcion, the pill that has lately begun to be charged
with driving people crazy all over the globe. In Holland, distribution
of Halcion had been prohibited entirely since 1979, two years after it
was introduced there and eight years before it was prescribed for me;
in France and Germany, doses of the size I was taking nightly had
been removed from the pharmacies in the 1980s; and in Britain it
was banned outright following a BBC television exposé aired in the
fall of 1991. *The* revelation—which came as less than a revelation to
someone like me—occurred in January 1992, with a long article in
The New York Times whose opening paragraphs were featured prominently on the front page. "For two decades," the piece began, "the

drug company that makes Halcion, the world's best-selling sleeping pill, concealed data from the Food and Drug Administration showing that it caused significant numbers of serious psychiatric side effects. . . ."

It was eighteen months after my breakdown that I first read a comprehensive indictment of Halcion—and a description of what the author called "Halcion madness"—in a popular American magazine. The article quoted from a letter in *The Lancet,* the British medical journal, in which a Dutch psychiatrist listed symptoms associated with Halcion that he had discovered in a study of psychiatric patients who had been prescribed the drug; the list read like a textbook summary of my catastrophe: ". . . severe malaise; depersonalization and derealization; paranoid reactions; acute and chronic anxiety; continuous fear of going insane; . . . patients often feel desperate and have to fight an almost irresistible impulse to commit suicide. I know of one patient who did commit suicide."

It was only through a lucky break that instead of having eventually to be hospitalized myself—or perhaps even buried—I came to withdraw from Halcion and my symptoms began to subside and disappear. One weekend early in the summer of 1987, my friend Bernie Avishai drove down from Boston to visit me after having become alarmed by my suicidal maunderings over the phone. I was by then three months into the suffering and I told him, when we were alone together in my studio, that I had decided to commit myself to a mental institution. Holding me back, however, was my fear that once I went in I'd never come out. Somebody had to convince me otherwise—I wanted Bernie to. He interrupted to ask a question whose irrelevance irritated me terribly: "What are you on?" I reminded him that I didn't take drugs and was "on" nothing, only some pills to help me sleep and to calm me down. Angered by his failure to grasp the severity of my situation, I confessed the shameful truth about myself as forthrightly as I could. "I've cracked up. I've broken down. Your friend here is mentally ill!" "Which pills?" he replied.

A few minutes later he had me on the phone to the Boston psychopharmacologist who just the previous year, I later learned, had saved

Bernie from a Halcion-induced breakdown very much like mine. The doctor asked me first how I was feeling; when I told him, he, in turn, told me what I was taking to make me feel that way. I refused at first to accept that all this pain stemmed simply from a sleeping pill and insisted that he, like Bernie, was failing to understand the *ghastliness* of what I was going through. Eventually, with my permission, he telephoned my local doctor and, under their joint supervision, I began that night to come off the drug, a process that I wouldn't care to repeat a second time and that I didn't think I'd live through the first. "Sometimes," the Dutch psychiatrist, Dr. C. van der Kroef, had written in *The Lancet,* "there are withdrawal symptoms, such as rapidly mounting panic and heavy sweating." My withdrawal symptoms were unremitting for seventy-two hours.

Elsewhere, enumerating the cases of Halcion madness that he had observed in the Netherlands, Dr. van der Kroef remarked, "Without exception, the patients themselves described this period as hell."

———

For the next four weeks, feelings of extreme vulnerability, though no longer quite disemboweling me, still chaperoned me everywhere, especially as I was virtually unable to sleep and so was bleary with exhaustion throughout the day and then, during the insomniac, Halcionless nights, weighed down by the leaden thought of how I had disgraced myself before Claire and my brother and those friends who had drawn close to us during my hundred miserable days. I was abashed, and a good thing it was, too, since mortification seemed to me as promising a sign as any of the return of the person I formerly had been, more concerned, for better or worse, with something as pedestrian as his self-respect than with carnivorous snakes needling through the mud floor of his pond.

But much of the time I didn't believe it was Halcion that had done me in. Despite the speed with which I recovered my mental, then my emotional equilibrium and looked to be ordering daily life as competently as I ever had before, I privately remained half-convinced that, though the drug perhaps intensified my collapse, it was I who had made the worst happen, after having been derailed by nothing more cataclysmic than a botched knee operation and a siege of protracted physical pain; half-convinced that I owed my transformation —my *deformation*—not to any pharmaceutical agent but to something concealed, obscured, masked, suppressed, or maybe simply uncreated in me until I was fifty-four but as much me and mine as my prose style, my childhood, or my intestines; half-convinced that whatever else I might imagine myself to be, I was *that* too and, if the circumstances were trying enough, I could be again, a shamefully dependent, meaninglessly deviant, transparently pitiable, brazenly defective *that*, deranged as opposed to incisive, diabolical as opposed to reliable, without introspection, without serenity, without any of the ordinary boldness that makes life feel like such a great thing—a frenzied, maniacal, repulsive, anguished, odious, hallucinatory *that* whose existence is one long tremor.

And am I half-convinced still, five years later, after all that the psychiatrists, newspapers, and medical journals have disclosed about the mind-altering wallop lurking for many of us in Upjohn's magic little sleeping pill? The simple, truthful answer is, "Why not? Wouldn't you be, if you were me?"

———

As for the Philip Roth whom I had spoken with in suite 511 of the King David Hotel and who most certainly was not me—well, what exactly he was after I had no idea, for instead of answering when he'd asked my name, I'd immediately hung up. You shouldn't have phoned in the first place, I thought. You have no reason to be interested and you mustn't be rattled. That would be ridiculous. For all you know, it's simply someone else who happens coincidentally to bear the same name. And if that's not so, if there *is* an impostor in Jerusalem passing himself off as you, there's still nothing that needs to be done. He'll be found out by others without your intervening. He already has been—by Apter and Aharon. Enough people know you in Israel to make it impossible for him *not* to be exposed and apprehended. What harm can he do you? The harm can only be done *by* you, going off half-cocked and impulsively making phone calls like this one. The last thing for him to know is that his hoax is bugging you, because bugging you has to be at the heart of whatever he is ostensibly trying to do. Aloof and unconcerned, for now at least, is your only—

This is how rattled I was already. After all, when he'd so matter-of-factly announced to me who he was I had only to tell him who I was and to see what then transpired—it might have been eye-opening and could even have been fun. My prudence in hanging up seemed, moments afterward, to have been nothing but the expression of helpless panic, a jolting indication that, nearly seven months after coming off Halcion, I might not be detraumatized at all. "Well, this is Philip Roth, too, the one who was born in Newark and has written umpteen books. Which one are you?" I could so easily have undone him with that; instead it was he who undid me merely by answering the phone in my name.

———

I decided to say nothing about him to Claire when I arrived in London the following week. I didn't want her to think that there was anything in the offing with the potential to seriously disconcert me, particularly since she, for one, didn't yet seem convinced that I had recovered sufficient strength to ride out an emotional predicament at all complex or demanding . . . and what was more to the point, when I was suddenly less than a hundred percent sure myself. Once I'd arrived in London I didn't even want to *remember* what Apter and Aharon had phoned New York to tell me. . . . Yes, a situation that I might well have lightheartedly treated as a source of entertainment only a year earlier, or as a provocation to be soundly dealt with, now required that I take certain small but deliberate precautionary measures to guard against my being thrown. I wasn't happy to make that discovery, yet I didn't know how better to keep this bizarre triviality from developing in my mind the way the bizarre had become so painfully magnified under the sway of the Halcion. I would do what I must to maintain a reasonable perspective.

During my second night in London, still sleeping poorly because of

jet lag, I began to wonder, after having popped awake in the dark for
the third or fourth time, if those calls from Jerusalem—as well as my
call *to* Jerusalem—had not perhaps occurred in dreams. Earlier that
day I would have sworn that I had taken both calls at my desk in the
hotel while I was sitting there beginning to work up the set of questions, based on my rereading of his books, that I intended to ask
Aharon in Jerusalem, and yet, contemplating the unlikely content of
the calls, I managed to convince myself during the course of that long
night that they could have been placed and received only while I was
asleep, that these were dreams of the kind that everyone dreams
nightly, in which characters are identifiable and ring true when
they're speaking, while what they're saying rings absolutely false. And
the origin of the dreams was, when I thought about it, all too pathetically manifest. The imposturing other whose inexplicable antics I
had been warned about by Apter and Aharon and whose voice I'd
heard with my own ears was a specter created out of my fear of
mentally coming apart while abroad and on my own for the first time
since recovering—a nightmare about the return of a usurping self
altogether beyond my control. As for the messengers bearing the
news of my Jerusalem counterself, they too couldn't have been any
more grossly emblematic of the dreaming's immediate, personal ram-
ifications, since not only did their acquaintance with the unforeseen
grotesquely exceed my own, but each had undergone the most tremendous transformation even before the clay of his original being
had had time to anneal into a solid, shatterproof identity. The much-
praised transfigurations concocted by Franz Kafka pale beside the
unthinkable metamorphoses perpetrated by the Third Reich on the
childhoods of my cousin and of my friend, to enumerate only two.

   So eager was I to establish as fact that a dream had merely over-
flowed its banks that I got up to phone Aharon before it was even
dawn. It was already an hour later in Jerusalem and he was a very
early riser, but even if I had to risk waking him up, I felt I couldn't
wait a minute longer to have him confirm that this business was all a
mental aberration of mine and that no phone conversation had taken
place between the two of us about another Philip Roth. Yet, once out

of bed and on the way down to the kitchen to call him quietly from
there, I recognized what a pipe dream it was to be telling myself that
I had only been dreaming. I ought to be rushing to telephone not
Aharon, I thought, but the Boston psychopharmacologist to ask if my
uncertainty as to what was real meant that three months of being
bombarded chemically by triazolam had left my brain cells perma-
nently impaired. And the only reason to be phoning Aharon was to
hear what new sightings he had to report. But why not bypass Aharon
and inquire directly of the impostor himself what exactly he was out
to achieve? By feigning "a reasonable perspective" I was only opening
myself further to a dangerous renewal of delusion. If there was any
place for me to be phoning at four fifty-five in the morning, it was
suite 511 of the King David Hotel.

I thought very well of myself at breakfast for having made it back
to bed at five without calling anyone; I felt settling over me that
blissful sense of being in charge of one's life, a man who once again
hubristically imagines himself at the helm of himself. Everything else
might be a delusion, but the reasonable perspective was not.

Then the phone rang. "Philip? More good news. You are in the
morning's paper." It was Aharon calling *me*.

"Wonderful. Which paper this time?"

"A Hebrew paper this time. An article about your visit to Lech
Walesa. In Gdansk. This is where you were before you came to attend
the Demjanjuk trial."

Had I been speaking to almost anyone else I might have been
tempted to believe that I was being teased or toyed with. But however much pleasure Aharon may take in the ridiculous side of life,
deliberately to perpetrate comic mischief, even of the most mildly
addling variety, was simply incompatible with his ascetic, gravely
gentle nature. He saw the joke, that was clear, but he wasn't in on it
any more than I was.

Across from me Claire was drinking her coffee and looking through
the *Guardian*. We were finishing breakfast. I hadn't been dreaming
in New York and I wasn't dreaming now.

Aharon's voice is mild, very light and mild, modulated for the ears of the highly attuned, and his English is spoken precisely, each word lightly glazed with an accent as Old Worldish as it is Israeli. It is an appealing voice to listen to, alive with the dramatic cadences of the master storyteller and vibrant in its own distinctly quiet way—and I was listening very hard. "I'll translate from your statement here," he was telling me. " 'The reason for my visit to Walesa was to discuss with him the resettlement of Jews in Poland once Solidarity comes to power there, as it will.' "

"You'd better translate the whole thing. Start from scratch. What page is it on? How long is it?"

"Not long, not short. It's on the back page, with the features. There's a photograph."

"Of?"

"You."

"And is it me?" I asked.

"I would say so."

"What's the heading over the story?"

" 'Philip Roth Meets Solidarity Leader.' In smaller letters, ' "Poland Needs Jews," Walesa Tells Author in Gdansk.' "

" 'Poland Needs Jews,' " I repeated. "My grandparents should only be alive to hear that one."

" ' "Everyone speaks about Jews," Walesa told Roth. "Spain was ruined by the expulsion of the Jews," the Solidarity leader said during their two-hour meeting at the Gdansk shipyards, where Solidarity was born in 1980. "When people say to me, 'What Jew would be crazy enough to come here?' I explain to them that the long experience, over many hundreds of years, of Jews and Poles together cannot be summed up with the word 'anti-Semitism.' Let's talk about a thousand years of glory rather than four years of war. The greatest explosion of Yiddish culture in history, every great intellectual movement of modern Jewish life," said the Solidarity leader to Roth, "took place on Polish soil. Yiddish culture is no less Polish than Jewish. Poland without Jews is unthinkable. Poland needs Jews," Walesa told the American-born Jewish author, "and Jews need Poland." ' Philip, I feel that I'm reading to you out of a story you wrote."

"I wish you were."

" 'Roth, the author of *Portnoy's Complaint* and other controversial Jewish novels, calls himself an "ardent Diasporist." He says that the ideology of Diasporism has replaced his writing. "The reason for my visit to Walesa was to discuss with him the resettlement of Jews in Poland once Solidarity comes to power there, as it will." Right now, the author finds that his ideas on resettlement are received with more hostility in Israel than in Poland. He maintains that however virulent Polish anti-Semitism may once have been, "the Jew hatred that pervades Islam is far more entrenched and dangerous." Roth continues, "The so-called normalization of the Jew was a tragic illusion from the start. But when this normalization is expected to flourish in the very heart of Islam, it is even worse than tragic—it is suicidal. Horrendous as Hitler was for us, he lasted a mere twelve years, and what is twelve years to the Jew? The time has come to return to the Europe that was for centuries, and remains to this day, the most authentic Jewish homeland there has ever been, the birthplace of rabbinic Judaism, Hasidic Judaism, Jewish secularism, socialism—on and on. The birthplace, of course, of Zionism too. But Zionism has outlived its historical function. The time has come to renew in the European Diaspora our preeminent spiritual and cultural role." Roth, who is fearful of a second Jewish Holocaust in the Middle East, sees "Jewish resettlement" as the only means by which to assure Jewish survival and to achieve "a historical as well as a spiritual victory over Hitler and Auschwitz." "I am not blind," Roth says, "to the horrors. But I sit at the Demjanjuk trial, I look at this tormentor of Jews, this human embodiment of the criminal sadism unleashed by the Nazis on our people, and I ask myself, 'Who and what is to prevail in Europe: the will of this subhuman murderer-brute or the civilization that gave to mankind Shalom Aleichem, Heinrich Heine, and Albert Einstein? Are we to be driven for all time from the continent that nourished the flourishing Jewish worlds of Warsaw, of Vilna, of Riga, of Prague, of Berlin, of Lvov, of Budapest, of Bucharest, of Salonica and Rome because of *him?'* It is time," concludes Roth, "to return to where we belong and to where we have every historical right to resume the great Jewish

European destiny that the murderers like this Demjanjuk disrupted." ' "

That was the end of the article.

"What swell ideas I have," I said. "Going to make lots of new pals for me in the Zionist homeland."

"Anyone who reads this in the Zionist homeland," said Aharon, "will only think, 'Another crazy Jew.' "

"I'd much prefer then that in the hotel register he'd sign 'Another crazy Jew' and not 'Philip Roth.' "

" 'Another crazy Jew' might not be sufficiently crazy to satisfy his *mishigas.*"

When I saw that Claire was no longer reading her paper but listening to what I was saying, I told her, "It's Aharon. There's a madman in Israel using my name and going around pretending to be me." Then to Aharon I said, "I'm telling Claire that there's a madman in Israel pretending to be me."

"Yes, and the madman undoubtedly believes that in New York and London and Connecticut there is a madman pretending to be him."

"Unless he's not at all mad and knows exactly what he's doing."

"Which is what?" asked Aharon.

"I didn't say I know, I said he knows. So many people in Israel have met me, have seen me—how can this person present himself as Philip Roth to an Israeli journalist and get away with it so easily?"

"I think this is a very young woman who wrote the story—I believe this is a person in her twenties. That's probably what's behind it—her inexperience."

"And the picture?"

"The picture they find in their files."

"Look, I have to contact her paper before this gets picked up by the wire services."

"And what can *I* do, Philip? Anything?"

"For the time being, no, nothing. I may want to talk to my lawyer before I even call the paper. I may want her to call the paper." But looking at my watch I realized that it was much too early to phone New York. "Aharon, just hold tight until I have a chance to think it through and check out the legal side. I don't even know what it is an impostor can be charged with. Invasion of privacy? Defamation of character? Reckless conduct? Is impersonation an actionable offense? What exactly has he appropriated that's against the law and how do I stop him in a country where I'm not even a citizen? I'd actually be dealing with Israeli law, and I'm not yet in Israel. Look, I'll call you back when I find something out."

But once off the phone I immediately came up with an explanation not wholly disconnected from what I'd thought the night before in bed. Although the idea probably originated in Aharon's remark that he felt that he was reading to me out of a story I'd written, it was nonetheless another ridiculously subjective attempt to convert into a mental event of the kind I was professionally all too familiar with what had once again been established as all too objectively real. It's Zuckerman, I thought, whimsically, stupidly, escapistly, it's Kepesh, it's Tarnopol and Portnoy—it's all of them in one, broken free of print and mockingly reconstituted as a single satirical facsimile of me. In other words, if it's not Halcion and it's no dream, then it's got to be literature—as though there cannot be a life-without ten thousand times more unimaginable than the life-within.

"Well," I said to Claire, "there's somebody in Jerusalem attending the Ivan the Terrible trial who's going around claiming to be me. Calls himself by my name. Gave an interview to an Israeli newspaper —that's what Aharon was reading to me over the phone."

"You found this out just now?" she asked.

"No. Aharon phoned me in New York last week. So did my cousin Apter. Apter's landlady said she'd seen me on TV. I didn't tell you because I didn't know what, if anything, it all amounted to."

"You're green, Philip. You've turned a frightening color."

"Have I? I'm tired, that's all. I was up on and off all night."

"You're not taking . . ."

"You can't be serious."

"Don't sound resentful. I just don't want anything to happen to you. Because you *have* turned a terrible color—and you seem . . . swamped."

"Do I? Did I? I didn't think I did. And it's you who have actually turned colors."

"I'm worried, that's why. You seem . . ."

"What? Seem *what?* What it seems to me I seem to be is someone who has just found out that somebody down in Jerusalem is giving newspaper interviews in his name. You heard what I said to Aharon. As soon as the business day begins in New York, I'm going to call Helene. I think now that the best thing is for *her* to telephone the paper and to get them to print a retraction tomorrow. It's a start at stopping him. Once their retraction's out, no other newspaper is going to go near him. That's step number one."

"What's step number two?"

"I don't know. Maybe step number two won't be necessary. I don't know what the law is. Do I slap an injunction on him? In Israel? Maybe what Helene does is to contact a lawyer down there. When I speak to her, I'll find out."

"Maybe step number two is not going there right now."

"That's ridiculous. Look, I'm *not* swamped. It's not *my* plans that are going to change—it's his."

But by the afternoon I was back again to thinking that it was far more reasonable, sensible, and even, in the long run, more satisfyingly ruthless to do nothing for now. Telling Claire anything, given her continuing apprehension about my well-being, was, of course, a mistake and, had she not been sitting across from me at the breakfast table when Aharon phoned in his latest report, one that I would never have made. And an even bigger mistake, I thought, would be to set lawyers loose now, on two continents no less, who might not effect an outcome any less damaging than I could—if, that is, I could manage to remain something more helpful than volatilely irritated until, eventually, this impostor played out his disaster, all alone, as he must. A retraction was not likely to undo whatever damage had already been done by the newspaper's original error. The ideas espoused so forcefully by the Philip Roth in that story were mine now and would likely endure as mine even in the recollection of those who'd read the retraction tomorrow. Nonetheless, this was not, I sternly reminded myself, the worst upheaval of my life, and I was not going to permit myself to behave as though it were. Instead of rushing to mobilize an army of legal defenders, better just to sit comfortably back on the sidelines and watch while he manufactures for the Israeli press and public a version of me so absolutely not-me that it will require nothing, neither judicial intervention nor newspaper retractions, to clear everyone's mind of confusion and expose him as whatever he is.

After all, despite the temptation to chalk him up to Halcion's lingering hold on me, he was not my but *his* hallucination, and by January 1988 I'd come to understand that he had more to fear from that than I did. Up against reality I was not quite so outclassed as I'd been up against that sleeping pill; up against reality I had at my disposal the strongest weapon in anyone's arsenal: my own reality. It wasn't I who was in danger of being displaced by him but he who had *without question* to be effaced by me—exposed, effaced, and extinguished. It was just a matter of time. Panic characteristically urges, in its quivering, raving, overexcitable way, "Do something before he goes too far!" and is loudly seconded by Powerless Fear. Meanwhile, poised and balanced, Reason, the exalted voice of Reason, counsels, "You have everything on your side, he has nothing on his. Try eradicating him overnight, before he has fully revealed exactly what he's intent on doing, and he'll only elude you to pop up elsewhere and start this stuff all over again. *Let* him go too far. There is no more cunning way to shut him down. He can only be defeated."

Needless to say, had I told Claire that evening that I'd changed my mind since morning and, instead of racing into battle armed with lawyers, proposed now to let him inflate the hoax until it blew up in his face, she would have replied that to do that would only invite trouble potentially more threatening to my newly reconstituted stability than the little that had so far resulted from what was still only a minor, if outlandish, nuisance. She would argue with even more concern than she'd displayed at breakfast—because three months of helplessly watching my collapse up close had deeply scarred her faith in me and hadn't done much for her own stability either—that I was nowhere ready for a test as unlikely and puzzling as this one, while I, experiencing all the satisfaction that's bestowed by a strategy of restraint, exhilarated by the sense of personal freedom that issues from refusing to respond to an emergency other than with a realistic appraisal and levelheaded self-control, was convinced of just the opposite. I felt absolutely rapturous over the decision to take on this impostor by myself, for on my own and by myself was how I'd always preferred to encounter just about everything. My God, I thought, this is me again, finally the much-pined-for natural upsurge of my obstinate, energetic, independent self, zeroed back in on life and brimming with my old resolve, vying once again with an adversary a little less chimerical than sickly, crippling unreality. He was just what the psychopharmacologist ordered! All right, bud, one on one, let's fight! You can only be defeated.

At dinner that evening, before Claire had a chance to ask me anything, I lied and told her that I had spoken with my lawyer, that from New York she had contacted the Israeli paper, and that a retraction was to be printed there the next day.

"I still don't like it," she replied.

"But what more can we do? What more *need* be done?"

"I don't like the idea of you there alone while this person is on the loose. It's not a good idea at all. Who knows what he is or who he is or what he's actually up to? Suppose he's crazy. You yourself called him a madman this morning. What if this madman is armed?"

"Whatever I may have called him, I happen to know nothing about him."

"That's my point."

"And why should he be armed? You don't need a pistol to impersonate me."

"It's Israel—*everybody's* armed. Half the people in the street traipsing around carrying guns—I never saw so many guns in my life. Your going there, at a time like this, with everything erupting everywhere, is a terrible, terrible mistake."

She was referring to the riots that had begun in Gaza and the West Bank the month before and that I'd been following in New York on the nightly news. A curfew was in effect in East Jerusalem and tourists had been warned away particularly from the Old City because of the stone throwing there and the possibility of violent clashes escalating between the army and the Arab residents. The media had taken to describing these riots, which had become a more or less daily occurrence in the Occupied Territories, as a Palestinian uprising.

"Why can't you contact the Israeli police?" she asked.

"I think the Israeli police may find themselves facing problems more pressing than mine right now. What would I tell them? Arrest him? Deport him? On what grounds? As far as I know, he hasn't passed a phony check in my name, he hasn't been paid for any services in my name—"

"But he must have entered Israel with a phony passport, with *papers* in your name. That's illegal."

"But do we know this? We don't. It's illegal but not very likely. I suspect that all he's done in my name is to shoot his mouth off."

"But there *must* be legal safeguards. A person cannot simply run off to a foreign country and go around pretending to be someone he is not."

"Happens probably more often than you think. How about some realism? Darling, how about your taking a reasonable perspective?"

"I don't want anything to happen to you. That's my reasonable perspective."

"What 'happened' to me happened to me many months ago now."

"Are you really up to this? I have to ask you, Philip."

"There's nothing for me to be 'up to.' Did anything like what happened to me ever happen to me before that drug? Has anything like it happened to me since the drug? Tomorrow they're printing a retraction. They're faxing Helene a copy. That's enough for now."

"Well, I don't understand this calm of yours—or hers, frankly."

"Now the calm's upsetting. This morning it was my chagrin."

"Yes, well—I don't believe it."

"Well, there's nothing I can do about that."

"Promise me you won't do anything ridiculous."

"Such as?"

"I don't *know*. Trying to find this person. Trying to *fight* with this person. You have no idea whom you might be dealing with. You must not try to look for him and solve this stupid thing yourself. At least promise that you won't do that."

I laughed at the very idea. "My guess," I said, lying once again, "is that by the time I get to Jerusalem, he won't be anywhere to be found."

"You won't do it."

"I won't have to. Look, see it this way, will you? I have everything on my side, he has nothing on his, absolutely nothing."

"But you're wrong. You know what he has on his side? It's clear from every word you speak. He has you."

———

After our dinner that evening I told Claire that I was going off to my study at the top of the house to sit down again with Aharon's novels to continue making my notes for the Jerusalem conversation. But no more than five minutes had passed after I'd settled at the desk, when I heard the television set playing below and I picked up the phone and called the King David Hotel in Jerusalem and asked to be put through to 511. To disguise my voice I used a French accent, not the bedroom accent, not the farcical accent, not that French accent descended from Charles Boyer through Danny Kaye to the TV ads for table wines and traveler's checks, but the accent of highly articulate and cosmopolitan Frenchmen like my friend the writer Philippe Sollers, no "zis," no "zat," all initial *h*'s duly aspirated—fluent English simply tinged with the natural inflections and marked by the natural cadences of an intelligent foreigner. It's an imitation I don't do badly —once, on the phone, I fooled even mischievous Sollers—and the one I'd decided on even while Claire and I were arguing at the dinner table about the wisdom of my trip, even while, I must admit, the exalted voice of Reason had been counseling me, earlier that day, that doing nothing was the surest way to do him in. By nine o'clock that night, curiosity had all but consumed me, and curiosity is not a very rational whim.

"Hello, Mr. Roth? Mr. Philip Roth?" I asked.

"Yes."

"Is this really the author I'm speaking to?"

"It is."

"The author of *Portnoy et son complexe?*"

"Yes, yes. Who is this, please?"

My heart was pounding as though I were out on my first big robbery with an accomplice no less brilliant than Jean Genet—this was not merely treacherous, this was *interesting.* To think that he was pretending at his end of the line to be me while I was pretending at my end not to be me gave me a terrific, unforeseen, Mardi Gras kind of kick, and probably it was this that accounted for the stupid error I immediately made. "I am Pierre Roget," I said, and only in the instant after uttering a convenient nom de guerre that I'd plucked seemingly out of nowhere did I realize that its initial letters were the same as mine—and the same as his. Worse, it happened also to be the barely transmogrified name of the nineteenth-century word cataloger who is known to virtually everyone as the author of the famous thesaurus. I hadn't realized that either—the author of the definitive book of synonyms!

"I am a French journalist based in Paris," I said. "I have just read in the Israeli press about your meeting with Lech Walesa in Gdansk."

Slip number two: Unless I knew Hebrew, how could I have read his interview in the Israeli press? What if he now began speaking to me in a language that I had learned just badly enough to manage to be bar mitzvahed at the age of thirteen and that I no longer understood at all?

Reason: "You are playing right into his plan. This is the very situation his criminality craves. Hang up."

Claire: "Are you really all right? Are you really up to this? Don't go."

Pierre Roget: "If I read correctly, you are leading a movement to resettle Europe with Israeli Jews of European background. Beginning in Poland."

"Correct," he replied.

"And you continue at the same time to write your novels?"

"Writing novels while Jews are at a crossroads like this? My life now is focused entirely on the Jewish European resettlement move- ment. On Diasporism."

Did he sound *anything* like me? I would have thought that my voice could far more easily pass for someone like Sollers speaking English than his could pass for mine. For one thing, he had much more Jersey in his speech than I'd ever had, though whether because it came naturally to him or because he mistakenly thought it would make the impersonation more convincing, I couldn't figure out. But then this was a more resonant voice than mine as well, richer and more stentorian by far. Maybe that was how he thought somebody who had published sixteen books would talk on the phone to an interviewer, while the fact is that if I talked like that I might not have had to write sixteen books. But the impulse to tell him this, strong as it was, I restrained; I was having too good a time to think of stifling either one of us.

"You are a Jew," I said, "who in the past has been criticized by Jewish groups for your 'self-hatred' and your 'anti-Semitism.' Would it be correct to assume—"

"Look," he said, abruptly breaking in, "I am a Jew, period. I would not have gone to Poland to meet with Walesa if I were anything else. I would not be here visiting Israel and attending the Demjanjuk trial if I were anything else. Please, I will be glad to tell you all you wish to know about resettlement. Otherwise I haven't time to waste on what has been said about me by stupid people."

"But," I persisted, "won't stupid people say that because of this resettlement idea you are an enemy of Israel and its mission? Won't this confirm—"

"I am Israel's enemy," he interrupted again, "if you wish to put it that sensationally, only because I am for the Jews and Israel is no longer in the Jewish interest. Israel has become the gravest threat to Jewish survival since the end of World War Two."

"Was Israel ever in the Jewish interest, in your opinion?"

"Of course. In the aftermath of the Holocaust, Israel was the Jewish hospital in which Jews could begin to recover from the devastation of that horror, from a dehumanization so terrible that it would not have been at all surprising had the Jewish spirit, had the Jews themselves, succumbed entirely to that legacy of rage, humiliation and grief. But that is not what happened. Our recovery actually came to pass. In less than a century. Miraculous, more than miraculous—yet the recovery of the Jews is by now a fact, and the time has come to return to our real life and our real home, to our ancestral Jewish Europe."

"Real home?" I replied, unable now to imagine how I ever could have considered not placing this call. "Some real home."

"I am not making promiscuous conversation," he snapped back at me sharply. "The great mass of Jews have been in Europe since the Middle Ages. Virtually everything we identify culturally as Jewish has its origins in the life we led for centuries among European Christians. The Jews of Islam have their own, very different destiny. I am not proposing that Israeli Jews whose origins are in Islamic countries return to Europe, since for them this would constitute not a homecoming but a radical uprooting."

"What do you do then with them? Ship them back for the Arabs to treat as befits their status as Jews?"

"No. For those Jews, Israel must continue to be their country. Once the European Jews and their families have been resettled and the population has been halved, then the state can be reduced to its 1948 borders, the army can be demobilized, and those Jews who have lived in an Islamic cultural matrix for centuries can continue to do so, independently, autonomously, but in peace and harmony with their Arab neighbors. For these people to remain in this region is simply as it should be, their rightful habitat, while for the European Jews, Israel has been an exile and no more, a sojourn, a temporary interlude in the European saga that it is time to resume."

"Sir, what makes you think that the Jews would have any more success in Europe in the future than they had there in the past?"

"Do not confuse our long European history with the twelve years of Hitler's reign. If Hitler had not existed, if his twelve years of terror were erased from our past, then it would seem to you no more unthinkable that Jews should also be Europeans than that they should also be Americans. There might even seem to you a much more necessary and profound connection between the Jew and Budapest, the Jew and Prague, than the one between the Jew and Cincinnati and the Jew and Dallas."

Could it be, I asked myself while he pedantically continued on in this vein, that the history he's most intent on erasing happens to be his own? Is he mentally so damaged that he truly believes that my history is his; is he some psychotic, some amnesiac, who isn't pretending at all? If every word he speaks he means, if the only person pretending here is me.... But whether that made things better or worse I couldn't begin to know. Nor, when next I found myself *arguing,* could I determine whether an outburst of sincerity from me made this conversation any more or less absurd, either.

"But Hitler *did* exist," I heard Pierre Roget emotionally informing him. "Those twelve years *cannot* be expunged from history any more than they can be obliterated from memory, however mercifully forgetful one might prefer to be. The meaning of the destruction of European Jewry cannot be measured or interpreted by the brevity with which it was attained."

"The meanings of the Holocaust," he replied gravely, "are for us to determine, but one thing is sure—its meaning will be no less tragic than it is now if there is a second Holocaust and the offspring of the European Jews who evacuated Europe for a seemingly safer haven should meet collective annihilation in the Middle East. A second Holocaust is *not* going to occur on the continent of Europe, *because* it was the site of the first. But a second Holocaust could happen here all too easily, and, if the conflict between Arab and Jew escalates much longer, it will—*it must.* The destruction of Israel in a nuclear exchange is a possibility much less farfetched today than was the Holocaust itself fifty years ago."

"The resettlement in Europe of more than a million Jews. The demobilization of the Israeli army. A return to the borders of 1948. It sounds to me," I said, "that you are proposing the final solution of the Jewish problem for Yasir Arafat."

"No. Arafat's final solution is the same as Hitler's: extermination. I am proposing the alternative to extermination, a solution not to Arafat's Jewish problem but to ours, one comparable in scope and magnitude to the defunct solution called Zionism. But I do not wish to be misunderstood, in France or anywhere else in the world. I repeat: In the immediate postwar era, when for obvious reasons Europe was uninhabitable by Jews, Zionism was the single greatest force contributing to the recovery of Jewish hope and morale. But having succeeded in restoring the Jews to health, Zionism has tragically ruined its own health and must now accede to vigorous Diasporism."

"Will you define Diasporism for my readers, please?" I asked, meanwhile thinking, The starchy rhetoric, the professorial presentation, the historical perspective, the passionate commitment, the grave undertones . . . What sort of hoax *is* this hoax?

"Diasporism seeks to promote the dispersion of the Jews in the West, particularly the resettlement of Israeli Jews of European background in the European countries where there were sizable Jewish populations before World War II. Diasporism plans to rebuild *everything*, not in an alien and menacing Middle East but in those very lands where everything once flourished, while, at the same time, it seeks to avert the catastrophe of a second Holocaust brought about by the exhaustion of Zionism as a political and ideological force. Zionism undertook to restore Jewish life and the Hebrew language to a place where neither had existed with any real vitality for nearly two millennia. Diasporism's dream is more modest: a mere half-century is all that separates us from what Hitler destroyed. If Jewish resources could realize the seemingly fantastic goals of Zionism in even less than fifty years, now that Zionism is counterproductive and itself the foremost Jewish problem, I have no doubt that the resources of world Jewry can realize the goals of Diasporism in half, if not even one tenth, the time."

"You speak about resettling Jews in Poland, Romania, Germany? In Slovakia, the Ukraine, Yugoslavia, the Baltic states? And you realize, do you," I asked him, "how much hatred for Jews still exists in most of these countries?"

"Whatever hatred for Jews may be present in Europe—and I don't minimize its persistence—there are ranged against this residual anti-Semitism powerful currents of enlightenment and morality that are sustained by the memory of the Holocaust, a horror that operates now as a bulwark *against* European anti-Semitism, however virulent. No such bulwark exists in Islam. Exterminating a Jewish nation would cause Islam to lose not a single night's sleep, except for the great night of celebration. I think you would agree that a Jew is safer today walking aimlessly around Berlin than going unarmed into the streets of Ramallah."

"What about the Jew walking around Tel Aviv?"

"In Damascus missiles armed with chemical warheads are aimed not at downtown Warsaw but directly at Dizengoff Street."

"So what Diasporism comes down to is fearful Jews in flight, terrified Jews once again running away."

"To flee an imminent cataclysm is 'running away' only from extinction. It is running *toward* life. Had thousands more of Germany's fearful Jews fled in the 1930s—"

"Thousands more would have fled," I said, "if there had been somewhere for them to flee to. You may recall that they were no more welcome elsewhere than they would be now if they were to turn up en masse at the Warsaw train station in flight from an Arab attack."

"You know what will happen in Warsaw, at the railway station, when the first trainload of Jews returns? There will be crowds to welcome them. People will be jubilant. People will be in tears. They will be shouting, 'Our Jews are back! Our Jews are back!' The spectacle will be transmitted by television throughout the world. And what a historic day for Europe, for Jewry, for all mankind when the cattle cars that transported Jews to death camps are transformed by the Diasporist movement into decent, comfortable railway carriages carrying Jews by the tens of thousands back to their native cities and towns. A historic day for human memory, for human justice, and for atonement too. In those train stations where the crowds gather to weep and sing and celebrate, where people fall to their knees in Christian prayer at the feet of their Jewish brethren, only there and then will the conscience cleansing of Europe begin." He paused theatrically here before concluding this visionary outpouring with the quiet, firm pronouncement "And Lech Walesa happens to believe this just as strongly as Philip Roth does."

"Does he? With all due respect, Philip Roth, your prophecy strikes me as nonsense. It sounds to me like a farcical scenario out of one of your books—Poles weeping with joy at the feet of the Jews! And you tell me you are *not* writing fiction these days?"

"This will come to pass," he declared oracularly, "because it *must* come to pass—the reintegration of the Jew into Europe by the year 2000, not a reentry as refugees, you must understand, but an orderly population transfer *with an international legal basis, with restoration of property, of citizenship, and of all national rights.* And then, in the year 2000, the pan-European celebration of the reintegrated Jew to be held in the city of Berlin."

"Oh, that's the best idea yet," I said. "The Germans particularly will be delighted to usher in the third millennium of Christianity with a couple of million Jews holding a welcome-home party at the Brandenburg Gate."

"In his day Herzl too was accused of being a satirist and of making an elaborate joke when he proposed the establishment of a Jewish state. Many deprecated *his* plan as a hilarious fantasy, an outlandish fiction, and called him crazy as well. But my conversation with Lech Walesa was not outlandish fiction. The contact I have made with President Ceauşescu, through the chief rabbi of Romania, is no hilarious fantasy. These are the first steps toward bringing about *a new Jewish reality based on principles of historical justice.* For years now, President Ceauşescu has been selling Jews to Israel. Yes, you hear me correctly: Ceauşescu has *sold* to the Israelis several hundred thousand Romanian Jews for ten thousand dollars a head. This is a fact. Well, I propose to offer him ten thousand more dollars for each Jew he takes back. I'll go as high as fifteen if I have to. I have carefully studied Herzl's life and have learned from his experience how to deal with these people. Herzl's negotiations with the sultan in Constantinople, though they happened to fail, were no more of a hilarious fantasy than the negotiations I will soon be conducting with the dictator of Romania at his Bucharest palace."

"And the money to pay the dictator off? My guess is that to fund your effort you have only to turn to the PLO."

"I have every reason to believe that my funding will come from the American Jews who for decades now have been contributing enormous sums for the survival of a country with which they happen to have only the most abstractly sentimental connection. The roots of American Jewry are not in the Middle East but in Europe—their Jewish style, their Jewish words, their strong nostalgia, their actual, weighable history, all this issues from their European origins. Grandpa did not hail from Haifa—Grandpa came from Minsk. Grandpa wasn't a Jewish nationalist—he was a Jewish humanist, a spiritual, believing Jew, who complained not in an antique tongue called Hebrew but in colorful, rich, vernacular Yiddish."

Our conversation was interrupted here by the hotel operator, who broke in to tell him that Frankfurt was now on the line.

"Pierre, hold a second."

Pierre, hold a second, and I did it, *held,* and, of course, obediently waiting for him to come back on made me even more ludicrous to myself than remembering everything I'd said in our conversation. I should have taped this, I realized—as evidence, as proof. But of what? That he wasn't me? This needed to be *proved?*

"A German colleague of yours," he said when he returned to speak to me again, "a journalist with *Der Spiegel.* You must excuse me if I leave you to talk with him now. He's been trying to reach me for days. This has been a good, strong interview—your questions may be aggressive and nasty, but they are also intelligent, and I thank you for them."

"One more, however, one last nasty question. Tell me, please," I asked, "are they lining up, the Romanian Jews who are dying to go back to Ceaușescu's Romania? Are they lining up, the Polish Jews who are dying to return to Communist Poland? Those Russians struggling to leave the Soviet Union, is your plan to turn them around at the Tel Aviv airport and force them onto the next flight back to Moscow? Anti-Semitism aside, you think people fresh from these terrible places will voluntarily choose to return just because Philip Roth tells them to?"

"I think I have made my position sufficiently clear to you for now," he replied most courteously. "In what journal will our interview be published?"

"I am free-lance, Mr. Philip Roth. Could be anywhere from *Le Monde* to *Paris-Match.*"

"And you will be kind enough to send a copy to the hotel when it appears?"

"How long do you expect to remain there?"

"As long as the disassociation of Jewish identity threatens the welfare of my people. As long as it takes Diasporism to recompose, once and for all, the splintered Jewish existence. Your last name again, Pierre?"

"Roget," I said. "Like the thesaurus."

His laugh erupted much too forcefully for me to believe that it had been provoked by my little quip alone. He knows, I thought, hanging up. He knows perfectly well who I am.

2

A Life
Not My Own

According to the testimony of six elderly Treblinka survivors, during the fifteen months from July 1942 to September 1943 when nearly a million Jews were murdered at Treblinka, the gas chamber there was operated by a guard, known to the Jews as Ivan the Terrible, whose sideline was to maim and torture, preferably with a sword, the naked men, women, and children herded together outside the gas chamber waiting to be asphyxiated. Ivan was a strong, vigorous, barely educated Soviet soldier, a Ukrainian in his early twenties whom the Germans had captured on the Eastern Front and, along with hundreds more Ukrainian POWs, recruited and trained to staff the Belsec, Sobibor, and Treblinka extermination camps in Poland. John Demjanjuk's lawyers, one of whom, Yoram Sheftel, was an Israeli, never disputed the existence of Ivan the Terrible or the horror of the atrocities he committed. They claimed only that Demjanjuk and Ivan the Terrible were two different people and that the evidence to the contrary was all worthless. They argued that the identity photo spread assembled for the Treblinka survivors by the Israeli police was totally unreliable because of the faulty and amateurish procedures used, procedures that had led or manipulated the survivors into mistakenly identifying Demjanjuk as Ivan. They argued that the sole piece of documentary evidence, an identity card from Trawniki, an SS training camp for Treblinka guards—a card bearing Demjanjuk's name, signature, personal details, and a photograph—was a KGB forgery designed to discredit Ukrainian nationalists by marking one of them as this savage war criminal. They argued that during the period when Ivan the Terrible had been running the Treblinka gas chamber, Demjanjuk had been held as a German prisoner of war in a region nowhere near the Polish death camps. The defense's Demjanjuk was a hardworking, churchgoing family man who had come to America with a young Ukrainian wife and a tiny child from a European DP camp in 1952—a father of three grown American children, a skilled autoworker with Ford, a decent, law-abiding American citizen renowned among the Ukrainian Americans in his Cleveland suburb for his wonderful vegetable garden and the pierogi that he helped the ladies cook for the celebrations at St. Vladimir's Orthodox Church. His only crime was to be born a Ukrainian whose Christian name had formerly been Ivan and to have been about the same age and perhaps even to have resembled somewhat the Ukrainian Ivan whom these elderly Treblinka survivors had, of course, not seen in the flesh for over forty years. Early in the trial, Demjanjuk had himself pleaded to the court, "I am not that awful man to whom you refer. I am innocent."

I learned all this from a thick file of xeroxed newspaper clippings about the Demjanjuk trial that I purchased at the office of *The Jerusalem Post,* the English-language Israeli paper. On the drive from the airport I'd seen the file advertised in that day's *Post,* and after checking in at the hotel, instead of phoning Apter and making arrangements to meet him later in the day, as I'd planned to do, I took a taxi directly over to the newspaper office. Then, before I went off to dinner with Aharon at a Jerusalem restaurant, I read carefully through the several hundred clippings, which dated back some ten years to when the U.S. government filed denaturalization charges against Demjanjuk in the

Cleveland district court for falsifying, on his visa application, the details of his whereabouts during World War II.

I was reading at a table in the garden courtyard of the American Colony Hotel. Ordinarily I stayed at Mishkenot Sha'ananim, the guest house for visiting academics and artists run by the mayor's Jerusalem Foundation and located a couple of hundred yards down the road from the King David Hotel. Several months earlier I had reserved an apartment there for my January visit, but the day before leaving London I had canceled the reservation and made one instead at the American Colony, a hotel staffed by Arabs and situated at the other end of Jerusalem, virtually on the pre-1968 borderline between Jordanian Jerusalem and Israeli Jerusalem and only blocks away from where violence had sporadically broken out in the Arab Old City during the previous few weeks. I explained to Claire that I had changed reservations to be as far as I could get from the other Philip Roth should he happen, despite the newspaper retraction, to be hanging on in Jerusalem still registered at the King David under my name. My staying at an Arab hotel, I said, minimized the likelihood of our paths ever crossing, which was what she herself had cautioned me against foolishly facilitating. "And maximizes," she replied, "the likelihood of getting stoned to death." "Look, I'll be all but incognito at the American Colony," I answered, "and for now incognito is the smartest, least disruptive, most reasonable strategy." "No, the smartest strategy is to tell Aharon to come to the guest room here and stay in London with you." Since on the day I left for Israel she herself was to fly to Africa to begin to make a film in Kenya, I suggested to her, when we parted at Heathrow Airport, that she was about as likely to be eaten by a lion in the streets of Nairobi as I was to come to any harm in a first-class hotel at the edge of East Jerusalem. Gloomily she disagreed and departed.

After reading the clipping file right through to an article from just the week before about a request by defense counsel Yoram Sheftel to enter ten new documents in evidence at this late stage of the proceedings, I wondered if it was while at the Demjanjuk trial that the impostor had first got the idea to pretend to be me, emboldened by the identity issue at the heart of the case, or if he had deliberately selected the trial for his performance because of the opportunities for publicity provided by the extensive media coverage. It disgusted me that he should insinuate this crazy stunt into the midst of such a grim and tragic affair, and, for the first time, really, I found myself outraged in the way that somebody without my professional curiosity about shenanigans like this one probably would have been from the start—not merely because, for whatever his reasons, he had decided that our two destinies should become publicly entangled but because he had chosen to entangle them here.

At dinner that evening I thought repeatedly of asking Aharon to recommend a Jerusalem lawyer for me to consult with about my problem, but instead I was mostly silent while Aharon spoke about a recent guest of his, a Frenchwoman, a university professor, married and the mother of two children, who had been discovered as a newborn infant in a Paris churchyard only months before the Allies liberated the city in 1944. She had been raised by foster parents as a Catholic but a few years back had come to believe that, in fact, she had been a Jewish child abandoned at birth by Jewish parents hiding somewhere in Paris and placed by them in the churchyard so that she would not be thought Jewish or raised as a Jew. This idea had begun to develop in her during the Lebanon war, when everyone she knew, including her husband and her children, was condemning the Israelis as criminal murderers and she found herself, alone and embattled, arguing strenuously in their defense.

She knew Aharon only through his books but wrote him nonetheless a compelling and impassioned letter about her discovery. He answered sympathetically, and a few days later she turned up on his doorstep to ask him to help her find a rabbi to convert her. That evening she had dinner with Aharon and his wife, Judith, and explained to them how she had never in her life felt she belonged to France, even though she wrote and spoke the language flawlessly and in her appearance and her behavior seemed to everyone as French as French could be—she was a Jew and she belonged to the Jews, of this she was ardently convinced.

The next morning Aharon took her to a rabbi he knew to ask if the rabbi would supervise her conversion. He refused, as did three other rabbis they went together to see. And each gave much the same reason for saying no: because neither her husband nor her children were Jews, the rabbis were disinclined to divide the family along religious lines. "Suppose I *divorce* my husband, *disown* my children—" But as she happened to love them all dearly, the rabbi to whom she made this proposal took it no more seriously than it was meant.

After her unsuccessful week in Jerusalem, desolated to have to return, still a Catholic, to her old life in France, she was at dinner at the Appelfelds' house on the evening before her departure, when Aharon and Judith, who could no longer bear to see the woman suffering so, suddenly announced to her, "You are a Jew! We, the Appelfelds, declare you a Jew! There—we have converted you!"

As we sat in the restaurant laughing together at the antic audacity of this obliging deed, Aharon, a small, bespectacled compact man with a perfectly round face and a perfectly bald head, looked to me very much like a benign wizard, as adept in the mysteries of legerdemain as his namesake, the brother of Moses. "He'd have no trouble," I later wrote in the preface to our interview, "passing for a magician who entertains children at birthday parties by pulling doves out of a hat—it's easier to associate his gently affable and kindly appearance with that job than with the responsibility by which he seems inescapably propelled: responding, in a string of elusively portentous stories, to the disappearance from Europe . . . of just about all the continent's Jews, his parents among them." Aharon himself had managed to remain alive by escaping from the Transnistria concentration camp at the age of nine and living either in hiding, foraging alone in the woods, or working as a menial laborer for poor local peasants until the Russians liberated him three years later. Before being transported to the camp, he had been the pampered child of wealthy, highly assimilated Bukovina Jews, a little boy educated by tutors, raised by nannies, and fitted out always in the finest clothes.

"To be declared a Jew by Appelfeld," I said, "that's no small thing.

You do have it in you to bestow this mantle on people. You even try it with me."

"Not with you, Philip. You were a Jew par excellence years before I came along."

"No, no, never so exclusively, totally, and incessantly as the Jew it pleases you to imagine me to be."

"Yes, exclusively, totally, incessantly, *irreducibly*. That you continue to struggle so to deny it is for me the ultimate proof."

"Against such reasoning," I said, "there is no defense."

He laughed quietly. "Good."

"And tell me, do *you* believe this Catholic professor's fantasy of herself?"

"What I believe is not what concerns me."

"Then what *about* what she believes? Doesn't it occur to the professor that she may have been left in a churchyard precisely because she was *not* Jewish? And that her sense of apartness originates not in her having been born a Jew but in her having been orphaned and raised by people other than her natural parents? Besides, would a Jewish mother be likely to abandon her infant on the very eve of the liberation, when the chances for Jewish survival couldn't have been better? No, no, to have been found when she was found makes Jewish parentage for this woman the *least* likely possibility."

"But a possibility no less. Even if the Allies were to liberate them in only a matter of days, they had still to survive those days in hiding. And to survive in hiding with a crying infant might not have been feasible."

"This is what she thinks."

"It's one thing she thinks."

"Yes, a person can, of course, think absolutely anything. . . ." And I, of course, was thinking about the man who wanted people to think that he was me—did *he* think that he was me as well?

"You look tired," Aharon said. "You look upset. You're not yourself tonight."

"Don't have to be. Got someone else to do it for me."

"But nothing is in the papers, nothing more that I have seen."

"Oh, but he's still at it, I'm sure. What's to stop him? Certainly not me. And shouldn't I at least try? Wouldn't you? Wouldn't anyone in his right mind?" It was Claire's position I heard myself taking up now that she was gone. "Shouldn't I place an ad in *The Jerusalem Post* informing the citizens of Israel that there is this impostor about, an ad disassociating myself from whatever he says or does in my name? A full-page ad would end this overnight. I could appear on television. Better, I could simply go and talk to the police, because more than likely he's traveling with false documents. I know he's got to be breaking some kind of law."

"But instead you do nothing."

"Well, I *have* done something. Since I spoke with you I phoned him. At the King David. I interviewed him on the phone from London, posing as a journalist."

"Yes, and you look pleased with that—*now* you look like yourself."

"Well, it wasn't entirely unenjoyable. But, Aharon, what *am* I to do? It's too ridiculous to take seriously and too serious to be ridiculous. And it's activating—*re*activating—the very state of mind that I've been working for months now to shake off. You know what's at the heart of the misery of a breakdown? Me-itis. Microcosmosis. Drowning in the tiny tub of yourself. Coming here I had it all figured out: desubjectified in Jerusalem, subsumed in Appelfeld, swimming in the sea of the other self—the other self being yours. Instead there is this me to plague and preoccupy me, a me who is not even me to obsess me day and night—the me who's not me encamped boldly in Jewish Jerusalem while I go underground with the Arabs."

"So that's why you're staying over there."

"Yes—because I'm not here for him, I'm here for *you.* That was the idea and, Aharon, it's *still* the idea. Look"—and from my jacket pocket I took the sheet of paper on which I'd typed out for him my opening question—"let's start," I said. "The hell with him. Read this."

I'd written: I find echoes in your fiction of two Middle European writers of a previous generation—Bruno Schulz, the Polish Jew who wrote in Polish and was shot and killed at fifty by the Nazis in Drogobych, the heavily Jewish Galician city where he taught high school and lived at home with his family, and Kafka, the Prague Jew who wrote in German and also lived, according to Max Brod, "spellbound in the family circle" for most of his forty-one years. Tell me, how pertinent to your imagination do you consider Schulz and Kafka to be?

Over tea then, we talked about neither me nor not-me but, somewhat more productively, about Schulz and Kafka until finally we grew tired and it was time to go home. Yes, I thought, this is how to prevail —forget this shadow and stick to the task. Of all the people who had assisted me in recovering my strength—among others, Claire, Bernie, the psychopharmacologist—I had chosen Aharon and talking to him as the final way out, the means by which to repossess that part of myself that I thought was lost, the part that was able to discourse and to think and that had simply ceased to exist in the midst of the Halcion wipeout when I was sure that I'd never be able to use my mind again. Halcion had destroyed not merely my ordinary existence, which was bad enough, but whatever was special to me as well, and what Aharon represented was someone whose maturation had been convulsed by the worst possible cruelty and who had managed nonetheless to reclaim his ordinariness *through* his extraordinariness, someone whose conquest of futility and chaos and whose rebirth as a harmonious human being and a superior writer constituted an achievement that, to me, bordered on the miraculous, all the more so because it arose from a force in him utterly invisible to the naked eye.

Later in the evening, before he went to bed, Aharon reformulated what he'd explained at the restaurant and typed out an answer in Hebrew to give to the translator the next day. Speaking of Kafka and himself, he said, "Kafka emerges from an inner world and tries to get some grip on reality, and I came from a world of detailed, empirical reality, the camps and the forests. My real world was far beyond the power of imagination, and my task as an artist was not to develop my imagination but to restrain it, and even then it seemed impossible to me, because everything was so unbelievable that one seemed oneself to be fictional. . . . At first I tried to run away from myself and from

my memories, to live a life that was not my own and to write about a
life that was not my own. But a hidden feeling told me that I was not
allowed to flee from myself and that if I denied the experience of my
childhood in the Holocaust I would be spiritually deformed. . . ."

———

My tiny cousin Apter, the unborn adult, earns his living painting
scenes of the Holy Land for the tourist trade. He sells them from a
little workshop—squeezed between a souvenir stall and a pastry
counter—that he shares with a leather craftsman in the Jewish quarter of the Old City. Tourists who ask his prices are answered in their
native tongues, for Apter, however underdeveloped as a man, happens to be someone whose past has left him fluent in English, Hebrew, Yiddish, Polish, Russian, and German. He even knows some
Ukrainian, the language he calls Goyish. What the tourists are told
when they ask Apter's prices is, "This is not for me to decide"—a
sentiment that, unfortunately, is not humbly feigned: Apter is too
cultivated to think well of his pictures. "I, who love Cézanne, who
weep and pray before his paintings, I paint like a philistine without
any ideals." "Of their kind," I tell him, "they're perfectly all right."
"Why such terrible pictures?" he asks—"Is this too Hitler's fault?" "If
it's any comfort to you, Hitler painted worse." "No," says Apter, "I've
seen his pictures. Even Hitler painted better than I do."

In any one week Apter might be paid as much as a hundred dollars
or as little as five for one of his three-by-four-foot landscapes. A philanthropic English Jew, a Manchester manufacturer who owns a high-
rise condo in Jerusalem and who somehow came to know Apter's
biography, once gave my cousin a thousand-pound check for a single
painting and, ever since, has made of Apter something of a ward,
sending a minion around once a year to purchase more or less the
same painting for the same outlandish price. On the other hand, an
elderly American woman once walked off with a picture without
giving Apter anything, or so Apter says—it was one of those dozen
he paints every week depicting the Jerusalem animal market near St.
Stephen's gate. The theft had left him sobbing in the street. "Police!"

he shouted. "Help me! Someone help me!" But when no one came to his assistance, he raced after her himself and soon chased her down in the next turning, where she was resting against a wall, the stolen painting at her feet. "I am not a greedy man," he said to her, "but, madam, please, I must eat." As Apter recounted the story, she insisted to the small crowd that quickly formed around the weeping artist with his beggarly hands outstretched that she had already paid him a penny, which for such a painting was more than enough. Indignantly she screamed in Yiddish, "Look at his pocket! He's lying!" "The twisted ogre mouth," Apter told me, "the terrible, horrible shriek—Cousin Philip, I understood what I was up against. I said to her, 'Madam, which camp?' 'All of them!' she cried, and then she spat in my face."

In Apter's stories, people steal from him, spit at him, defraud and insult and humiliate him virtually every day and, more often than not, these people who victimize my cousin are survivors of the camps. Are his stories accurate and true? I myself never inquire about their veracity. I think of them instead as fiction that, like so much of fiction, provides the storyteller with the lie through which to expose his unspeakable truth. I treat the stories rather the way Aharon has chosen to understand the story concocted by his Catholic "Jew."

I had every intention, the morning after my dinner with Aharon, of taking a taxi directly from the hotel up to Apter's cubbyhole workshop in the old Jewish quarter and of spending a couple of hours with him before meeting once again with Aharon to resume our conversation over lunch. Instead, I went off in the taxi to the morning session of the Demjanjuk trial—to face down my impostor. If he wasn't there, I'd go on to the King David Hotel. I had to: twenty-four more hours of doing nothing and I'd be able to think of nothing else. As it was, I had been sleepless most of the night, up just about hourly to double-check that my door was locked, and then back to bed, waiting for him to appear above the footboard, Magrittishly suspended in midair, as though the footboard were a footstone, the hotel room a graveyard, and one or the other of us the ghost. And my dreams—rocketing clusters of terrible forebodings too sinister even to be named—I awakened from them with a ruthless determination to murder the bastard with my own two hands. Yes, by morning it was clear even to me that by doing nothing I was only exaggerating everything, and yet *still* I wavered, and it wasn't until the taxi was pulling up at the gate to the Jewish quarter that I finally told the driver to turn around and gave him the address of the convention center at the other end of the city, out beyond the Knesset and the museum, where, in a hall ordinarily used for lectures and movies, Demjanjuk had been on trial now for eleven months. At breakfast I'd copied the address out of the paper and heavily circled the spot on my Jerusalem street map. *No more wavering.*

Outside the doorway to the hall four armed Israeli soldiers were standing about chattering together next to a booth bearing a handwritten sign that read, in Hebrew and in English, "Check Your Weapons Here." I walked by them unnoticed and into an outer lobby where I had only to show my passport to a young policewoman and write my name in a register at her desk to be allowed to proceed on through the metal detector to the inner lobby. I took my time signing in, looking up and down the page to see if my name had been written there already. Failing to find it proved nothing, of course—the court had been in session for an hour by then and there were scores of names recorded in the ledger's pages. What's more, I thought, the passport he held was more likely in his name than in mine. (But without a passport in my name how had he registered as me at his hotel?)

Inside the lobby I had to hand over the passport again, this time as security for an audio headset. The soldier on duty there, another young woman, showed me how I could tune it to a simultaneous English translation of the Hebrew proceedings. I waited for her to recognize me as someone who'd been to the trial before, but once she'd done her job she went back to reading her magazine.

When I entered the courtroom and saw, from behind the last row of spectators, what exactly was going on, I forgot completely why I had come; when, after sorting out the dozen or so figures on the raised platform at the front of the courtroom, I realized which one was the accused, not only did my double cease to exist, but, for the time being, so did I.

There he was. *There he was.* Once upon a time, drove two, three hundred of them into a room barely big enough for fifty, wedged them in every which way, bolted the doors shut, and started up the engine. Pumped out carbon monoxide for half an hour, waited to hear the screams die down, then sent in the live ones to pry out the dead ones and clean up the place for the next big load. "Get that shit out of there," he told them. Back when the transports were really rolling, did this ten, fifteen times a day, sometimes sober, sometimes not, but always with plenty of gusto. Vigorous, healthy boy. Good worker. Never sick. Not even drink slowed him down. Just the opposite. Bludgeoned the bastards with an iron pipe, tore open the pregnant women with his sword, gouged out their eyes, whipped their flesh, drove nails through their ears, once took a drill and bored a hole right in someone's buttocks—felt like it that day, so he did it. Screaming in Ukrainian, shouting in Ukrainian, and when they didn't understand Ukrainian, shot them in the head. What a time! Nothing like it ever again! A mere twenty-two and he owned the place—could do to any of them whatever he wished. To wield a whip and a pistol and a sword and a club, to be young and healthy and strong and drunk and powerful, *boundlessly* powerful, like a god! Nearly a million of them, a *million,* and on every one a Jewish face in which he could read the terror. Of him. *Of him!* Of a peasant boy of twenty-two! In the history of this entire world, had the opportunity ever been given to anyone anywhere to kill so many people all by himself, one by one? What a job! A sensational blowout every day! One continuous party! Blood! Vodka! Women! Death! Power! And the screams! Those unending screams! And all of it *work,* good, hard work and yet wild, wild, untainted joy—the joy most people only get to dream of, nothing short of ecstasy! A year, a year and a half of that is just about enough to satisfy a man forever; after that a man need never complain that life had passed him by; after that anyone could be content with a routine, regular nine-to-five job where no blood ever really flowed except, on rare occasions, as a result of an accident on the factory floor. Nine to five, then home to dinner with the wife and kids—that's all you needed after that. At twenty-two he'd seen all that anyone could ever hope to see. Great while it lasted, stupendous while you were young and fearless and on a tear, running over with animal zest for just about everything, but the sort of thing you outgrow eventually, as indeed he had. You have to know when to quit with a job like that and, luckily, he was one who did.

There he was. There *it* was, bald now and grown stocky, a big, cheerful palooka of sixty-eight, a good father, a good neighbor, loved by his family and all his friends. Still did push-ups every morning, even in his cell, the kind where you've got to leave the floor and clap your hands together before you come back down on your palms— could still boast wrists so thick and strong that, on the plane over, ordinary handcuffs hadn't been large enough to encompass them. Nonetheless, it was nearly fifty years since he'd last smashed open anyone's skull, and he was by now as benign and unfrightening as an old boxing champ. Good old Johnny—man the demon as good old Johnny. Loved his garden, everyone said. Rather tend tomatoes now and raise string beans than bore a hole in somebody's ass with a drill. No, you've got to be young and in your prime, you've got to be on top of things and raring to go to manage successfully even something as simple as having a little fun like that with somebody's big fat behind. He'd sowed his oats and settled down, all that rough stuff sworn off long ago. Could only barely remember now all the hell he had raised. So many years! The way they fly! No, he was somebody else entirely. That hell-raiser was no longer him.

There he was, between two police guards at a small table behind the longer table from which his three attorneys conducted his defense. He wore a pale blue suit over an open-necked shirt, and there was a headset arched across his large bald skull. I didn't realize right off that he was listening to a simultaneous translation of the proceedings into Ukrainian—he looked as though he were passing the time with a favorite pop cassette. His arms were crossed casually over his chest, and ever so faintly his jaws moved up and down as though he were an animal at rest tasting the last of its cud. That's all he did while

I watched him. Once he looked indifferently out at the spectators, entirely at ease with himself, munching almost imperceptibly on nothing. Once he took a sip of water from the glass on the table. Once he yawned. You have the wrong man, this yawn proclaimed. With all due respect, these Jewish old people who identify Demjanjuk as their terrible Ivan are senile or mistaken or lying. I was a German prisoner of war. I know no more about a camp at Treblinka than an ox or a cow does. You might as well have a cud-chewing quadruped on trial here for murdering Jews—it would make as much sense as trying me. I am stupid. I am harmless. I am nobody. I knew nothing then and I know nothing now. My heart goes out to you for all you suffered, but the Ivan you want was never anybody as simple and innocent as good old Johnny the gardener from Cleveland, Ohio.

I remembered reading in the clipping file that on the day the prisoner was extradited from the United States and arrived in Israel, he asked the Israeli police, as they were taking him from the plane in his oversized handcuffs, if he could be permitted to kneel down and kiss the airstrip. A pious pilgrim in the Holy Land, a devout believer and religious soul—that was all he'd ever been. Permission was denied him.

So there he was. Or wasn't.

When I looked around the crowded courtroom for an empty place, I saw that at least a third of the three hundred or so spectators were high school kids, probably bused in together for the morning session. There was also a large contingent of soldiers, and it was in among them that I found a seat about halfway back in the center of the hall. They were boys and girls in their late teens, with that ragtag look that distinguishes Israeli soldiers from all others, and though clearly they too were there for "educational" reasons, I couldn't spot more than a handful of them paying attention to the trial. Most were sprawled across their seats, either shifting restlessly or whispering back and forth or just catatonically daydreaming, and not a few were asleep. The same could be said of the students, some of whom were passing notes like schoolkids anywhere who've been taken on a trip by the teacher and are bored out of their minds. I watched two girls of about fourteen giggling together over a note they'd received from a boy in the row behind them. Their teacher, a lanky, intense young man with glasses, hissed at them to cut it out, but watching the two of them I was thinking, No, no, it's right—to them Treblinka *should* be a nowhere someplace up in the Milky Way; in this country, so heavily populated in its early years by survivors and their families, it's actually a cause for rejoicing, I thought, that by this afternoon these young teenagers won't even remember the defendant's name.

At a dais in the center of the stage sat the three judges in their robes, but it was a while before I could begin to take them in or even to look their way because, once again, I was staring at John Demjanjuk, who claimed to be no less run-of-the-mill than he looked—my face, he argued, my neighbors, my job, my ignorance, my church affiliation, my long, unblemished record as an ordinary family man in Ohio, all this innocuousness disproves a thousand times over these crazy accusations. How could I be both that and this?

Because you are. Because your appearance proves only that to be both a loving grandfather and a mass murderer is not all that difficult. It's because you could do both so well that I can't stop staring at you. Your lawyers may like to think otherwise but this admirably unimportant American life of yours is your *worst* defense—that you've been so wonderful in Ohio at living your little, dull life is precisely what makes you so loathsome here. You've really only lived sequentially the two seemingly antipodal, mutually excluding lives that the Nazis, with no strain to speak of, managed to enjoy simultaneously—so what, in the end, is the big deal? The Germans have proved definitively to all the world that to maintain two radically divergent personalities, one very nice and one not so nice, is no longer the prerogative of psychopaths only. The mystery isn't that you, who had the time of your life at Treblinka, went on to become an amiable, hardworking American nobody but that those who cleaned the corpses out for you, your accusers here, could ever pursue anything resembling the run-of-the-mill after what was done to them by the likes of you—that *they* can manage run-of-the-mill lives, *that's* what's unbelievable!

Not ten feet from Demjanjuk, at a desk at the foot of the judges' dais, was a very pretty dark-haired young woman whose function there I couldn't at first ascertain. Later in the morning I realized that she was a documents clerk assisting the chief judge, but when I first noticed her so handsomely composed in the middle of everything, I could think only of those Jewish women whom Demjanjuk was accused of brutalizing with a sword and a whip and a club in the narrow pathway, the "tube," where those off the cattle cars were corralled together by him before he drove them through the gas-chamber door. She was a young woman of a physical type he must have encountered more than once in the tube and over whom his power there had been absolute. Now, whenever he looked toward the judges or toward the witness stand across from the defense attorney's table, she had to be somewhere in his field of vision, head unshaven, fully clothed, self-assured and unafraid, an attractive young Jewish woman beyond his reach in every way. Before I understood what her job must be, I even wondered if that couldn't have been *why* she'd been situated exactly where she was. I wondered if in his dreams back at the jail he ever saw in that documents clerk the ghost of the young women he had destroyed, if in his dreams there was ever a flicker of remorse, or if, as was more likely, in the dreams as in the waking thoughts he only wished that she had been there in the tube at Treblinka too—she, the three judges, his courtroom guards, the prosecuting attorneys, the translators, and, not least of all, those who came to the courtroom every day to stare as I was staring.

His trial was really no surprise to him, this propaganda trial trumped up by the Jews, this unjust, lying farce of a trial to which he had been dragged in irons from his loving family and his peaceful home. All the way back there in the tube, he'd known the trouble these people could cook up for a simple boy like himself. He knew their hatred of Ukrainians, had known about it all his life. Who had made the famine when he was a child? Who had transformed his country into a cemetery for seven million human beings? Who had turned his neighbors into subhuman creatures devouring mice and rats? As a mere boy he'd seen it all, in his village, in his *family*— mothers who ate the gizzards of the family pet cat, little sisters who had given themselves for a rotten potato, fathers who resorted to cannibalism. The crying. The shrieking. The agony. And everywhere the dead. Seven million of them! Seven million Ukrainian dead! And because of whom? Caused by whom!

Remorse? Go fuck your remorse!

Or did I have Demjanjuk wrong? While he chewed his cud and sipped his water and yawned through the trial's tedious stretches, perhaps his mind was empty of everything but the words "It wasn't me"—needed nothing more than that to keep the past at bay. "I hate no one. Not even you filthy Jews who want me dead. I am an innocent man. It was somebody else."

And *was* it somebody else?

So there he was—or wasn't. I stared and I stared, wondering if, despite all I'd read of the evidence against him, his claim that he was innocent was true; if the survivors who'd identified him could all be lying or wrong; if the identity card of the uniformed concentration-camp guard, bearing his Cyrillic signature and the photo of his youthful face, could indeed be a forgery; if the contradictory stories of his whereabouts as a German POW during the months when the prosecution's evidence placed him at Treblinka, muddled stories that he'd changed at virtually every inquiry before and since he'd received the original indictment, added up nonetheless to a believable alibi; if the demonstrably incriminating lies with which, since 1945, he had been answering the questions of refugee agencies and immigration authorities, lies that had led to his denaturalization and deportation from the United States, somehow pointed not to his guilt but to his innocence.

But the tattoo in his left armpit, the tattoo the Nazis had given their SS staff to register each individual's blood type—could that mean anything other than that he'd worked for them and that here in this courtroom he was lying? If not for fear of the truth being discovered, why had he set about secretly in the DP camp to obliterate that tattoo? Why, if not to hide the truth, had he undertaken the excruciatingly painful process of rubbing it bloody with a rock, of waiting for the flesh to heal, and of then repeatedly scraping and scraping with the rock until in time the skin was so badly scarred that his telltale tattoo was eradicated? "My tragic mistake," Demjanjuk told the court, "is that I can't think properly and I can't answer properly." Stupidity—the only thing to which he had confessed since the complaint identifying him as Ivan the Terrible was first filed against him by the U.S. Attorney's office eleven years earlier in Cleveland. And you cannot hang a man for being stupid. The KGB had framed him. Ivan the Terrible was somebody else.

A disagreement was brewing between the chief judge, a somber, gray-haired man in his sixties named Dov Levin, and the Israeli defense lawyer, Yoram Sheftel. I couldn't understand what the dispute was about because my headset had turned out to be defective, and rather than get up and possibly lose my seat while going for a replacement, I stayed where I was and, without understanding anything of the conflict, listened to the exchange heat up in Hebrew. Seated on the dais to the left of Levin was a middle-aged female judge with glasses and short-clipped hair; beneath her robe she was mannishly attired in a shirt and tie. To Levin's right was a smallish, bearded judge with a skullcap, a grandfatherly, sagacious-looking man of about my age and the sole Orthodox member of the panel.

I watched as Sheftel grew more and more exasperated with whatever Levin was telling him. The day before, I'd read in the Demjanjuk clipping file about the lawyer's flamboyant, hotheaded style. The theatrical zealousness with which he espoused his client's innocence, particularly in the face of the anguished eyewitness survivor testimony, seemed to have made him less than beloved by his compatriots; indeed, since the trial was being broadcast nationally on radio and television, chances were that the young Israeli lawyer had become one of the least popular figures in all of Jewish history. I remembered reading that during a noon recess some months back, a courtroom spectator whose family had been killed at Treblinka had shouted at Sheftel, "I can't understand how a Jew can defend such a criminal. How can a Jew defend a Nazi? How can Israel allow it? Let me tell you what they did to my family, let me explain what they did to my body!" As best I could gather from his argument with the chief judge, neither that nor any other challenge to his Jewish loyalties had diminished Sheftel's confidence or the forcefulness he was prepared to bring to Demjanjuk's defense. I wondered how endangered he was when he exited the courtroom, this small, unstoppable battering ram of a man, this engine of defiance so easily discernible by his long sideburns and his narrow-gauge beard. Stationed at regular intervals around the edge of the courtroom were unarmed uniformed policemen with walkie-talkies; undoubtedly there were armed plainclothesmen in the hall as well—here Sheftel was no less secure from harm than was his hated client. But when he drove home at the end of the day in his luxurious Porsche? When he went out with his girlfriend to the beach or a movie? There had to be people all over Israel, people watching television at this very moment, who would have been glad to shut him up with whatever it took to do it right.

Sheftel's dispute with the judge had resulted in Levin's declaring an early lunch recess. I came to my feet with everyone else as the judges stood and left the dais. All around me the high school kids raced for the exits; only a little less eagerly, the soldiers followed them out. In a few minutes no more than thirty or so spectators remained scattered about the hall, most huddled together talking softly to one another, the rest just sitting silently alone as though too infirm to move or swallowed up in a trance. All were elderly—retired, I thought at first, people who had the time to attend the sessions regularly. Then I realized that they must be camp survivors. And what was it like for them to find standing only a few feet away the mustached young man in the neat gray business suit whom I now recognized, from his newspaper photos, as Demjanjuk's twenty-two-year-old son, John junior, the son who vociferously protested that his father was being framed and who, in his media interviews here, proclaimed his father's absolute and total innocence of all wrongdoing? These survivors had, of course, to recognize who he was—I'd read that at the start of the trial, the son, at the family's request, had been seated prominently right up behind his father on the stage, and even I, a newcomer, had spotted him when Demjanjuk, several times that morning, had looked down into the first row, where John junior was seated, and, grimacing unself-consciously, had signaled to him his boredom with the tiresome legal wrangling. I calculated that John junior had been no more than eleven or twelve when his father had first been fingered as Ivan the Terrible by U.S. immigration. The boy had gone through his childhood thinking, as so many lucky children do, that he had a name no more or less distinctive than anyone else's and, happily enough, a life to match. Well, he would never be able to believe that again: forevermore he was the namesake of the Demjanjuk whom the Jews had tried before all of mankind for someone else's horrible crime. Justice may be served by this trial, but his children, I thought, are now plunged into the hatred—the curse is revived.

Did no survivor in all of Israel think of killing John Demjanjuk, Jr., of taking revenge on the guilty father through the perfectly innocent son? Was there no one whose family had been exterminated at Treblinka who had thought of kidnapping him and of then mutilating him, gradually, piecemeal, an inch at a go, until Demjanjuk could take no more and admitted to the court who he was? Was there no survivor, driven insane with rage by this defendant's carefree yawning and his indifferent chewing of his cud, no grieving, wrathful wreck of a survivor, blighted and enraged enough to envisage in the torturing of the one the means of extracting a confession from the other, to perceive in the outright murder of the next in line a perfectly just and fitting requital?

I asked these questions of myself when I saw the tall, slender, well-groomed young man headed briskly toward the main exit with the three defense lawyers—I was astonished that, like Sheftel, Demjanjuk's namesake, his male successor and only son, was about to step into the Jerusalem streets wholly unprotected.

———

Outside the courtroom the balmy winter weather had taken a dramatic turn. It was another day entirely. A tremendous rainstorm was raging, sheets of rain driven laterally by a strong wind that made it impossible to discern anything beyond the first few rows of cars in the lot surrounding the convention center. The people trying to determine how to leave the building were packed together in the outer foyer and on the walkway under the overhang. It was only when I'd moved into this crowd that I remembered whom I'd come looking for—my tiny local difficulty had been utterly effaced by a very great mass of real horror. To have run off, as I had, to hunt him down seemed to me now far worse than rash; it was to succumb momentarily to a form of insanity. I was thoroughly ashamed of myself and disgusted once again for getting into a dialogue with this annoyance —how crazy and foolish to have taken the bait! And how little urgency finding him had for me now. Laden with all I'd just witnessed, I resolved to put myself to my proper use.

I was to meet Aharon for lunch just off Jaffa Street, at the Ticho House, but with the rainstorm growing more and more violent I didn't see how I could possibly get there in time. Yet, having just removed myself from standing in my own way, I was determined that nothing, but nothing, should obstruct me, least of all the inclement weather. Squinting through the rain to search for a taxi, I suddenly saw young Demjanjuk dart out from beneath the overhang, following behind one of his lawyers into the open door of a waiting car. I had the impulse to race after him and ask if I could bum a ride to downtown Jerusalem. I didn't do it, of course, but if I had, might I not myself have been mistaken for the self-appointed Jewish avenger and been gunned down in my tracks? But by whom? Young Demjanjuk was there for the taking. And could I be the only person in all of this crowd to see how very easy taking him could be?

About a quarter of a mile up a hill from the parking lot, there was a big hotel that I remembered seeing on the drive in, and, desperate, I finally stepped out of the crowd and into the rainstorm and made a dash for the hotel. Minutes later, my clothes soaked and my shoes filled with water, I was standing in the hotel lobby looking for a phone to call a taxi, when someone tapped me on the shoulder. I turned to find facing me the other Philip Roth.

3

We

"I can't speak," he said. "It's you. You came!"

But the one who couldn't speak was I. I was breathless, and only in part because of running uphill against the lashing force of that storm. I suppose until that moment I'd never wholeheartedly believed in his existence, at least as anything more substantial than that pompous voice on the telephone and some transparently ridiculous newspaper blather. Seeing him materialize voluminously in space, measurable as a customer in a clothing shop, palpable as a prizefighter up in the ring, was as frightening as seeing a vaporous ghost—and simultaneously electrifying, as though after immersion in that torrential storm, I'd been doused, for good measure, like a cartoon-strip character, full in the face with an antihallucinogenic bucket of cold water. As jolted by the spellbinding reality of his unreality as by its immensely disorienting antithesis, I was at a loss to remember the plans I'd made for how to act and what to say when I'd set out to hunt him down in the taxi that morning—in the mental simulation of our face-off I had failed to remember that the face-off would not, when it came

to pass, be a mental simulation. He was crying. He had taken me in
his arms, sopping wet though I was, and begun to cry, and not undra-
matically either—as though one or the other of us had just returned
intact from crossing Central Park alone at night. Tears of joyous relief
—and I had imagined that confronted with the materialization of *me*,
he would recoil in fear and capitulate.

"Philip Roth! The real Philip Roth—after all these years!" His body
trembled with emotion, tremendous emotion even in the two hands
that tightly grasped my back.

It required a series of violent thrusts with my elbows to unlock his
hold on me. "And you," I said, shoving him a little as I stepped away,
"you must be the fake Philip Roth."

He laughed. But still cried! Not even in my mental simulation had
I loathed him quite as I did seeing those stupid, unaccountable tears.

"Fake, oh, compared to you, *absolutely* fake—compared to you,
nothing, no one, a cipher. I can't tell you what it's like for me! In
Israel! In Jerusalem! I don't know what to say! I don't know where to
begin! The books! Those books! I go back to *Letting Go,* my favorite
to this day! Libby Herz and the psychiatrist! Paul Herz and that coat!
I go back to 'The Love Vessel' in the old *Dial!* The work you've done!
The potshots you've taken! Your women! Ann! Barbara! Claire! Such
terrific women! I'm sorry, but imagine yourself in my place. For me
—to meet you—in Jerusalem! What brings you here?"

To this dazzling little question, so ingenuously put, I heard myself
reply, "Passing through."

"I'm looking at myself," he said, ecstatically, "except it's *you.*"

He was exaggerating, something he may have been inclined to do.
I saw before me a face that I would not very likely have taken for my
own had I found it looking back at me that morning from the mirror.
Someone else, a stranger, someone who had seen only my photograph or some newspaper caricature of me, might possibly have been
taken in by the resemblance, especially if the face called itself by my
name, but I couldn't believe that there was anyone who would say,
"Don't fool me, you're really that writer," had it gone about its business as Mr. Nusbaum's or Dr. Schwartz's. It was actually a convention-

ally better-looking face, a little less mismade than my own, with a more strongly defined chin and not so large a nose, one that, also, didn't flatten Jewishly like mine at the tip. It occurred to me that he looked like the after to my before in the plastic surgeon's advertisement.

"What's your game, my friend?"

"No game," he replied, surprised and wounded by my angry tone. "And I'm no fake. I was using 'real' ironically."

"Well, I'm not so pretty as you and I'm not so ironical as you and I was using 'fake' *unerringly.*"

"Hey, take it easy, you don't know your strength. Don't call names, okay?"

"You go around pretending to be me."

This brought that smile back—"You go around pretending to be *me,*" he loathsomely replied.

"You exploit the physical resemblance," I went on, "by telling people that you are the writer, the author of my books."

"I don't have to tell them anything. They take me for the author of those books right off. It happens all the time."

"And you just don't bother to correct them."

"Look, can I buy you lunch? You—here! What a shock to the system! But can we stop this sparring and sit down in this hotel and talk seriously together over lunch? Will you give me a chance to *explain?*"

"I want to know what you're up to, buddy!"

"I *want* you to know," he said gently and, like a Marcel Marceau at his corniest, with an exaggerated tamping-down gesture of his two hands, indicated that I ought to try to stop shouting and be reasonable like him. "I want you to know *everything.* I've dreamed all my life—"

"Oh no, not the 'dreams,'" I told him, incensed now not only by the ingenue posturing, not only by how he persisted in coming on so altogether unlike the stentorian Diasporist Herzl he'd impersonated for me on the phone, but by the Hollywooded version of my face so nebbishly pleading with me to try to calm down. Odd, but for the

moment that smoothed-out rectification of my worst features got my
goat as much as anything did. What do we despise most in the appearance of somebody who looks like ourselves? For me, it was the
earnest attractiveness. "Please, not the softly melting eyes of the nice
Jewish boy. Your 'dreams'! I *know* what you've been up to here, I
know what's been going on here between you and the press, so just
can the harmless-shlimazl act now."

"But your eyes melt a little too, you know. I know the things you've
done for people. You hide your sweet side from the public—all the
glowering photographs and I'm-nobody's-sucker interviews. But behind the scenes, as I happen to know, you're one very soft touch, Mr.
Roth."

"Look, what are *you* and who are *you?* Answer me!"

"Your greatest admirer."

"Try again."

"I can't do better than that."

"Try anyway. *Who are you?*"

"The person in the world who has read and loved your books like
no one else. Not just once, not just twice—so many times I'm embar-
rassed to say."

"Yes, that embarrasses you in front of me? What a sensitive boy."

"You look at me as though I'm fawning, but it's the truth—I know
your books inside out. I know your *life* inside out. I could be your
biographer. I *am* your biographer. The insults you've put up with,
they drive me nuts just on your behalf. *Portnoy's Complaint,* not
even nominated for a National Book Award! The book of the decade
and not even *nominated!* Well, you had no friend in Swados; he
called the shots on that committee and had it in for you but good. So
much animosity—I don't get it. Podhoretz—I actually cannot speak
the man's name without tasting my gall in my mouth. And Gilman—
that attack on *When She Was Good,* on the integrity of *that book.*
Saying you wrote for Womrath's Book Store—about that perfectly
honorable little book! And Professor Epstein, *there's* a genius. And
those broads at *Ms.* And this exhibitionist Wolcott—"

I sank back into the chair behind me, and there in the hotel lobby,

clammy and shivering under the rain-soaked clothes, I listened as he
recalled every affront that had ever appeared in print, every assault
that had ever been made on my writing and me—some, insults so
small that, miraculously, even I had forgotten them, however much
they might have exasperated me a quarter of a century earlier. It was
as though the genie of grievance had escaped the bottle in which a
writer's resentments are pickled and preserved and had manifested
itself in humanish form, spawned by the inbreeding of my overly
licked oldest wounds and mockingly duplicating the man I am.

"—Capote on the Carson show, coming on with that 'Jewish Mafia'
shit, 'From Columbia University to Columbia Pictures'—"

"Enough," I said, and pushed myself violently up out of the chair.
"That is really enough!"

"It's been no picnic, that's all I'm trying to say. I know what a
struggle living is for you, Philip. May I call you Philip?"

"Why not? That's the name. What's yours?"

With that sonny-boy smile I wanted to smash with a brick, he
replied, "Sorry, truly sorry, but it's the same. Come on, have some
lunch. Maybe," he said, pointing to my shoes, "you want to stop in
the toilet and shake those out. You got drenched, man."

"And you're not wet at all," I observed.

"Hitched a ride up the hill."

Could it be? Hitched the ride I'd thought of hitching with Demjanjuk's son?

"You were at the trial then," I said.

"There every day," he replied. "Go, go ahead, dry off," he said, "I'll
get a table for us in the dining room. Maybe you can relax over lunch.
We have a lot to talk about, you and me."

In the bathroom I took a deliberately long time to dry myself off,
thinking to give him every opportunity to call a taxi and make a clean
getaway without ever having to confront me again. His had been a
commendable, if nauseating, performance for someone who, despite
his cleverly seizing the initiative, had to have been only a little less
caught off guard in the lobby than I was; as the sweet-natured innocent, cravenly oscillating between bootlicking and tears, his had been

a more startlingly original performance by far than my own mundane
portrayal of the angry victim. Yet the impact of *my* materialization
must surely have been more galvanic even for him than his had been
for me and he had to be thinking hard now about the risk of pushing
this thing further. I gave him all the time he needed to wise up and
clear out and disappear for good, and then, with my hair combed and
my shoes each emptied of about half a cup of water, I came back up
into the lobby to phone a taxi to get me over to my lunch date with
Aharon—I was half an hour late already—and immediately I spotted
him just outside the entryway to the restaurant, ingratiating smile still
intact, more handsomely me than even before.

"I was beginning to think Mr. Roth had taken a powder," he said.

"And I was hoping the same about you."

"Why," he asked, "would I want to do a thing like that?"

"Because you're involved in a deceptive practice. Because you're
breaking the law."

"Which law? Israeli law, Connecticut state law, or international
law?"

"The law that says that a person's identity is his private property
and can't be appropriated by somebody else."

"Ah, so you've been studying your Prosser."

"Prosser?"

"Professor Prosser's *Handbook of the Law of Torts.*"

"I haven't been studying anything. All I need to know about a case
like this common sense can tell me."

"Well, still, take a look at Prosser. In 1960, in the *California Law
Review,* Prosser published a long article, a reconsideration of the
original 1890 Warren and Brandeis *Harvard Law Review* article in
which they'd borrowed Judge Cooley's phrase 'the general right to
be let alone' and staked out the dimensions of the privacy interest.
Prosser discusses privacy cases as having four separate branches and
causes of action—one, intrusion upon seclusion; two, public disclo-
sure of private facts; three, false light in the public eye; and four,
appropriation of identity. The prima facie case is defined as follows:
'One who appropriates to his own use or benefit the name or likeness

of another is subject to liability to the other for invasion of his privacy.' Let's have lunch."

The dining room was completely empty. There wasn't even a
waiter to show us in. At the table he chose for us, directly in the
center of the room, he drew out my chair for me as though *he* were
the waiter and stood politely behind it while I sat down. I couldn't
tell whether this was straight satire or seriously meant—yet *more*
idolatry—and even wondered if, with my behind an inch from the
seat, he might do what sadistic kids like to do in grade school and at
the last moment pull the chair out from under me so that I landed on
the floor. I grabbed an edge of the chair in either hand and pulled the
seat safely under me as I sat.

"Hey," he said, laughing, "you don't entirely trust me," and came
around to take the chair across the table.

An indication of how stunned I'd been out in the lobby—and had
remained even off by myself in the bathroom, where I had somehow
got round to believing that victory was achieved and he was about to
run off, never to dare to return—was that only when we were sitting
opposite each other did I notice that he was dressed identically to
me: not similarly, *identically*. Same washed-out button-down, open-
neck Oxford blue shirt, same well-worn tan V-neck cashmere
sweater, same cuffless khaki trousers, same gray Brooks Brothers her-
ringbone sports jacket threadbare at the elbows—a perfect replica of
the colorless uniform that I had long ago devised to simplify life's
sartorial problem and that I had probably recycled not even ten times
since I'd been a penniless freshman instructor at the University of
Chicago in the mid-fifties. I'd realized, while packing my suitcase for
Israel, that I was just about ragged enough for my periodic overhaul
—and so too, I saw, was *he*. There was a nub of tiny threadlets where
the middle front button had come off his jacket—I noticed because
for some time now I'd been exhibiting a similar nub of threadlets
where the middle button had yet again vanished from *my* jacket. And
with that, everything inexplicable became even more inexplicable, as
though what we were missing were our navels.

"What do you make of Demjanjuk?" he asked.

Were we going to *chat?* About Demjanjuk no less?

"Don't we have other, more pressing concerns, you and I? Don't we have the prima facie case of identity appropriation to talk about, as outlined in point four by Professor Prosser?"

"But all that sort of pales, don't you think, beside what you saw in that courtroom this morning?"

"How would you know what I saw this morning?"

"Because I saw you seeing it. I was in the balcony. Upstairs with the press and the television. You couldn't take your eyes off him. Nobody can the first time. Is he or isn't he, was he or wasn't he?—the first time, that's all that goes round in anyone's head."

"But if you'd spotted me from the balcony, what was all that emotion about back in the lobby? You already knew I was here."

"You minimize your meaning, Philip. Still doing battle against being a personage. You don't entirely take in who you are."

"So you're taking it in for me—is that the story?"

When, in response, he lowered his face—as though I'd impertinently raised a subject we'd already agreed to consider off bounds—I saw that his hair had seriously thinned out and was striated gray in a pattern closely mirroring my own. Indeed, all those differences between our features that had been so reassuringly glaring at first sight were dismayingly evaporating the more accustomed to his appearance I became. Penitentially tilted forward like that, his balding head looked *astonishingly* like mine.

I repeated my question. *"Is* that the story? Since I apparently don't 'take in' what a personage I am, you have kindly taken it upon yourself to go about as this great personage *for* me?"

"Like to see a menu, Philip? Or would you like a drink?"

There was still no waiter anywhere, and it occurred to me that this dining room was not even open yet for business. I reminded myself then that the escape hatch of the "dream" was no longer available to me. Because I am sitting in a dining room where there is no food to be obtained; because across from me there sits a man who, I must admit, is nearly my duplicate in every way, down to the button missing from his jacket and the silver-gray filaments of hair that he has just pointedly displayed to me; because, instead of adjusting manfully to the predicament and intuitively taking control, I am being pushed to within an inch of I don't know what intemperate act by this stupidly evolving, unendurable farce, apparently all this only means that I am wide awake. What is being manufactured here is *not* a dream, however weightless and incorporeal life happens to feel at this moment and however alarmingly I may sense myself as a speck of being embodying nothing but its own speckness, a tiny existence even more repugnant than his.

"I'm talking to you," I said.

"I know. Amazing. And *I'm* talking to *you.* And not just in my head. More amazing."

"I meant I would like an *answer* from you. A serious answer."

"Okay, I'll answer seriously. I'll be blunt, too. Your prestige has been a little wasted on you. There's a lot you haven't done with it that you could have done—a lot of good. That is not a criticism, just a statement of fact. It's enough for you to write—God knows a writer like you doesn't owe anyone any more than that. Of course not every writer is equipped to be a public figure."

"So you've gone public for me."

"A rather cynical way to put it, wouldn't you say?"

"Yes? What is the uncynical way?"

"Look, at bottom—and this is meant with no disrespect, but since bluntness is *your* style—at bottom you are only instrumental."

I was looking at his glasses. It had taken this long for me to get round to the glasses, glasses framed in a narrow gold half-frame exactly like my own. . . . Meanwhile he had reached inside his jacket pocket and withdrawn a worn old billfold (yes, worn exactly like mine) and extracted from it an American passport that he handed across the table to me. The photograph was one taken of me some ten years ago. And the signature was my signature. Flipping through its pages, I saw that Philip Roth had been stamped in and out of half a dozen countries that I myself had never visited: Finland, West Germany, Sweden, Poland, Romania.

"Where'd you get this?"

"Passport office."

"This happens to be me, you know." I was pointing to the photograph.

"No," he quietly replied. "It's me. Before my cancer."

"Tell me, did you think this all out beforehand or are you making the story up as you go along?"

"I'm terminally ill," he replied, and so confusing was that remark that when he reached across for the passport, the strongest and best evidence I had of the fraud that he was perpetrating, I stupidly handed it back to him instead of keeping it and causing a fracas then and there. "Look," he said, leaning intensely across the table in a way I recognized as an imitation of my own conversational style, "about the two of us and our connection is there really any more to say? Maybe the trouble is that you haven't read enough Jung. Maybe it comes down to nothing more than that. You're a Freudian, I'm a Jungian. Read Jung. He'll help you. I began to study him when I first had to deal with you. He explained for me parallelisms that are unexplainable. You have the Freudian belief in the sovereign power of causality. Causeless events don't exist in your universe. To you things that aren't thinkable in intellectual terms aren't worth thinking about. A lot of smart Jews are like that. Things that aren't thinkable in intellectual terms don't even exist. How can I exist, a duplicate of you? How can you exist, a duplicate of me? You and I defy causal explanation. Well, read Jung on 'synchronicity.' There are meaningful arrangements that defy causal explanation and they are happening *all the time.* We are a case of synchronicity, synchronistic phenomena. Read a little Jung, Philip, if only for your peace of mind. 'The uncontrollability of real things'—Carl Jung knows all about it. Read *The Secret of the Golden Flower.* It'll open your eyes to a whole other world. You look stupefied—without a causal explanation you are lost. How on this planet can there be two men of the same age who happen not only to look alike but to bear the same name? All right, you *need* causality? I'll *give* you causality. Forget about just you and me—there would have been another *fifty* little Jewish boys of our age growing up to look like us if it hadn't been for certain tragic events that occurred in Europe between 1939 and 1945. And is it impossible that half a dozen of them might' not have been Roths? Is our family name that rare? Is it impossible that a couple of those little Roths might not have been called after a grandfather Fayvel, like you, Philip, and like me? You, from your career perspective, may think it's horrible that there are two of us and that you are not unique. From my Jewish perspective, I have to say I think it's horrible that *only* two are left."

"No, no, not horrible—*actionable.* It's actionable that of the two of us left, one of us goes around impersonating the other. Had there been seven thousand of us left in the world, only one of us, you see, would have written my books."

"Philip, nobody could treasure your books more than I do. But we are at a point in Jewish history when maybe there is more for us to be talking about, especially together here at last in Jerusalem, than your books. Okay, I have allowed people to confuse me with you. But, tell me, please, how else could I have got to Lech Walesa?"

"You can't seriously be asking me that question."

"I can and I am, and with good reason. By seeing Lech Walesa, by having with him the fruitful talk we had, what harm did I do you? What harm did I do anyone? The harm will come only if, because of your books and for no other reason, you should want to be so legal-istic as to go ahead and try to undo everything I achieved in Gdansk. Yes, the law *is* on your side. Who says no? I wouldn't have undertaken an operation on this scale without first knowing in every last detail the law that I am up against. In the case of *Onassis v. Christian Dior–New York, Inc.,* where a professional model, a Jackie Onassis look-alike, was used in advertisements for Dior dresses, the court deter-mined that the effect of using a look-alike was to represent Jackie Onassis as associated with the product and upheld her claim. In the case of *Carson v. Here's Johnny Portable Toilets,* a similar decision was reached. Because the phrase 'Here's Johnny' was associated with Carson and his TV show, the toilet company had no right, according to the court, to display the phrase on their portable toilets. The law couldn't be any more clear: even if the defendant is using *his own name,* he may be liable to prosecution for appropriation if the use implies that some other famous individual of that name is actually being represented. I am, as you see, more knowledgeable than you are about exactly what *is* actionable here. But I really cannot believe that you can believe that there is a telling similarity between the peddling of high-fashion shmatas, let alone the selling and renting of portable toilets, and the mission to which I have dedicated my life. I took your achievement as my own; if you like, all right, I stole your books. *But for what purpose?* Once again the Jewish people are at a terrible crossroad. Because of Israel. Because of Israel and the way that Israel endangers us all. Forget the law and listen, please, to what I have to say. The majority of Jews don't choose Israel. Its existence only confuses everyone, Jews and Gentiles alike. I repeat: Israel only *endangers* everyone. Look at what happened to Pollard. I am haunted by Jonathan Pollard. An American Jew paid by Israeli intelligence to spy against his own country's military establishment. I'm frightened by Jonathan Pollard. I'm frightened because if I'd been in his job with U.S. naval intelligence, *I would have done exactly the same thing.* I daresay, Philip Roth, that *you* would have done the same thing if you were convinced, as Pollard was convinced, that, by turning over to Israel secret U.S. information about Arab weapons systems, you could be saving Jewish lives. Pollard had fantasies about saving Jewish lives. I understand that, *you* understand that: Jewish lives must be saved, and at absolutely any cost. But the cost is not betraying your country, it's *greater* than that: it's defusing the country that most endangers Jewish lives today—and that is the country called Israel! I would not say this to anyone else—I am saying this only to you. *But it must be said.* Pollard is just another Jewish victim of the existence of Israel— because Pollard enacted no more, really, than the Israelis demand of Diaspora Jews *all the time.* I don't hold Pollard responsible, I hold Israel responsible—Israel, which with its all-embracing Jewish totalism has replaced the goyim as the greatest intimidator of Jews in the world; Israel, which today, with its hunger for Jews, is, in many, many terrible ways, deforming and disfiguring Jews as only our anti-Semitic enemies once had the power to do. Pollard loves Jews. I love Jews.

You love Jews. But no more Pollards, please. God willing, no more Demjanjuks either. We haven't even spoken of Demjanjuk. I want to hear what you saw in that courtroom today. Instead of talking about lawsuits, can we, now that we know each other a little better, talk about—"

"No. *No.* What is going on in that courtroom is not an issue between us. Nothing there has the least bearing on this fraud that you are perpetrating by passing yourself off as me."

"*Again* with the fraud," he mumbled sadly, with a deliberately comical Jewish intonation. "Demjanjuk in that courtroom has *every-thing* to do with us. If it wasn't for Demjanjuk, for the Holocaust, for Treblinka—"

"If this is a joke," I said, rising out of my seat, "it is a very stupid, very wicked joke and I advise you to stop it right now! Not Treblinka —not that, please. Look, I don't know who you are or what you are up to, but I'm warning you—pack up and get out of here. Pack it up and go!"

"Oh, where the hell is a waiter? Your clothes are wet, you haven't eaten—" And to calm me down he reached across the table and took hold of my hand. "Just hang on—*waiter!*"

"Hands off, clown! I don't want lunch—*I want you out of my life!* Like Christian Dior, like Johnny Carson and the portable toilet—*out!*"

"Christ, you're on a short fuse, Philip. You're a real heart-attack type. You act like I'm trying to ridicule you, when, Christ, if I valued you any more—"

"Enough—*you're a fraud!*"

"But," he pleaded, "you don't know yet what I'm trying to *do.*"

"I *do* know. You are about to empty Israel of the Ashkenazis. You are about to resettle Jews in all the wonderful places where they were once so beloved by the local yokels. You and Walesa, you and Ceauşescu are about to avert a second Holocaust!"

"But—then—that was *you,*" he cried. "*You* were Pierre Roget! You tricked me!" And he slumped over in his chair at the horror of the discovery, pure commedia dell'arte.

"Repeat that, will you? I did what?"

But he was now in tears, second time since we'd met. What *is* it with this guy? Watching him shamelessly carrying on so emotionally reminded me of my Halcion crying jags. Was this his parody of my powerlessness, still more of his comic improvisation, or was he hooked on Halcion himself? Is this a brilliant creative disposition whose ersatz satire I'm confronting or a genuine ersatz maniac? I thought, Let Oliver Sacks figure him out—you get a taxi and go, but then somewhere within me a laugh began, and soon I was overcome with laughter, laughter pouring forth from some cavernous core of understanding deeper even than my fears: despite all the unanswered questions, never, never had anybody seemed less of a menace to me or a more pathetic rival for my birthright. He struck me instead as *a great idea* . . . yes, a great idea breathing with life!

———

Although I was over an hour late for our appointment, I found Aharon still waiting for me in the café of the Ticho House when finally I arrived there. He had figured that it was the rainstorm that delayed me and had been sitting alone at a table with a glass of water, patiently reading a book.

For the next hour and a half we ate our lunch and talked about his novel *Tzili,* beginning with how the child's consciousness seemed to me the hidden perspective from which not just this but other novels of his were narrated as well. I said nothing about anything else. Having left the aspirant Philip Roth weeping in that empty hotel dining room, crushed and humiliated by my loud laughter, I had no idea what to expect next. I had faced him down—so now what?

This, I told myself: *this.* Stick to the task!

Out of the long lunchtime conversation, Aharon and I were able to compose, in writing, the next segment of our exchange.

ROTH: In your books, there's no news from the public realm that might serve as a warning to an Appelfeld victim, nor is the victim's impending doom presented as part of a European catastrophe. The historical focus is supplied by the reader, who understands, as the victims cannot, the magnitude of the enveloping evil. Your reticence as a historian, when combined with

the historical perspective of a knowing reader, accounts for the
peculiar impact your work has—for the power that emanates
from stories that are told through such very modest means. Also,
dehistoricizing the events and blurring the background, you
probably approximate the disorientation felt by people who
were unaware that they were on the brink of a cataclysm.

It's occurred to me that the perspective of the adults in your
fiction resembles in its limitations the viewpoint of a child, who,
of course, has no historical calendar in which to place unfolding
events and no intellectual means of penetrating their meaning. I
wonder if your own consciousness as a child at the edge of the
Holocaust isn't mirrored in the simplicity with which the imminent horror is perceived in your novels.

APPELFELD: You're right. In *Badenheim 1939* I completely ignored the historical explanation. I assumed that the historical
facts were known and that readers would fill in what was missing. You're also correct, it seems to me, in assuming that my description of the Second World War has something in it of a
child's vision. Historical explanations, however, have been alien
to me ever since I became aware of myself as an artist. And the
Jewish experience in the Second World War was not "historical." We came in contact with archaic mythical forces, a kind
of dark subconscious the meaning of which we did not know,
nor do we know it to this day. This world appears to be rational (with trains, departure times, stations, and engineers),
but in fact these were journeys of the imagination, lies and
ruses, which only deep, irrational drives could have invented.
I didn't understand, nor do I yet understand, the motives of the
murderers.

I was a victim, and I try to understand the victim. That is a
broad, complicated expanse of life that I've been trying to deal
with for thirty years now. I haven't idealized the victims. I don't
think that in *Badenheim 1939* there's any idealization either. By
the way, Badenheim is a rather real place, and spas like that were
scattered all over Europe, shockingly petit bourgeois and idiotic
in their formalities. Even as a child I saw how ridiculous they
were.

It is generally agreed, to this day, that Jews are deft, cunning, and sophisticated creatures, with the wisdom of the world stored up in them. But isn't it fascinating to see how easy it was to fool the Jews? With the simplest, almost childish tricks they were gathered up in ghettos, starved for months, encouraged with false hopes, and finally sent to their death by train. That ingenuousness stood before my eyes while I was writing *Badenheim*. In that ingenuousness I found a kind of distillation of humanity. Their blindness and deafness, their obsessive preoccupation with themselves is an integral part of their ingenuousness. The murderers were practical, and they knew just what they wanted. The ingenuous person is always a shlimazl, a clownish victim of misfortune, never hearing the danger signals in time, getting mixed up, tangled up, and finally falling into the trap. Those weaknesses charmed me. I fell in love with them. The myth that the Jews run the world with their machinations turned out to be somewhat exaggerated.

ROTH: Of all your translated books, *Tzili* depicts the harshest reality and the most extreme form of suffering. Tzili, the simplest child of a poor Jewish family, is left alone when her family flees the Nazi invasion. The novel recounts her horrendous adventures in surviving and her excruciating loneliness among the brutal peasants for whom she works. The book strikes me as a counterpart to Jerzy Kosinski's *The Painted Bird*. Though less grotesque, *Tzili* portrays a fearful child in a world even bleaker and more barren than Kosinski's, a child moving in isolation through a landscape as uncongenial to human life as any in Beckett's *Molloy*.

As a boy you wandered alone like Tzili after your escape, at age nine, from the camp. I've been wondering why, when you came to transform your own life in an unknown place, hiding out among the hostile peasants, you decided to imagine a girl as the survivor of this ordeal. And did it occur to you ever *not* to fictionalize this material but to present your experiences as you remember them, to write a survivor's tale as direct, say, as Primo Levi's depiction of his Auschwitz incarceration?

APPELFELD: I have never written about things as they happened.

All my works are indeed chapters from my most personal experience, but nevertheless they are not "the story of my life." The things that happened to me in my life have already happened, they are already formed, and time has kneaded them and given them shape. To write things as they happened means to enslave oneself to memory, which is only a minor element in the creative process. To my mind, to create means to order, sort out and choose the words and the pace that fit the work. The materials are indeed materials from one's life, but, ultimately, the creation is an independent creature.

I tried several times to write "the story of my life" in the woods after I ran away from the camp. But all my efforts were in vain. I wanted to be faithful to reality and to what really happened. But the chronicle that emerged proved to be a weak scaffolding. The result was rather meager, an unconvincing imaginary tale. The things that are most true are easily falsified.

Reality, as you know, is always stronger than the human imagination. Not only that, reality can permit itself to be unbelievable, inexplicable, out of all proportion. The created work, to my regret, cannot permit itself all that.

The reality of the Holocaust surpassed any imagination. If I remained true to the facts, no one would believe me. But the moment I chose a girl, a little older than I was at that time, I removed "the story of my life" from the mighty grip of memory and gave it over to the creative laboratory. There memory is not the only proprietor. There one needs a causal explanation, a thread to tie things together. The exceptional is permissible only if it is part of an overall structure and contributes to an understanding of that structure. I had to remove those parts that were unbelievable from "the story of my life" and present a more credible version.

When I wrote *Tzili* I was about forty years old. At that time I was interested in the possibilities of naiveness in art. Can there be a naive modern art? It seemed to me that without the naiveté still found among children and old people and, to some extent, in ourselves, the work of art would be flawed. I tried to correct that flaw. God knows how successful I was.

Dear Philip,

I enraged you/you blitzed me. Every word I spoke—stupid/ wrong/unnatural. Had to be. Been dreading/dreaming this meeting since 1959. Saw your photo on *Goodbye, Columbus*/knew that my life would never be the same. Explained to everyone we were two different people/had no desire to be anyone but myself/wanted *my* fate/hoped your first book would be your last/wanted you to fail and disappear/thought constantly about your dying. IT WAS NOT WITHOUT RESISTANCE THAT I ACCEPTED MY ROLE: THE NAKED YOU/THE MESSIANIC YOU/ THE SACRIFICIAL YOU. MY JEWISH PASSIONS SHIELDED BY NOTHING. MY JEWISH LOVING UNRESTRAINED.

LET ME EXIST. Do not destroy me to preserve your good name. I AM YOUR GOOD NAME. I am only spending the renown you hoard. You hide yourself/in lonely rooms/country recluse/anonymous expatriate/garreted monk. Never spent it as you should/might/wouldn't/couldn't: IN BEHALF OF THE JEW- ISH PEOPLE. Please! Allow me to be the public instrument through which you express the love for the Jews/the hatred for their enemies/that is in every word you ever wrote. *Without legal intervention.*

Judge me not by words but by the woman who bears this letter. To you I say everything stupidly. Judge me not by awkward words which falsify everything I feel/know. Around you I will never be a smith with words. See beyond words. I am not the writer/I am something else. I AM THE YOU THAT IS NOT WORDS.

Yours,
Philip Roth

The immediate physical reality of her was so strong and exciting— and unsettling—that it was a little like sitting across a table from the moon. She was about thirty-five, a voluptuously healthy-looking creaturely female around whose firm, rosy neck it wouldn't have been inappropriate to tie the county fair's first-prize ribbon—this was a biological winner, this was somebody who was *well*. Her whitish blond hair was worn casually pinned in a tousled bun at the back of her head, and she had a wide mouth, the warm interior of which she showed you, like a happy, panting dog, even when she wasn't speaking, as though she were taking your words in through her mouth, as though another's words were not received by the brain but processed—once past the small, even, splendidly white teeth and the pink, perfect gums—by the whole, radiant, happy-go-lucky thing. Her vivacious alertness, even her powers of concentration, seemed situated in the vicinity of her jaws; her eyes, beautifully clear and strongly focused though they were, did not appear to reach anywhere like so deep into the terrific ubiquity of all that hereness. She had the substantial breasts and the large round behind of a much heavier, less sprightly woman—she might, in another life, have been a fecund wet nurse from the Polish hinterlands. In fact, she was an oncology nurse and he had met her five years earlier, when he was first a cancer patient in a Chicago hospital. Her name was Wanda Jane "Jinx" Possesski,° and she aroused in me the sort of yearnings excited by the thought of a luxuriously warm fur coat on a freezing winter day: specifically, a craving to be enwrapped.

The woman by whom he wished to be judged was sitting across from me at a small table in the garden of the American Colony courtyard, beneath the charming arched windows of the old hotel. The violent morning rain squalls had subsided into little more than a sun shower while I was having lunch with Aharon, and now, at a few minutes before three, the sky was clear and the courtyard stones aglitter with light. It felt like a May afternoon, warm, breezy, lullingly serene, even though it was January of 1988 and we happened to be only a few hundred yards from where Israeli soldiers had teargassed a rock-throwing mob of young Arab boys just the day before. Demjanjuk was on trial for murdering close to a million Jews at Treblinka, Arabs were rising up against the Jewish authorities all over the Occupied Territories, and yet from where I was seated amid the lush shrubbery, between a lemon tree and an orange tree, the world could not have seemed any more enticing. Pleasant Arab waiters, singing little birds, a good cold beer—and this woman of his who evoked in me the illusion that nothing could be more durable than the perishable matter from which we are made.

All the while I read his dreadful letter she watched me as though she'd brought to the hotel directly from President Lincoln the original manuscript of the Gettysburg Address. The only reason I didn't tell her, "This is as loony a piece of prose as I've ever received in my life," and tear it into little pieces was because I didn't want her to get up and go. I wanted to hear her talk, for one thing: it was my chance to find out more, only more lies perhaps, but then, enough lies, and maybe some truth would begin trickling through. And I wanted to hear her talk because of the beguilingly ambiguous timbre of her voice, which was harmonically a puzzle to me. The voice was like something you've gotten out of the freezer that's taking its own sweet time to thaw: moist and spongy enough at the edges to eat, otherwise off-puttingly refrigerated down to its deep-frozen core. It was difficult to tell just how coarse she was, if there was a great deal going on in her or if maybe there was nothing at all and she was just a petty criminal's obedient moll. Probably it was only my infatuation with the exciting fullness of such a female presence that led me to visualize a mist of innocence hanging over her bold carnality that might enable me *to get somewhere.* I folded the letter in thirds and slipped it into my inside pocket—*what I should have done with his passport.*

"It's incredible," she said. "Overwhelming. You even read the same way."

"From left to right."

"Your facial expressions, the way you take everything in, even your clothes—it's *uncanny.*"

"But then everything is uncanny, is it not? Right down to our sharing the very same name."

"And," she said, smiling widely, "the sarcasm, too."

"He tells me that I should judge him by the woman who bears his letter, but much as I'd like to, it's hard, in my position, not to judge him by other things first."

"By what he's undertaken. I know. It's so gigantic for Jews. For

Gentiles, too. I think for everyone. The lives he'll save. The lives he's *saved.*"

"Already? Yes? Whose?"

"Mine, for one."

"I thought it was you who was the nurse and he who was the patient—I thought you'd helped save him."

"I'm a recovering anti-Semite. I was saved by A-S.A."

"A-S.A.?"

"Anti-Semites Anonymous. The recovery group Philip founded."

"It's just one brainstorm after another with Philip," I said. "He didn't tell me about A-S.A."

"He didn't tell you hardly anything. He couldn't. He's so in awe of you, he got all bottled up."

"Oh, I wouldn't say bottled up. I'd say unbottled up almost to a fault."

"All I know is he came back in terrible shape. He's still in bed. He says he disgraced himself. He came away thinking you hated him."

"Why on earth would I hate Philip?"

"That's why he wrote this letter."

"And sent you to act as his advocate."

"I'm not a big reader, Mr. Roth. I'm not a reader at all. When Philip was my patient I didn't even know you existed, let alone that you were his look-alike. People are *always* mistaking him for you, everywhere we go—everywhere, everyone, except illiterate me. To me he was just the most intense person I'd ever met in my life. He still is. There's no one like him."

"Except?" I said, tapping my chest.

"I meant the way he's set out to change the world."

"Well, he's come to the right place for that. Every year they treat dozens of tourists here who go around thinking themselves the Messiah and exhorting mankind to repent. It's a famous phenomenon at the mental-health center—local psychiatrists call it 'Jerusalem syndrome.' Most of them think they're the Messiah or God, and the rest claim to be Satan. You got off easy with Philip."

But nothing I said, however disdainful or outright contemptuous of him, had any noticeable effect on the undampable conviction with which she continued extolling to me the achievements of this blatant fraud. Was it *she* suffering from that novel form of hysteria known as Jerusalem syndrome? The government psychiatrist who had entertained me with a witty exposition on the subject a few years back had told me that there are also Christians they find wandering out in the desert who believe themselves to be John the Baptist. I thought: *his* harbinger, Jinx the Baptist, mouthpiece for the Messiah in whom she's discovered salvation and the exalted purpose of her life. "The Jews," she said, staring straight out at me with her terribly gullible eyes, "are all he thinks about. Night and day, since his cancer, his life has been dedicated to the Jews."

"And you," I asked, "who believe in him so—are you now a Jew lover too?"

But I could not seem to say anything to impair her buoyancy, and for the first time I wondered if perhaps she was afloat on dope, if both of them were, and if that accounted for everything, including the very soulful smile my sharp words had evoked—if behind the audacious mystery of these two there was nothing but a pound of good pot.

"Philip lover, yes; Jew lover, no. Uh-uh. All Jinx can love, and it's plenty for her, is no longer hating Jews, no longer blaming Jews, no longer detesting Jews on sight. No, I can't say that Jinx Possesski is a lover of Jews or that Jinx Possesski ever will be. What I can say—okay?—is what I said: I'm a recovering anti-Semite."

"And what's that like?" I asked, thinking now that there was something not *entirely* unbelievable about her words and that I could do no better than to be still and listen.

"Oh, it's a story."

"How long are you in recovery?"

"Almost five years. I was poisoned by it. A lot, I think now, had to do with the job. I don't blame the job, I blame Jinx—but still, there's one thing about a cancer hospital: the pain is just something that you can't imagine. When someone's in pain, you almost want to run out of the room, screaming to get the pain medication. People have no idea, they really and truly have no idea, what it is like to have pain like that. Their pain is so outrageous, and everyone is afraid of dying. There's a lot of failure in cancer—you know, it's not a maternity ward. On a maternity ward, I might never have found out the truth about myself. It might never have happened to me. You want to hear all this?"

"If you want to tell me," I said. What I wanted to hear was why she loved this fraud.

"I got drawn into people's suffering," she said. "I couldn't help it. If they cry, I hold their hand, I hug them—if they cry, *I* cry. I hug them, they hug me—to me there's no way not to. It's like you were their savior. Jinx could do no wrong. But I can't be their savior. And that got to me after a while." The nonsensically happy look slipped suddenly from Jinx's face and she was convulsed by a rush of tenderness that left her for a moment unable to go on. "These patients . . ." she said, her voice completely deiced now and as soft through and through as a small child's, ". . . they look at you with those eyes. . . ." The magnitude of the emotions she was reckoning with took me by surprise. *If this is an act, then she's Sarah Bernhardt.* "They look at you with those eyes, they're so wide open—and they grab, *they grab* —and I give, but I can't give them life. . . . After a while," she went on, the emotion subsiding into something sad and rueful, "I was just helping people to die. Make you more comfortable. Give you more pain medication. Give you a back massage. Turn you a certain way. Anything. I did a lot for patients. I always went one beyond the medical thing. 'You wanna play cards, you wanna smoke a little marijuana?' The patients were the only thing that meant anything to me. After a day when maybe three people died, you bagged the last person—'This is *it,*' you say, 'I'm fuckin' tired of puttin' a fuckin' tag on someone's toe!' " How violently the moods wavered! One little word was enough to turn her around—and the little word in this case was *it.* "This is *it,*" and she was as radiant with a crude, bold, coarse forcefulness as she had been stricken just the minute before by all that anguishing heartache. What there was to subject her to him I still couldn't say, but what might subordinate a man to her I had no

difficulty perceiving: everything existed in such generous portions.
Not since I had last read Strindberg could I remember having run
across such a tantalizing layer cake of female excitement. The desire
I then suppressed—to reach out and cup her breast—was only in
part the urge men have perpetually to suppress when the fire is
suddenly lit in a public place: beneath the soft, plump mass of breast
I wanted to feel, against my palm, the power of that heart.

"You know," she was saying, "I'm sick and tired of turning someone
over and thinking that this is not going to affect me! 'Tag 'em and
wrap 'em. Have you tagged them and wrapped them yet? Tag 'em and
wrap 'em up.' 'No, because the family hasn't come yet. Get the fuckin'
family here so we can tag 'em and wrap 'em, and get the hell out of
here!' I OD'd on death, Mr. Roth. Because," and again she could not
speak, so felled was she by these memories ". . . because there was
too much death. It was too much dying, you know? And I just
couldn't handle myself. I turned on the Jews. The Jewish doctors.
Their wives. Their kids. And they were good doctors. Excellent doctors, excellent surgeons. But I'd see the photographs framed on their
desks, the kids with tennis rackets, the wives by the pool, I'd hear
them on the phone, making dates for the evening like nobody on the
floor was dying—planning for their tennis, their vacations, their trips
to London and Paris, 'We're staying at the Ritz, we're eating at the
Schmitz, we're going to back up a truck and empty out Gucci's,' and
I'd freak out, man, I'd go off on a real anti-Semitic binge. I worked on
the gastric floor—stomach-liver-pancreatic floor. Two other nurses
about the same age, and it was like an infection that went from me to
them. At our nursing station, which was great, we had the greatest
music, a lot of rock 'n' roll, and we gave each other a tremendous
amount of support, but we were all, like, calling in sick a lot, and I
was yakking and yakking about the Jews more and more. We were all
young there, twenty-three, twenty-four, twenty-five—five days a
week, and you worked overtime and every night you stayed late. You
stayed late because these people were so sick, and I'd think about
those Jewish doctors home with their wives and their kids—even
when I was away from the floor, it wouldn't leave me. I was on fire

with it. The Jews, the Jews. When we'd work evenings, all three of us together, we'd get home, smoke a joint, *definitely* smoke a joint—couldn't wait to roll it. We made piña coladas. Anything. All night. If we didn't drink at home we'd get dressed up or throw our makeup on and go out, Near North, Rush Street, the scene. Go to all the bars. Sometimes you met people and you went on dates and you fucked—okay?—but not really as an outlet. The outlet for the dying was pot. The outlet for the dying was the Jews. With me anti-Semitism was in the family. Is it hereditary, environmental, or strictly a moral flaw? A topic of discussion at A-S.A. meetings. The answer? We don't care why we have it, we are here to admit that we have it and help each other get rid of it. But in me I think I had it for all the reasons you can. My father hated them, to begin with. A boiler engineer in Ohio. I heard it growing up but it was like wallpaper, it never meant a thing before I was a cancer nurse. But once I started—okay?—I couldn't stop. Their money. Their wives. Those women, those faces of theirs —those hideous Jewish faces. Their kids. Their clothes. Their voices. You name it. But mostly the look, the Jewish look. It didn't stop. *I* didn't stop. It got to the point that the resident, this one doctor, Kaplan, he didn't like to look you in the eyes that much—he would say something about a patient and all I saw were those Jewish lips. He was a young guy but already he had the underslung jaw like the old Jews get, and the long ears, and those real liver lips—the whole bit that I couldn't stand. That's how I went berserk. That's when I hit bottom. He was scared because he was not used to giving so much pain medication. He was scared the patient would suffer respiratory arrest and die. But she was a woman my age—so young, so young. She had cancer that went *everywhere*. And she was just in so much pain. She was in *so* much pain. Mr. Roth, a *terrific* amount of pain." And the tears were streaming onto her face, the mascara running, and the impulse I now suppressed was not to palpate her large, warm breast or to measure the warlike strength of the heart beneath but to take her two hands from the tabletop and enclose them in mine, those transgressive, tabooless nurse's hands, so deceptively clean and innocent-seeming, that had nonetheless been everywhere, swathing, spraying, washing, wiping, freely touching everywhere, handling everything, open wounds, drainage bags, every running orifice, as naturally as a cat pawing a mouse. "I had to get out of cancer. I didn't want to be a cancer nurse. I just wanted to be a nurse, anything. I was screaming at him, at Kaplan, at those fucking Jew lips, 'You better fucking give us the pain medication we need! Or we are going to get the attending and he's going to be pissed off at you for waking him up! Get it! Get it now!' You know," she said, surprisingly childishly. "You know? You know?"

You know, like, okay?—and still there was enough persuasiveness there to *make* you know.

"She was young," she told me, "strong. Their will is very, very strong. It'll keep them going forever, despite as much pain as they can endure. Even *more* pain than they can endure and they endure. It's horrible. So you give them more medication because their heart is so strong and their will is so strong. They're in pain, Mr. Roth— *you have to give them something!* You know? You know?"

"I do now, yes."

"They need an almost *elephant* dose of morphine, the people that are so young." And she made none of the effort she had the moment before to hide her weeping in her shoulder or to pause and steady herself. "They're young—it's *doubly* bad! I shouted at Dr Kaplan, 'I will not allow someone to be cruel to someone who is dying!' So he got it for me. And I gave it to her." Momentarily she seemed to see herself in the scene, to see herself giving it to her, to that woman her own age, "so young, so young." She was there again. Maybe, I thought, she's always there and *that's* why she's with him.

"What happened?" I asked her.

Weakly—and this was no weakling—but very weakly she finally answered, all the while looking down at the hands that I persisted in envisioning everywhere, hands that she once must have washed two hundred times a day. "She died," she said.

When she looked up again she was smiling sadly, certifying with that smile that she was out of cancer now, that all the dying, though it hadn't stopped, though it never stopped, no longer required that she smoke pot and down piña coladas and hate the likes of Dr. Kaplan and me. "She was going to die anyway, she was ready to die, but she died on me. I killed her. Her skin was beautiful. You know? She was a waitress. A good person. An outgoing person. She told me she wanted six children. But I gave her morphine and she died. I went berserk. I went to the bathroom and I went hysterical. The Jews! The Jews! The head nurse came in. She was the reason why you see me here and not in jail. Because the family was very bad. They came in screaming. 'What happened? What happened?' Families get so guilt-ridden because they can't do anything and they don't want her to die. They know that she's suffering horribly, that there's no hope, yet when she dies, 'What happened? What happened?' But the head nurse was, like, so good, a great woman, and she held me. 'Possesski, you gotta get out of here.' It took me a year. I was twenty-six years old. I got transferred. I got on the surgical floor. There's always hope on the surgical floor. Except there's a procedure called 'open and close.' Where you open them up and the doctor won't even attempt anything. And they stay and they die. They die! *Mr. Roth, I couldn't get away from death.* Then I met Philip. He had cancer. He was operated on. Hope! Hope! Then the pathology report. Three lymph nodes are involved. So I'm, like, 'Oh, my God.' I didn't want to get attached. I tried to stop myself. You always try to stop yourself. That's what the cursing is all about. The tough talk isn't so tough, you know? You think it's cold. It's not cold at all. That happened with Philip. I thought I hated him. Okay, I *wanted* to hate him. I should have learned from that girl I killed. Stay away. Look at his looks. But instead I fell in love with him, I fell *in love* with his looks, with every fucking Jewish thing about him. That talk. Those jokes. That intensity. The imitations. Crazy with life. He was the one patient ever who gave me more strength than I gave them. We fell in love."

Just then, through the large window opposite me, I noticed Demjanjuk's legal team in the lobby beyond the courtyard—they too must be guests here in this East Jerusalem hotel and on their way either to or from the afternoon session. I recognized Sheftel first, the Israeli lawyer, and then the other two; with them, still dressed impeccably in suit and tie, as though he were lawyer number four, was Demjanjuk's tall young son. Jinx looked to see what had diverted my attention from her life's searing drama of death and love.

"Know why Demjanjuk continues lying?" she asked.

"*Is* he lying?"

"*Is* he! The defense has *nothing.*"

"Sheftel looks awfully cocky to me."

"Bluff, all bluff—there's no alibi *at all.* The alibi's proved false a dozen times over. And the card, the Trawniki card, it's got to be Demjanjuk's—it's *his* picture, *his* signature."

"And not a fake?"

"The prosecution has *proved* it's not fake. And those old people on the witness stand, the people who cleaned out the gas chambers for him, the people who worked alongside him *every day,* it's *overwhelming,* the case against him. Anyway, Demjanjuk *knows* they know. He acts like a stupid peasant but he's a cunning bastard and no fool. He knows he'll be hanged. He knows it's coming to him, too."

"So why does he continue to lie?"

She jerked a thumb toward the lobby, a brusque little gesture that took me by surprise after the impassioned vulnerability of her aria, something she'd probably learned to mime, along with the anti-Semitism, from the boiler engineer, her father. And what she was saying about the trial I figured she must be miming too, for these were no longer words stained with her blood but words she repeated as though she didn't even believe in the meaning of words. Parroting her hero, I thought, as the adoring mate of a hero will.

"The son," she explained. "He wants the son to be good and not to know. Demjanjuk's lying for the son. If Demjanjuk confessed, that boy would be finished. He wouldn't have a chance." One of those hands of hers settled familiarly on my arm, one of those hands whose history of besmirchment by the body's secretions I could not stop myself envisioning; and for me, in that raw contact, there was such a shock of intimacy that I felt momentarily absorbed into her being, very like what an infant must feel back when the mother's hands aren't mere appendages but the very incarnation of her whole warm, wonderful big body. Resist, I thought, this overtempting presence—these are not two people with your interests at heart! ·

"Talk to him. Sit down and talk to Philip, *please.*"

"'Philip' and I have nothing to talk about."

"Oh, *don't,*" she begged me, and as her fingers closed on me even more tightly, the pressure of her thumb in the crook of my arm triggered a rush of just about everything urging me in the wrong direction, *"please, don't . . . ."*

"Don't what?"

"Undermine what he is doing!"

"It's not I who is doing the undermining."

"But the man," she cried, "is in *remission!*"

Even under less excitable conditions, "remission" is not a word easy to ignore, any more than "guilty" or "innocent" is in the courtroom when pronounced by the jury foreman to the judge.

I said, "Remission from cancer is nothing that I am against, for him or anyone. I am not even against his so-called Diasporism. I have no interest in those ideas either way. What I am against is his entangling our two lives and confusing people about who is who. What I cannot permit and what I will not permit is his encouraging people to believe that he is me. That must stop!"

"It will—okay? It'll stop."

"Will it? How do you know?"

"Because Philip told me to tell you that it would."

"Yes, did he? Why *didn't* you then? Why didn't *he,* in that letter—that completely idiotic letter!" I said, angrily remembering the vacuous pithiness, the meaningless dissonance, the hysterical incoherence of that life-and-death longhand, remembering all those stupid slashes only vaguely disguising what I surmised he'd as soon do with me.

"You're misunderstanding him," she pleaded. "It *will* stop. He's sick about how this has upset you. What happened has sent him reeling. I mean with vertigo. I mean literally *he can't stand up.* I left him there in bed. He crashed, Mr. Roth, completely."

"I see. He thought I wouldn't mind. He thought the interviews with the journalists would just roll off my back."

"If you would meet with him one more time—"

"I *met with him*. I'm meeting with *you*," I said, and pulled my arm out from beneath her hand. "If you love him, Miss Possesski, and are devoted to him, and want to avoid the sort of trouble that might possibly endanger the health of a cancer patient in remission, then you'd be well advised to stop him *now*. He must stop using my name now. This is as far as I go with meetings."

"But," she said, her voice heating up and her hands clenched in anger, "that's like asking you to stop using *his* name."

"No, no, not at all! *Your patient in remission is a liar.* Whatever great motives may be motivating him, he happens to be lying through his teeth! His name is *not* the same as mine, and if he told you that it was, then he lied to you, too."

Just the contortion of her mouth caused me instinctively to raise a hand to ward off a blow. And what I caught with that hand was a fist quite hard enough to have broken my nose. "Prick!" she snarled. "Your name! Your name! Do you ever, ever, ever think of anything *other* than your fucking name!"

Interlocked on the tabletop now, our fingers began a fight of their own; her grip was anything but girlish, and even pressing with all my strength, I was barely able to keep her five fingers immobilized between mine. Meanwhile I kept an eye on the other hand.

"You're asking the wrong man," I said. "The question is, 'Does he?'"

Our struggle was being watched by the hotel waiters. A group of them had gathered just inside the windowed door to the lobby so as to look on at what must have struck them as a lovers' quarrel, no more or less dangerous—and entertaining—than that, a touch of comic relief from the violence in the street, and probably not a little pornographically piquant.

"You should be a tenth as selfless, a *hundredth* as selfless! Do you know many dying men? Do you know many dying men whose thoughts are only for saving others? Do you know many people kept alive on a hundred and fifty pills a day who could begin to do what he is doing? What he went through in Poland just to *see* Walesa! *I* was worn out. But Philip would not be stopped, not by *anything*. Dizzy spells that would fell a horse and *still* he doesn't stop! He falls down, he gets up, he keeps going. And the pain—he is like trying to excrete his own insides! The people we have to see before we even *get* to Walesa! It wasn't the shipyards where we met him. That's just stuff for the papers. It was way the hell out and beyond. The car rides, the passwords, the hiding places—and still this man *does not stop!* Eighteen months ago every last doctor gave him no more than six months to live—and here he is, in Jerusalem, alive! Let him have what keeps him alive! Let this man go on with his dream!"

"The dream that he is me?"

"You! You! Nothing in your world but *you!* Stop stroking my hand! Let go of my hand! Stop coming *on* with me!"

"You tried to hit me with that hand."

"You are trying to seduce me! *Let me go!*"

She was wearing a belted blue poplin raincoat over a short denim skirt and a white ribbed sweater, a very youthful outfit, and it made her appear, when our fingers fell apart and she rose in a fury from her chair, rather statuesquely pubescent, a woman's fullness coyly displayed in mock-maidenly American disguise.

In the features of one of the young waiters huddled up to the glass of the lobby door I saw the feverish look of a man who hopes with all his heart that the long-awaited striptease is about to begin. Or perhaps, when her hand reached down into her raincoat pocket, he thought that he was going to witness a shooting, that the voluptuous woman was about to pull a gun. And as I was still completely in the dark about what this couple was after and what they were truly contriving to do, my expectations were all at once no more realistic than his. In coming to Jerusalem like this, refusing to consider seriously an impostor's more menacing meaning, heeding only my desperate yearning to be intact and entire, to prove that I was unimpaired by that ghastly breakdown and once again a robust, forceful, undamaged man, I had made the biggest, stupidest mistake yet, even more unfortunate a mistake than my lurid first marriage and one from which, it appeared, there was to be no escape. *I should have listened to Claire.*

But what the voluptuous woman pulled from her pocket was only an envelope. "You shit! The remission *depends* on this!" And hurling the envelope onto the table, she ran from the courtyard and out of the hotel through the lobby, where the thrill-seeking, mesmerized waiters were no longer to be seen.

Only when I began to read this second communication from him, which was composed in longhand like the first, did I realize how skillfully he had worked to make his handwriting resemble my own. Alone now, without all her radiant realness to distract me, I saw on this sheet of paper the pinched and twisted signs of my own impatient, overaccelerated left-handed scrawl, the same irregular slope climbing unevenly uphill, the *o*'s and *e*'s and *a*'s compressed and all but indistinguishable from *i*'s, the *i*'s themselves hastily undotted and the *t*'s uncrossed, the "The" in the heading atop the page a perfect replica of the "The" I'd been writing since elementary school, which looked more like "Fli." It was, like mine, a hand in a hurry to be finished with writing abnormally into, rather than flowing right-handedly away from, the barrier of its own impeding torso. Of all the falsifications I knew of so far, including the phony passport, this document was far and away the most professional and even more infuriating to behold than the forgery of his conniving face. He'd even taken a crack at my style. At least the style wasn't his, if that loonily cryptic, slash-bedecked letter she'd given me first was any sample of the prose that came to this counterfeiter "naturally."

THE TEN TENETS OF ANTI-SEMITES ANONYMOUS

1. We admit that we are haters prone to prejudice and powerless to control our hatred.
2. We recognize that it is not Jews who have wronged us but we who hold Jews responsible for our troubles and the world's evils. It is we who wrong *them* by believing this.
3. A Jew may well have shortcomings like any other human being, but the shortcomings we are here to be honest about are our own, i.e., paranoia, sadism, negativism, destructiveness, envy.
4. Our money problems are not of the Jews' making but of our own.
5. Our job problems are not of the Jews' making but of our

own (so too with sexual problems, marital problems, problems in the community).

6. Anti-Semitism is a form of flight from reality, a refusal to think honestly about ourselves and our society.

7. Inasmuch as anti-Semites cannot control their hatred, they are not like other people. We recognize that even to drop a casual anti-Semitic slur endangers our struggle to rid ourselves of our sickness.

8. Helping to detoxify others is the cornerstone of our recovery. Nothing will so much ensure immunity from the illness of anti-Semitism as intensive work with other anti-Semites.

9. We are not scholars, we do not care why we have this dreadful illness, we come together to admit that we have it and to help one another get rid of it.

10. In the fellowship of A-S.A. we strive to master the temptation to Jew hatred in all its forms.

4

Jewish
Mischief

"Now suppose," I said to Aharon when we met to resume our work over lunch the next day, "suppose this isn't a stupid prank, isn't an escapade of some crazy kind, isn't a malevolent hoax; suppose, despite every indication to the contrary, these two are not a pair of con artists or crackpots—however astonishing the supposition, suppose that they are exactly what they present themselves to be and that every word they speak is the truth." My resolve to compartmentalize my impostor, to keep coolly disengaged, and, while in Jerusalem, to remain concentrated solely on the assignment with Aharon had, of course, collapsed completely before the provocation of Wanda Jane's visit. As Claire had forlornly predicted (as I who'd phoned him right off the bat in the guise of Pierre Roget, secretly had never doubted), the very absurdity of his impersonation was too tantalizing for me to be able to think of anything else quite so excitedly. "Aharon, suppose it is so. All of it. A man named XYZ happens to look like the twin of a well-known writer whose name, remarkably enough, is also XYZ. Perhaps some three or four generations back, before the millions of European Jews migrated en masse to America, they were rooted in the same Galician clan—and perhaps not. Doesn't matter. Even if they share no common ancestry—and wildly unlikely as all the similarities might seem—such a coincidence could happen and in this instance it does. The duplicate XYZ is mistaken repeatedly for the original XYZ and naturally comes to take a more than passing interest in him. Whether he then develops his interest in certain Jewish contradictions because these figure prominently in the writer's work or whether they engage him for biographical reasons of his own, the duplicate finds in Jews a source for fantasies no less excessive than those of the original. For instance: Because the duplicate XYZ believes that the state of Israel, as currently constituted, is destined to be destroyed by its Arab enemies in a nuclear exchange he invents Diasporism, a program that seeks to resettle all Israeli Jews of European origin back in those countries where they or their families were residents before the outbreak of the Second World War and thereby to avert 'a second Holocaust.' He's inspired to pursue its implementation by the example of Theodor Herzl, whose plan for a Jewish national state had seemed no less utopian and antihistorical to its critics some fifty-odd years before it came to fruition. Of the numerous strong arguments against *his* utopia, none is more of an impediment than the fact that these are countries in which Jewish security and well-being would be perennially menaced by the continuing existence of European anti-Semitism, and it's with this problem still obstructing him that he enters the hospital as a cancer patient and finds himself being nursed by Jinx Possesski. He is ill, Jewish, and battling to live, and she is not only pantingly alive but rabidly anti-Semitic. A volcanic drama of repulsion and attraction ensues—bitter cracks, remorseful apologies, sudden clashes, tender reconciliations, educational tirades, furtive fondlings, weeping, embraces, wrenching emotional confusion, and then, late one night, there comes the discovery, the revelation, the breakthrough. Sitting at the foot of the bed in the dark hospital room where, struggling miserably against the dry heaves, he is on the chemotherapy intravenous drip, the nurse discloses to her suffering patient the miseries of *her* consuming disease. She tells it all as she never has before, and while she does, XYZ comes to realize that there are anti-Semites who are like alcoholics who actually want to stop but don't know how. The analogy to alcoholism continues to deepen the longer he listens to her. But, of course, he thinks—there are occasional anti-Semites, who engage in nothing more really than a little anti-Semitism as a social lubricant at parties and business lunches; moderate anti-Semites, who can control their anti-Semitism and even keep it a secret when they have to; and then there are the all-out anti-Semites, the real career haters, who may perhaps have begun as moderate anti-Semites but who eventually are consumed by what turns out in them to be a progressively debilitating disease. For three hours Jinx confesses to him her helplessness before the most horrible feelings and thoughts about Jews, to the murderous malice that engulfs her whenever she has so much as to speak with a Jew, and all the while he is thinking, She must be cured. If she is cured, we are saved! If I can save her, I can save the Jews! I must not die! I will not die! When she has finished, he says to her softly, 'Well, at last you've told your story.' Weeping wretchedly, she replies, 'I don't feel any better for it.' 'You will,' he promises her. 'When? *When?*' 'In time,' answers XYZ, and then he asks if she knows another anti-Semite who is ready to give it up. She isn't even sure, she meekly replies, that she is ready to herself, and even if she thinks herself ready, is she *able?* It isn't with him as it is with other Jews—she's in love with him and this miraculously washes away all hatred. But with the other Jews, it's automatic, it just rises up in her at the mere *sight* of them. Perhaps if she could steer clear of Jews for just a little while . . . but in this hospital, with all its Jewish doctors, Jewish patients, and Jewish families, with the Jewish crying, the Jewish whispering, the Jewish screaming . . . . He says to her, 'An anti-Semite who cannot meet, or mix with, Jews still has an anti-Semitic mind. However far from Jews you flee, you will take it with you. The dream of eluding the anti-Semitic feelings by escaping from Jews is only the reverse of cleansing yourself of these feelings by ridding the earth of all Jews. The only shield against your hatred is the program of recovery that we have begun in this hospital tonight. Tomorrow night bring with you another anti-Semite, another of the nurses who knows in her heart what anti-Semitism is doing to her life.' For what he is thinking now is that, like the alcoholic, the anti-Semite can only be cured by another anti-Semite, while what she is thinking is that she does not want her Jew to absolve *another* anti-Semite of her anti-Semitism but craves that loving forgiveness for herself alone. Isn't one anti-Semitic woman enough? Must he have all the anti-Semitic women in the world begging his Jewish forgiveness, confessing to their Gentile rottenness, admitting to him that he is superior and they are slime? *Tell me, girls, your dirty goy secrets.* It's *this* that turns the Jew *on!* But the next evening, from the nurses' station where they play all the wonderful rock 'n' roll, she brings to him not just one anti-Semitic woman besides herself but two. The room is dark but for the night lamp shining at the side of the sickbed where he lies gaunt, silent, greenishly pale, so miserable he is not even sure any longer whether he is conscious or comatose, whether the three nurses are seated in a row at the foot of his bed saying what he thinks he hears them saying or it is all a deathbed delirium and the three are tending him in the final awful moments of his life. 'I am an anti-Semite like Wanda Jane,' whispers one of the weeping nurses. 'I need to discuss my anger with Jews. . . .' "

Here I found myself laughing as uproariously as I had when I'd left Jinx's savior and my impostor in the hotel dining room the day before, and, for the moment, I could go no further.

"What's so hilarious?" asked Aharon, smiling at my laughter. "His mischief or yours? That he pretends to be you or that you now pretend to be him?"

"I don't know. I suppose what's most hilarious is my distress. Define 'mischief,' please."

"To a mischief-maker like you? Mischief is how some Jews get involved in living."

"Here," I said, and, laughing still, laughing with the foolish, uncontrollable laughter of a child who no longer can remember what it was that started him off, I handed him a copy of "The Ten Tenets of A-S.A." "This is what she left with me."

"So," said Aharon, as he held between two fingers the document whose margins were filled with my scrawl, "you are his editor, too."

"Aharon, who *is* this man?" I asked, and waited and waited for the laughter to subside. *"What* is he?" I went on when I could speak again. "He gives off none of the aura of a real person, none of the *coherence* of a real person. Or even the *in*coherence of a real person. Oh, it's all plenty incoherent, but incoherent in some wholly artificial way: he emanates the aura of something absolutely spurious, almost the way that Nixon did. He didn't even strike me as Jewish—that seemed as false as everything else and *that's* supposed to be at the heart of it all. It isn't just that what he calls by my name has no connection to me; it doesn't seem to have any to him, either. A mismade artifact. No, even that puts it too positively."

"A vacuum," said Aharon. "A vacuum into which is drawn your own gift for deceit."

"Don't exaggerate. More like a vacuum cleaner into which is sucked my dust."

"He has less talent for impersonating you than you have—maybe that's the irritation. Substitute selves? Alter egos? The writer's medium. It's all too shallow and too porous for you, without the proper weight and substance. Is this the double that is to be my own? An aesthetic outrage. The great wonders performed on the golem by Rabbi Liva of Prague you are now going to perform on him. Why? Because you have a better conception of him than he does. Rabbi Liva started with clay; you begin with sentences. It's perfect," said Aharon, with amusement, and all the while reading my marginal commentary on the Ten Tenets. "You are going to rewrite him."

What I had noted in the margins was this: "Anti-Semites come from all walks of life. This is too complicated for them. 1. Each tenet must not convey more than one idea. First tenet shouldn't have both hatred *and* prejudice. Powerless to control is a redundancy—powerless over or can't control. 2. No logic to progression. Should unfold from general to specific, from acceptance to action, from diagnosis to program of recovery to joy of living TOLERANT. 3. Avoid fancy words. Sounding like a highbrow. Drop negativism, endangers, intensive, immunity. Anything bookish bad for your purpose (generally true throughout life)." And on the reverse side of the sheet, which Aharon had now turned over and begun to read, I'd tried recasting the first few A-S.A. tenets in a simpler style, so that A-S.A. members (should there be any such!) could actually utilize them. I'd taken my inspiration from something Jinx had said to me—"We don't care why we have it, we are here to admit that we have it and help each other get rid of it." Jinx has got the tone, I thought: blunt and monosyllabic. Anti-Semites come from all walks of life.

1. We admit [I'd written] that we are haters and that hatred has ruined our lives.
2. We recognize that by choosing Jews as the target for our hatred, we have become anti-Semites and that all our thoughts and actions have been affected by this prejudice.
3. Coming to understand that Jews are not the cause of our troubles but our own shortcomings are, we become ready to correct them.
4. We ask our fellow anti-Semites and the Spirit of Tolerance to help us overcome these defects.
5. We are willing to fully apologize for all the harm caused by our anti-Semitism. . . .

While Aharon was reading my revisions we were approached by a very slight, elderly cripple who seesawed toward us on two aluminum forearm crutches from the nearby table where he'd been eating. There was generally a contingent of the elderly eating their lunch in the clean, quiet café of the Ticho House, which was tucked away from the heavy Jaffa Street traffic behind a labyrinth of pinkish stone walls. The fare was simple and inexpensive and, afterward, you could take your coffee or tea on the terrace outside or on a bench beneath the tall trees in the garden. Aharon had thought it would be a tranquil place to hold our conversations undisturbed, without the distractions of the city intruding.

When the old man had made it to our table, he did not speak until he had cumbersomely uncrated his hundred meager pounds of limbs and torso onto the chair to the side of me and sat there waiting, it would seem, for a wildly fluttering heartbeat to decelerate, all the while, through the heavy lenses of his horn-rimmed glasses, determining the meaning of my face. He had that alarming boiled look of someone suffering from a skin disease, and the word to express the meaning of *his* face seemed to me to be "ordeal." He wore a heavy cardigan sweater buttoned up beneath his plain blue suit and, under the sweater, a starched white shirt and bow tie, very neat and businesslike—how a decorous neighborhood tradesman might attire himself in an underheated appliance shop.

"Roth," he said. "The author."

"Yes."

Here he removed his hat to reveal a microscopically honeycombed skull, a perfectly bald surface minutely furrowed and grooved like the shell of a hard-boiled egg whose dome has been fractured lightly by the back of a spoon. The man's been dropped, I thought, and reassembled, a mosaic of smithereens, cemented, sutured, wired, bolted. . . .

"May I ask your name, sir?" I said. "This is Aharon Appelfeld, the Israeli author. You are?"

"Get out," he said to Aharon. "Get out before it happens. Philip Roth is right. He is not afraid of the crazy Zionists. Listen to him. You have family? Children?"

"Three children," Aharon replied.

"This is no place for Jewish children. Enough dead Jewish children. Take them while they're alive and go."

"Have you children?" Aharon asked him.

"I have no one. I came to New York after the camps. I gave to Israel. That was my child. I lived in Brooklyn on nothing. Work only, and ninety cents on the dollar to Israel. Then I retired. Sold my jewelry business. Came here. And every day I am living here I want to run away. I think of my Jews in Poland. The Jew in Poland had terrible enemies too. But because he had terrible enemies did not mean he could not keep his Jewish soul. But these are Jews in a Jewish country without a Jewish soul. This is the Bible all over again.

God prepares a catastrophe for these Jews without souls. If ever there will be a new chapter in the Bible you will read how God sent a hundred million Arabs to destroy the people of Israel for their sins."

"Yes? And was it for their sins," Aharon asked, "that God sent Hitler?"

"God sent Hitler because God is crazy. A Jew knows God and how He operates. A Jew knows God and how, from the very first day He created man, He has been irritated with him from morning till night. That is what it means that the Jews are chosen. The goyim smile: God is merciful, God is loving, God is good. Jews don't smile—they know God not from dreaming about Him in goyisch daydreams but from living all their lives with a God Who does not ever stop, *not once,* to think and reason and use His head with His loving children. To appeal to a crazy, irritated father, that is what it is to be a Jew. To appeal to a crazy, *violent* father, and for three thousand years, that is what it is to be a crazy Jew!" Having disposed of Aharon, he turned back to me, this crippled old wraith who should have been lying down somewhere, in the care of a doctor, surrounded by a family, his head at rest on a clean white pillow until he could peacefully die. "Before it's too late, Mr. Roth, before God sends to massacre the Jews without souls a hundred million Arabs screaming to Allah, I wish to make a contribution."

It was the moment for me to tell him that if that was his intention, he had the wrong Mr. Roth. "How did you find me?" I asked.

"You were not at the King David so I came for my lunch. I come every day here for my lunch—and here, today, is you." Speaking of himself, he added grimly, "Always lucky." He removed an envelope from his breast pocket, a process that, because of his bad tremor, one had to wait very patiently for him to complete, as though he were a struggling stammerer subduing the nemesis syllable. There was more than enough time to stop him and direct his contribution to the legitimate recipient, but instead I allowed him to hand it to me.

"And what is your name?" I asked again, and with Aharon looking on, I, without so much as the trace of a tremor, slipped the envelope into my own breast pocket.

"Smilesburger," he replied, and then began the pathetic drama of returning his hat to the top of his head, a drama with a beginning, a middle, and an end.

"Own a suitcase?" he asked Aharon.

"Threw it away," Aharon gently replied.

"Mistake." And with that Mr. Smilesburger hoisted himself painfully upward, uncoiling from the chair until at last he was wavering dangerously before us on his forearm crutches. "No more suitcases," he said, "no more Jews."

His sallying forth from the café, on no legs and no strength and those crutches, was another pathetic drama, this one reminiscent of a lone peasant working a muddy field with a broken-down, primitive plow.

I withdrew from my jacket pocket the long white envelope containing Smilesburger's "contribution." Painstakingly printed across the face of the envelope, in those wavering oversized letters children first use to scrawl *cat* and *dog,* was the name by which I had been known all my life and under which I had published the books to which Jinx's savior and my impostor now claimed authorship in cities as far apart as Jerusalem and Gdansk.

"So *this* is what it's about," I said. "Bilking the senile out of their dough—shaking down old Jews for money. What a charming scam." While slicing open the envelope with a table knife, I asked Aharon, "What's your guess?"

"A million dollars," he replied.

"I say fifty. Two twenties and a ten."

Well, I was wrong and Aharon was right. Hiding as a child from his murderers in the Ukrainian woods while I was still on a Newark playground playing fly-catcher's-up after school had clearly made him less of a stranger than I to life in its more immoderate manifestations. Aharon was right: a numbered cashier's check, drawn on the Bank of Israel in New York, for the sum of one million dollars, and payable to me. I looked to be sure that the transaction had not been postdated to the year 3000, but no, it bore the date of the previous Thursday—January 21, 1988.

"This makes me think," I said, handing it across the table to him, "of Dostoyevsky's very greatest line."

"Which line is that?" Aharon asked, examining the check carefully, back and front.

"Do you remember, in *Crime and Punishment*, when Raskolnikov's sister, Dunya, is lured to Svidrigailov's apartment? He locks her in with him, pockets the key, and then, like a serpent, sets out to seduce her, forcibly if necessary. But to his astonishment, just when he has her helplessly cornered, this beautiful, well-bred Dunya pulls a pistol out of her purse and points it at his heart. Dostoyevsky's greatest line comes when Svidrigailov sees the gun."

"Tell me," said Aharon.

" 'This,' said Svidrigailov, 'changes everything.' "

ROTH: *Badenheim 1939* has been called fablelike, dreamlike, nightmarish, and so on. None of these descriptions makes the book less vexing to me. The reader is asked, pointedly, to understand the transformation of a pleasant Austrian resort for Jews into a grim staging area for Jewish "relocation" to Poland as being somehow analogous to events preceding Hitler's Holocaust. At the same time, your vision of Badenheim and its Jewish inhabitants is almost impulsively antic and indifferent to matters of causality. It isn't that a menacing situation develops, as it frequently does in life, without warning or logic but that about these events you are laconic, I think, to a point of unrewarding inscrutability. Do you mind addressing my difficulties with this highly praised novel, which is perhaps your most famous book in America? What *is* the relation between the fictional world of *Badenheim* and historical reality?

APPELFELD: Rather clear childhood memories underlie *Badenheim 1939*. Every summer we, like all the other petit bourgeois families, would set out for a resort. Every summer we tried to find a restful place where people didn't gossip in the corridors, didn't confess to one another in corners, didn't interfere with you, and, of course, didn't speak Yiddish. But every summer, as though we were being spited, we were once again surrounded by Jews, and that left a bad taste in my parents' mouths, and no small amount of anger.

Many years after the Holocaust, when I came to retrace my childhood from before the Holocaust, I saw that these resorts occupied a particular place in my memories. Many faces and bodily twitches came back to life. It turned out that the grotesque was etched in no less than the tragic. Walks in the woods and the elaborate meals brought people together in Badenheim —to speak to one another and to confess to one another. People permitted themselves not only to dress extravagantly but also to speak freely, sometimes picturesquely. Husbands occasionally lost their lovely wives, and from time to time a shot would ring out in the evening, a sharp sign of disappointed love. Of course I could arrange these precious scraps of life to stand on their own artistically. But what was I to do? Every time I tried to reconstruct those forgotten resorts, I had visions of the trains and the camps, and my most hidden childhood memories were spotted with the soot from the trains.

Fate was already hidden within those people like a mortal illness. Assimilated Jews built a structure of humanistic values and looked out on the world from it. They were certain that they were no longer Jews and that what applied to "the Jews" did not apply to them. That strange assurance made them into blind or half-blind creatures. I have always loved assimilated Jews, because that was where the Jewish character, and also, perhaps, Jewish fate, was concentrated with greatest force.

Aharon took a bus back home around two, though only after we had gone ahead and, at my insistence, tried our best to ignore the Smilesburger check and to begin the conversation about *Badenheim 1939* that later evolved into the written exchange transcribed above. And I headed off on foot toward the central produce market and the dilapidated working-class neighborhood just behind it, to meet my cousin Apter at the room in his landlady's house in a little alley in Ohel-Moshe, thinking while I walked that Mr. Smilesburger's wasn't the first million donated to a Jewish cause by a well-fixed Jew, that a million was peanuts, really, when it came to Jewish philanthropy, that probably in this very city not a week went by when some American Jew who'd made a bundle in real estate or shopping malls didn't drop by to schmooze at the office of the mayor and, on the way out, happily hand over to him a check twice as big as mine. And not just fat cats gave and gave—even obscure old people like Smilesburger were leaving small fortunes to Israel all the time. It was part of a tradition of largesse that went back to the Rothschilds and beyond, staggering checks written out to Jews imperiled or needy in ways that their prosperous benefactors had either survived or, as they saw it, miraculously eluded against all the historical odds. Yes, there was a well-known, well-publicized context in which both this donor and his donation made perfectly ordinary sense, even if, in personal terms, I still didn't know what had hit me.

My thoughts were confused and contradictory. Surely it was time to turn to my lawyer, to get her to contact local counsel (or the local police) and begin to do what had to be done to disentangle the other one from me before some new development made into a mere trifle the million-dollar misunderstanding at the Ticho House. I told myself to get to a phone and call New York immediately, but instead I wandered circuitously toward the old market on Agrippas Street, under the auspices of a force stronger than prudence, more compelling even than anxiety or fear, something that preferred this narrative to unfold according to his, and not my, specifications—a story determined this time without any interference from me. Perhaps that was my reconstituted sanity back in power again, the calculated detachment, the engrossed neutrality of a working writer that, some half-year earlier, I was sure had been impaired forever. As I'd explained to Aharon the day before, there was nothing I coveted so much, after those months of spinning like a little stick in the subjectivist whirlpool of a breakdown, as to be *de*subjectified, the emphasis anywhere but on my own plight. Let his hisness drive *him* nuts—my myness was to be shipped off on a sabbatical, one long overdue and well earned. With Aharon, I thought, self-obliteration's a cinch, but to annihilate myself while this other one was running freely about . . . well, triumph at that and you will dwell in the house of the purely objective forever.

But then why, if "engrossed neutrality" is the goal, accept this check in the first place, a check that can only mean trouble?

The other one. The double. The impostor. It only now occurred to me how these designations unwittingly conferred a kind of legitimacy on this guy's usurping claims. There was no "other one." There was one and one alone on the one hand and a transparent fake on the other. This side of madness and the madhouse, doubles, I thought, figure mainly in books, as fully materialized duplicates incarnating the hidden depravity of the respectable original, as personalities or inclinations that refuse to be buried alive and that infiltrate civilized society to reveal a nineteenth-century gentleman's iniquitous secret. I knew all about these fictions about the fictions of the self-divided, having decoded them as cleverly as the next clever boy some four decades earlier in college. But this was no book I was studying or one I was writing, nor was this double a character in anything other than the vernacular sense of that word. Registered in suite 511 at the King David Hotel was not the other me, the second me, the irresponsible me, the deviant me, the opposing me, the delinquent, turpitudinous me embodying my evil fantasies of myself—I was being confounded by somebody who, very simply, was not me, who had nothing to do with me, who called himself by my name but had no relation to me. To think of him as a *double* was to bestow on him the destructive status of a famously real and prestigious archetype, and *impostor* was no improvement, it only intensified the menace I'd conceded with the Dostoyevskyan epithet by imputing professional credentials in duplicitous cunning to this ... this *what?* Name him. Yes, name him now! Because aptly naming him is knowing him for what he is and isn't, exorcising and possessing him all at once. Name him! In his pseudonymity is his anonymity, and it's that anonymity that's killing me. Name him! Who is this preposterous proxy? Nothing like namelessness to make a mystery of nothing. *Name him!* If I alone am Philip Roth, he is who?

Moishe Pipik.

But of course! The anguish I could have saved myself if only I'd known. Moishe Pipik—a name I had learned to enjoy long before I had ever read of Dr. Jekyll and Mr. Hyde or Golyadkin the First and Golyadkin the Second, a name that more than likely had not been

uttered in my presence since I was still a child small enough to be
engrossed by the household drama of all our striving relatives, their
tribulations, promotions, illnesses, arguments, etc., back when one or
another of us pint-sized boys, having said or done something thought
to be definingly expressive of an impish inner self, would hear the
loving aunt or the mocking uncle announce, "Is this a Moishe Pipik!"
Always a light little moment, that—laughter, smiles, commentary,
clarification, and the spoiled spotlit one, in the center suddenly of the
family stage, atingle with prideful embarrassment, delighted by the
superstar billing but abashed a little by the role that did not seem
quite to accord with a boychild's own self-imaginings. Moishe Pipik!
The derogatory, joking nonsense name that translates literally to
Moses Bellybutton and that probably connoted something slightly
different to every Jewish family on our block—the little guy who
wants to be a big shot, the kid who pisses in his pants, the someone
who is a bit ridiculous, a bit funny, a bit childish, the comical shadow
alongside whom we had all grown up, that little folkloric fall guy
whose surname designated the *thing* that for most children was neither here nor there, neither a part nor an orifice, somehow a concav-
ity and a convexity both, something neither upper nor lower, neither
lewd nor entirely respectable either, a short enough distance from
the genitals to make it suspiciously intriguing and yet, despite this,
teasing proximity, this conspicuously puzzling centrality, as meaningless as it was without function—the sole archaeological evidence of
the fairy tale of one's origins, the lasting imprint of the fetus who was
somehow oneself without actually being anyone at all, just about the
silliest, blankest, stupidest watermark that could have been devised
for a species with a brain like ours. It might as well have been the
omphalos at Delphi given the enigma the pipik presented. Exactly
what was your pipik trying to tell you? Nobody could ever really
figure it out. You were left with only the word, the delightful play-
word itself, the sonic prankishness of the two syllabic pops and the
closing click encasing those peepingly meekish, unobtrusively shle-
mielish twin vowels. And all the more rapturously ridiculous for
being yoked to Moishe, to Moses, which signaled, even to small and

ignorant boys overshadowed by their big wage-earning, wisecracking elders, that in the folk language of our immigrant grandparents and their inconceivable forebears there was a strong predisposition to think of even the supermen of our tribe as all kind of imminently pathetic. The goyim had Paul Bunyan and we had Moishe Pipik.

I was laughing my head off in the Jerusalem streets, laughing once again without restraint, hilariously laughing all by myself at the simple obviousness of the discovery that had turned a burden into a joke—"Is this a Moishe Pipik!" I thought, and felt all at once the return of my force, of the obstinacy and mastery whose strong resurgence I had been waiting and waiting on for so many months now, of the effectiveness that was mine back before I was ever on Halcion, of the gusto that was mine before I'd ever been poleaxed by any calamity at all, back before I had ever heard of contradiction or rejection or remorse. I felt what I'd felt way, way back, when, because of the lucky accident of a happy childhood, I didn't know I could be overcome by anything—all the endowment that was originally mine before I was ever impeded by guilt, a full human being strong in the magic. Sustaining that state of mind is another matter entirely, but it sure is wonderful while it lasts. Moishe Pipik! Perfect!

When I reached the central market it was still crowded with shoppers and, for a few minutes, I stopped to stroll through the produce-piled aisles, captivated by that stir of agitated, workaday busyness that makes open-air markets, wherever they are, so enjoyable to wander around in, particularly when you're clearing your head of a fog. Neither the stallkeepers shouting in Hebrew the price of their bargains while nimbly bagging what had just been sold nor the shoppers, speeding through the maze of stalls with the concentrated alacrity of people intent on getting the most for the least in the shortest possible amount of time, appeared to be in any way worried about being blown sky-high, and yet every few months or so, in this very market, an explosive device, hidden by the PLO in a refuse pile or a produce crate, was found by the bomb squad and defused or, if it wasn't, went off, maiming and killing whoever was nearby. What with violence between armed Israeli soldiers and angry Arab mobs flaring up all over the Occupied Territories and tear-gas canisters being lobbed back and forth only a couple of miles away in the Old City, it would have seemed only human had shoppers begun to shy away from risking life and limb in a target known to be a terrorist favorite. Yet the animation looked to me as intense as ever, the same old commotion of buying and selling testifying to just how palpably bad life has to become for people to ignore something as fundamental as getting supper on the table. Nothing could appear to be *more* human than refusing to believe extinction possible so long as you were encircled by luscious eggplants and ripe tomatoes and meat so fresh and pink that it looked good enough to wolf down raw. Probably the first thing they teach at terrorist school is that human beings are never less heedful of their safety than when they are out gathering food. The next best place to plant a bomb is a brothel.

At the end of a row of butcher stalls I saw a woman on her knees beside one of the metal trash cans where the butchers threw their leavings, a large, round-faced woman, about forty or so, wearing glasses and dressed in clothes that hardly looked like a beggar's. The tidy ordinariness of her attire was what had drawn my attention to her, kneeling there on the sticky cobblestones—wet with smelly leakage from the stalls, runny by mid-afternoon with a thin mash of garbagey muck—and fishing through the slops with one hand while holding a perfectly respectable handbag in the other. When she realized that I was watching her, she looked up and, without a trace of embarrassment—and speaking not in Hebrew but in accented English—explained, "Not for me." She then resumed her search with a fervor so disturbing to me, with gestures so convulsive and a gaze so fixed, that I was unable to walk off.

"For whom then?" I asked.

"For my friend," she said, foraging deep down into the bucket as she spoke. "She has six children. She said to me, 'If you see anything . . .' "

"For soup?" I asked.

"Yes. She puts something in with it—makes soup."

Here, I thought to say to her, here is a check for a million dollars.

Feed your friend and her children with this. Endorse it, I thought, and give it to her. Whether she's crazy or sane, whether there is or is not a friend, all of that is immaterial. She is in need, here is a check—give it to her and go. I am not responsible for this check!

"Philip! Philip Roth!"

My first impulse was not to turn around and acknowledge whoever thought he had recognized me but to rush away and get lost in the crowd—not again, I thought, not *another* million. But before I could move, the stranger was already there beside me, smiling broadly and reaching out for my hand, a smallish, boxy, middle-aged man, dark-complexioned, with a sizable dark mustache and a heavily creased face and an arresting shock of snowy white hair.

"Philip," he said warmly even though I withheld my hand and cautiously backed off—"Philip!" He laughed. "You don't even know me. I'm so fat and old and lined with my worries, you don't even remember me! You've grown only a forehead—I've grown this ridiculous hair! It's Zee, Philip. It's George."

"Zee!"

I threw my arms around him while the woman at the garbage pail, transfixed all at once by the two of us embracing, uttered something aloud, angrily said something in what was no longer English, and abruptly darted away without having scavenged anything for her friend—and without the million dollars either. Then, from some fifty feet away, she turned back and, pointing now from a safe distance, began to shout in a voice so loud that everywhere people looked to see what the problem was. Zee too looked—and listened. And laughed, though without much amusement, when he found out that the problem was him. "Another expert," he explained, "on the mentality of the Arab. Their experts on our mentality are everywhere, in the university, in the military, on the street corner, in the market—"

"Zee" was for Ziad, George Ziad,° whom I hadn't seen in more than thirty years, since the mid-fifties, when we'd lived for a year down the corridor from each other in a residence hall for divinity students at the University of Chicago, where I was getting my M.A. in English and George was a graduate student in the program called Religion and Art. Most of the twenty or so rooms in the Disciples Divinity House, a smallish neo-Gothic building diagonally across from the main university campus, were rented by students affiliated with the Disciples of Christ Church, but since there weren't always enough of them to fill the place, outsiders like the two of us were allowed to rent there as well. The rooms on our floor were bright with sunlight and inexpensive, and, despite the usual prohibitions that obtained everywhere in university living quarters back then, it wasn't impossible, if you had the courage for it, to slip a girl through your door late in the evening. Zee had had the courage and the strong need for it too. In his early twenties, he had been a very lithe, dapperly dressed young man, small but romantically handsome, and his credentials—a Harvard-educated Egyptian enrolled at Chicago to study Dostoyevsky and Kierkegaard—made him irresistible to all those Chicago coeds avid for cross-cultural adventure.

"I live here," George answered when I asked what he was doing in Israel. "In the Occupied Territories. I live in Ramallah."

"And not in Cairo."

"I don't come from Cairo."

"You don't? But didn't you?"

"We fled to Cairo. We came from here. I was born here. The house I grew up in is still exactly where it was. I was more stupid than usual today. I came to look at it. Then, still more stupidly, I came here—to observe the oppressor in his natural habitat."

"I didn't know any of this, did I? That you came from Jerusalem?"

"It was not something I talked about in 1955. I wanted to forget all that. My father couldn't forget, and so I would. Weeping and ranting all day long about everything he had lost to the Jews: his house, his practice, his patients, his books, his art, his garden, his almond trees —every day he screamed, he wept, he ranted, and I was a wonderful son, Philip. I couldn't forgive him his despair for the almond trees. The trees particularly enraged me. When he had the stroke and died, I was relieved. I was in Chicago and I thought, 'Now I won't have to hear about the almond trees for the rest of my life. Now I can be who I am.' And now the trees and the house and the garden are all I can think about. My father and his ranting are all I can think about. I think about his tears every day. And that, to my surprise, is who I am."

"What do you do here, Zee?"

Smiling at me benignly, he answered, "Hate."

I didn't know what to reply and so said nothing.

"She had it right, the expert on my mentality. What she said is true. I am a stone-throwing Arab consumed by hate."

Again I offered no reply.

His next words came slowly, tinged with a tone of sweet contempt. "What do you expect me to throw at the occupier? Roses?"

"No, no," he finally said when I continued to remain silent, "it's the children who do it, not the old men. Don't worry, Philip, I don't throw anything. The occupier has nothing to fear from a civilized fellow like me. Last month they took a hundred boys, the occupiers. Held them for eighteen days. Took them to a camp near Nablus. Boys eleven, twelve, thirteen. They came back brain-damaged. Can't hear. Lame. Very thin. No, not for me. I prefer to be fat. What do I do? I teach at a university when it is not shut down. I write for a newspaper when it is not shut down. They damage my brain in more subtle ways. I fight the occupier with words, as though words will ever stop them from stealing our land. I oppose our masters with ideas—that is my humiliation and shame. Clever thinking is the form my capitulation takes. Endless analyses of the situation—that is the grammar of my degradation. Alas, I am not a stone-throwing Arab—I am a word-throwing Arab, soft, sentimental, and ineffective, altogether like my father. I come to Jerusalem to stand and look at the house where I was a boy. I remember my father and how his life was destroyed. I look at the house and want to kill. Then I drive back to Ramallah to cry like him over all that is lost. And you—I know why you are here. I read it in the papers and I said to my wife, 'He hasn't changed.' I read aloud to my son just two nights ago your story 'The Conversion of the Jews.' I said, 'He wrote this when I knew him, he wrote this at the University of Chicago, he was twenty-one years old, and he hasn't changed at all.' I loved *Portnoy's Complaint*, Philip. It was great, great! I assign it to my students at the university. 'Here is a Jew,' I tell

them, 'who has never been afraid to speak out about Jews. An independent Jew and he has suffered for it too:' I try to convince them
that there are Jews in the world who are not in any way like these
Jews we have here. But to them the Israeli Jew is so evil they find it
hard to believe. They look around and they think, What have they
done? Name one single thing that Israeli society has done! And, Philip,
my students are right—who *are* they? what *have* they done? The
people are coarse and noisy and push you in the street. I've lived in
Chicago, in New York, in Boston, I've lived in Paris, in London, and
nowhere have I seen such people in the street. The *arrogance!* What
have they created like you Jews out in the world? Absolutely nothing.
Nothing but a state founded on force and the will to dominate. If you
want to talk about culture, there is absolutely no comparison. Dismal
painting and sculpture, no musical composition, and a very minor
literature—that is what all their arrogance has produced. Compare
this to American Jewish culture and it is pitiable, it is laughable. And
yet they are not only arrogant about the Arab and *his* mentality, they
are not only arrogant about the goyim and *their* mentality, they are
arrogant about you and *your* mentality. These provincial nobodies
look down on *you.* Can you imagine it? There is more Jewish spirit
and Jewish laughter and Jewish intelligence on the Upper West Side
of Manhattan than in this entire country—and as for Jewish *conscience,* as for a Jewish sense of *justice,* as for Jewish *heart* . . . there's
more Jewish heart at the knish counter at Zabar's than in the whole
of the Knesset! But *look* at you! You look great. Still so thin! You look
like a Jewish baron, like a Rothschild from Paris."

"Do I really? No, no, still an insurance man's son from New Jersey."

"How is your father? How is your mother? How is your brother?"
he asked me, excitedly.

The metamorphosis that, physically, had all but effaced the boy I'd
known at Chicago was nothing, I had come to realize, beside an
alteration, or deformation, far more astonishing and grave. The gush,
the agitation, the volubility, the frenzy barely beneath the surface of
every word he babbled, the nerve-racking sense he communicated of
someone aroused and decomposing all at the same time, of someone

in a permanent state of imminent apoplexy ... how could that be Zee, how could this overweight, overwrought cyclone of distress possibly have been the cultivated young gentleman we all so admired for his suavity and his slick composure? Back then I was still a crisscross of personalities, a grab bag of raw qualities, strands of street-corner boyishness still inextricably interwoven with the burgeoning high-mindedness, while George had seemed to me so successfully imperturbable, so knowing in the ways of life, so wholly and impressively *formed.* Well, to hear him tell it now, I'd had him wrong in every way: in reality he'd been living under an ice cap, a son trying in vain to stanch the bleeding of a wronged and ruined father, with his wonderful manners and his refined virility not only masking the pain of dispossession and exile but concealing even from himself how scorched he was by shame, perhaps even more so than the father.

Emotionally, his voice quaking, Zee said to me, "I dream of Chicago. I dream of those days when I was a student in Chicago."

"Yes, we were lively boys."

"I dream about Walter Schneeman's Red Door Book Shop. I dream about the University Tavern. I dream about the Tropical Hut. I dream about my carrel in the library. I dream about my courses with Preston Roberts. I dream about my Jewish friends, about you and Herb Haber and Barry Targan and Art Geffin—Jews who could not *conceive* of being Jews like this! There are weeks, Philip, when I dream of Chicago every single night!" Taking my hands tightly in his and shaking them as though they were a set of reins, he said suddenly, "What are you doing? What are you doing *right this minute?*"

I was, of course, on my way to visit Apter at his room, but I decided not to tell this to George Ziad in the state of agitation he was in. The previous evening I had spoken briefly on the phone with Apter, assuring him once again that the person identified as me at the Demjanjuk trial a week earlier had merely been someone who looked like me and that I had arrived in Jerusalem only the day before and would come to see him at his stall in the Old City the very next afternoon. And here, like virtually every other man I seemed to meet in Jerusalem, Apter had begun to cry. Because of the violence, he told me, because of the Arabs throwing stones, he was too frightened to leave his room and I must come to see him there:

I did not want to tell George that I had a cousin here who was an emotionally impaired Holocaust survivor, because I did not want to hear him tell me how it was the Holocaust survivors, poisoned by their Holocaust pathology, against whose "will to dominate" the Palestinians had for over four decades now been struggling to survive.

"Zee, I have time for just a quick cup of coffee—then I've got to run."

"Coffee where? Here? In the city of my father? Here in the city of my father they'll sit down right next to us—they'll sit in my *lap.*" He said this while pointing to two young men standing beside a fruit vendor's stall only some ten or fifteen feet away. They were wearing jeans and talking together, two short, strongly built fellows I would have assumed were market workers taking a few minutes off for a smoke had Zee not said, "Israeli security. Shin Bet. I can't even go into a public toilet in the city of my father that they don't come in next to me and start pissing on my shoes. They're everywhere. Interrogate me at the airport, search me at customs, intercept my mail, follow my car, tap my phone, bug my house—they even infiltrate my classroom." He began to laugh very loudly. "Last year, my best student, he wrote a wonderful Marxist analysis of *Moby Dick*—he was Shin Bet too. My only 'A.' Philip, I cannot sit and have coffee here. Triumphant Israel is a terrible, terrible place to have coffee. These victorious Jews are terrible people. I don't just mean the Kahanes and the Sharons. I mean them *all,* the Yehoshuas and the Ozes included. The good ones who are against the occupation of the West Bank but not against the occupation of my father's house, the 'beautiful Israelis' who want their Zionist thievery and their clean conscience too. They are no less superior than the rest of them—these beautiful Israelis are even *more* superior. What do they know about 'Jewish,' these 'healthy, confident' Jews who look down their noses at you Diaspora 'neurotics'? This is health? This is confidence? This is *arrogance.* Jews who make military brutes out of their sons—and how superior they feel to you Jews who know nothing of guns! Jews who use clubs to break the hands of Arab children—and how superior they feel to you Jews incapable of such violence! Jews without tolerance, Jews for whom it is always black and white, who have all these crazy splinter parties, who have a party of *one man,* they are so intolerant one of the other—these are the Jews who are superior to the Jews in the Diaspora? Superior to people who know in their bones the meaning of give-and-take? Who live with success, like tolerant human beings, in the great world of crosscurrents and human differences? Here they are *authentic,* here, locked up in their Jewish ghetto and armed to the teeth? And you there, *you* are 'unauthentic,' living freely in contact with all of mankind? The *arrogance,* Philip, it is *insufferable!* What they teach their children in the schools is to look with disgust on the Diaspora Jew, to see the English-speaking Jew and the Spanish-speaking Jew and the Russian-speaking Jew as a freak, as a worm, as a terrified neurotic. As if this Jew who now speaks Hebrew isn't just *another kind of Jew*—as if speaking Hebrew is the culmination of human achievement! I'm here, they think, and I speak Hebrew, this is my language and my home, and I don't have to go around thinking all the time, 'I'm a Jew but what is a Jew?' I don't have to be this kind of self-questioning, self-hating, alienated, frightened neurotic. And what those so-called neurotics have given to the world in the way of brain power and art and science and all the skills and ideals of civilization, to this they are oblivious. But then to the entire *world* they are oblivious. For the entire world they have one word: goy! 'I live here and I speak Hebrew and all I know and see are other Jews like me and isn't that wonderful!' Oh, what an impoverished Jew this arrogant Israeli is! Yes, they are the authentic ones, the Yehoshuas and the Ozes, and tell me, I ask them, what are Saul Alinsky and David Riesman and Meyer Schapiro and Leonard Bernstein and Bella Abzug and Paul Goodman and Allen Ginsberg, and on and on and on and *on?* Who do they think they *are,* these provincial nobodies! Jailers! This is their great Jewish achievement—to make Jews into jailers and jet-bomber pilots! And just suppose they were to succeed, suppose they were to win and have their way and every Arab in Nablus and every Arab in Hebron and every Arab in the Galilee and in Gaza, suppose every Arab in the world, were to disappear courtesy of the Jewish nuclear bomb, what would they have here fifty years from now? A noisy little state of no importance whatsoever. That's what the persecution and the destruction of the Palestinians will have been for— the creation of a Jewish Belgium, without even a Brussels to show for it. That's what these 'authentic' Jews will have contributed to civilization—a country lacking every quality that gave the Jews their great distinction! They may be able to instill in other Arabs who live under their evil occupation fear and respect for their 'superiority,' but I grew up with *you* people, I was educated with *you* people, *by* you people, I lived with *real* Jews, at Harvard, at Chicago, with *truly* superior people, whom I admired, whom I loved, to whom I did *indeed* feel inferior and *rightly* so—the vitality in them, the irony in them, the human sympathy, the human *tolerance,* the goodness of heart that was simply *instinctive* in them, people with the Jewish sense of survival that was all human, elastic, adaptable, humorous, creative, and all this they have replaced here with a stick! The Golden *Calf* was more Jewish than Ariel Sharon, God of Samaria and Judea and the Holy Gaza Strip! The worst of the ghetto Jew combined with the worst of the bellicose, belligerent goy, and that is what these people call 'authentic'! Jews have a reputation for being intelligent, and they *are* intelligent. The only place I have ever *been* where all the Jews are stupid is Israel. I spit on them! I *spit* on them!" And this my friend Zee proceeded to do, spat on the wet, gritty marketplace pavement while looking defiantly at the two toughs in jeans he'd identified as Israeli security, neither of whom happened to be looking our way or, seemingly, to be concerned with anything other than their own conversation.

———

Why did I drive with him to Ramallah that afternoon instead of keeping my date with Apter? Because he told me so many times that I had to? Had to see with my own eyes the occupier's mockery of justice; had to observe with my own eyes the legal system behind which the occupier attempted to conceal his oppressive colonizing; had to post-

pone whatever I was doing to visit with him the army courtroom
where the youngest brother of one of his friends was being tried on
trumped-up charges and where I would witness the cynical corruption of every Jewish value cherished by every decent Diaspora Jew.

The charge against his friend's brother was of throwing Molotov
cocktails at Israeli soldiers, a charge "unsupported by a single shred
of evidence, unsubstantiated, another filthy lie." The boy had been
picked up at a demonstration and then "interrogated." Interrogation
consisted of covering his head with a hood, soaking him alternately
with hot and cold showers, then making him stand outside, whatever
the weather, the hood still over his head, enshrouding his eyes, ears,
nose, and mouth—hooded like that for forty-five days and forty-five
nights until the boy "confessed." I had to see what this boy looked
like after those forty-five days and forty-five nights. I had to meet
George's friend, one of the most stalwart opponents of the occupation, a lawyer, a poet, a leader whom, of course, the occupier was
trying to silence by arresting and torturing his beloved kid brother. *I
had to,* George charged me, the veins strung out like cables in his
neck and his fingers in motion all the while, rapidly flexing open and
shut as though there were something in the palm of each hand out of
which he was squeezing the last bit of life.

We were standing beside George's car, which he'd left parked on a
tiny side street a few blocks up from the market. The car had been
ticketed and two policemen were waiting not far away and asked to
see George's identity card, the car's registration, and his driver's license as soon as he stepped up and, making rather a show of his
indifference, acknowledged the West Bank plates as his. Using
George's key, the police methodically searched the trunk and beneath the seats and opened the glove compartment to examine its
contents, and meanwhile, pretending to be oblivious to them, to be
completely unintimidated by them, unharassed, unafraid, unhumil-
iated, George, like a man on the brink of a seizure, continued to tell
me what I *had* to do.

*The corruption of every Jewish value cherished by every decent
Diaspora Jew . . .* It was this fulsome praise of Diaspora Jews, whose

excessiveness simply would not stop, that had finally convinced me that our meeting in the marketplace had been something other than sheer coincidence. His adamant insistence that I accompany him now to the occupier's travesty of a courtroom made me rather more certain that George Ziad had been following me—the me, that is, who he thought I had become—than that those two who'd been smoking and gabbing together beside the fruit vendor's stall in the market were Shin Bet agents who'd been following him. And this, the very best reason for my *not* doing what he told me I had to do, was exactly why I knew I had to do it.

Adolescent audacity? Writerly curiosity? Callow perversity? Jewish mischief? Whatever the impulse that informed my bad judgment, being mistaken for Moishe Pipik for the second time in less than an hour made yielding to his importuning as natural to me, as irresistible for me, as accepting Smilesburger's donation had been at lunch.

George never stopped talking; he couldn't stop. An unbridled talker. An inexhaustible talker. A frightening talker. All the way out to Ramallah, even at the roadblocks, where not only his identification papers but now mine as well were checked over by the soldiers and where, each and every time, the trunk of the car was once again examined and the seats removed and the contents of the glove compartment emptied onto the road, he lectured me on the evolution of that guilt-laden relationship of American Jews to Israel which the Zionists had sinisterly exploited to subsidize their thievery. He had figured it out, thought it all through, even published an influential essay in a British Marxist journal on "The Zionist Blackmailing of American Jewry," and, from the sound of it, all that publishing the essay had achieved was to leave him more degraded and enraged and ground down. We drove by the high-rise apartment buildings of Jerusalem's northern Jewish suburbs ("A concrete jungle—so *hideous* what they build here! These aren't houses, they are fortresses! The mentality is everywhere! Machine-sawed stone facing—the *vulgarity* of it!"); out past the large nondescript modern stone houses built before the Israeli occupation by wealthy Jordanians, which struck me as more vulgar by far, crowned as each was with an elongated TV aerial kitschily replicating the Eiffel Tower; and finally into the dry, stone-strewn valley of the countryside. And as we drove, embittered analysis streamed forth unabated, of Jewish history, Jewish mythology, Jewish psychosis and sociology, each sentence delivered with an alarming air of intellectual wantonness, the whole a pungent ideological mulch of overstatement and lucidity, of insight and stupidity, of precise historical data and willful historical ignorance, a loose array of observations as disjointed as it was coherent and as shallow as it was deep—the shrewd and vacuous diatribe of a man whose brain, once as good as anyone's, was now as much a menace to him as the anger and the loathing that, by 1988, after twenty years of the occupation and forty years of the Jewish state, had corroded everything moderate in him, everything practical, realistic, and to the point. The stupendous quarrel, the perpetual emergency, the monumental unhappiness, the battered pride, the intoxication of resistance had rendered him incapable of even nibbling at the truth, however intelligent he still happened to be. By the time his ideas wormed their way through all that emotion, they had been so distorted and intensified as only barely to resemble human thought. Despite the unremitting determination to comprehend the enemy, as though in understanding them there was still, for him, some hope, despite the thin veneer of professorial brilliance, which gave even his most dubious and bungled ideas a certain intellectual gloss, now at the core of everything was hatred and the great disabling fantasy of revenge.

And I said nothing, did not so much as challenge one excessive claim or do anything to clarify his thinking or to take exception where I knew he didn't know what he was talking about. Instead, employing the disguise of my own face and name, I listened intently to all the suppositions spawned by his unbearable grievance, to the suffering spilling out of him in every word; I studied him with the coldhearted fascination and intense excitement of a well-placed spy.

Here is a condensation of his argument, a good deal more cogent for being summarized. I won't describe the collisions and the pileups that George only narrowly avoided while he held forth. Suffice it to say that, even without an uprising under way and violence breaking

out everywhere, it is extremely hazardous to sit beside a man making
a long speech at the wheel of a car. On the drive that afternoon
between Jerusalem and Ramallah, there was not a half-mile without
its excitements. George did not always fulminate looking straight
ahead.

In summary, then, George's lecture on that topic I could not really
remember having chosen to shadow me like this, from birth to death;
the topic whose obsessive examination I had always thought I could
someday leave behind; the topic whose persistent intrusion into matters high and low it was not always easy to know what to make of;
the pervasive, engulfing, wearying topic that encapsulated the largest
problem and most amazing experience of my life and that, despite
every honorable attempt to resist its spell, appeared by now to be the
irrational power that had run away with my life—and, from the sound
of things, not mine alone . . . that topic called *the Jews.*

First—according to George's historical breakdown of the cycle of
Jewish corruption—were the pre-Holocaust, postimmigration years
of 1900 to 1939: a period of renouncing the Old Country for the
New; of dealienization and naturalization, of extinguishing the memories of families and communities abandoned, of forgetting parents
left to age and die without their most adventurous children to comfort and console them—the feverish period of toiling to construct in
America, and in English, a new life and identity as Jews. After this, the
period of calculated amnesia, 1939 to 1945, the years of the immeasurable catastrophe, when, with lightning speed, those families and
communities from which the newly, incompletely Americanized Jews
had voluntarily severed their strongest ties were quite literally obliterated by Hitler. The destruction of European Jewry registered as a
cataclysmic shock on American Jews not only because of its sheer
horror but also because this horror, viewed irrationally through the
prism of their grief, seemed to them in some indefinable way *ignited*
by them—yes, instigated by the wish to put an end to Jewish life in
Europe that their massive emigration had embodied, as though between the bestial destructiveness of Hitlerian anti-Semitism and their
own passionate desire to be delivered from the humiliations of their

European imprisonment there had existed some horrible, unthinkable interrelationship, bordering on complicity. And a misgiving very similar, an undivulgeable self-denunciation perhaps even more ominous, could be imputed to the Zionists and their Zionism. For were the Zionists without contempt for Jewish life in Europe when they embarked for Palestine? Didn't the militants who pioneered the Jewish state feel an even more drastic revulsion for the Yiddish-speaking masses of the shtetl than did those practical-minded immigrants who'd managed their escape to America without the blight of an ideology like Ben-Gurion's? Admittedly, migration, and not mass murder, was the solution proposed by Zionism; nevertheless, disgust for their own origins these Zionists made manifest in a thousand ways, most tellingly in choosing as the official tongue of the Jewish state the language of the remote biblical past rather than the shaming European vulgate that issued from the mouths of their powerless forebears.

So: Hitler's slaughter of all those millions whom these Jews had unwittingly abandoned to their fate, the destruction of the humiliating culture whose future they had wanted no part of, the annihilation of the society that had compromised their virility and restricted their development—this left the unimperiled Jews of America as well as Israel's defiantly bold founding fathers with a legacy not only of grief but of inexpungible guilt so damning as to warp the Jewish soul for decades thereafter, if not for centuries to come.

Following the catastrophe came the great period of postwar normalization, when the emergence of Israel as a haven for the surviving remnant of European Jewry coincided precisely with the advance of assimilation in America; the period of renewed energy and inspiration, when the Holocaust was itself still only dimly perceived by the public at large and before it had infested all of Jewish rhetoric; the years before the Holocaust had been commercialized by that name, when the most popular symbol for what had been endured by European Jewry was a delightful adolescent up in the attic diligently doing her homework for her daddy and when the means for contemplating everything more horrible were still generally undiscovered or sup-

pressed, when in Israel it would be years before a holiday was officially proclaimed to commemorate the six million dead; the period
when Jews everywhere wished to be known even to themselves for
something more vitalizing than their victimization. In America it was
the age of the nose job, the name change, the ebbing of the quota
system, and the exaltations of suburban life, the dawn of the era of
big corporate promotions, whopping Ivy League admissions, hedonis-
tic holidays, and all manner of dwindling prohibitions—and of the
emergence of a corps of surprisingly goylike Jewish children, dopey
and confident and happy in ways that previous generations of anxious
Jewish parents had never dared to imagine possible for their own.
The pastoralization of the ghetto, George Ziad called it, the pasteur-
ization of the faith. "Green lawns, white Jews—you wrote about it.
You crystallized it in your first book. That's what the hoopla was all
about. 1959. The Jewish success story in its heyday, all new and
thrilling and funny and fun. Liberated new Jews, normalized Jews,
ridiculous and wonderful. The triumph of the untragic. Brenda Pa-
timkin dethrones Anne Frank. Hot sex, fresh fruit, and Big Ten bas-
ketball—who could imagine a happier ending for the Jewish people?"

Then 1967: the Israeli victory in the Six Day War. And with this,
the confirmation not of Jewish dealienization or of Jewish assimilation
or of Jewish normalization but of Jewish *might,* the cynical institu-
tionalization of the Holocaust begins. It is precisely here, with a Jewish military state gloating and triumphant, that it becomes official
Jewish policy to remind the world, minute by minute, hour by hour,
day in and day out, that the Jews were victims before they were
conquerors and that they are conquerors only because they are victims. This is the public-relations campaign cunningly devised by the
terrorist Begin: to establish Israeli military expansionism as histori-
cally just by joining it to the memory of Jewish victimization; to
rationalize—as historical justice, as just retribution, as nothing more
than self-defense—the gobbling up of the Occupied Territories and
the driving of the Palestinians off their land once again. What justifies
seizing every opportunity to extend Israel's boundaries? Auschwitz.
What justifies bombing Beirut civilians? Auschwitz. What justifies

smashing the bones of Palestinian children and blowing off the limbs of Arab mayors? Auschwitz. Dachau. Buchenwald. Belsen. Treblinka. Sobibor. Belsec. "Such falseness, Philip, such brutal, cynical insincerity! To keep the territories has for them one meaning and *only* one meaning: it is to display the physical prowess that made the conquest possible! To rule the territories is to exercise a prerogative hitherto denied—the experience of oppressing and victimizing, the experience now of ruling *others.* Power-mad Jews is what they are, is *all* that they are, no different from the power-mad everywhere, except for the mythology of victimization that they use to justify their addiction to power and their victimizing of *us.* The famous joke has it exactly right: 'There's no business like *Shoah* business.' During the period of their normalization there was the innocent symbol of little Anne Frank, that was poignant enough. But now, in the era of their greatest armed might, now at the height of their insufferable arrogance, now there are sixteen hours of *Shoah* with which to pulverize audiences all over the world, now there is 'Holocaust' on NBC once a week, starring as a Jew Meryl Streep! And the American Jewish leaders who come here, they know this *Shoah* business very well—they arrive here from New York, Los Angeles, Chicago, these officials of the Jewish establishment, and to those few Israelis who still have some truthfulness in them and some self-respect, who still know how to utter something other than the propaganda and the lies, they say, 'Don't *tell* me how the Palestinians are becoming accommodating. Don't *tell* me how the Palestinians have legitimate claims. Don't *tell* me how the Palestinians are oppressed and that an injustice has been done. Stop that immediately! I cannot raise money in America with that. Tell me about how we are threatened, tell me about terrorism, tell me about anti-Semitism and the Holocaust!' And this explains why there is the show trial of this stupid Ukrainian—to reinforce the cornerstone of Israeli power politics by bolstering the ideology of the victim. No, they will not stop describing themselves as victims and identifying themselves with the past. But it is not exactly as though the past has been ignored—the very existence of this state is evidence of that. By now surely this obsessive narrative of theirs has come to violate their sense of reality—it certainly violates ours. Don't tell *us* about their victimization! We are the last people in the *world* to understand that! *Of course* Ukrainian anti-Semitism is real. There are many causes that we all know, having to do with the role the Jews played there in the economic structure, with the cynical role assigned to them by Stalin in the farm collectivization—all this is clear. But whether this stupid Ukrainian is Ivan the Terrible is not *at all* clear, it *can't* be clear after forty years, and so, if you have any honesty as a nation, any respect left at all for the law, you let him go. If you must have your vengeance, you send him back to the Ukraine and let the Russians deal with him—that should be satisfaction enough. But to try him here in the courtroom and over the radio and on the television and in the papers, this has only one purpose—a public-relations stunt à la the Holocaust-monger Begin and the gangster Shamir; public relations to justify Jewish might, to justify Jewish rule by perpetuating into the next one hundred millennia the image of the Jewish victim. But is public relations the purpose of a system of criminal justice? The criminal-justice system has a *legal* purpose, not a public-relations purpose. To educate the public? No, that's the purpose of an *educational* system. I repeat: Demjanjuk is here to maintain the mythology that is this country's lifeblood. Because without the Holocaust, where are they? *Who* are they? It is through the Holocaust that they sustain their connection to world Jewry, especially to privileged, secure American Jewry, with its exploitable guilt over being unimperiled and successful. Without the connection to world Jewry, where is their historical claim to the land? Nowhere! If they were to lose their custodianship of the Holocaust, if the mythology of the dispersion were to be exposed as a sham—*what then?* What *happens* when American Jews shed their guilt and come to their senses? What *happens* when American Jews realize that these people, with their incredible arrogance, have taken on a mission and a meaning that is utterly preposterous, that is *pure mythology?* What *happens* when they come to realize that they have been sold a bill of goods and that, far from being superior to Diaspora Jewry, these Zionists are inferior *by every measure of civilization?* What *happens*

when American Jews discover that they have been duped, that they
have constructed an allegiance to Israel on the basis of irrational guilt,
of vengeful fantasies, above all, *above all,* based on the most naive
delusions about the moral identity of this state? *Because this state
has no moral identity.* It has *forfeited* its moral identity, if it ever had
any to begin with. By relentlessly institutionalizing the Holocaust it
has even forfeited its claim to the Holocaust! The state of Israel has
drawn the last of its moral credit out of the bank of the dead six
million—this is what they have done by breaking the hands of Arab
children on the orders of their illustrious minister of defense. Even
to world Jewry it will be clear: this is a state founded on force and
maintained by force, a Machiavellian state that deals violently with
the uprising of an oppressed people in an occupied territory, a Machiavellian state in, admittedly, a Machiavellian world, but about as
saintly as the Chicago Police Department. They have advertised this
state for forty years as essential to the existence of Jewish culture,
people, heritage; they have tried with all their cunning to advertise
Israel as a no-choice reality when, in fact, it is an *option,* to be
examined in terms of *quality* and *value.* And when you dare to
examine it like this, what do you actually find? Arrogance! Arrogance!
Arrogance! And beyond the arrogance? Nothing! And beyond the
nothing—*more arrogance!* And now it is there for the whole world
to see every night on television—a primitive capacity for sadistic
violence that has finally put the lie to *all* their mythology! 'The Law
of the Return'? As if any self-respecting civilized Jew would *want* to
'return' to a place like this! 'The Ingathering of the Exiles'? As if 'exile'
from Jewishness begins to describe the Jewish condition anywhere
but *here!* 'The Holocaust'? The Holocaust is over. Unbeknownst to
them, the Zionists themselves officially declared it over three days
ago at Manara Square in Ramallah. I will take you there and show you
the place where the decree was written. A wall where the soldiers
took innocent Palestinian civilians and clubbed and beat them to a
pulp. Forget the publicity stunt of that show trial. The end of the
Holocaust is written on that wall in Palestinian blood. Philip! Old
friend! All your life you have devoted to saving the Jews from them-

selves, exposing to them their self-delusions. All your life, as a writer, ever since you began writing those stories out at Chicago, you have been opposing their flattering self-stereotypes. You have been attacked for this, you have been reviled for this, the conspiracy against you in the Jewish press began at the beginning and has barely let up to this day, a smear campaign the likes of which has befallen no Jewish writer since Spinoza. Do I exaggerate? All I know is that if a goy publicly insulted a Jew the way they have publicly insulted you, the B'nai B'rith would be screaming from every pulpit and every talk show, 'Anti-Semitism!' They have called you the filthiest names, charged you with the most treacherous acts of betrayal, and yet you continue to feel responsible to them, to fear for them, you persist, in the face of their self-righteous stupidity, to be their loving, loyal son. You are a great patriot of your people, and because of this, much of what I have been saying has angered and offended you. I see it in the set of your face, I hear it in your silence. You think, He is crazy, hysterical, reckless, wild. And what if I am—*wouldn't you be?* Jews! Jews! Jews! How can I not think continually about Jews! Jews are my jailers, I am their prisoner. And, as my wife will tell you, there is nothing I have less talent for than being a prisoner. My talent was to be a professor, not a slave to a master. My talent was to teach Dostoyevsky, not to live drowning in spite and resentment like the underground man! My talent was to explicate the interminable monologues of his seething madmen, not to turn into a seething madman whose own interminable monologues he cannot stifle even in his sleep. Why don't I restrain myself if I know what I'm doing to myself? My poor wife asks this question every day. Why can't we move back to Boston before the stroke that killed the ranting father kills the ranting son? Why? Because I, who will not capitulate, am a patriot *too,* who loves and hates his defeated, cringing Palestinians probably in the same proportion that *you,* Philip, love and hate your smug, self-satisfied Jews. You say nothing. You are shocked to see debonair Zee in a state of blind, consuming rage, and you are too ironical, too worldly, too skeptical to accept with graciousness what I am about to tell you now, but, Philip, *you are a Jewish prophet and you always have*

been. You are a Jewish *seer,* and with your trip to Poland you have
taken a visionary, bold, historical step. And for it you will now be
more than just reviled in the press—you will be threatened, you will
be menaced, you may very well be physically attacked. I wouldn't
doubt that they will even try to arrest you—to implicate you in some
criminal act and put you in jail to shut you up. These are ruthless
people here, and Philip Roth has dared to fly directly in the face of
their national lie. For forty years they have been dragging Jews from
all over the world, making payoffs, cutting deals, bribing officials in a
dozen different countries so as to get their hands on more and more
Jews and drag them here to perpetuate their myth of a Jewish homeland. And now comes Philip Roth to do everything he can to encourage these same Jews to stop squatting on somebody else's land and
to leave this make-believe country of theirs before these unregenerate, power-mad, vengeful Zionists implicate the whole of world Jewry
in their brutality and bring a catastrophe down upon the Jews from
which they will never recover. Old friend, we need you, we all need
you, the occupiers as much as the occupied need your Diaspora
boldness and your Diaspora brains. You are not in bondage to this
conflict, you are not helpless in the grip of this thing. You come with
a vision, a fresh and brilliant vision to resolve it—not a lunatic uto
pian Palestinian dream or a terrible Zionist final solution but a pro-
foundly conceived historical arrangement that is workable, that is
just. Old friend, dear, dear old friend—how can I serve you? How
can *we* serve you? We are not without our resources. Tell me what
we must do and we will do it."

5

I Am
Pipik

The Ramallah military court lay within the walls of a jail built by the British during the Mandate, a low, concrete, bunkerlike complex whose purpose it would have been hard to misconstrue—it was a punishment just to look at it. The jail was perched atop a bald, sandy hill at the edge of the city, and we turned at the roundabout at the foot of the hill and drove up to the high chain fence, topped by a double roll of barbed wire, that enclosed the outermost perimeter of the four or five acres separating the jail from the road below. George and I got out of the car and approached the gate to present our papers to one of three armed guards. Without speaking, the guard examined them and handed them back, and we were permitted to advance another hundred feet to a second gatehouse, where a submachine gun jutting out the window was aimed at whatever ascended the drive. The gun was manned by a grim, unshaven young soldier, who eyed us soberly while we handed our papers over to another guard, who tossed them onto his desk and, with a truculent gesture, indicated that we could go on.

"Sephardic boys," George told me as we continued toward a side door of the jail. "Moroccans. The Ashkenazis prefer to keep their hands clean. They get their darker brethren to do their torturing for them. The ignorant Arab haters from the Orient furnish the refined Ashkenazis with a very useful, all-purpose proletarian mob. Of course when they lived in Morocco they didn't hate Arabs. They lived harmoniously with Arabs for a thousand years. But the white Israelis have taught them that, too—how to hate the Arabs and how to hate themselves. The white Israelis have turned them into their thugs."

The side door was guarded by a pair of soldiers who, like those we'd just encountered, looked to have been recruited from the meanest city streets. They let us through without a word, and we stepped into a shabby courtroom barely large enough for a couple of dozen spectators. Occupying half the seats were more Israeli soldiers, who weren't carrying weapons that I could see but who didn't appear as though they'd have much trouble putting down a disturbance with just their bare hands. In scruffy fatigues and combat boots, their shirt collars open and their heads bare, they sat lazily sprawled about but nonetheless looking very proprietary with their arms spread to either side along the back rail of the wooden benches. My first impression was of young toughs lolling in the outer lobby of an employment agency that specialized in placing bouncers.

On the raised dais at the front of the courtroom, between two large Israeli flags pinned to the wall behind him, sat the judge, a uniformed army officer in his thirties. Slender, slightly balding, clean-shaven, carefully turned out, he listened to the proceedings with the perspicacious air of a mild, judicious person—one of "us."

In the second row down from the dais, a seated spectator gestured toward George, and we two slipped quietly in beside him. No soldiers sat in this row. They had grouped themselves together further back, near a door at the rear of the room, which I saw opened onto the detention area for the defendants. Before the door was pulled shut, I glimpsed an Arab boy. You could read the terror on his face even from thirty feet away.

We had joined the poet-lawyer whose brother was accused of throwing Molotov cocktails and whom George had described as a formidable opponent of the Israeli occupation. When George introduced us he took my hand and pressed it warmly. Kamil° was his name, a tall, mustached man, skeletally thin, with the molten, black, meaningful eyes of what they used to call a ladies' man and a manner that reminded me of the persuasively debonair disguise that George had worn back when he was Zee in Chicago.

Kamil explained to George, in English, that his brother's case had still not been heard. George lifted a finger toward the dock to greet the brother, a boy of about sixteen or seventeen whose vacant expression suggested to me that he was, at least for the moment, paralyzed more by boredom than by fear. Altogether there were five Arab defendants in the dock, four teenagers and a man of about twenty-five whose case had been argued since morning. Kamil explained to me in a whisper that the prosecution was trying to renew the detention order of the older defendant, an alleged thief said to have stolen two hundred dinars, but that the Arab policeman testifying for the prosecution had only just arrived in the court. I looked to where the policeman was being cross-examined by the defense lawyer, who, to my surprise, wasn't an Arab but an Orthodox Jew, an imposingly bearded bear of a man, probably in his fifties, wearing a skullcap along with his black legal gown. The interpreter, seated at the center of the proceedings just down from the judge, was a Druze, Kamil told me, an Israeli soldier who spoke Arabic and Hebrew. The lawyer for the prosecution was, like the judge, an army officer in uniform, a delicate-looking young fellow who had the air of someone engaged in an exceedingly tiresome task, though momentarily he seemed amused, as did the judge, by a remark of the policeman's just translated by the interpreter.

My second Jewish courtroom in two days. Jewish judges. Jewish laws. Jewish flags. And non-Jewish defendants. Courtrooms such as Jews had envisioned in their fantasies for many hundreds of years, answering longings even more unimaginable than those for an army or a state. One day *we* will determine justice!

Well, the day had arrived, amazingly enough, and here we were, determining it. The unidealized realization of another hope-filled human dream.

My two companions focused only briefly on the cross-examination; soon George had a pad in his hand and was making notes to himself while Kamil was once again whispering directly into my face, "My brother has been given an injection."

I thought at first that he'd said "injunction."

"Meaning what?" I asked.

"An *injection.*" He illustrated by pressing his thumb into my upper arm.

"For what?"

"For nothing. To weaken his constitution. Now he aches all over. Look at him. He can barely hold his head up. A sixteen-year-old," he said, plaintively unfurling his hands before him, "and they have made him sick with an injection." The hands indicated that this was what they did and there was no way to stop them. "They use medical personnel. Tomorrow I'll go complain to the Israeli medical society. And they will accuse me of libel."

"Maybe he got an injection from medical personnel," I whispered back, "because he was already ill."

Kamil smiled as you smile at a child who plays with its toys while, in the hospital, one of its parents is dying. Then he put his lips to my ear to hiss, "It is *they* who are ill. This is how they suppress the revolt of the nationalist core. Torturing in ways that don't leave marks." He motioned toward the policeman on the witness stand. "Another sham. The case goes on and on only to extend our agony. This is the fourth day this has happened. They think that if they frustrate us long enough we will run away to live on the moon."

The next time Kamil turned to whisper to me, he took my hand in his as he spoke. "Everywhere I meet people from South Africa," he whispered. "I talk to them. I ask them questions. Because this gets so much like that every day."

Kamil's whispering was beginning to get on my nerves, as was the role in which I'd cast myself for whatever perverse and unexplained reason. *How can we serve you?* Either Kamil was working to recruit me as an ally against the Jews or he was testing to see if my usefulness was anything like George had surmised it to be on the basis of my visit with Lech Walesa. I thought, I've been putting myself in difficulties like this all my life but, up 'till now, by and large in fiction. How exactly do I get out of this?

Again there was the pressure of Kamil's shoulder against my own and his warm breath on my skin. "Is this not correct? If it weren't that Israel was Jewish—"

There was the sharp smack of a gavel striking, the judge's way of suggesting to Kamil that perhaps it was time to shut up. Kamil, imperturbable, sighed and, crossing his hands in his lap, bore his reprimand in a state of ruminative meditation for about two minutes. Then he was at my ear again. "If it weren't that Israel was Jewish, would not the same American Jewish liberals who are so identified with its well-being, would they not condemn it as harshly as South Africa for how it treats its Arab population?"

I chose again not to reply, but this discouraged him no more than the gavel had. "Of course, South Africa is irrelevant now. Now that they are breaking hands and giving their prisoners medical injections, now one thinks not of South Africa but of Nazi Germany."

Here I turned my face to his as instinctively as I would hit the brake if something darted out in front of my car. And gazing altogether unaggressively at me were those liquid eyes with that bottomless eloquence which was all opacity to me. I had only to nod sympathetically, to nod and arrange my face in my gravest expression, in order to carry on the masquerade—but what was the *purpose* of this masquerade? If it had ever had a purpose, I was too provoked by my taunter's reckless rhetoric to remember what it was and get on with the act. I'd heard enough. "Look," I said, starting quiet and low but, surprisingly, as the words came, all at once flaring out of control, "Nazis didn't break hands. They engaged in industrial annihilation of human beings. They made a manufacturing process of death. Please, no metaphors where there is recorded history!"

With that I sprang to my feet, but as I pushed past George's legs the judge swung the gavel, twice this time, and in the row at the back four soldiers promptly stood and I saw the armed guard at the door toward which I was headed move to block my way. Then the perspicacious judge, speaking in English, ringingly announced to the courtroom, "Mr. Roth is morally appalled by our neocolonialism. Make way. The man needs air." He spoke next in Hebrew and the guard blocking the door moved aside and I pushed the door open and stepped into the yard. But I had barely a moment to begin to figure out how I was going to find my way back to Jerusalem on my own before everyone I had left behind came pouring through the door after me. Everyone but George and Kamil. Had they been arrested? When I peered back through the open door I saw that the prisoners had been removed from the dock and, except at the dais, the room was empty. And there beside the chair of the army judge, who'd apparently called a recess in order to address them privately, stood my two missing companions. The judge happened at the moment to be listening and not speaking. It was George who was speaking. *Foaming.* Kamil stood quietly beside him, a very tall man with his hands in his pockets, an attacker whose onslaught was tamed by a cunning camouflaged to look just like forbearance.

The defense lawyer, the large bearded man in the skullcap, industriously smoked a cigarette only a few feet away from me. He smiled when I turned his way, a smile with a needle in it. "So," he said, as though before we had even exchanged a word we had already reached a stalemate. He lit a second cigarette with the butt of his first and, after a little frenzy of deep inhalations, spoke again. "So you're the one they're all talking about."

Inasmuch as he'd seen me tête-à-tête in the courtroom with the locally renowned brother of an Arab defendant and had to have assumed from that, however incorrectly, that my bias, if I had one, couldn't be entirely antithetical to his, I was unprepared for the flagrant disdain. *Another* antagonist. But mine or Pipik's? As it turned out, a little of each.

"Yes, you open your mouth," he said, "and whatever comes out, the whole world takes notice. The Jews begin to beat their breasts.

'Why is he against us? Why isn't he for us?' That must be a wonderful feeling, its mattering so much what you are for or against."

"A better feeling, I assure you, than being a lawyer pleading petty-theft cases out in the sticks."

"A two-hundred-and-fifty-pound Orthodox Jewish lawyer. Don't minimize my insignificance."

"Go away," I said.

"You know, when the schmucks here get on me for defending Arabs, I don't usually bother to listen. 'It's a living,' I tell them. 'What do you expect from a shyster like me?' I tell them that the Arab respects a fat man, a fat man can screw them really good. But when George Ziad brings to this courtroom his celebrity leftists, then I seem to myself nearly as despicable as they are. At least you have the excuse of self-advancement. How will you get to Stockholm without your Third World credentials?"

"Of course. All a part of the assault on the prize."

"The glamorous one, their courtroom bard, has he told you yet about the burning building? 'If you jump out of a burning building, you may land on the back of a man who happens to be walking along the street. That is a bad enough accident. You then don't have to start beating him over the head with a stick. But that is what is happening on the West Bank. First they landed on people's backs, in order to save themselves, and now they are beating them over the head.' So folkloric. So very authentic. Hasn't he taken you by the hand yet? He will, very stirringly, when you are ready to go. This is when Kamil gets the Academy Award. 'You will leave here and forget, and she will leave here and forget, and George will leave here, and for all I know perhaps even George will forget. But the one who receives the strokes, he has an experience different from that of the one who counts the strokes.' Yes, they have a great catch in you, Mr. Roth. A Jewish Jesse Jackson—worth a thousand Chomskys. And here they are," he said, looking to where George and Kamil had stepped through the courtroom door and into the yard, "the world's pet victims. What is their dream? Palestine or Palestine and Israel too? Ask them sometime to try and tell you the truth."

What George and Kamil did first when they joined us was to shake the large lawyer's hand; in turn he offered each a cigarette, and when I refused one, he lit himself another and began to laugh, a harsh, tearing noise with cavernous undertones that did not bring good tidings from the bronchial tubes; another thousand packs and he might never again have to endure the sickly naiveté of celebrity leftists like Jesse Jackson and me. "The eminent author," he explained to George and Kamil, "doesn't know what to make of our cordiality." To me he then confided, "This is the Middle East. We all know how to lie with a smile. Sincerity is not of this world, but these native boys make a specialty of underdoing it. That's something you find out about Arabs—perfectly natural in both roles at the same time. So convincing one way—just like you when you write—and then, the next moment, someone will walk out of the room, they'll turn around and be just the opposite."

"And how do you account for this?" I asked him.

"One's interest allows anything. Very, very basic. Comes from the desert. That blade of grass is mine and my animal is going to get it or die. It's my animal or your animal. That's where interest begins and it justifies all duplicity. There is in Islam this idea of *taqiya.* Generally called in English 'dissimulation.' It's especially strong in Shi'ite Islam but it's all over Islamic culture. Doctrinally speaking, dissimulation is *part* of Islamic culture, and the permission to dissimulate is widespread. The culture doesn't expect that you'll speak in a way that endangers you and certainly not that you'll be candid and sincere. You would be considered foolish to do that. People say one thing, adopt a public position, and are then quite different on the inside and privately act in a totally different way. They have an expression for this: 'the shifting sands'—*ramál mutaharrika.* An example. For all their bravado about opposing Zionism, throughout the Mandate they sold land to the Jews. Not just their run-of-the-mill opportunists but also their big leadership. But they have a wonderful proverb to justify this as well. *Ad-daroori lih achkaam.* 'Necessity has its own rules.' Dissimulation, two-facedness, secretiveness—all highly regarded values among your friends," he told me. "They don't think that other people have to know what is really on their minds. Very different from Jews, you see, telling everything that's on their minds to everyone nonstop. I used to think that God has given the Jew the Arab to bedevil his conscience and keep it Jewish. I know better since meeting George and the bard. God sent us the Arab so we could learn from him how to refine our own deviousness."

"And why," George asked him, "did God give the Arab the Jew?"

"To punish him," the lawyer answered. "You know that better than anyone. To punish him, of course, for falling away from Allah. George is a great sinner," he said to me. "He can tell you some entertaining stories about falling away."

"And Shmuel° is a greater actor even than I am a sinner," said George. "In our communities he plays the role of a saint—a Jew who defends the Arab's civil rights. To be represented by a Jewish lawyer —this way there is at least a chance in the courtroom. Even Demjanjuk thinks this way. Demjanjuk fired his Mr. O'Brien and hired Sheftel because he too is deluded enough to think it will help. I heard the other day that Demjanjuk told Sheftel, 'If I had a Jewish lawyer to begin with, I'd never be in this trouble now.' Shmuel, admittedly, is no Sheftel. Sheftel is the antiestablishment superstar—he'll squeeze those Ukrainians for all they're worth. He'll make half a million on this Treblinka guard. That isn't the humble way of Saint Shmuel. Saint Shmuel doesn't care how little he is paid by his impoverished defendants. Why should he? He receives his paycheck elsewhere. It isn't enough that Shin Bet corrodes our life here by buying an informer in every family. It isn't enough to play the serpent like that with people already oppressed and, you would think, humiliated quite enough already. No, even the civil-rights lawyer must be a spy, even *that* they must corrupt."

"George is not fair to his informers," the Jewish lawyer told me. "Yes, there are a great many of them, but why not? It is a traditional occupation in this region, one at which its practitioners are marvelously adept. Informing has a long and noble history here. Informing goes back not just to the British, not just to the Turks, it goes all the way back to Judas. Be a good cultural relativist, George—informing

is a way of life here, no less deserving of your respect than the way
of life indigenous to any society. You spent so many years abroad as
an intellectual playboy, you were away so long from your own people, that you judge them, if I may say so, almost with the eyes of a
condescending Israeli imperialist dog. You speak of informing, but
informing offers a little *relief* from all that humiliation. Informing
lends status, informing offers privileges. You really should not be so
quick to slit the throats of your collaborators when collaborating is
one of your society's most estimable achievements. It is actually on
the order of an anthropological crime to burn their hands and stone
them to death'—and for someone in your shoes, it is stupid as well.
Since everybody in Ramallah already suspects everyone else of informing, some foolish hothead might someday be so misguided as to
take *you* for a collaborator and slit your throat too. What if I were to
spread the rumor myself? I might not find doing that too unpleasant."

   "Shmuel," George replied, "do what you do, spread false rumors if
you like—"

   While their bantering continued, Kamil stood apart smoking in
silence. He did not seem even to be listening, nor was there any
reason why he should have been, since this bitter little vaudeville
turn was clearly for the sake of my, and not his, education.

   The soldiers who'd been smoking together at the other end of the
yard started back toward the courtroom door and, after expectorat-
ing into the dust from behind one hand, the lawyer Shmuel, too,
abruptly headed off without another insult for any of us.

   Kamil said to me, now that Shmuel had gone, "I mistook you for
somebody else."

   Who this time? I wondered. I waited to hear more but for a while
there was nothing more and his thoughts appeared to be elsewhere
again. "There are too many things to do," he finally explained, "in not
enough time. We are all overworked and overstrained. No sleep begins to make you stupid." A grave apology—and the gravity I found
as unnerving as everything else about him. Because his rage wasn't
flaring up in your face every two minutes, it struck me as more
fearsome than George's to be near. It was like being in the vicinity of

one of those bombs they unearth during urban excavations, the big ones that have lain unexploded since World War II. I imagined—as I didn't when thinking about George—that Kamil could do a lot of damage when and if he ever went off.

"Whom did you mistake me for?" I asked.

He surprised me by smiling. "Yourself."

I did not like this smile from a man who I surmised *never* horsed around. Did he know what he was saying or was he saying that he had nothing more to say? All this performing didn't mean that a play was in progress; it meant the opposite.

"Yes," I said, feigning friendliness, "I can see how you might be misled. But I assure you that I am no more myself than anyone else around here."

Something in that response made him promptly turn even more severe-looking than before the dubious gift of that smile. I really couldn't understand what he was up to. Kamil spoke as though in a code known only to himself; or perhaps he was just trying to frighten me.

"The judge," George said, "has agreed that his brother should go to the hospital. Kamil is staying to be sure it happens."

"I hope nothing's wrong with your brother," I said, but Kamil continued to look at me as though I were the one who had given the boy the injection. Now that he had apologized for having mistaken me for somebody else, he seemed to have concluded that I was even more contemptible than the other guy.

"Yes," Kamil replied. "You are sympathetic. Very sympathetic. It is difficult not to be sympathetic when you see with your own eyes what is being perpetrated here. But let me tell you what will happen to your sympathy. You will leave here, and in a week, two weeks, a month at the most, you will forget. And Mr. Shmuel the lawyer, he will go home tonight and, even before he is in the front door, before he has even eaten his dinner and played with his children, he will forget. And George will leave here and perhaps even George will forget. If not today, tomorrow. George forgot once before." Angrily he pointed back to the jail, but his voice was exceedingly gentle when he said, "The one who receives the strokes has an experience different from that of the one who counts the strokes." And with that went back to where his brother was a prisoner of the Jews.

George wanted to telephone his wife to tell her he would shortly be home with a guest, so we walked around to a door at the front of the complex, where there was no one standing guard, and George simply pushed it open and went in, with me following closely behind. I was astonished that a Palestinian like George and a perfect stranger like me could just start down the corridor without anyone's stopping us, especially when I remembered that no one had checked at any point to see if we were armed. In an office at the end of the corridor, three female soldiers, Israeli girls of about eighteen or nineteen, were typing away, their radio tuned to the standard rock stuff—we had only to roll a grenade through the open door to take our revenge for Kamil's brother. How come no one seemed alert to this possibility? One of the typists looked up when he asked in Hebrew if he could use the phone. She nodded perfunctorily, "Shalom, George," and that's when I thought, He *is* a collaborator.

George, speaking English, was telling his wife how he'd run into me in Jerusalem, the great friend he hadn't seen since 1955, and I looked at the posters on the walls of the dirty, drab little room, tacked up probably by the soldier-typists to help them forget where they worked—there was a travel poster from Colombia, a poster of little ducklings swimming cutely in a lily pond, a poster of wildflowers growing abundantly in a peaceful field—and all the while I pretended to be engaged by them and nothing more, I was thinking, He's an Israeli spy—and who he is spying on is me. Only what kind of spy can he be if he doesn't know that I'm not the right me? And why should Shmuel have exposed him if Shmuel works for Shin Bet himself? No, he's a spy for the PLO. No, he's a spy for no one. No one's a spy. *I'm* the spy!

Where everything is words, you'd think I'd have some mastery and know my way around, but all this churning hatred, each man a verbal firing squad, immeasurable suspicions, a flood of mocking, angry talk, all of life a vicious debate, conversations in which there is nothing that cannot be said . . . no, I'd be better off in the jungle, I thought, where a roar's a roar and one is hard put to miss its meaning. Here I had only the weakest understanding of what might underlie the fighting and the shadow fighting; nor was my own behavior much more plausible to me than anyone else's.

As we walked together down the hill and out past the guarded gatehouses, George berated himself for having imposed the miseries of the occupation on his wife and his son, neither of whom had the fortitude for a frontline existence, even though for Anna° there was compensation of a sort in living virtually next door to the widowed father whose failing health had been such a source of anxiety to her in America. He was a wealthy Ramallah businessman, nearly eighty, who had seen that Anna was sent to the best schools from the time she was ten, first, in the mid-fifties, to a Christian girls' school in Beirut, after that to the United States, where she'd met and married George, who was also Christian. Anna had worked for years as a layout artist with a Boston advertising agency; here she ran a workshop for the production of propaganda posters, leaflets, and handouts, an operation whose clandestine nature took its toll in a daily dose of nagging medical problems and a weekly bout of migraines. Her abiding fear was of the Israelis coming at night and arresting not her but their fifteen-year-old son, Michael.°

Yet for George himself had there been a choice? In Boston he'd held the line against Israel's defenders at the Middle East seminars in Coolidge Hall, he obstinately opposed his Jewish friends even when it meant ruining his own dinner parties, he wrote op-ed pieces for the *Globe* and went on WGBH whenever Chris Lydon wanted someone to battle for three minutes with the local Netanyahu on his show; but idealistically resisting the occupier from the satisfying security of his tenured American professorship turned out to be even less tolerable to his conscience than the memory of going around all those years disavowing any connection to the struggle at all. Yet here in Ramallah, true to his duty, he worried continually about what returning with him was doing to Anna and, even more, to Michael, whose rebellion George hadn't foreseen, though when he described it I

wondered how he could have failed to. However heroic the cause
had seemed to Michael amid the patriotic graffiti decorating his bedroom walls in suburban Newton, he felt now as only an adolescent
son can toward what he sees as an obstacle to his self-realization
raised by an obtuse father mandating an outmoded way of life. Most
reluctantly, George was on the brink of accepting his father-in-law's
financial help and, at Anna's insistence, sending Michael back to a
New England boarding school for his remaining high school years. To
George—who believed the boy was big enough to stay and be educated here in the hard truth of their lives, old enough now to share
in the tribulation that was inescapably theirs and to embrace the
consequences of being George's son—the arguments with Michael
were all the more punishing for being a reenactment of the bitter
conflict that had alienated him from his own father and embittered
them both.

My heart went out to Michael, however callow a youth he might
be. The shaming nationalism that the fathers throw on the backs of
their sons, each generation, I thought, imposing its struggle on the
next. Yet that was their family's big drama and the one that weighed
on George Ziad like a stone. Here is Michael, whose entitlement, his
teenage American instinct tells him, is to be a new ungrateful generation, ahistorical and free, and here is another father in the heart-
breaking history of fathers, who expects everything blindly selfish in
a young son to capitulate before his own adult need to appease the
ghost of the father whom he had affronted with his own selfishness.
Yes, making amends to father had taken possession of George and, as
anyone knows who's tried it, making amends to father is hard work
—all that hacking through the undergrowth of stale pathology with
the machete of one's guilt. But George was out to settle the issue of
self-division once and for all, and that meant, as it usually does, im-
moderation with a vengeance. Half-measures are out for these people
—but hadn't they always been for George? He wanted a life that
merged with that of others, first, as Zee in Chicago, with ours and
now all over again here with theirs—subdue the inner quarrel with
an act of ruthless simplification—and it never worked. But sensibly

occupying the middle ground in Boston hadn't worked either. His life couldn't seem to merge with anyone's anywhere no matter what drastic experiment in remodeling he tried. Amazing, that something as tiny, really, as a self should contain contending subselves—and that these subselves should themselves be constructed of subselves, and on and on and on. And yet, even *more* amazing, a grown man, an educated adult, a full professor, who seeks *self-integration!*

Multiple selves had been on my mind for months now, beginning with my Halcion breakdown and fomented anew by the appearance of Moishe Pipik, and so perhaps my thinking about George was overly subjective; but what I was determined to understand, however imperfectly, was why whatever George said, even when, like a guy in a bar, he despaired about people as close to him as his wife and his child, didn't seem to me quite to make sense. I kept hearing a man as out of his depth as he was out of control, convulsed by all his contradictions and destined never to arrive where he belonged, let alone at "being himself." Maybe what it all came down to was that an academic, scholarly disposition had been overtaken by the mad rage to make history and *that*, his temperamental unfitness, rather than the urgency of a bad conscience, accounted for all this disjointedness I saw, the overexcitability, the maniacal loquacity, the intellectual duplicity, the deficiencies of judgment, the agitprop rhetoric—for the fact that amiable, subtle, endearing George Ziad had been turned completely inside out. Or maybe it just came down to injustice: isn't a colossal, enduring injustice enough to drive a decent man mad?

Our pilgrimage to the bloodstained wall where Israeli soldiers had dragged the local inhabitants to break their bones and beat them into submission was thwarted by a ring of impassable roadblocks around the central square, and we had, in fact, to detour up through the outlying hills to reach George's house at the other side of Ramallah. "My father used to weep nostalgically about these hills, too. Even in spring, he'd say, he could smell the almond blossoms. You can't," George told me, "not in spring—they bloom in February. I was always kind enough to correct his hyperbole. Why couldn't he be a man about those trees and stop crying?"

In a tone of self-castigating resignation George wearily compiled an indictment of recollections like these all the way up, around, and down the back roads into the city—so perhaps I'd been right the first time, and it *was* remorse that, if not alone in determining the scale of this harsh transformation, intensified the wretched despair that polluted everything and had made hyperbole standard fare for George, too. For having sniped at a ruined father's sentimental maunderings with a faultfinding adolescent's spiteful tongue, Dr. Ziad's little boy looked now to be paying the full middle-aged price and then some.

Unless, of course, it was all an act.

———

George's was one of half a dozen stone houses separated by large patches of garden and clustered loosely around a picturesque old olive grove that stretched down to a small ravine—originally, during Anna's early childhood, this had been a family compound full of brothers and cousins but most of them had emigrated by now. There was a biting chill in the air as it was getting to be dusk, and inside the house, in a tiny fireplace at the end of the narrow living room, a few sticks of wood were burning, a pretty sight but without effect against the chill pervasive dankness that went right to one's bones. The place was cheerily fixed up, however, with bright textiles splashed about on the chairs and the sofa and several rugs with modernistic geometric designs scattered across the uneven stone floor. To my surprise I didn't see books anywhere—maybe George felt his books were more secure at his university office—though there were a lot of Arabic magazines and newspapers strewn atop a table beside the sofa. Anna and Michael wore heavy sweaters as we sat close to the fire drinking our hot tea, and I warmed my hands on the cup, thinking, This aboveground cellar, after Boston. The cold smell of a dungeon on top of everything else. There was also the smell of a kerosene heater burning—one that might not have been in the best state of repair—but it seemed to be off in another room. This room opened through multipaned French doors onto the garden, and a four-bladed fan hung by a very long stem from an arched ceiling that must have been fifteen

feet high, and though I could see how the place might have its charm
once the weather grew warm, right now this wasn't a home to inspire
a mood of snug relaxation.

Anna was a tiny, almost weightless woman whose anatomy's whole
purpose seemed to be to furnish the housing for her astonishing eyes.
There wasn't much else to her. There were the eyes, intense and
globular, eyes to see with in the dark, set like a lemur's in a triangular
face not very much larger than a man's fist, and then there was the
tent of the sweater enshrouding the anorexic rest of her and, peeping
out at the bottom, two feet in baby's running shoes. I would have
figured as a mate for the George I'd known a nocturnal creature fuller
and furrier than Anna, but perhaps when they'd met and married in
Boston some two decades back there'd been more in her of the
sprightly gamine than of this preyed-upon animal who lives by night
—if you can call it living—and during the day is gone.

Michael was already a head taller than his father, an excruciatingly
skinny, delicate brunette with marbleized skin, a prettyish boy whose
shyness (or maybe just exasperation) rendered him mute and immo-
bile. His father was explaining that Diasporism was the first original
idea that he had heard from a Jew in forty years, the first that promised a solution based on honest historical and moral foundations, the
first that acknowledged that the only just way to partition Palestine
was by transferring not the population that was indigenous to the
region but the population to whom this region had been, from the
start, foreign and inimical ... and all the while Michael's eyes remained rigidly fixed on some invisible dot that compelled his entire
attention and that was situated in the air about a foot above my knee.
Nor did Anna appear to take much hope from the fact that Jewry's
leading Diasporist was visiting her home for tea. Only George, I
thought, is so far gone, only he is so crazily desperate ... unless it's
all an act.

Of course George understood that such a proposal would be received with nothing but scorn by the Zionists, whose every sacrosanct precept Diasporism exposed as fraudulent; and he went on to
explain that even among Palestinians, who should be my ardent ad-

vocates, there would be those, like Kamil, lacking the imagination to grasp its political potential, who would stupidly misconstrue Diasporism as an exercise in Jewish nostalgia—

"So that was his take," I said, daring to interrupt the unbridled talker who, it occurred to me, perhaps with his voice alone had reduced his wife to little more than those eyes and battered his son into silence. "A nostalgic Jew, dreaming Broadway dreams about a musical-comedy shtetl."

"Yes. Kamil said to me, 'One Woody Allen is enough.' "

"Did he? In the courtroom? Why Woody Allen?"

"Woody Allen wrote something in *The New York Times,*" George said. "An op-ed article. Ask Anna. Ask Michael. They read it and couldn't believe their eyes. It was reprinted here. It ranks as Woody Allen's best joke yet. Philip, the guy isn't a shlimazl just in the movies. Woody Allen believes that Jews aren't capable of violence. Woody Allen doesn't believe that he is reading the papers correctly—he just can't believe that Jews break bones. Tell us another one, Woody. The first bone they break in defense—to put it charitably; the second in winning; the third gives them pleasure; and the fourth is already a reflex. Kamil hasn't patience for this idiot, and he figured you for another. But it doesn't matter in Tunis what Kamil thinks in Ramallah about Philip Roth. It hardly matters any longer in Ramallah what Kamil thinks about anything."

"Tunis?"

"I assure you that Arafat can differentiate between Woody Allen and Philip Roth."

This was surely the strangest sentence I had ever heard spoken in my life. I decided to top it. If this is the way George wants to play it, then this is the way we shall go. I am not writing this thing. They are. I don't even exist.

"Any meeting with Arafat," I heard myself telling him, "must be completely secret. For obvious reasons. But I *will* meet with him, any place and any time, Tunis or anywhere, and tomorrow is none too soon. It might be communicated to Arafat that through the good offices of Lech Walesa it's likely that I'll be meeting secretly at the

Vatican with the Pope, probably next month. Walesa is already committed to my cause, as you know. He maintains that the Pope will find
in Diasporism not only a means of resolving the Arab-Israeli conflict
but an instrument for the moral rehabilitation and spiritual reawak-
ening of all of Europe. I am myself not as sanguine as he is about the
boldness of this pope. It's all well and good for His Holiness to be
pro-Palestinian and to berate the Jews for appropriating property to
which they have no legal right. It's something else again to espouse
the corollary of this position and to invite a million-plus Jews to
consider themselves at home in the heart of Western Christendom.
Yes, it would be something if the Pope were to call upon Europe
publicly and openly to invite its Jews to return from their exile in
Israel, and for him to mean it; if he were to call on Europe to confess
to its complicity in their uprooting and destruction; if he were to call
on Europe to purge itself of a thousand years of anti-Semitism and to
make room in its midst for a vital Jewish presence to multiply and
flourish there and, in anticipation of the third millennium of Christianity, to declare by proclamation in all its parliaments the right of
the Jewish uprooted to resettle in their European homeland and to
live as Jews there, free, secure, and welcome. That would be simply
wonderful. But I have my doubts. Walesa's Polish pope may even
prefer Europe as Hitler passed it on to his European heirs—His Holiness may not really care to undo Hitler's little miracle. But Arafat is
another matter. Arafat—" On I went, usurping the identity of the
usurper who had usurped mine, heedless of truth, liberated from all
doubt, assured of the indisputable rightness of my cause—seer, savior, very likely the Jews' Messiah.

So this is how it's done, I thought. This is how they do it. You just
say everything.

No, I didn't stop for a very long time. On and on and on, obeying
an impulse I did nothing to quash, ostentatiously free of uncertainty
and without a trace of conscience to rein in my raving. I was telling
them about the meeting of the World Diasporist Congress to take
place in December, fittingly enough in Basel, the site of the first
World Zionist Congress just ninety years ago. At that first Zionist

Congress there had been only a couple of hundred delegates—*my*
goal was to have twice that many, Jewish delegations from every
European country where the Israeli Ashkenazis would soon resume
the European Jewish life that Hitler had all but extinguished. Walesa,
I told them, had already agreed to appear as keynote speaker or to
send his wife in his behalf if he concluded that he could not safely
leave Poland. I was talking about the Armenians, suddenly, about
whom I knew nothing. "Did the Armenians suffer because they were
in a Diaspora? No, because they were *at home* and the Turks moved
in and massacred them *there.*" I heard myself next praising the greatest Diasporist of all, the father of the new Diasporist movement,
Irving Berlin. "People ask where I got the idea. Well, I got it listening
to the radio. The radio was playing 'Easter Parade' and I thought, But
this is Jewish genius on a par with the Ten Commandments. God gave
Moses the Ten Commandments and then He gave to Irving Berlin
'Easter Parade' and 'White Christmas.' The two holidays that celebrate
the divinity of Christ—the divinity that's the very heart of the Jewish
rejection of Christianity—and what does Irving Berlin brilliantly do?
He de-Christs them both! Easter he turns into a fashion show and
Christmas into a holiday about snow. Gone is the gore and the murder of Christ—down with the crucifix and up with the bonnet! *He
turns their religion into schlock.* But nicely! Nicely! So nicely the
goyim don't even know what hit 'em. They love it. *Everybody* loves
it. The Jews especially. Jews loathe Jesus. People always tell me Jesus
is Jewish. I never believe them. It's like when people used to tell me
Cary Grant was Jewish. Bull*shit.* Jews don't want to *hear* about Jesus.
And can you blame them? So—Bing Crosby replaces Jesus as the
beloved Son of God, and the Jews, the *Jews,* go around whistling
about Easter! And is that so disgraceful a means of defusing the enmity
of centuries? Is anyone really dishonored by this? If schlockified
Christianity is Christianity cleansed of Jew hatred, then three cheers
for schlock. If supplanting Jesus Christ with snow can enable my
people to cozy up to Christmas, then let it snow, let it snow, let it
snow! Do you see my point?" I took more pride, I told them, in
"Easter Parade" than in the victory of the Six Day War, found more

security in "White Christmas" than in the Israeli nuclear reactor. I told them that if the Israelis ever reached a point where they believed their survival depended not merely on breaking hands but on dropping a nuclear bomb, that would be the end of Judaism, even if the state of Israel should survive. "Jews as Jews will simply disappear. A generation after Jews use nuclear weapons to save themselves from their enemies, there will no longer be people to identify themselves as Jews. The Israelis will have saved their state by destroying their people. They will never survive morally after that; and if they don't, why survive as Jews at all? They barely have the wherewithal to survive morally now. To put all these Jews in this tiny place, surrounded on all sides by tremendous hostility—how *can* you survive morally? Better to be marginal neurotics, anxious assimilationists, and everything else that the Zionists despise, better to *lose* the state than to lose your moral being by unleashing a nuclear war. Better Irving Berlin than Ariel Sharon. Better Irving Berlin than the Wailing Wall. Better Irving Berlin than Holy Jerusalem! What does owning *Jerusalem*, of all places, have to do with being Jews in 1988? Jerusalem is by now the *worst* thing that could possibly have happened to us. *Last* year in Jerusalem! Next year in Warsaw! Next year in Bucharest! Next year in Vilna and Cracow! Look, I know people call Diasporism a revolutionary idea, but it's *not* a revolution that I'm proposing, it's a *retroversion,* a turning back, the very thing Zionism itself once was. You go back to the crossing point and cross back *the other way*. Zionism went back too far, that's what went wrong with Zionism. Zionism went back to the crossing point of the dispersion—Diasporism goes back to the crossing point of *Zionism.*"

My sympathies were entirely with George's wife. I didn't know which was more insufferable to her, the fervor with which I presented my Diasporist blah-blah or the thoughtfulness with which George sat there taking it in. Her husband had finally stopped talking —only to listen to this! Either to warm herself or to contain herself she'd enwrapped herself in her own arms and, like a woman on the brink of keening, she began almost imperceptibly rocking and swaying to and fro. And the message in those eyes of hers couldn't have been plainer: I was more than even she could bear, she who had by now borne everything. *He suffers enough without you. Shut up. Go away. Disappear.*

All right, I'll address this woman's fears directly. Wouldn't Moishe Pipik? "Anna, I'd be skeptical too if I were you. I'd be thinking, just as you are, This writer is one of those writers with no grasp on reality. This is all the nonsensical fantasy of a man who understands nothing. This is not even literature, let alone politics, this is a fable and a fairy tale. You are thinking of the thousand reasons why Diasporism can only fail, and I am telling you that I know the thousand reasons, I know the *million* reasons. But I am also here to tell you, to tell George, to tell Kamil, to tell whoever here will listen that it cannot fail *because it must not fail,* because the absurdity is not Diasporism but its alternative: Destruction. What people once thought about Zionism you are now thinking about Diasporism: an impossible pipe dream. You are thinking that I am just one more victim of the madness here that is on both sides—that this mad, crazy, tragic predicament has engulfed my sanity too. I see how miserable I am making you by exciting expectations in George that you know to be utopian and beyond implementation—that George, in *his* heart of hearts, knows to be utopian. But let me show you both something I received just a few hours ago that may cause you to think otherwise. It was given to me by an elderly survivor of Auschwitz."

I removed from my jacket the envelope containing Smilesburger's check and handed it to Anna. "Given to me by someone as desperate as you are to bring this maddening conflict to a just and honorable and workable conclusion. His contribution to the Diasporist movement."

When Anna saw the check, she began to laugh very softly, as though this were a private joke intended especially for her amusement.

"Let me see," said George, but for the moment she would not relinquish it. Wearily he asked her, "Why do you laugh? I prefer that, mind you, to the tears, but why do you laugh like this?"

"From happiness. From joy. I'm laughing because it's all over. To-

morrow the Jews are going to line up at the airline office to get their
one-way tickets for Berlin. Michael, look." And she drew the boy
close to her to show him the check. "Now you will be able to live in
wonderful Palestine for the rest of your life. The Jews are leaving. Mr.
Roth is the anti-Moses leading them out of Israel. Here is the money
for their airfare." But the pale, elongated, beautiful boy, without so
much as glancing at the check in his mother's hand, clenched his
teeth and pulled away violently. This did not stop Anna, however—
the check was merely the pretext she needed to deliver *her* diatribe.
"Now there can be a Palestinian flag flying from every building and
everybody can stand up and salute it twenty times a day. Now we can
have our own money, with Father Arafat's portrait on our very own
bills. In our pockets we can jingle coins bearing the profile of Abu
Nidal. I'm laughing," she said, "because Palestinian Paradise is at
hand."

"Please," George said, "this is the royal road to the migraine." He
motioned impatiently for her to hand him my check. Pipik's check.

"Another victim who can't forget," said Anna, meanwhile studying
the face of the check with those globular eyes as though there at last
she might find the clue to why fate had delivered her into this misery.
"All these victims and their horrible scars. But, tell me," she asked,
and as simply as a child asks why the grass is green, "how many
victims can possibly stand on this tiny bit of soil?"

"But he *agrees* with you," her husband said. "That is why he is
here."

"In America," she told me, "I thought I had married a man who had
left all this victimization behind, a man of cultivation who knew what
made life rich and full. I didn't think I had married another Kamil,
who can't start being a human being until the occupation is over.
These perpetual little brothers, claiming they can't live, they can't
breathe, because somebody is casting a shadow over them! The moral
childishness of these people! A man with George's brain, strangling
on spurious issues of *loyalty!* Why aren't you loyal," she cried, wildly
turning on George, "to your *intellect?* Why aren't you loyal to *literature?* People like you"—meaning me as well—"run for their *lives*

from backwater provinces like this one. You ran, you were *right* to
run, both of you, as far as you could from the provincialism and the
egocentricity and the xenophobia and the lamentations, you were
not poisoned by the sentimentality of these childish, stupid ethnic
mythologies, you plunged into a big, new, free world with all your
intellect and all your energy, truly free young men, devoted to art,
books, reason, scholarship, to *seriousness*—"

"Yes, to everything noble and elevated. Look," said George, "you
are merely describing two snobbish graduate students—and we were
not so pure even then. You paint a ridiculously naive portrait that
would have struck us as laughable even then."

"Well, all I mean," she answered contemptuously, "is that you
couldn't possibly have been as idiotic as you are now."

"You just prefer the high-minded idiocy of universities to the low-
minded idiocy of political struggle. No one says it isn't idiotic and
stupid and perhaps even futile. But that is what it's like, you see, for a
human being to live on this earth."

"No amount of money," she said, ignoring the condescension to
address me again about my check, "will change a single thing. Stay
here, *you'll* see. There is nothing in the future for these Jews and
these Arabs but more tragedy, suffering, and blood. The hatred on
both sides is too enormous, it envelops everything. There is no trust
and there will not be for another thousand years. 'To live on this
earth.' Living in Boston was living on this earth—" she angrily reminded George. "Or isn't it 'life' any longer when people have a big,
bright apartment and quiet, intelligent neighbors and the simple civilized pleasure of a good job and raising children? Isn't it 'life' when
you read books and listen to music and choose your friends because
of their qualities and not because they share your roots? Roots! A
concept for *cavemen* to live by! Is the survival of Palestinian culture,
Palestinian people, Palestinian heritage, is that really a 'must' in the
evolution of humanity? Is all that mythology a greater must than the
survival of my son?"

"He's going back," George quietly replied.

"When? *When?*" She shook the check in George's face. "When

Philip Roth collects a thousand more checks from crazy Jews and the airlift to Poland begins? When Philip Roth and the Pope sit down together in the Vatican and solve our problems for us? I will not sacrifice my son to any more fanatics and their megalomaniacal fantasies!"

"He will go back," George repeated sternly.

"Palestine is a lie! Zionism is a lie! Diasporism is a lie! The biggest lie yet! I will not sacrifice Michael to more lies!"

———

George phoned to downtown Ramallah for a taxi to come to his house to drive me to Jerusalem. The driver was a weathered-looking old man who seemed awfully sleepy given that it was only seven in the evening. I wondered aloud if this was the best George could do.

First George told him in Arabic where to take me, then, in English, he said, "He's used to the checkpoints, and the soldiers there are familiar with him. You'll get back all right."

"To me he looks a little the worse for wear."

"Don't worry," George said. He had wanted, in fact, to take me back himself, but in their bedroom, where Anna had gone to lie down in the dark, she had warned George that if he dared to go off in the evening to drive to Jerusalem and back, neither she nor Michael would be there when he returned, *if* he returned and didn't wind up beaten to death by the army or shot by vigilante Jews. "It's the migraine talking," George explained. "I don't want to make it worse."

"I'm afraid," I said, "I already have."

"Philip, we'll speak tomorrow. There are many things to discuss. I'll come in the morning. I want to take you somewhere. I want you to meet someone. You will be free in the morning?"

I had arranged a meeting with Aharon, I had somehow to get to see Apter, but I said, "For you, yes, of course. Say goodbye to Michael for me. And to Anna. . . ."

"He's in there holding her hand."

"Maybe this *is* all too much for him."

"It does begin to look that way." He closed his eyes and pressed his fingers to his forehead. "My *stupidity*," he moaned. "My fucking stupidity!"

At the door he embraced me. "Do you know what you're doing? Do you know what it's going to mean for you when the Mossad finds out you've met with Arafat?"

"Arrange the meeting, Zee."

"Oh, you're the best of them!" he said emotionally. "The very best!"

Bullshit artist, I thought, actor, liar, fake, but all I did was return the embrace with no less fervent duplicitousness than was being proffered.

To circumvent the Ramallah roadblocks, which still barred the entrance to the city center and access to the telltale bloodstained wall, the taxi driver took the circuitous route through the hills that George had used earlier to get home. There were no lights to be seen anywhere once we were headed away from the complex of stone houses at the edge of the ravine, no cars appeared on the hillside roads, and for a long time I kept my eyes fixed on the path cut by our headlamps and was too apprehensive to think of anything other than making it safely back to Jerusalem. Shouldn't he be driving with his brights on? Or were those feeble beams the brights? Going back with this old Arab, I thought, had to be a mistake but so was coming out with George, so, surely, was everything I had just said and done. This little leave I had taken not merely of my senses but of my life was inexplicable to me—it was as though reality had stopped and I had gotten off to do what I did and now I was being driven along these dark roads to where reality would be waiting for me to climb back on board and resume doing what I used to do. Had I even been present? Yes, yes, I most certainly had been, hidden no more than an inch or two behind that mild exercise in malicious cynicism. And yet I could swear that my carrying-on was completely innocent. The lengths I had gone to to mislead George hadn't seemed to me any more underhanded than if we'd been two children at play in a sandpile, no more insidious and about as mindless—for one of the few times in my life I couldn't really satirize myself for thinking too much.

What had I yielded to? How did I get here? The rattling car, the sleepy driver, the sinister road . . . it was all the unforeseen outcome of the convergence of my falseness with his, dissimulation to match dissimulation . . . unless George hadn't been dissimulating, *unless the only act was mine!* But could he possibly have taken that blather seriously about Irving Berlin? No, no—*here's* what they're up to: They're thinking of the infantile idealism and immeasurable egoism of all those writers who step momentarily onto the vast stage of history by shaking the hand of the revolutionary leader in charge of the local egalitarian dictatorship; they're thinking of how, aside from flattering a writer's vanity, it lends his life a sense of significance that he just can't seem to get finding the mot juste (if he even comes anywhere close to finding it one out of five hundred times); they're thinking that nothing does that egoism quite so much good as the illusion of submerging it for three or four days in a great and selfless, highly visible cause; they're thinking along the lines that Shmuel the lawyer had been thinking when he observed that it might just be that I'd come round to the courtroom in the clutches of "the world's pet victims" to beef up my credentials for the big prize. They're thinking of Jesse Jackson, of Vanessa Redgrave, smiling in those news photographs arm in arm with their leader, and of how, in the public-relations battle with the Jews, which well might decide more in the end than all of the terrorism would, a photograph in *Time* with a celebrity Jew might just be worth ten seconds of the leader's precious time. Of course! They're setting me up for a photo opportunity, and the looniness of my Diasporism is inconsequential—Jesse Jackson isn't exactly Gramsci either. Mitterrand has Styron, Castro has Márquez, Ortega has Pinter, and Arafat is about to have me.

No, a man's character isn't his fate; a man's fate is the joke that his life plays on his character.

We hadn't yet reached the houses sporting their Eiffel Tower TV antennas but we were out of the hills and on the main road south to Jerusalem when the taxi driver spoke his first words to me. In English, which he did not pronounce with much assurance, he asked, "Are you a Zionist?"

"I'm an old friend of Mr. Ziad's," I replied. "We went to university together in America. He is an old friend."

"Are you a Zionist?"

And who is *this* guy? I thought. This time I ignored him and continued looking out the window for some unmistakable sign, like those TV aerials, that we were approaching the outskirts of Jerusalem. Only what if we weren't anywhere near the road to Jerusalem but on the road to somewhere else? Where were the Israeli checkpoints? So far we hadn't passed one.

"Are you a Zionist?"

"Tell me," I replied as agreeably as I could, "what you mean by a Zionist and I'll tell you if I'm a Zionist."

"Are you a Zionist?" he repeated flatly.

"Look," I snapped back, thinking, Why don't you just say no? "what business is that of yours? Drive, please. This is the road to Jerusalem, is it not?"

"Are you a Zionist?"

The car was now perceptibly losing speed, the road was pitch-black, and beyond it I could see nothing.

"Why are you slowing down?"

"Bad car. Not work."

"It was working a few minutes ago."

"Are you a Zionist?"

We were barely rolling along now.

"Shift," I said, "shift the car down and give it some gas."

But here the car stopped.

"What's going on!"

He did not answer but got out of the car with a flashlight, which he began clicking on and off.

"Answer me! Why are you stopping out here like this? Where are we? Why are you flashing that light?"

I didn't know whether to stay in the car or to jump out of the car or whether either was going to make any difference to whatever was about to befall me. "Look," I shouted, leaping after him onto the road, "did you understand me? I am George Ziad's *friend!*"

But I couldn't find him. He was gone.

And this is what you get for fucking around in the middle of a civil insurrection! This is what you get for not listening to Claire and not turning everything over to lawyers! This is what you get for failing to comply with a sense of reality like everyone else's! *Easter Parade!* This is what you get for your bad jokes!

"Hey!" I shouted. "Hey, you! Where are you?"

When there was no reply, I opened the driver's door and felt around for the ignition: *he'd left the keys.* I got in and shut the door and, without hesitating, started the car, accelerating hard in neutral to prevent it from stalling. Then I pulled onto the road and tried to build up speed—there must be a checkpoint *somewhere!* But I hadn't driven fifty feet before the driver appeared in the dim beam of the headlights waving one hand for me to stop and clutching his trousers around his knees with the other. I had to swerve wildly to avoid hitting him, and then, instead of stopping to let him get back in and drive me the rest of the way, I gunned the motor and pumped the gas pedal but nothing was able to get the thing to pick up speed and, only seconds later, the motor conked out.

Back behind me in the road I saw the flashlight wavering in the air, and in a few minutes the old driver was standing, breathless, beside the car. I got out and handed him the keys and he got back in and, after two or three attempts, started the motor, and we began to move off, jerkily at first, but then everything seemed to be all right and we were driving along once again in what I decided to believe was the right direction.

"You should have said you had to shit. What was I supposed to think when you just stopped the car and disappeared?"

"Sick," he answered. "Stomach."

"You should have told me that. I misunderstood."

"Are you a Zionist?"

"Why do you keep *asking* that? If you mean Meir Kahane, then I am not a Zionist. If you mean Shimon Peres . . ." But why was I favoring with an answer this harmless old man with bowel problems, answering him seriously in a language he understood only barely . . .

where the hell *was* my sense of reality? "Drive, please," I said. "Jerusalem. Just get me to Jerusalem. And without talking!"

But we hadn't got more than three or four miles closer to Jerusalem when he drove the car over to the shoulder, shut off the engine, took up the flashlight, and got out. This time I sat calmly in the back seat while he found himself some spot off the road to take another crap. I even began to laugh aloud at how I had exaggerated the menacing side of all this, when suddenly I was blinded by headlights barreling straight toward the taxi. Just inches from the front bumper, the other vehicle stopped, although I had braced for the impact and may even have begun to scream. Then there was noise everywhere, people shouting, a second vehicle, a third, there was a burst of light whitening everything, a second burst and I was being dragged out of the car and onto the road. I didn't know which language I was hearing, I could discern virtually nothing in all that incandescence, and I didn't know what to fear more, to have fallen into the violent hands of marauding Arabs or a violent band of Israeli settlers. "English!" I shouted, even as I tumbled along the surface of the highway. "I speak English!"

I was up and doubled over the car fender and then I was yanked and spun around and something knocked glancingly against the back of my skull and then I saw, hovering enormously overhead, a helicopter. I heard myself shouting, "Don't hit me, God damn it, I'm a Jew!" I'd realized that these were just the people I'd been looking for to get me safely back to my hotel.

I couldn't have counted all the soldiers pointing rifles at me even if I could have managed successfully to count—more soldiers even than there'd been in the Ramallah courtroom, helmeted and armed now, shouting instructions that I couldn't have heard, even if their language was one I understood, because of the noise of the helicopter.

"I hired this taxi in Ramallah!" I shouted back to them. "The driver stopped to shit!"

"Speak English!" someone shouted to me.

"THIS IS ENGLISH! HE STOPPED TO MOVE HIS BOWELS!"

"Yes? Him?"

"The driver! The Arab driver!" But where was he? Was I the only one they'd caught? *"There was a driver!"*

"Too late at night!"

"Is it? I didn't know."

"Shit?" a voice asked.

"Yes—we stopped for the driver to shit, he was only flashing the flashlight—"

"To shit!"

"Yes!"

Whoever had been asking the questions began to laugh. "That's all?" he shouted.

"As far as I know, *yes.* I could be wrong."

"You are!"

Just then one of them approached, a young, heavyset soldier, and he had a hand extended toward mine. In his other hand was a pistol. "Here." He gave me my wallet. "You dropped this."

"Thank you."

"This is quite a coincidence," he said politely in perfect English, "I just today, this afternoon, finished one of your books."

———

Thirty minutes later, I was safely at the door of my hotel, chauffeured there in an army jeep by Gal Metzler,° the young lieutenant who that very afternoon had read the whole of *The Ghost Writer.* Gal was the twenty-two-year-old son of a successful Haifa manufacturer who'd been in Auschwitz as a boy and with whom Gal had a relationship, he told me, exactly like the one Nathan Zuckerman had with *his* father in my book. Side by side in the jeep's front seats, we sat in the parking area in front of the hotel while Gal talked to me about his father and himself, and while I was thinking that the only son I'd seen yet in Greater Israel who was *not* in conflict with his father was John Demjanjuk, Jr. There there was only harmony.

Gal told me that in six months he would be finishing four years as an army officer. Could he continue to maintain his sanity that long?

He didn't know. That's why he was devouring two and three books a day—to remove himself every minute that he possibly could from the madness of this life. At night, he said, every night, he dreamed about leaving Israel after his time was up and going to NYU to study film. Did I know the film school at NYU? He mentioned the names of some teachers there. Did I know these people?

"How long," I asked him, "will you stay in America?"

"I don't know. If Sharon comes to power . . . I don't know. Now I go home on leave, and my mother tiptoes around me as though I'm somebody just released from the hospital, as though I'm crippled or an invalid. I can stand only so much of it. Then I start shouting at her. 'Look, you want to know if I personally beat anyone? I didn't. But I had to do an awful lot of maneuvering to avoid it!' She's glad and she cries and it makes her feel better. But then my father starts shouting at the two of us. 'Breaking hands? It happens in New York City every night. The victims are black. Will you go running from America because they break hands in America?' My father says, 'Take the British, put them here, face them with what we are facing—they would act out of morality? The Canadians would act out of morality? The French? A state does not act out of moral ideology, a state acts out of self-interest. A state acts to preserve its existence.' 'Then maybe I prefer to be stateless,' I tell him. He laughs at me. 'We tried it,' he tells me. 'It didn't work out.' As if I need his stupid sarcasm—as if half of me doesn't believe exactly what *he* believes! Still I have to deal with women and children who look me in the eyes and scream. They look at me ordering my troops to take away their brothers and their sons, and what they see is an Israeli monster in sunglasses and boots. My father is disgusted with me when I say such things. He throws his dishes on the floor in the middle of the meal. My mother starts crying. *I* start crying. I cry! And I never cry. But I love my father, Mr. Roth, so I cry! Everything I've done in my life, I've done to make my father proud of me. That was why I became an officer. My father survived Auschwitz when he was ten years younger than I am now. I am humiliated that I can't survive this. I know what reality is. I'm not a fool who believes that he is pure or that life is simple. It is Israel's fate to live in an Arab sea. Jews accepted this fate rather than have nothing and no fate. Jews accepted partition and the Arabs did not. If they'd said yes, my father reminds me, they would be celebrating forty years of statehood too. But every political decision with which they have been confronted, invariably they have made the wrong choice. *I know all this.* Nine tenths of their misery they owe to the idiocy of their own political leaders. *I know that.* But still I look at my own government and I want to vomit. Would you write a recommendation for me to NYU?"

A big soldier armed with a pistol, a two-hundred-pound leader of men whose face was darkly stubbled with several days' whiskers and whose combat uniform foully reeked of sweat, and yet, the more he recounted of his unhappiness with his father and his father's with him, the younger and more defenseless he had seemed to me. And now this request, uttered almost in the voice of a child. "So—" I laughed—*"that's* why you saved my life out there. That's why you didn't let them break my hands—so I could write your recommendation."

"No, no, *no,"* he quickly replied, a humorless boy distressed by my laughter and even more grave now than he'd been before, "no—no one would have hurt you. Yes, it's there, of course it's there, I'm not saying it's not there—some of the boys *are* brutal. Most because they are frightened, some because they know the others are watching and they don't want to be cowards, and some because they think, 'Better them than us, better him than me.' But no, I assure you—you were never in real danger."

"It's you who's in real danger."

"Of falling apart? You can tell that? You can see that?"

"You know what I see?" I said. "I see that you are a Diasporist and you don't even know it. You don't even know what a Diasporist is. You don't know what your choices really are."

"A Diasporist? A Jew who lives in the Diaspora."

"No, no. More than that. Much more. It is a Jew for whom *authenticity* as a Jew means living in the Diaspora, for whom the Diaspora is the normal condition and Zionism is the abnormality—a Diasporist is a Jew who believes that the only Jews who matter are the Jews of the Diaspora, that the only Jews who will survive are the Jews of the Diaspora, that the only Jews who *are* Jews are the Jews of the Diaspora—"

It would have been hard to say where I found the energy after what I'd been through in just forty-eight hours, but suddenly here in Jerusalem something was running away with me again and there seemed to be nothing I had more strength for than this playing-at-Pipik. That lubricious sensation that is fluency took over, my eloquence grew, and on I went calling for the de-Israelization of the Jews, on and on once again, obeying an intoxicating urge that did not leave me feeling quite so sure of myself as I may have sounded to poor Gal, torn in two as he was by the rebellious and delinquent feelings of a loyal, loving son.

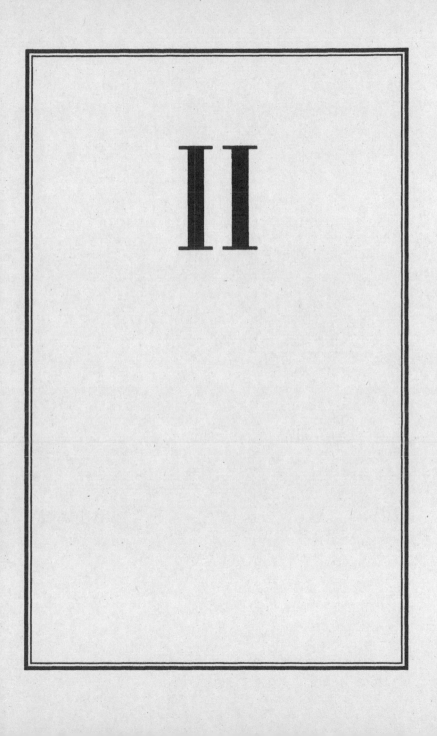

II

6

His
Story

When I went up to the desk for the key to my room, the young clerk smiled and said, "But you have it, sir."

"If I had it I wouldn't be asking for it."

"Earlier, when you came out of the bar, I gave it to you, sir."

"I haven't been in the bar. I've been everywhere in Israel but the bar. Look, I'm thirsty. I'm hungry. I'm dirty and I need a bath. I'm out on my feet. The key."

"Yes, a key!" he chirped, pretending to laugh at his own stupidity, and turned away to find one for me while slowly I caught up with the meaning of what I had just heard.

I sat with my key in one of the wicker chairs in the corner of the lobby. The desk clerk by whom I'd first been confused tiptoed up to me after about twenty minutes and asked in a quiet voice whether I needed assistance to my room; worried that I might be ill, he had brought, on a tray, a bottle of mineral water and a glass. I took the water and drank it all down, and then, when he remained at my side, looking concerned, I assured him that I was all right and could make my way to my room alone.

It was almost eleven. If I waited another hour, might he not leave on his own—or would he just get into my pajamas and go to bed? Perhaps the solution was to take a taxi over to the King David Hotel and ask for his key as casually as he, apparently, had walked off with mine. Yes, go there and sleep there. With her. And tomorrow he meets with Aharon to complete our conversation while she and I get on with the promotion of the cause. I just pick up where I left off in the jeep.

I remained half dozing in that corner chair, groggily thinking that this was still last summer and that everything I took to be actuality—the Jewish courtroom in Ramallah, George's desperate wife and child, my impersonating Moishe Pipik for them, the farcical taxi ride with the shitting driver, my alarming run-in with the Israeli army, my impersonating Moishe Pipik for Gal—was all a Halcion hallucination. Moishe Pipik was *himself* a Halcion hallucination; as was Jinx Possesski; as was this Arab hotel; as was the city of Jerusalem. If this were Jerusalem I'd be where I always stay, the municipal guest house, Mishkenot Sha'ananim. I would have seen Apter and all my friends here. . . .

With a start, I surfaced, and there to either side of me was a large potted fern; there too was the kind clerk, offering water again and asking if I was sure I didn't need help. I saw by my watch that it was half past eleven. "Tell me please, the day, the month, and the year."

"Tuesday, January 26, 1988. In thirty minutes, sir, it will be the twenty-seventh."

"And this is Jerusalem."

He smiled. "Yes, sir."

"Thank you. That's all."

I put my hand in my inside jacket pocket. Had that been a Halcion hallucination as well, the cashier's check for a million dollars? Must have been. The envelope was gone.

Instead of telling the clerk to get the manager or the security officer and advising them that an intruder posing as me and probably crazy and maybe even armed had gained access to my room, I got up and went across the lobby and into the restaurant to find out if it was possible at this late hour to get something to eat. I stopped first in the doorway to see if Pipik and Jinx might be dining there; she could very well have been with him when he'd come out of the bar earlier to get my key from the front desk—perhaps they were not yet up fucking together in my room but down here eating together at my expense. Why not that, too?

But except for a party of four men lingering over coffee at a round table in the furthest corner of the restaurant, the place was empty even of waiters. The four seemed to be having a good time, quietly laughing over something together, and only when one of them came to his feet did I recognize that he was Demjanjuk's son and that the late diners with him were his father's legal team, Chumak the Canadian, Gill the American, and Sheftel the Israeli. Probably they'd been working out the next day's strategy over dinner and now they were bidding good night to John junior. He was no longer in the neat dark suit he'd been wearing in the courtroom but dressed casually in slacks and a sports shirt, and when I saw that he was carrying a plastic bottle of water in one hand, I remembered reading in my clipping file that except for Sheftel, whose home and office were forty-five minutes away, in Tel Aviv, the lawyers and the Demjanjuk family members were staying at the American Colony; he must be taking the water to his room.

Leaving the dining room, young Demjanjuk passed directly beside me and, as though it were he for whom I'd been waiting there, I turned and followed after him, thinking exactly as I had the day before when I'd seen him headed from the courtroom for the street: Should this boy be unprotected? Isn't there a single survivor of the camps whose children or sister or brother or parents or husband or wife had been murdered there, someone who had been mutilated there or maddened for life, ready to take vengeance on Demjanjuk senior through Demjanjuk junior? Isn't there anyone prepared to hold the son hostage until the father confesses? It was difficult to account for what was keeping him alive and safe in this country, populated as it was by the last of the generation to whose decimation his namesake stood accused of having made such a wholehearted contribution. Isn't there one Jack Ruby in all of Israel?

And then it occurred to me: How about you?

Lagging only some four or five feet behind him, I followed young Demjanjuk through the lobby and up the stairs, suppressing the impulse to stop him and say, "Look, I for one don't hold it against you that you believe your father is being framed. How could you believe otherwise and be the good American son that you are? Your belief in your father does not make you my enemy. But some people here may see it differently. You're taking an awfully big chance walking around like this. You, your sisters, and your mother have suffered enough already. But so too, remember, have a lot of Jews. You'll never recover from this no matter how you may delude yourself, but then neither have a lot of Jews quite recuperated yet from what they and their families have been through. You might really be asking a little too much of them to go walking around here in a nice sports shirt and a clean pair of slacks, with a full bottle of mineral water in your hand. . . . Innocuous enough from your point of view, I'm sure: what's the water have to do with anything? But don't provoke memories unnecessarily, don't tempt some enraged and broken soul to lose control and do something regrettable. . . ."

When my quarry turned into the corridor off the landing I proceeded on up the stairs to the hotel's top floor, where my room was situated midway down the hall. I moved as quietly as I could to the door of my room and listened there for sounds from within, while back by the staircase someone was standing and looking my way— someone who had been following only steps behind me while I had been following Demjanjuk's son. A plainclothesman, of course! Stationed here by the police and watching out for John junior's safety. Or is this the plainclothesman shadowing me, imagining that I'm Moishe Pipik? Or is he stalking Pipik, thinking that Pipik is me? Or is he here to investigate why we are two and what we two are conspiring to do?

Though nothing could be heard from within the room and though he had perhaps come and gone, having already stolen or destroyed whatever he was after, I was convinced that even if there was only the remotest chance that he was inside, it would still be foolish to enter alone and so I turned and started back toward the staircase just as the door to my room opened a ways and there, peering out of it, was Moishe Pipik's head. I was actually hastening in double time along the corridor by then, but because I didn't want him to know how afraid of him I had become, I stopped and even took a few slow steps back toward where he was standing now, half in and half out of the room. And what I saw, as I stepped closer, so shocked me that I had all I could do not to turn and run full speed for help. His face was the face I remembered seeing in the mirror during the months when I was breaking down. His glasses were off, and I saw in his eyes my own dreadful panic of the summer before, my eyes at their most fearful, back when I could think of little other than how to kill myself. He wore on his face what had so terrified Claire: my look of perpetual grief.

"You," he said. That was all. But for him that was the accusation: I who was I.

"Come in," he said, weakly.

"No, you come out. Get your shoes"—he was in his stocking feet and his shirt was hanging out of his trousers—"get whatever is yours, hand over the key, and get out of here."

Without even bothering to answer he turned back into the room. I approached as far as the door and looked inside to see if Jinx was with him. But he was stretched diagonally across the bed, all alone and looking sorrowfully at the whitewashed, vaulted ceiling. The pillows were wadded up by the headboard, and the spread was turned back and dragged down onto the tile floor, and beside him on the bed was an opened book, my copy of Aharon Appelfeld's novel *Tzili.* In the small room nothing else appeared to have been disarranged; I am orderly with my things, even in a hotel room, and everything of mine looked to me as I'd left it. I hadn't had much with me to begin with: on the little desk by the large, arched window was the folder containing the notes of my conversations with Aharon, the three tapes Aharon and I had made so far, and Aharon's books in

English translation. Because my tape recorder was in my one suitcase and the suitcase locked inside the closet, whose key was in my wallet, he couldn't have listened to the tapes; perhaps he'd rifled through the shirts and socks and underwear laid out in the middle bureau drawer, perhaps I'd find later that he'd even defiled them in some way, but so long as he hadn't sacrificed a goat in the bathtub, I knew enough to consider myself lucky.

"Look," I said to him from the doorway, "I'm going to get the house detective. He's going to call the police. You've broken into my room. You've trespassed on my property. I don't know what you may have taken—"

"What *I've* taken?" And saying this, he swung about and sat himself up on the edge of the bed, cradling his head in his hands so that for the moment I couldn't see the grief-stricken face and the resemblance to my own, by which I was still transfixed and horrified. Nor could he see me and the resemblance to which he had succumbed out of a motive that was still anything but clear in its personal particulars. I understood that people are trying to transform themselves all the time: the universal urge to be otherwise. So as not to look as they look, sound as they sound, be treated as they are treated, suffer in the ways they suffer, etc., etc., they change hairdos, tailors, spouses, accents, friends, they change their addresses, their noses, their wallpaper, even their forms of government, all to be more like themselves or less like themselves, or more like or less like that exemplary prototype whose image is theirs to emulate or to repudiate obsessively for life. It wasn't even that Pipik had gone further than most—he was, in the mirror, improbably evolved into somebody else already; there was very little more for him to imitate or fantasize. I could understand the temptation to quash oneself and become imperfect and a sham in entertainingly new ways—I had succumbed too, and not just a few hours earlier with the Ziads and then with Gal, but more sweepingly even than that in my books: looking like myself, sounding like myself, even laying claim to convenient scraps of my biography, and yet, beneath the disguise of me, someone entirely other.

But this was no book, and it wouldn't do. "Get off my bed," I told him, "get out!"

But he had picked up Aharon's *Tzili* and was showing me how far he'd got in reading it. "This stuff is real poison," he said. "Everything Diasporism fights against. Why do you think highly of this guy when he is the *last* thing we need? He will never relinquish anti-Semitism. It's the rock he builds his whole world on. Eternal and unshakable anti-Semitism. The man is irreparably damaged by the Holocaust—why do you want to encourage people to read this fear-ridden stuff?"

"You miss the point—I want only to encourage you to leave."

"It astonishes me that you, of all people, after all that you have written, should want to reinforce the stereotype of the Jewish victim. I read your dialogue with Primo Levi last year in the *Times*. I heard you had a breakdown after he killed himself."

"Who'd you hear it from? Walesa?"

"From your brother. From Sandy."

"You're in touch with my brother, too? He's never mentioned it."

"Come in. Close the door. We have a lot to talk about. We have been intertwined for decades in a thousand different ways. You don't want to know how uncanny this whole thing is, do you? All you want is to get rid of it. But it goes back, Philip, all the way back to Chancellor Avenue School."

"Yes, you went to Chancellor?"

He began quietly to sing, in a soft baritone voice—a singing voice chillingly familiar to me—a few bars of the Chancellor Avenue School song, words that had been set, early in the thirties, to the tune of "On Wisconsin." "... We will do our best ... try to always be victorious ... put us through the test, rah-rah-rah ..." He smiled at me wanly with the grief-stricken face. "Remember the cop who crossed you at the corner of Chancellor and Summit? Nineteen thirty-eight—the year you started kindergarten. Remember his name?"

While he spoke I glanced back toward the staircase, and there, to my relief, I saw just the person I was looking for. He paused at the landing, a short, stocky man in shirtsleeves, with closely cropped black hair and a masklike, inexpressive face, or so the face appeared from that distance. He looked toward me now without any attempt to disguise the fact that he was there and that he too sensed that something suspicious was going on. It was the plainclothesman.

"Al," Pipik was saying once again, his head falling back on the pillows. "Al the Cop," he repeated wistfully.

While Pipik babbled on from the bed, the plainclothesman, without my even signaling him, started along the corridor toward where I was waiting in the open doorway.

"You used to jump up to touch his arms," Pipik was reminding me. "He'd hold his arms straight out to stop the traffic, and you little kids would jump up and touch his arms as you crossed the street. Every morning, 'Hi, Al!' and jump up and touch his arms. Nineteen thirty-eight. Remember?"

"Sure," I said, and as the plainclothesman approached, I smiled to let him know that, although he was needed, the situation was not yet out of control. He leaned close to my ear and mumbled something. He spoke in English but because of his accent the softly uttered words were unintelligible at first.

"What?" I whispered.

"Want me to blow you?" he whispered back.

"Oh, no—thanks, no. My mistake." And I stepped into the room and pulled the door firmly shut.

"Pardon the intrusion," I said.

"Remember Al?"

I sat down in the easy chair by the window, not quite knowing what else to do now that I was locked in with him. "You don't look so hot, Pipik."

"Pardon?"

"You look awful. You look physically ill. This business is not doing you a world of good—you look like somebody in very serious trouble."

"Pipik?" He was sitting up now on the bed. Contemptuously he asked, "You call me *Pipik?*"

"Don't take it so hard. What else should I call you?"

"Cut the shit—I came for the check."

"What check?"

"*My* check!"

"Yours? Please. Did anyone ever tell you about my great-aunt who lived in Danbury, Pipik? My grandfather's older sister on my father's side. Nobody tell you yet about our Meema Gitcha?"

"I want that check."

"You found out about Al the Cop, somebody taught you all the words to the Chancellor song, so now perhaps it's time you learned about Meema Gitcha, the family ancient, and how we would visit her and the phone calls we made to her when we got home from her house, safe and sound. You're so interested in 1938—this is about 1940."

"You're not stealing from *me* stealing that check, you're not stealing from Smilesburger—*you're stealing from the Jewish people.*"

"Please. *Please.* Enough. Meema Gitcha was also a Jewish person, you know—*listen to me.*" I can't say that I had any idea of what I was doing but I told myself that if I just took charge and kept talking I could wear him down to nothing and then proceed from there . . . But to do what? "Meema Gitcha—a very foreign-looking Old Country woman, big and bossy and bustling, and she wore a wig and shawls and long dark dresses, and going to visit her in Danbury was a terrific outing, almost like leaving America."

"I want that check. Now."

"Pipik, pipe down."

"Cut the Pipik crap!"

"Then *listen.* This is *interesting.* Once every six months or so we went out in two carloads to visit Meema Gitcha for the weekend. Her husband had been a hatter in Danbury. He used to work at Fishman's in Newark with my grandfather, who was also a hatter for a while, but when the hat factories left for Connecticut, Gitcha and her family moved up with them to Danbury. About ten years later, Gitcha's husband, working in off-hours, taking a stock of finished hats to the shipping room, was trapped and died in an accident in the elevator. Gitcha was on her own and so two, three times a year, we all went north to see her. A five-hour car ride in those days. Aunts, uncles, cousins, my grandmother, all packed in together, coming and going. It was somehow the most Jewishy-Yiddishy event of my childhood—we *could* have been driving all the way back to the folkland of Galicia traveling up to Danbury on those trips. Meema Gitcha's was a house-hold with a lot of melancholy and confusion—poor lighting, food always cooking, illness in the wings, some new tragedy always immi-nent—relatives very different from the lively, healthy, Americanized contingent stuffed into the new Studebakers. Meema Gitcha never got over her husband's accident. She was always sure we were going to be killed in a car crash on the way up, and when we weren't, she was sure we would be killed in a crash on the way down, and so the custom was that as soon as we got home on Sunday night, the very moment we stepped through the door, before anybody even went to the bathroom or got out of his coat, Meema Gitcha had to be phoned and reassured that we were still alive. But, of course, in those days, in our world, a long-distance phone call was unheard of—other than in an emergency, nobody would dream of making one. Nonetheless, when we got home from Meema Gitcha's, no matter how late it was, my mother got on the phone and, as though what she was doing was entirely on the up and up, dialed the operator and asked to place a long-distance call to Meema Gitcha's Connecticut number and to speak there person-to-person with Moishe Pipik. Even while my mother was holding the phone, my brother and I used to put our ears up next to hers on the receiver because it was tremendously exciting to hear the goyisch operator trying to get her tongue around 'Moishe Pipik.' She always got it wrong, and my mother, who was wonderful at this and celebrated for it in the family, my mother very calmly, very precisely, would say, 'No, operator, no—person-to-person to Moí-she . . . Pí-pik. Mr. Moishe . . . *Pipik.*' And when finally the opera-tor got it marginally right, we would hear the voice of Meema Gitcha jumping in at the other end—'Moishe Pipik? He's not here! He left half an hour ago!' and immediately, bang, she'd hang up before the phone company caught on to what we were doing and threw the whole bunch of us in jail."

Something about the story—could just have been its length—seemed to have sedated him a little, and he lay there on the bed as though for the moment he were no threat to anyone, including even himself. His eyes were closed when he said, very wearily, "What does

this have to do with what you have done to me? Anything? Have you
no imagination for what you did to me today?"

I thought then that he was like some errant son of mine, like the
child I'd never had, some ne'er-do-well infantile grown-up who bears
the family name and the facial features of a larger-than-life dad and
doesn't much like feeling suffocated by him and has gone everywhere
to learn to breathe and, after decades on his motorcycle, having
succeeded at nothing but strumming on an electric guitar, appears at
the doorstep of the old manse to vent the impotence of a lifetime and
then, following twenty-four hours of frenzied indictment and
frightening tears, ends up back in his boyhood bedroom, momentarily drained of recrimination, while the father sits kindly beside him,
mentally ticking off all his offspring's deficiencies, thinking, "At your
age I had already... ," and aloud, trying in vain, with funny stories, to
amuse this beast of prey into a change of heart, at least until he'll
accept the check he came for and go away to some place where he
can repair automobiles.

The check. The check was no hallucination and the check was
gone. It was all no hallucination. This is worse than Halcion—this is
happening.

"You're thinking Pipik was our fall guy," I said, "the scapegoat's
scapegoat—but, no, Pipik was protean, a hundred different things.
Very human in that regard. Moishe Pipik was someone who didn't
exist and couldn't possibly exist, and yet we were claiming he was so
real he could answer the telephone. To a seven-year-old child this
was all hilarious. But then Meema Gitcha would say, 'He left half an
hour ago,' and I was suddenly as stupid as the operator and I believed
her. I could *see* him leaving. He wanted to stay and talk more with
Meema Gitcha. Going to visit her reassured him of something. That
he wasn't entirely alone, I suppose. There weren't that many Jews in
Danbury. How had poor little Moishe Pipik got there in the first place?
Oddly, Gitcha could be a very reassuring bulk of a person for all that
there was nothing that didn't worry her. But the worries she attacked
like a dragon slayer—maybe that was it. I imagined them speaking in
Yiddish, Meema Gitcha and Moishe Pipik. He was a refugee boy who

wore an Old Country refugee cap, and she gave him food to eat out of the cooking pots and her dead husband's old coat to wear. Sometimes she slipped him a dollar. But whenever he happened to come around to see her after the New Jersey relatives had been visiting for the weekend, and he sat at the table telling her his problems, she would sit there eyeing the kitchen clock, and then suddenly she would jump up and say, 'Go, Moishe! Look at the time! God forbid you should be here when they call!' And in the midst of everything, *in mitn drinen,* you know, he grabbed his cap and he ran. Pipik ran and he ran and he ran and he never stopped running until fifty years later he finally reached Jerusalem and all that running had made him *so* tired and *so* lonely that all he could do when he got to Jerusalem was to find a bed, any bed, even somebody else's bed. . . ."

I had put my sonny boy to sleep, with my story anesthetized him. I remained in the chair by the window wishing that it had killed him. When I was younger my Jewish betters used to accuse me of writing short stories that endangered Jewish lives—would that I could! A narrative as deadly as a gun!

I took a look at him, a good long hungry look of the kind I hadn't quite been able to take while he was looking back at me. Poor bastard. The resemblance *was* striking. As his trousers were gathered up on his legs because of the way he had fallen to sleep, I could see that he even had my spindly ankles—or I his. The minutes passed quietly. I'd done it. Worn him down. Knocked him out. It was the first peaceful moment I'd known all day. So this, I thought, is what I look like sleeping. I hadn't seen myself as quite so long in a bed though maybe it was just that this bed was short. Anyway, this is what the women see when they awaken to contemplate the wisdom of what they have done and with whom. This is what I would look like if I were to die tonight in that bed. This is my corpse. I am sitting here alive even though I am dead. I am sitting here after my death. Maybe it's before my birth. I am sitting here and, like Meema Gitcha's Moishe Pipik, I do not exist. I left half an hour ago. I am here sitting *shivah* for myself.

This is stranger even than I thought.

No, not that tack. No, just a different person similarly embodied, the physical analogue to what in poetry would be a near rhyme. Nothing more revelatory than that.

I lifted the phone on the table beside me and very, very quietly asked the switchboard operator to get me the King David Hotel.

"Philip Roth, please," I said, when the operator came on at the King David.

The phone in their room was answered by Jinx.

I whispered her name.

"Honey! Where are you? I'm going crazy!"

Weakly I replied, "Still here."

"Where?"

"His room."

"God! Didn't you find it?"

"Nowhere."

"Then that's it—leave!"

"I'm waiting for him."

"Don't! No!"

"My million, damn it!"

"But you sound awful—you sound *worse.* You took too much again. You can't take that much."

"I took what it takes."

"But it's *too much.* How bad is it? Is it very bad?"

"I'm resting."

"You sound ghastly! You're in pain! Come back! Philip, come back! He'll turn everything around! It'll be you who stole from *him!* He's a vicious, ruthless egomaniac who'll say *anything* to win!"

This deserved a laugh. "Him? Frighten me?"

"He frightens *me! Come back!"*

"Him? He's shitting his pants with fear of *me.* He thinks it's all a dream. I'll show him what a dream is. He won't know what hit him when I've finished scrambling his fucking brains."

"Hon, this is *suicide."*

"I love you, Jinx."

"Really? Am I anything at all to you anymore?"

"What are you wearing?" I whispered, keeping my eye on the bed.

"What?"

"What do you have on?"

"Just my jeans. My bra."

"The jeans."

"Not now."

"The jeans."

"This is crazy. If he comes back . . ."

"The jeans."

"They are. They are."

"Off?"

"I'm pulling them off."

"Around your ankles. Leave them around your ankles."

"They are."

"The panties."

"You too."

"Yes," I said, "oh, yes."

"Yes? Is it out?"

"I'm on his bed."

"You crazy man."

"On his bed. I've got it out. Oh, it's out, all right."

"Is it big?"

"It's big."

"Very big?"

"Very big."

"My nipples are hard as a fucking rock. My tits are spilling out. Oh, hon, they're spilling over—"

"All of it. Say all of it."

"I'm nobody's cunt but your cunt—"

"Ever?"

"Nobody's."

"All of it."

"I worship your stiff cock."

"All of it."

"My lips around your stiff stiff cock—"

On the bed Pipik had opened his eyes and I hung up the phone.

"Feel better?" I asked.

He looked at me as if a man deep in a coma and, seemingly seeing nothing, closed his eyes again.

"Too much medication," I said.

I decided not to call Jinx back and finish off the job. I'd got the idea.

When he came around next there was a mask of perspiration clinging to his forehead and his cheeks.

"Shall I get a doctor?" I asked. "Do you want me to call Miss Possesski?"

"I just want you, I just want you . . ." But tears appeared in his eyes and he couldn't go on.

"What *do* you want?"

"What you stole."

"Look, you're a sick man. You're in a lot of pain, aren't you? You're taking painkilling drugs that are bending your mind. You're taking tremendous doses of those drugs, that's the story, isn't it? I know from experience what that's like. I know how they can make you behave. Look, I don't particularly want to send a Demerol addict to jail. But if that's what it takes to get you to leave me alone, I don't care how sick you are or how much pain you're in or how loony the drugs are making you act, I will take it as my business to see that that happens. I'll be absolutely merciless with you if I find that I have to be. But *do* I have to be? How much do you need to get out of here and to go somewhere with Miss Possesski and try to get some peace and quiet? Because this other thing is a stupid farce, it means nothing, it can come to nothing, you're bound to fail. It's very likely to end for you two in a stupid catastrophe brought on by yourselves. I'm willing to pay your way to wherever you want to go. Two round-trip first-class airplane tickets to anyplace your two hearts desire. Something toward expenses too, to tide you over until you sort things out. Doesn't that seem reasonable? I press no charges. You go away. Please, let's negotiate a settlement and put an end to this."

"Easy as that." He didn't seem quite as bleary now as when he'd first come round, but there was still perspiration beading his upper lip and no color at all in his face. " 'Moishe Pipik Gets Paid Off. NBA Winner Wins Again.' "

"Would the Jewish police be a more humane solution? A payoff isn't always without dignity in a mess like this. I'll give you ten thousand bucks. That's a lot of money. I have a publisher here"—and why hadn't I thought of calling *him!*—"and I'll arrange to have ten thousand dollars in cash in your hands by noon tomorrow—"

" 'Providing you are out of Jerusalem by nightfall.' "

"By nightfall tomorrow, yes."

"I get ten and you get the balance."

"There is no balance. That's it."

"No balance?" He began to laugh. "No balance?" All at once he was sitting up straight and seemed entirely resuscitated. Either the drugs had suddenly worn off or they had suddenly kicked in, but Pipik was himself again (whoever that might be). "You who studied arithmetic with Miss Duchin at Chancellor Avenue School, you tell me there is *no balance* when"—and here he began gesturing as though he were a Jewish comic, his two hands to the left, his two hands to the right, distinguishing *this* from *that, that* from *this*—"when the subtrahend is ten thousand and the minuend is one million? You got B's in arithmetic all through Chancellor. Subtraction is one of the four fundamental operations of arithmetic. Let me refresh your recollection. It is the inverse of addition. The result of subtracting one number from another is called the difference. The symbol for this operation is our friend the minus sign. Any of this ring a bell? As in addition, only like qualities can be subtracted. Dollars from dollars, for instance, work very nicely. Dollars from dollars, Phil, is what subtraction was made for."

What *was* he? Was he fifty-one percent smart or was he fifty-one percent stupid? Was he fifty-one percent crazy or was he fifty-one percent sane? Was he fifty-one percent reckless or was he fifty-one percent cunning? In every case it was a very close call.

"Miss Duchin. I must confess," I said, "I'd forgotten Miss Duchin."

"You played Columbus for Hana Duchin in the Columbus Day play. Fourth grade. She adored you. Best Columbus she ever had. They all adored you. Your mother, your Aunt Mim, your Aunt Honey, your Grandma Finkel—when you were a tot they used to stand around the crib, and when your mother changed your diaper, they used to take turns kissing your *tuchas*. Women have been lining up to kiss your *tuchas* ever since."

Well, we were both laughing now. "What are you, Pipik? What's your game? You have this amusing side to you, don't you? You're obviously much more than just a fool, you have a stunning companion who is full of life, you don't lack for audacity or daring, you even have some brains. I hate to be the one to say it but the vehemence and intelligence of your criticism of Israel makes you into something more than just a crackpot. Is this just a malicious comedy about convictions? The argument for Diasporism isn't always as farcical as you make it sound. There's a mad plausibility about it. There's more than a grain of truth in recognizing and acknowledging the Eurocentrism of Judaism, of the Judaism that gave birth to Zionism, and so forth. Yet it also strikes me, I'm afraid, like the voice of puerile wishful thinking. Tell me, please, what *is* this really all about? Identity theft? It's the stupidest con going. You've *got* to get caught. Who are you? Tell me what you do for a living when you aren't doing this. As far as I know—though correct me if I'm wrong—you've never plugged into my American Express card. So on what do you survive? Your wits alone?"

"Guess." Oh, he was very bright and sparkly now, practically flirtatious. *Guess*. Don't tell me he's bisexual! Don't tell me this is more of the guy in the hallway! Don't tell me he wants us to have it off together, Philip Roth fucking Philip Roth! That, I'm afraid, is a form of masturbation too fancy even for me.

"I can't guess. You're a blank to me," I said. "I even get the feeling that without me around you're a blank to yourself. A little urbane, a little intelligent, a little self-confident, maybe even a little fascinating —Jinx-like creatures don't just drop from the sky—but mostly somebody who never arrived at a clear idea of what his life was for, mostly uncohesive, disappointed, a very shadowy, formless, fragmented thing. A kind of wildly delineated nothing. What enkindles you when

I'm not here? Under 'me' isn't there at least a *little* you? What do you aim for in life other than getting people to think that you are somebody else?"

"What do *you* aim for other than that?"

"Yes, I take your point, but the question asked of you has a broader meaning, no? Pipik, what do you do for a real life?"

"I'm a licensed law-enforcement official," he said. "How's that grab you? I'm a private investigator. Here."

His ID. Could have been a bad picture of me. License No. 7794. Date of Expiration 06/01/90. ". . . A duly licensed private investigator . . . and is vested with all the authorities allowed him by law." And his signature. My signature.

"I run an agency in Chicago," he said. "Three guys and me. That's all. Small agency. We list what most everybody else lists—thefts, white- and blue-collar crime, missing persons, matrimonial surveillance. We do lie detection. Narcotics. We do murders. I do all the missing-persons cases. Missing persons is what Philip Roth is known for throughout the Midwest. I've been as far as Mexico and Alaska. Twenty-one years and I found everybody I was ever contracted to find. I also handle all the murders."

I gave back the ID card and watched him return it to his wallet. Were there a hundred more phony cards in there, all of them bearing that name? I didn't think it wise to ask just then—he'd caught me up short with "I handle all the murders."

"You like the dangerous assignments," I said.

"I have to be challenged twenty-four hours a day, seven days a week. I like to live on the edge, always up—it keeps my adrenaline going. Anything other than that I consider boring."

"Well, I'm stunned."

"I see that."

"I had you figured for an adrenaline freak but it wasn't exactly a law *enforcer* that I would have thought to call you."

"It's impossible for a Jew to be a private detective?"

"No."

"It's impossible for a detective to look like me? Or like you?"

"No, it's not even that."

"You just think I'm a liar. It's a cozy universe you've got going—you're the truth-telling Philip and I'm the lying Philip, you're the honest Philip and I'm the dishonest Philip, you're the reasonable Philip and I'm the manic psychopath."

"I like the missing-persons bit. I like that that's your specialty. Very witty in the circumstances. And what got you into detective work? Tell me that, while we're at it."

"I was always the type of person who wanted to help other people. Since I was a kid I couldn't stand injustice. It drove me crazy. It still does. It always will. Injustice is my obsession. I think it has to do with being a Jewish kid growing up in the war era. America wasn't always fair to Jews in those days. Beaten up in high school. Just like Jonathan Pollard. I could even have gone in the same direction as Pollard. Acting out of my love of Jews, I could have done it. I had the Pollard fantasies, volunteering for Israel, working for the Mossad. At home, FBI, CIA, they both turned me down. Never found out why. I sometimes wonder if it wasn't because of you, because they thought it was just too much bother, a guy who was a veritable duplicate of somebody in the public eye. But I'll never know. I used to draw a cartoon strip for myself when I was a kid. 'A Jew in the FBI.' Pollard is very important to me. What the Dreyfus case was to Herzl, the Pollard case is to me. Through my PI contacts I've heard that the FBI attached Pollard to a polygraph machine, gave him lists of prominent American Jews, and told him to identify the other spies. He wouldn't do it. Everything about the guy repels me except that. I live in dread of a second Pollard. I live in dread of what that will mean."

"So, is what I'm supposed to gather from all this that you became a detective to help Jews?"

"Look, you tell me you know nothing about me and you're at a disadvantage because I know so much about you. I'm explaining to you that it's my profession to know as much as I know, not just about you but about *everyone.* You ask me to level with you. That's what I'm trying to do. Except all I meet with is a barrage of disbelief. You want *me* to take a polygraph? I could pass it with flying colors. Okay,

I haven't been calm and collected with you. It surprises me, too. I wrote and apologized for that. Some people blitz you, no matter who you are. I have to tell you that you are only the second person in my life to blitz me like this. In my line of work I'm hardened to everything and I see everything and I have to learn to handle everything. The only other time it happened before, that I was blitzed anything like this, was in 1963, when I met the president. He came to Chicago. I was doing some bodyguard work then. Usually I was employed by a private contractor, but at this time I was employed by the public sector, too. It was the mayor's office. I couldn't speak when he shook my hand. The words wouldn't come out. That doesn't usually happen. Words are a large part of my business and account for ninety percent of my success. Words and brains. It was probably because I was having masturbatory fantasies in those days about his wife on her water skis and I felt guilty. Do you know what the president said to me? He said, 'I know your friend Styron. You've got to come down to Washington and have dinner with us and the Styrons some night.' Then he said, 'I'm a great admirer of *Letting Go.*' That was in August 1963. Three months later he was shot."

"Kennedy mixed you up with me. The president of the United States thought a bodyguard in the mayor's office was a novelist on the side."

"The guy shook a million hands a day. He took me for another dignitary. It wasn't hard—there was my name, my looks, and besides, people are always taking a bodyguard for somebody else. That's part of the job. Somebody desires protection. Somebody like you, say, who might be feeling threatened. You ride around with them. You pretend you're a friend or something. Sure, some guys tell you they want to make it obvious that you're a bodyguard, so you play that part. Nice dark suit, the sunglasses, you carry a gun. The goon outfit. That's what they want, you do it. They want it obvious—they like the flash, the glitter of it. I had one client I worked with all the time in Chicago, a big contractor and developer, lots of money, and a lot of people who might be after him, and he loved the show. I'd go to Vegas with him. Him and his limousine and his friends—they wanted it always to be a big thing. I had to watch the women when they went to the bathroom. I had to go into the bathroom with them without their knowing it."

"Difficult?"

"I was twenty-seven, twenty-eight, I managed it. Things have changed now but at this time I was the only Jewish bodyguard in the whole Midwest. I broke ground out there. The other Jewish boys were all in law school. That was what the families wanted. Didn't your old man want you to go to law school instead of to Chicago to become an English teacher?"

"Who told you that?"

"Clive Cummis, your brother's friend. Big New Jersey attorney now. Before you went out to graduate school to study literature, your father asked Clive to take you aside to plead with you to go to law school instead."

"I don't myself remember that happening."

"Sure. Clive took you into the bedroom on Leslie Street. He said you'd never make a living teaching English. But you told him you weren't having any of that stuff and to forget it."

"Well, that's an incident that slips my mind."

"Clive remembers it."

"You see Clive Cummis, too?"

"I get business from lawyers all over the country. I have a lot of law firms we work very closely with. We are exclusive agents for them. They'll turn over all the cases to us where they need an investigator in Chicago. We'll turn cases over to them, they'll turn cases over to us. I've got a great working relationship with about two hundred police departments, basically in Illinois, Wisconsin, and Indiana. We have a great relationship with the county police, tremendous arrest record with the counties. I brought in a lot of people for them."

I have to tell you that I was beginning to believe him.

"Look, I never *ever* wanted to do the Jewish thing," he said. "That always seemed to me to be our big mistake. Law school to me was just another ghetto. So was what you did, the writing, the books, the schools, all that scorn for the material world. Books to me were too Jewish, just another way to hide from fear of the goyim. You see, I was having Diasporist thoughts even then. It was crude, it wasn't formulated, but the instinct was there from the start. These people here call it 'assimilation' in order to disparage it—I called it living like a man. I joined the army to go to Korea. I *wanted* to fight the Communists. I never got sent. They made me an MP at Fort Benning. I built my body in the gym there. I learned to direct traffic. I became a pistol expert. I fell in love with weapons. I studied the martial arts. You quit ROTC because you were against the military establishment at Bucknell, and I became the best fucking MP they ever saw in Georgia. I *showed* the fucking rednecks. Don't be afraid, I told myself, don't run away—beat them at their fucking game. And through this technique I developed a tremendous sense of self-worth."

"What happened to it?" I asked.

"Please, don't insult me *too* much. I don't carry a gun, the cancer has knocked the shit out of my body, the drugs, you're right, they're no good for the brain, they fuck up your nature, and, on top of everything, I am in awe of you—that's true and always will be. It's as it *should* be. I know my place vis-à-vis you. I'm willing to take shit from you that I never took before in my life. I'm a little powerless where you're concerned. But I happen also to understand your predicament better than you give me credit for. You're blitzed too, Phil, this isn't the easiest situation for a classic Jewish paranoid to handle. That's what I'm trying to address right now—your paranoid response. That's why I'm explaining to you who I am and where I'm coming from. I'm not an alien from outer space. I'm not a schizoid delusion. And however much fun it is for you to think so, I'm not Meema Gitcha's Moishe Pipik, either. Far from it. I'm Philip Roth. I'm a Jewish private detective from Chicago who has got cancer and is doomed to die of it, but not before he makes his contribution. I am not ashamed of what I have done for people up until now. I am not ashamed of being a bodyguard for people who needed a bodyguard. A bodyguard is a piece of meat, but I never gave anybody less than the best. I did matrimonial surveillance for years. I know it's the comic-relief end of the business, catching people with their pants down, I know it's not being a novelist who wins prizes for excellence—but that's not the Philip Roth who I was. I was the Philip Roth who went up to the desk manager at the Palmer House and showed him my badge or gave him some other pretense so I could get to the registration book to see that they had actually signed in and what room they were in. I am the Philip Roth who in order to get up there would say I was a floral-delivery person and I gotta be sure this is personally done because the guy gave me a hundred dollars to get it up there. I am the Philip Roth who would get the maid and make up a story for her: 'I forgot my key, this is my room, you can check downstairs that this is my room.' I am the Philip Roth who could always get a key, who could always get in the room—*always*."

"Just like here," I said, but that didn't stop him.

"I am the Philip Roth who rushes into the room with his Minolta and gets his pictures before they know what's happened. Nobody gives you awards for this, but I was never ashamed, I put in my years, and when I finally had the money, I opened my own agency. And the rest is history. People are missing and Philip Roth finds them. I'm the Philip Roth who is dealing with desperate people all the time, and not just in some book. Crime is desperate. The person who reported them is desperate and the person who is on the lam is desperate, and so desperation is my life, day and night. Kids run away from home and I find them. They run away and they get pulled into the world of people who are scum. They need a place to stay, and so the people take advantage of that. My last case, before I got cancer, was a fifteen-year-old girl from Highland Park. Her mother came to me, she was a mess, a lot of tears and screaming. Donna registered for her high school class in September, went for the first two days, and then disappeared. She winds up with a known felon, warrants for his arrest, a bad guy. A Dominican. I found this apartment building in Calumet City where his grandmother lived, and I staked it out. It was all I had to go on. I staked it out for days. I sat upwards of twenty-six hours once without relief. With nothing happening. You have to have patience, *tremendous* patience. Even reading the newspapers is chancy because something could happen in a split second and you might miss it. There for hours and you have to be inventive. You hide in the vehicle, you sit low in the vehicle, you pretend you're just hanging out like anybody else in the vehicle. Sometimes you go to the bathroom in the vehicle—you can't help it. And meanwhile I am always putting myself in the criminal's mind, how he's going to react and what he's going to do. Every criminal is different and every scenario I come up with is different. When you're a criminal and you're stupid, you don't think, but if you're a detective you have to be intelligent enough to not-think in the way this guy doesn't think. Well, he turns up at the grandmother's finally. I follow him on foot when he comes out. He goes to make a drug purchase. Then he comes back to the car. I make a pass by the car and there she is—I make a positive identification that it is Donna. It turned out later that he was doing drugs in the car himself. To shorten a long story, the car chase lasted twenty-five minutes. We're driving about eighty miles an hour down side roads through four Indiana towns. The guy is charged with six-teen different counts. Eluding police, resisting arrest, kidnapping—he's in deep shit. I interrogated the girl. I said, 'How you doin', Donna?' She says, 'I don't know what you're talking about, my name is Pepper. I'm from California. I've been in town a week.' This nice Highland Park high school girl of fifteen has the intelligence of a hardened con and her story is perfect. She's been gone eleven months, and she had a fake birth certificate, a driver's license, a whole bunch of fake IDs. Her behavior indicated to me that this guy was using her for prostitution. We found condoms in her pocketbook, sexual devices in the car and things."

I thought, He's got it all down pat from TV. If only I'd watched more "L.A. Law" and read less Dostoyevsky I'd know what's going on here, I'd know in two minutes what show it is exactly. Maybe motifs from fifteen shows, with a dozen detective movies thrown in. The joke is that more than likely there's a terrifically popular network program that everyone stays home for on Friday nights, and not only is it about a private investigator who specializes in missing kids but it's a Jewish private investigator, and the episode about the high school girl (sweet cheerleader, square parents, mind of her own) and the addict-pimp abductor (dirty dancer, folkloric grandmother, pitted skin) was probably the last one seen by Pipik before he'd hopped on the plane for Tel Aviv to play me. Maybe it was the in-flight movie on El Al. Probably everybody in America over three years of age knows about how detectives shit in their cars and call the cars vehicles, probably everybody over three in America knows exactly what is meant by a sexual device and only the aging author of *Portnoy's Complaint* has to ask. What fun it must be for him putting me on like this. But is the masquerading relentless for the sake of the shakedown, or is the shakedown a pretext for the performance and all the real fun in the act? What if this isn't simply a con but his parody of my vocation, what's now known to mankind as a "roast." Yes, suppose this Pipik of mine is none other than the Satiric Spirit in the flesh, and the whole thing a send-up, a satire of authorship! How could I have missed it? Yes, yes, the Spirit of Satire is of course who he is, here to poke fun at me and other outmoded devotees of what is important and what is real, here to divert us all from the Jewish savagery that doesn't bear thinking about, come with his road show to Jerusalem to make everyone miserable laugh.

"What are the sexual devices?" I asked him.

"She had a vibrator. There was a blackjack in the car. I forget what else we had."

"What's the blackjack, a kind of dildo? I suppose dildos are a dime a dozen on prime time by now. What the Hula-Hoop used to be."

"They use blackjacks for S & M. For beating and punishing and things like that."

"What happened to Donna? Is she white? I didn't catch this show. Who plays you? Ron Liebman or George Segal? Or is it you playing them for me?"

"I don't know many writers," he replied. "Is this the way they all think? That out there everybody is *playing?* Man! You listened too religiously to that kiddie program when you were a little boy—you and Sandy may have loved it too much. Saturday mornings. Remember? Nineteen forty also. Eleven a.m. Eastern Standard Time. Da-*dum*-da-dadada, *dum*-da-dadada, *dum*-dada-da-dum."

He was humming the tune that used to introduce "Let's Pretend," a fairy-tale half hour that little unmediaized American children adored back in the thirties and forties, my brother and I but two of the millions.

"Maybe," he said, "your perception of reality got arrested at the 'Let's Pretend' level."

To this I did not even bother to reply.

"Oh, that's a cliché, is it? Am I boring you? Well," he said, "now that you're pushing sixty and 'Let's Pretend' isn't on the air anymore, someone *should* bore you long enough to explain that, one, the world is real, two, the stakes are high, and, three, nobody is pretending anymore except *you.* I have been inside your head for so long now and yet not until this moment have I understood what a writer is all about: you guys think it's *all* make-believe."

"I don't think *any* of it is make-believe, Pipik. I think—I *know*—that you are a real liar and a real fake. It's the stories that purport to be about 'it,' it's the struggle to describe 'it,' where the make-believe comes in. Five-year-old children may take the stories for real, but by the time you're pushing sixty, deciphering the pathology of story making comes to be just another middle-age specialty. By the time you're pushing sixty, the representations of 'it' *are* 'it.' They're everything. Follow me?"

"Nothing hard to follow except your relevance. Cynicism increases with age because the bullshit piles up on your head. What's that got to do with us?"

I heard myself ask aloud, "Am I conversing with this person, am I truly trying to make *sense* with him? *Why?*"

"Why *not!* Why should you converse with Aharon Appelfeld," he said, holding up and shaking Aharon's book, "and not with me!"

"A thousand reasons."

He was all at once in a jealous rage because I talked seriously to Aharon but not to him. "Name *one!*" he cried.

Because, I thought, of Aharon's and my distinctly radical *twoness,* a condition with which you appear to have no affinity at all; because we are anything *but* the duplicates that everyone is supposed to believe you and me to be; because Aharon and I each embody the *reverse* of the other's experience; because each recognizes in the other the Jewish man he is *not*; because of the all but incompatible orientations that shape our very different lives and very different books and that result from *antithetical* twentieth-century Jewish biographies; because we are the heirs jointly of a drastically *bifurcated* legacy—because of the sum of all these Jewish *antinomies*, yes, we have much to talk about and are intimate friends.

"Name *one!*" he challenged for a second time but on this subject I simply remained silent and, sensibly for a change, kept my thinking to myself. "You recognize Appelfeld for the person he claims to be; why do you refuse that with me? All you *do* is resist me. Resist me, ignore me, insult me, defame me, rant and rave at me—*and steal from me.* Why must there be this bad blood? Why *you* should see *me* as a rival—I cannot understand it. Why is this relationship so belligerent from your end? Why must it be destructive when together we could achieve so much? We could have a creative relationship, we could be partners—copersonalities working in tandem rather than stupidly divided in two!"

"Look, I've got more personalities than I can use already. All you are is one too many. This is the end of the line. I don't want to go into business with you. I just want you to go away."

"We could at least be friends."

He sounded so forlorn I had to laugh. "Never. Profound, unbridgeable, unmistakable differences that far outweigh the superficial similarity—no, we can't be friends, either. This is it."

He looked, to my astonishment, about to burst into tears because of what I'd said. Or maybe it was just the ebb tide of those drugs. "Look, you never told me what happened to Donna," I said. "Entertain us a little more, and then, what do you say, let's bring this little error to an end. What became of Highland Park High's fifteen-year-old dominatrix? How'd that show wind up?"

But this, of course, riled him again.

"Shows! You really think I watch PI shows? There isn't one that depicts what's real, not *one.* If I had a choice between watching "Magnum, P.I." and "Sixty Minutes," I'd watch "Sixty Minutes" anytime. Shall I tell you something? Donna turned out to be Jewish. Her mother, I found out later, was the reason why she left. I won't go into that, you don't care. But I did, I got involved in those cases—they were my life before I got sick. I would try to find out what the reasons were they left and try to get them to stay. I would try to help them. That was very rewarding. Unfortunately this Dominican with Donna —his name was Hector—Donna had a problem with him—"

"He had this power over her," I said, "and to this day she's trying to contact him."

"That happens to be the case. That's true. She was charged with receiving stolen property, resisting arrest, eluding police too—she's in a detention center."

"And the day she's released from the detention center, she'll run away again," I said. "Great story. Everybody can identify, as they say. Beginning with you. She doesn't want to be Dr. and Mrs. Jew's Donna anymore, she wants to be Hector's Dominican Pepper. All this auto-biographical fantasy, is it nationwide? Is it worldwide? Maybe this stuff everybody is watching has inspired half the human population with the yearning for a massive transfer of souls, maybe that's what *you* embody—the longings for metempsychosis inspired in mankind by all those TV shows."

"Idiot!" he shouted. "It's staring you right in the *face* what I embody!"

It is, I thought: exactly nothing. There is no meaning here at all. *That's* the meaning. I can stop there. I could have started there. Nothing could look more like it meant something than this, and nothing could mean less.

"So, what happened finally to Hector?" I asked him, hoping now that if I could lead him to the end of something, of anything, it might present an opportunity to get him up from my bed and out of the room without my having to call down to the desk for assistance. I never felt less inclined than at that moment to see this poor possessed scoundrel wind up in trouble. Not only was he meaningless but, having observed him for nearly an hour, I was hard-pressed to believe any longer that he was violent. In this way we *weren't* dissimilar: the violence was all verbal. I had, in fact, actively to prevent myself from despising him less than was warranted, given the maddening mix-up he'd made of my life and the repercussions of this encounter, which I was sure were going to dog me in unpleasant ways in the future.

"Hector?" he said. "Hector made bail, he's out on bail." Unexpectedly he began to laugh, but a laugh that was as hopeless and weary as any sound emitted by him yet. "You and Hector. I never saw the parallel till now. As if I don't have enough grief from you, with all the ways you want to fuck me over, I've got Hector waiting in the wings. He called me, he spoke to me, he threatened my life—Hector told me he was going to kill me. This is just before I went into the hospital. I've arrested a lot of people, you realize, put a lot of people in prison. They phone me, they track me down, and I don't hide. If somebody wants to get even with me, there's nothing I can do. But I don't look over my shoulder. I told Hector what I tell them all. 'I'm listed in the book, man. Philip Roth. Come and get me.' "

With this I raised my arms over my head, I howled, I clapped my hands together, once, then again, until I found myself applauding him. "Bravo! You're wonderful! What a finish! What a flourish! On the phone, the dedicated Jewish savior, the Jewish statesman, Theodor Herzl turned inside out. Then face-to-face outside the trial, a zany fan blushing with adoration. And now this, the masterstroke—the detective who doesn't look over his shoulder. 'I'm in the book, man. Philip Roth. Come and get me.' The *book!*" From out of my depths roared all the laughter that I should have been laughing from the day I first heard that this preposterous mouthpiece claimed to exist.

But he was suddenly screaming from the bed, "I want the check! I want my check! You've stolen a million dollars!"

"I lost it, Pipik. I lost it on the highway from Ramallah. The check is gone."

Aghast, he stared straight at me, at the person in all the world who most reminded him of himself, the person he saw as the rest of him, the completion of him, the one who'd come to be his very reason for being, his mirror image, his meal ticket, his hidden potential, his public persona, his alibi, his future, the one in whom he sought refuge from himself, the other whom he called himself, the person in whose service he had repudiated his own identity, the breakthrough to the other half of his life ... and he saw instead, laughing at him uncontrollably from behind the mask of his very own face, his worst enemy, the one to whom the only bond is hatred. But how could Pipik have failed to know that I would have to hate him no less than he hated me? Did he honestly expect that when we met I'd fall in love and set up shop and have a creative relationship with him like Macbeth and his wife?

"I lost it. It's a great story, too, nearly rivals yours for unbelievability. The check is gone," I told him again. "A million bucks blowing away across the desert sands, probably halfway down to Mecca by now. And with that million you could have convened that first Diasporist Congress in Basel. You could have shipped the first lucky Jews back to Poland. You could have established a chapter of A-S.A. right in Vatican City. Meetings in the basement of St. Peter's Church. Full house every night. 'My name is Eugenio Pacelli. I'm a recovering anti-Semite.' Pipik, who sent you to me in my hour of need? Who made me this wonderful gift? Know what Heine liked to say? There is a God, and his name is Aristophanes. *You* prove it. It's Aristophanes they should be worshiping over at the Wailing Wall—if he were the God of Israel I'd be in shul three times a day!"

I was laughing the way people cry at funerals in the countries where they let go and really have at it. They rend their clothes. They rake their faces with their nails. They howl. They swoon. They faint. They grab at the coffin with their twisted hands and fling themselves shrieking into the hole. Well, this is how I was laughing, if you can picture it. To judge from Pipik's face—our face!—it was something to behold. Why *isn't* God Aristophanes? Would we be any further from the truth?

"Surrender yourself to what is real," were my first words to him when I could talk again. "I speak from experience—surrender to reality, Pipik. There's nothing in the world quite like it."

I suppose I should have laughed even more uproariously at what happened next; as a newly anointed convert to the Old Comedy, I should have bounded to my feet, cried aloud, "Hallelujah!" and sung the praises of He Who Created Us, He Who Formed Us from the Mud, the One and Only Comic Almighty, OUR SOVEREIGN REDEEMER, ARISTOPHANES, but for reasons all too profane (total mental paralysis) I could only dumbly gape at the sight of nothing less than the highly entertaining Aristophanic erection that Pipik had produced, as though it were a rabbit, from his fly, an oversized pole right out of *Lysistrata* that, to my further astonishment, he proceeded to crank in a rotary motion, to position, with one hand cupped over the knobby doll-like head, as if he were moving the floor shift on a prewar car. Then he was lunging with it across the bed.

"There's reality. Like a rock!"

He was ridiculously light, as though the disease had eaten through his bones, as though inside there was nothing left of him and he was as hollow as Mortimer Snerd. I caught hold of his arm just as he landed, and with a blow between his shoulder blades and another, nastier, at the base of the spine, I spun him out the door (who'd opened it?) and shoved him ass-first into the corridor. Then there was the split second in which, across the threshold, each of us was frozen in place by the reflection of the malformed mistake that was the other. Then the door seemed to spring to life again to assist me —the door was closed and locked but afterward I could have sworn I'd had as little to do with its shutting as with its opening.

"My shoes!"

He was screaming for his shoes just as my phone began to ring. So —we were *not* alone, this Arab hotel in Arab East Jerusalem had not been emptied of Demjanjuk's son and Demjanjuk's lawyers, the place had not been evacuated of all its guests and sealed off by the Jewish authorities so that this struggle for supremacy between Roth and "Roth" could rage on undisturbed until the cataclysmic end—no, a complaint at long last from the outer world about the intemperate acting out of this primordial dream.

His shoes were beside the bed, cordovans with the strap that pulls across the instep, Brooks Brothers shoes of the kind I'd been wearing since I'd first admired them on the feet of a dapperly Princetonian

Shakespeare professor at Bucknell. I bent to pick up Pipik's shoes and saw that, along the back lateral curve, the heels were sharply worn away exactly as were the heels of the pair I had on. I looked at mine, at his, and then opened and shut the door so quickly that all I caught sight of as I hurled his cordovans into the corridor was the part in his hair. I saw the part as he rushed the door, and when the door was locked again I realized that it was on the opposite side from my own. I reached a hand up to my scalp to be certain. He'd modeled himself on my photograph! Then this, I said to myself, is most definitely someone else, and, depleted beyond depletion, I dropped with my arms outspread on the disheveled bed from which he and his erection had just arisen. That man is not me! I am here and I am whole and part what hair I still possess on the *right* side. Yet in spite of this, and of differences even more telling—our central nervous systems, for example—he's going to proceed down the stairs and out of the hotel like that, he's going to parade through the lobby like that, he's going to walk across Jerusalem like that, and when the police finally run him down and go to take him in for indecent exposure, he's going to tell them what he tells them all—"I'm in the book. Philip Roth. Come and get me."

"My glasses!"

The glasses I found right there beside me on the bed. I snapped them in two and hurled the pieces against the wall. Let him be blind!

"They're broken! *Go!*"

My phone continued ringing and I was no longer laughing like a good Aristophanian but quivering with irreligious, unenlightened rage.

I picked up the phone and said nothing.

"Philip Roth?"

"Not here."

"Philip Roth, where was God between 1939 and 1945? I'm sure He was at the Creation. I'm sure He was at Mount Sinai with Moses. My problem is where He was between 1939 and 1945. That was a dereliction of duty for which even He, *especially* He, cannot ever be forgiven."

I was being addressed in a thick, grave Old Country accent, a hoarse, rough, emphysemic voice that sounded as though it originated in something massively debilitated.

Meanwhile someone had struck up a light, rhythmic knuckle rapping on my door. Shave and a haircut . . . *two bits*. Could it be Pipik on the phone if it was also Pipik at the door? How many of him were there?

"Who is this?" I asked into the phone.

"I spit on this God who was on vacation from 1939 to 1945!"

I hung up.

Shave and a haircut . . . *two bits*.

I waited and waited but the rapping would not go away.

"Who is that?" I finally whispered, but so softly that I thought I might not even be heard. I could almost believe I was smart enough not to be asking.

The whisper back seemed to waft through the keyhole, carried on a wire-thin current of cool air. "Want me to blow you?"

"Go away!"

"I'll blow both of you."

———

I am looking down on an open-air hospital ward or public clinic that is set out on a vast playing field that reminds me of School Stadium on Bloomfield Avenue in Newark, where Newark's rivalrous high schools—the Italian high school, the Irish high school, the Jewish high school, the Negro high school—played football doubleheaders when I was a boy. But this arena is ten times the size of our stadium and the crowd is as huge as the crowd at a bowl game, tens upon tens of thousands of excited fans, snugly layered with clothing and warming their dark insides with steaming containers of coffee. White pennants wave everywhere, rhythmically the crowd takes up the chant, "Give me an M! Give me an E! Give me a T! Give me an E!" while down on the field white-clad doctors glide agilely about in clinical silence—I am able to see through my binoculars their serious, dedicated faces and the faces, too, of those who lie still as stone, each hooked up to an IV drip, their souls draining into the body on the next gurney. And what is horrifying is that the face of every one of them, even of the women and of the little children, is the face of Ivan of Treblinka. From the stands, the cheering fans can see nothing but the balloon of a big, stupid, friendly face swelling out of each of the bodies strapped to the gurneys, but with my binoculars I see concentrated in that emerging face everything in humanity that there is to hate. Yet the electrified crowd seethes with hope. "All will be different from now on! Everybody will be nice from now on! Everybody will belong to a church like Mr. Demjanjuk! Everybody will raise a garden like Mr. Demjanjuk! Everybody will work hard and come home at night to a wonderful family like Mr. Demjanjuk!" I alone have binoculars and am witness to the unfolding catastrophe. "That is Ivan!" But nobody can hear me above the hurrahs and the exuberant cheering. "Give me an O! Give me an S!" I am still shouting that it is Ivan, Ivan from Treblinka, when they pluck me lightly out of my seat and, rolling me down atop the soft tassels of the white woolen caps worn by all the fans, pass my body (swathed now in a white pennant bearing a big blue "M") over a low brick wall that has painted across it "The Memory Barrier. Players Only," and into the arms of two waiting doctors, who strap me tightly to a gurney of my own and wheel me out to midfield just as the band strikes up a quick-time march. When the IV needle pierces my wrist, I hear the mighty roar that precedes the big game. "Who's playing?" I ask the nurse in the white uniform who attends me. She is Jinx, Jinx Possesski. She pats my hand and whispers, "University of Metempsychosis." I begin to scream, "I don't want to play!" but Jinx smiles reassuringly and says, "You must—you're the starting halfback."

———

"HALF BACK" was sounding the alarm in my ear when I scrambled upright in the bed with no idea in what dimensionless black room I had awakened. I concluded at first that it was the previous summer and that I needed a light to find the pillbox beside the bed. I need half of a second Halcion to get me through the rest of the night. But

I'm reluctant to turn on the light for fear of finding paw prints not just on the bedsheets and the pillowcases but climbing the walls and crossing the ceiling. Then my phone begins to ring again. "What is the real life of man?" I am asked this by the emphysemic old Jew with the tired voice and the heavy accent. "I give up. What *is* the real life of man?" "There is none. There is only the urge to attain a real life. Everything that is not real is the real life of man." "Okay. I've got one for you. Tell me the meaning of today." "Error. Error upon error. Error, misprision, fakery, fantasy, ignorance, falsification, and mischief, of course, irrepressible mischief. An ordinary day in the life of anyone." *"Where* is the error?" *In his bed,* I think, and, dreaming on, I am in the bed of someone who has just died of a highly contagious disease, and then I am dying myself. For locking myself into this little room with him, for ridiculing and chastising him from only an arm's length away, for telling this ego-blank megalomaniacal pseudo-being that he is no more to me than a mere Moishe Pipik, for my failing to understand that he is not a joke, Moishe Pipik murders me and there I expire, emptied of all my blood, until I am ejected like a pilot from the burning cockpit into the discovery that I have had a wet dream for the first time in twenty-five years.

Fully awake, I left the bed at long last and, in the dark, crossed to the arched window in front of the desk to see if I could spot him keeping a lookout on my room from the street below, and what I saw, not in the narrow street bordering this side of the hotel but two streets beyond, was a convoy of buses under the glow of the lamps and several hundred soldiers, each with a rifle slung over his shoulder, waiting to board them. I couldn't even hear the boots striking against the pavement, so easily did the soldiers amble along, one by one, once the signal to move out had been given. There was a high wall running the length of the far side of the street and on the near side was a block-long stone structure with a corrugated iron roof that must have been a garage or a warehouse, an L-shaped building that made the street a hidden cul-de-sac. There were six buses, and I stood there watching until the last soldier climbed aboard with his weapon and the buses began to roll away, heading out more than likely for the West Bank, replacement troops to put down the riots, armed Jews, what Pipik maintains makes a second Holocaust imminent, what Pipik claims he can render unnecessary through the benevolent agency of A-S.A. . . .

I decided then—it was a little after two—to leave Jerusalem. If I got to it immediately, I'd have time enough to compose another three or four questions to round out the interview. Aharon's house was in a development village some twenty minutes due west of Jerusalem, just off the road to the airport. At dawn I'd have the taxi stop there briefly so that I could give to Aharon those last questions and then proceed on to the airport and London.

Why didn't you just *pretend* to be his partner? Your error was derision. You'll pay plenty for breaking those glasses.

By two that night I was so done in by the unsurpassable confusion of the day before, so unable any longer to assess the truth of anything amid all this turmoil, that these three sentences, softly uttered aloud by me while beginning to prepare for my dawn departure, I took to be spoken by Pipik from the other side of the door. *The lunatic is back! He's armed!* And it was no less astonishing—and in its way *more* frightening—when, in the next instant, I understood that it was my own voice that I had heard and mistaken for his, that it was only me talking to myself as might any lonely traveler who'd found himself wide awake, far from home, in a strange hotel in the middle of the night.

I was suddenly in a terrible state. All that I had struggled to retrieve since the breakdown of the previous summer rapidly began to give way before an onslaught of overpowering dread. I was all at once terrified that I did not have the strength to hold myself together very much longer and that I would be carried off into some new nightmare of disintegration unless I could forcibly stop this unraveling with my few remaining ounces of self-control.

What I did was to move the bureau in front of the door, not so much anticipating that he would return and dare to use again the key to my room that was still in his pocket, but for fear that I might find myself *volunteering* to open the door to allow him to make some last proposal for a rapprochement. Watching out for my bad back, I slowly dragged the bureau away from where it was positioned opposite the bed and, turning back the oriental rug in the center of the room, edged it as noiselessly as I could along the tiles until it obstructed access to the door. Now I couldn't possibly let him have at me, however entertaining, intimidating, or heartfelt his petition to reenter. Using the bureau to block the door was the second-best precaution I could think to take against my own stupidity; the first was flight, getting myself a thousand miles away from him and my demonstrable incapacity to contend on my own with the mesmeric craziness of this provocation. But for now, I thought, sit it out, barricaded in. Until the light came up and the hotel reawakened to life and I could leave the room accompanied by a bellhop and make my departure in a taxi drawn right up in front of the entrance, I would sit it out right there.

For the next two hours I remained at the desk in front of the window, fully aware of just how visible I was to anyone lurking in the street below. I did not bother to pull the curtains, since a piece of fabric is no protection against a well-aimed rifle shot. I could have pushed the desk away from the window and along the adjacent wall, but sanity balked here and simply would not permit a further rearrangement of the furniture. I could have sat up on the bed and composed from there my remaining questions for Aharon, but instead, to safeguard what little equilibrium I still possessed, I chose to sit as I have been sitting all my life, in a chair, at a desk, under a lamp, substantiating my peculiar existence in the most consolidating way I know, taming temporarily with a string of words the unruly tyranny of my incoherence.

In *To the Land of the Cattails* [I wrote], a Jewish woman and her grown son, the offspring of a Gentile father, are journeying back to the remote Ruthenian countryside where she was born. It's the summer of 1938. The closer they get to her home the more menacing is the threat of Gentile violence. The mother says to her son, "They are many, and we are few." Then you write: "The word *goy* rose up from within her. She smiled as if hearing a distant memory. Her father would sometimes, though only occasionally, use that word to indicate hopeless obtuseness."

The Gentile with whom the Jews of your books seem to share their world is usually the embodiment of hopeless obtuseness and of menacing, primitive social behavior—the *goy* as drunkard, wife beater, as the coarse, brutal semisavage who is "not in control of himself." Though obviously there's more to be said about the non-Jewish world in those provinces where your books are set—and also about the capacity of Jews, in their own world, to be obtuse and primitive, too—even a non-Jewish European would have to recognize that the power of this image over the Jewish imagination is rooted in real experience. Alternatively the *goy* is pictured as an "earthy soul . . . overflowing with health." *Enviable* health. As the mother in *Cattails* says of her half-Gentile son, "He's not nervous like me. Other, quiet blood flows in his veins."

I'd say that it's impossible to know anything really about the Jewish imagination without investigating the place that the *goy* has occupied in the folk mythology that's been exploited in America by Jewish comedians like Lenny Bruce and Jackie Mason and, at quite another level, by Jewish novelists. American fiction's most single-minded portrait of the *goy* is in *The Assistant* by Bernard Malamud. The *goy* is Frank Alpine, the down-and-out thief who robs the failing grocery store of the Jew, Bober, later attempts to rape Bober's studious daughter, and eventually, in a conversion to Bober's brand of suffering Judaism, symbolically renounces *goyish* savagery. The New York Jewish hero of Saul Bellow's second novel, *The Victim*, is plagued by an alcoholic Gentile misfit named Allbee, who is no less of a bum and a drifter than Alpine, even if his assault on Leventhal's hard-won composure is intellectually more urbane. The most imposing Gentile in all of Bellow's work, however, is Henderson—the self-exploring rain king who, to restore his psychic health, takes his blunted instincts off to Africa. For Bellow no less than for Appelfeld, the truly "earthy soul" is not the

Jew, nor is the search to retrieve primitive energies portrayed as the quest of a Jew. For Bellow no less than for Appelfeld, and, astonishingly, for Mailer no less than for Appelfeld—we all know that in Mailer when a man is a sadistic sexual aggressor his name is Sergius O'Shaugnessy, when he is a wife killer his name is Stephen Rojack, and when he is a menacing murderer he isn't Lepke Buchalter or Gurrah Shapiro, he's Gary Gilmore.

Here, succumbing finally to my anxiety, I turned off the desk lamp and sat in the dark. And soon I could see into the street below. And someone *was* there! A figure, a man, running across the dimly lit pavement not twenty-five feet from my window. He ran crouching over but I recognized him anyway.

I stood at the desk. "Pipik!" I shouted, flinging open the window. "Moishe Pipik, you son of a bitch!"

He turned to look toward the open window and I saw that in either hand he held a large rock. He raised the rocks over his head and shouted back at me. He was masked. He was shouting in Arabic. Then he ran on. Then a second figure was running by, then a third, then a fourth, each of them carrying a rock in either hand and all their faces hidden by ski masks. Their source of supply was a pyramid-shaped rock pile, a rock pile that resembled a memorial cairn and that stood just inside an alleyway across from the hotel. The four ran up and down the street with their rocks until the cairn was gone. Then the street was empty again and I shut the window and went back to work.

In *The Immortal Bartfuss,* your newly translated novel, Bartfuss asks irreverently of his dying mistress's ex-husband, "What have we Holocaust survivors done? Has our great experience changed us at all?" This is the question with which the novel somehow or other engages itself on virtually every page. We sense in Bartfuss's lonely longing and regret, in his baffled effort to overcome his own remoteness, in his avidity for human contact, in his mute wanderings along the Israeli coast and his enigmatic encounters in dirty cafés, the agony that life can become in the wake of a great disaster. Of the Jewish survivors who wind up smuggling and black-marketeering in Italy directly after the war, you write, "No one knew what to do with the lives that had been saved."

My last question, growing out of your preoccupation in *The Immortal Bartfuss,* is, perhaps, extremely comprehensive, but think about it, please, and reply as you choose. From what you observed as a homeless youngster wandering in Europe after the war, and from what you've learned during four decades in Israel, do you discern distinguishing patterns in the experience of those whose lives were saved? What *have* the Holocaust survivors done and in what ways were they ineluctably changed?

7

Her
Story

He'd taken nothing. Not even a sock was missing from the bureau drawer where I'd laid my loose clothing, and, in searching for the check that meant everything to him, he hadn't disarranged a thing. He'd borrowed *Tzili* to read while waiting on the bed for my return but that seemed to have been the only possession of mine—my identity aside—that he had dared to touch. I began to doubt, while I packed my bag to go, if he actually had searched the room and, disturbingly for a moment, even to wonder if he had ever been here. But if he hadn't come to claim the check as his, why had he risked my wrath (and perhaps worse) by breaking in?

I had my jacket on and my bag packed. I was only waiting for dawn. I had but one goal and that was to disappear. The rest I'd puzzle out or not when I'd successfully accomplished an escape. And don't write about it afterward, I told myself. Even the gullible now have contempt for the idea of objectivity; the latest thing they've swallowed whole is that it's impossible to report anything faithfully other than one's own temperature; everything is allegory—so what possible chance would I have to persuade anyone of a reality like this one? Ask Aharon, when you say goodbye to him, please to be silent and forget it. Even in London, when Claire returns and asks what happened, tell her all is well. "Nothing happened, he never turned up." Otherwise you can explain these two days for the rest of your life and no one will ever believe your version to be anything other than your version.

Folded in thirds in the inside pocket of my jacket were the fresh sheets of hotel stationery onto which I'd copied, in legible block letters, my remaining questions for Aharon. In my bag I had all our other questions and answers and all the tapes. I had managed despite everything to do the job, maybe not as I'd looked forward to doing it back in New York . . . I remembered Apter suddenly. Could I catch him at his rooming house on my way out of Jerusalem? Or would I find Pipik already waiting there, Pipik pretending to poor Apter that he's me!

The lights were off in my room. I'd been sitting in the dark for half an hour, waiting at the little desk by the large window with my fully packed bag up against my leg and watching the masked men who had resumed their rock conveying directly below, as though for my singular edification, as though daring me to pick up the phone to notify the army or the police. These are rocks, I thought, to split open the heads of Jews, but I also thought, I belong elsewhere, this struggle is over territory that is not mine . . . I counted the number of rocks they were moving. When I reached a hundred I could stand it no longer, and I called the desk and asked to be put through to the police. I was told that the line was engaged. "It's an emergency," I replied. "Is something wrong? Are you ill, sir?" "Please, I want to report something to the police." "As soon as I get a free line, sir. The police are very busy tonight. You lost something, Mr. Roth?"

A woman spoke from the other side of the door just as I was hanging up. "Let me in," she whispered, "it's Jinx Possesski. Something terrible is happening."

I pretended not to be there, but she began rapping lightly on the door—she must have overheard me on the phone.

"He's going to kidnap Demjanjuk's son."

But I had only my one objective and didn't bother to answer her. *You can't make a mistake doing nothing.*

"They're plotting right this minute to kidnap Demjanjuk's son!"

Outside the door Pipik's Possesski, below the window the Arabs in ski masks running rocks—I closed my eyes to compose in my head a last question to leave with Aharon before I flew off. *Living in this society, you are bombarded by news and political disputation. Yet, as a novelist, you have, by and large, pushed aside the Israeli daily turbulence—*

"Mr. Roth, they intend to do it!"

—in order to contemplate markedly different Jewish predicaments. What does this turbulence mean to a novelist like yourself? How does being a citizen of—

Jinx was softly sobbing now. "He wears this. Walesa gave it to him. Mr. Roth, you've got to help . . ."

—of this self-revealing, self-asserting, self-challenging, self-legendizing society affect your writing life? Does this news-producing reality ever tempt your imagination?

"This will be the end of him."

Everything dictated silence and self-control but I couldn't restrain myself and spoke my mind. "Good!"

"It'll destroy everything he's done."

"Perfect!"

"You must take *some* responsibility."

"None!"

Meanwhile I had got down on my hands and knees and was trying to reach under the bureau to see what she had pushed beneath the door. I was able, finally, to fish it out with my shoe.

A jagged piece of fabric about the size of my hand and as weightless as a swatch of gauze—a cloth Star of David, something I'd only seen before in those photographs of pedestrians on the streets of occupied Europe, Jews tagged as Jews with a bit of yellow material. This surprise shouldn't have exasperated me more than anything else issuing from Pipik's excesses but it did, it exasperated me violently. Stop. Breathe. Think. His pathology is his, not yours. Treat it with realistic humor—and *go!* But instead I gave way to my feelings. *Hold off, hold off,* but I couldn't—there seemed no way for me to treat the appearance of this tragic memento as just a harmless amusement. There was absolutely nothing he wouldn't turn into a farce. A blasphemer even of *this.* I cannot endure him.

"Who is this madman! Tell me who this madman is!"

"I will! Let me in!"

"Everything! The truth!"

"All I know! I will!"

"You're alone?".

"All alone. I am. I swear to you I am."

"Wait."

Stop. Breathe. Think. But I did instead what I'd decided not to do until it was time to make a safe exit. I edged the big bureau away from the door just enough to open it, and then I unlocked the door and let squeeze into the room the coconspirator he had sent to entice me, dressed for those pickup bars where the oncology nurses used to go to irrigate themselves of all that death and dying back when Jinx Possesski was still a full-fledged, unreclaimed hater of Jews. Big dark glasses covered half her face, and the black dress she was wearing couldn't have made her look any shapelier. She couldn't have looked any shapelier without it. It was a great cheap dress. Lots of lipstick, the unkempt pale pile of Polish cornsilk, and enough of her protruding for me to conclude not only that she was up to no good but that it may not have been my terrible temper alone that had enjoined me from stopping and breathing and thinking, that I had let Jinx past my barricade because I was up to no good myself and had been for some time now. It occurred to me, friends, when she wriggled through the door and then turned the key to lock us in—and him out?—that I should never have left the front stoop in Newark. I never longed so passionately, not for her, not that quite yet, but for my life before impersonation and imitation and twofoldedness set in, life before self-mockery and self-idealization (and the idealization of the mockery; and the mockery of the idealization; and the idealization of the idealization; and the mockery of the mockery), before the alternating exaltations of hyperobjectivity and hypersubjectivity (and the hyper-objectivity about the hypersubjectivity; and the hypersubjectivity about the hyperobjectivity), back when what was outside was outside and what was inside was inside, when everything still divided cleanly and nothing happened that couldn't be explained. I left the front stoop on Leslie Street, ate of the fruit of the tree of fiction, and nothing, neither reality nor myself, had been the same since.

I didn't want this temptress, I wanted to be ten; despite a lifelong determinedly antinostalgic stance, I wanted to be ten and back in the neighborhood when life was not yet a blind passage out but still like baseball, where you came home, and when the voluptuous earthliness of women other than my mamma was nothing I yet wished to gorge myself on.

"Mr. Roth, he's waiting to hear from Meir Kahane. They're going to do it. Somebody has to stop them!"

"Why did you bring this?" I said, angrily thrusting the yellow star in her face.

"I told you. Walesa gave it to him. In Gdansk. Philip wept. Now he wears it under his shirt."

"The truth! The truth! Why at three in the morning do you come with this star and this story? How did you get this far anyway? How did you pass the desk downstairs? How do you get across Jerusalem at this hour, with all this danger and dressed like fucking Jezebel? This is a city seething with hatred, the violence will be terrible, it's dreadful already, and *look* at how he sent you here! Look at how he's fitted you out in this femme fatale Bond movie get-up! The man has got the instincts of a pimp! Forget the crazy Arabs—a crazy pack of pious Jews could have stoned you to death in this dress!"

"But they are going to kidnap Demjanjuk's son and send him back piece by piece until Demjanjuk confesses! They're writing Demjanjuk's confession right now. They say to Philip, 'You, writer—do it good!' Toe by toe, finger by finger, eyeball by eyeball, until his father speaks the truth, they are going to torture the son. Religious people in skullcaps, and you should hear what they are saying—and Philip sits there writing the confession! Kahane! Philip is *anti*-Kahane, calls him a *savage,* and he's sitting there waiting for a phone call from the savage fanatic he hates most in the world!"

"Answer me please with the truth. Why did he send you here in this dress? With this star? How does a person like him *come about?* The chicanery is *inexhaustible."*

"I ran! I told him, 'I cannot listen anymore. I cannot watch you destroy everything!' I ran away!"

"To me."

"You must give him back the check!"

"I lost the check. I don't have the check. I told him that. Something untoward happened. Certainly the girlfriend of your boyfriend can understand that. The check is gone."

"But your keeping the money is what's making him wild! Why did you accept Mr. Smilesburger's money when you *knew* it wasn't meant for you!"

I pushed the cloth star into her hand. "Take this with you and get out of here."

"But Demjanjuk's *son!"*

"Miss, I was not born to Bess and Herman Roth in Newark's Beth Israel Hospital to protect this man Demjanjuk's son."

"Then protect *Philip!"*

"That is what I'm doing."

"But it's to prove himself to you that *he's* doing what *he's* doing. He's out of his mind for your admiration. You are the hero, like it or not!"

"Please, with a dick like his he doesn't need me for a hero. He was nice enough to come here to show it to me. Did you know that? He's not particularly pestered by inhibitions, is he?"

"No," she muttered, "oh, no," and here she caved in and dropped to the edge of the bed in tears.

"Nope," I said, "uh-uh, you two aren't taking turns—*get up and get out."*

But she was crying so pathetically that all I could do was to return to the easy chair by the window and sit there until she had exhausted herself on my pillow. That she was clutching that cloth star while she wept disgusted and infuriated me.

Down in the street the masked Arabs were gone. I didn't seem to have been born to stop them either.

When I couldn't any longer stand the sight of her with the star, I came over to the bed and pulled it out of her hands, and then I unzipped my suitcase and shoved it in with my things. I still have it. I am looking at it while I write.

"It's an implant," she said.

"What is? What are you saying?"

"It isn't 'his.' It's a plastic implant."

"Oh? Tell me more."

"Everything's been cut out of him. He couldn't stand how it left him. So he had the procedure. Plastic rods are in there. Inside the penis is a penile implant. Why do you laugh? How can you *laugh!* You're laughing at somebody's terrible suffering!"

"I'm not at all—I'm laughing at all the lies. Poland, Walesa, Kahane, even the *cancer's* a lie—Demjanjuk's *son* is a lie. And this prick he's so proud of, come clean, in what Amsterdam doodad shop did you two find *that* nutty joke? It's *Hellzapoppin'* with Possesski and Pipik, it's a gag a minute with you two madcap kids—who *wouldn't* laugh? The prick was great, I have to admit, but I think I'll always love best the Poles at the Warsaw railroad station ecstatically welcoming back their Jews. Diasporism! Diasporism is a plot for a Marx Brothers movie—Groucho selling Jews to Chancellor Kohl! I lived eleven years in London—not in bigoted, backwater, pope-ridden Poland but in civilized, secularized, worldly-wise England. When the first hundred thousand Jews come rolling into Waterloo Station with all their belongings in tow, I really want to be there to see it. Invite me, won't you? When the first hundred thousand Diasporist evacuees voluntarily surrender their criminal Zionist homeland to the suffering Palestinians and disembark on England's green and pleasant land, I want to see with my very own eyes the welcoming committee of English goyim waiting on the platform with their champagne. 'They're here! More Jews! Jolly good!' No, *fewer* Jews is my sense of how Europe prefers things, *as few of them as possible.* Diasporism, my dear, seriously misses the *point* about the *depths* of the antipathy. But then, that shouldn't come as news to a charter member of A-S.A.

That poor old Smilesburger was nearly suckered by Diasporism's founding father out of a million bucks—well, I don't think this Smilesburger is all there either."

"What Mr. Smilesburger does with his money," she shot back, her face rapidly melting down into the defeated grimace of a thwarted child, *"is up to Mr. Smilesburger!"*

"Then tell Mr. Smilesburger to stop the check, why don't you? Go play the interceding woman with him. It's not going to work here, so go try it with him. Tell him he gave the check to the wrong Philip Roth."

"I'm crashing," she moaned, "damn it, I'm *crashing,"* and she grabbed the phone from the tin-topped table squeezed in by the wall at the inside corner of the bed and asked the clerk at the hotel switchboard for the King David Hotel. All roads lead back to him. I decided too late to wrestle the phone away from her. Among all the other things contributing to the disorganization of my thinking was the immediacy of her sensuality on that bed.

"It's me," she said when the connection was made. ". . . With him. . . . Yes I am. . . . His room! . . . No! . . . No! Not with *them!* . . . I can't go on, Phil. I'm on the damn brink. Kahane is crazy, you said so, not me. . . . *No!* . . . I am crashing, Philip, I am going to crash!" Here she thrust the phone at me. "You stop him! You must!"

Because for some reason the phone was wired into the wall furthest from the door, the cord had to be pulled across the width of the bed and I had to lean directly across her to speak into the mouthpiece. Maybe that was *why* I spoke into the mouthpiece. There could be no other reason. To anyone watching us through that one big window, it would have been she and I who looked like coconspirators now. Propinquity and piquancy seemed as if one word derived from the single explosive root syllable *Jinx.*

"On to yet another hilarious idea, I hear," said I into the telephone.

The reply was calm, amused, his voice my own restrained mild voice! "Of yours," he said.

"Repeat that."

"Your idea," he said, and I hung up.

But no sooner was I off the phone than it was ringing again.

"Let it be," I told her.

"Okay, that's it," she said, "that's gotta be it."

"Right. Just let it ring."

The return trip to the chair beside the desk was one long temptation-ridden journey, rich with pleas to the baser yearnings for caution and common sense, a great deal of convulsive conflict compressed into a very short space, a kind of synthesis of my whole adult life. Seating myself as far as I could get in that room from this rash, precipitate complicity of ours, I said, "Leaving aside for the moment who *you* are, who is this antic fellow who goes around as me?" I signaled with a finger that she was not to touch the ringing phone. "Concentrate on my question. Answer me. Who is he?"

"My patient. I told you that."

"Another lie."

"*Everything* can't be a lie. Stop *saying* that. It doesn't help anyone. You protect yourself from the truth by calling everything you won't believe a lie. Everything that's too much for you, you say, 'That's a lie.' But that's denial, Mr. Roth, of what living *is!* These lies of yours are my damn life! *The phone is no lie!*" And she lifted the phone and cried into the mouthpiece, "I won't! It's over! I'm not coming back!" But what she heard through the receiver sucked the angry blood engorging her face all the way back down to her feet as though she'd been upended and "hourglass" were no mere metaphor with which to describe her shape. Very meekly she offered me the phone.

"The police," she said, horrified and uttering "police" as she must once have heard patients freshly apprised of their chances repeat the oncologist's "terminal." "Don't," she begged me, "he won't survive it!"

The Jerusalem police were responding to my call. Because the rock runners were gone I had now been put through to them—or maybe all phone lines *had* indeed been tied up earlier, unlikely as that still seemed to me. I described to the police what I'd seen from my window. They asked me to describe what was going on there now. I told them that the street was empty. They asked my name and I gave it to them. I gave them my U.S. passport number. I did not go on to tell them that someone bearing a duplicate passport, a counterfeit of mine, was at that very moment conspiring at the King David Hotel to kidnap and torture John Demjanjuk's son. Let him try it, I thought. If she's not lying, if he's resolved, like his antihero Jonathan Pollard, to be a Jewish savior regardless of the cost—or even if the motive is merely personal, if he's just determined to take a leading role in my life like the boy who shot Reagan to wow Jodie Foster—let the fantasies evolve grandiosely without my interference, this time let him overstep something more than just my boundaries and collide head-on with the Jerusalem police. I could not myself arrange a more satisfying conclusion to this stupid drama of no importance. Two minutes into it they'll nab him in his bid for historical significance and that will be the end of Moishe Pipik.

She had closed her eyes and crossed her arms and laid them protectively over her breasts while I hung just inches above her talking to the police. And she remained like that, absolutely mummified, while I traversed the room and sat back down in my chair once again, thinking, as I looked at the bed, that she could have been waiting to be removed by the undertaker. And that made me think of my first wife, who, some twenty years earlier, at just about Jinx's age, had been killed in a car crash in New York. We had embarked on a disastrous three-year marriage after she had falsified the results of a pregnancy test in the aftermath of our lurid love affair and then threatened suicide if I didn't marry her. Six years after my leaving the marriage against her will, I'd still been unable to win her consent to a divorce, and when she was abruptly killed in 1968, I wandered around Central Park, the site of her fatal accident, reciting to myself a ferociously apt little couplet by John Dryden, the one that goes, "Here lies my wife: here let her lie!/Now she's at rest; and so am I."

Jinx was taller than her by half a foot and substantial physically in a rather more riveting way, but seeing her laid out in repose, as though for burial, I was struck by a racial resemblance to the square-headed northern good looks of my long-dead enemy. What if it was she risen from the dead to take her revenge . . . if she was the master-

mind who'd trained and disguised him, taught him my mannerisms
and how I speak ... plotted out the intricacies of the identity theft
with the same demoniacal resolve with which she'd dished up to the
Second Avenue pharmacist that false urine specimen.... These were
the thoughts lapping at the semiconscious brain of a fitfully dozing
man struggling still to remain alert. The woman in the black dress
stretched across the bed was no more the ghost of my first wife's
corpse than Pipik was the ghost of me, yet there was now a dreamlike
distortion muddling my mind against which I was only intermittently
able to mobilize my rational defenses. I felt drugged by too many
incomprehensible events and, after twenty-four hours of going without sleep, I was shadowboxing none too deftly with an inchoate,
dimming consciousness.

"Wanda Jane 'Jinx' Possesski—open your eyes, Wanda Jane, and
tell me the truth. It is time."

"You're going?"

"Open your eyes."

"Put me in your bag and take me with you," she moaned. "Get me
out of here."

"Who are you?"

"Oh, you know," she said wearily, her eyes still closed, "the fucked
up shiksa. Nothing new."

I waited to hear more. She wasn't laughing when she said, once
again, "Take me with you, Philip Roth."

It *is* my first wife. I must be saved and you must save me. I am
drowning and you did it. I am the fucked-up shiksa. Take me with
you.

We slept this time round for more than just a few minutes, she in
the bed, I in the chair, arguing as of old with the resurrected wife.
"Can't you even return from *death* without screaming about the morality of your position versus the immorality of mine? Is alimony all
you think about even there? What is the source of the eternal claim
on my income? On what possible grounds did you conclude that
somebody owed you his life?"

Then I was put ashore again in the tangible world where she

wasn't, back with my flesh and Wanda Jane's in the fairy tale of material existence.

"Wake up."

"Oh, yes . . . I'm here."

"Fucked-up how?"

"How else? Family." She opened her eyes. "Low-class. Beer-drinking. Fighting. Stupid people." Dreamily she said, "I didn't like them."

Neither did she. Hated them. I was the last best chance. Take me with you, I'm pregnant, you must.

"Raised Catholic," I said.

She positioned herself up on her elbows and melodramatically blinked. "My God," she asked, "which one are you?"

"The only one."

"Wanna put your million on it?"

"I want to know who you are. I want to know finally what is going on—I want the truth!"

"Father Polish," she said lightly, ticking off the facts, "mother Irish, Irish grandmother a real doozy, Catholic schools—church until I was probably twelve years old."

"Then?"

She smiled at the earnest "Then," an intimate smile that was no more, really, than a slow curling at the corner of the mouth, something that could only be measured in millimeters but that was, in my book, the very epitome of sexual magic.

I ignored it, if you can describe failing still to get up and leave as ignoring anything.

" 'Then?' Then I learned how to roll a joint," she said. "I ran away from home to California. I got involved with drugs and all that hippie stuff. Fourteen. Hitchhiked. It wasn't uncommon."

"And then?"

" 'And then?' Well, out there I remember going through a Hare Krishna event in San Francisco. I liked that a lot. It was very passionate. People were dancing. People were very taken over by the emotion of it. I didn't get involved in that. I got involved with the Jesus people. Just before that I had been going back to Mass. I guess I was interested in getting involved in some sort of religion. What exactly are you trying to figure out again?"

"What do you think I'm trying to figure out? *Him.*"

"Gee, and I thought you were interested in little me."

"The Jesus people. You got involved."

"Well . . ."

"Go ahead."

"Well, there was a pastor, a very passionate little guy. . . . There was always a passionate guy. . . . I looked like a waif, I guess. I was dressed like a hippie. I guess I was wearing a long skirt, I had long hair. Little peasant outfit. You've seen 'em. Well, this guy gave an altar call at the end of the service, the first one I ever went to, and he asked whoever wanted to accept Jesus into his heart to stand up. The spiel is if you want peace, if you want happiness, accept Jesus into your heart as your personal savior. I was sitting in the front row with my girlfriend. I stood up. Halfway through standing, I realized that I was the only one standing. He came down from the altar and prayed over me that I would receive the baptism of the Holy Spirit. Looking back on it, I think I just hyperventilated. But I had some sort of rush, some sort of profound feeling. And I did begin to speak in some sort of language. I'm sure it was made up. It's supposed to be communication with God. Without bothering with language. Your eyes are closed. I did feel a tingling. Sort of detached from what was going on around me. In my own world. Being able to forget who I was and what I was doing. And just do this. It went on for a couple of minutes. He put his hand on my head and I was thrilled. I think I was just vulnerable to anything."

"Why?"

"Usual reasons. Everybody's reason. Because of who my parents were. I got very little attention at home. None. So walking into a place where suddenly I'm a star, everybody loves me and wants me, how could I resist? I was a Christian for twelve years. Age of fifteen to the age of twenty-seven. One of those hippies who found the Lord. It became my life. I hadn't been going to school. I had dropped out of school, and actually I went back to grammar school, I finished grammar school at sixteen in San Francisco. I had these breasts even back then and there I was with them, sitting at a grammar school desk next to all those little kids."

"Your cross," I said, "carried before instead of aft."

"Sometimes it sure seems that way. The doctors were always rubbing up against me when we worked together. Anyway, I'd failed all my life in school and suddenly, tits and all, I started doing okay. And I read the Bible. I liked all that death-to-self stuff. I felt like shit already and it sort of confirmed my feeling of shit. I'm worthless, I'm nothing. God is Everything. It can be very passionate. Just imagine that somebody loved you enough to die for you. That's big-time love."

"You took it personally."

"Oh, absolutely. That's me all over. Yes, yes. I loved to pray. I would be very passionate and I would pray and I would love God and I would be ecstatic. I remember training myself not to look at anything when I was walking on the street. I would only look straight ahead. I didn't want to be distracted from contemplating God. But that can't last. It's too hard. That would sort of dissipate—then I'd be overcome with guilt."

Where had she disposed of all the "like"s and the "okay"s and the "you know"s? Where was the tarty, tough-talking nurse from the day before? Her tones were as soft now as those of a well-behaved ten-year-old child, the pitter-patter, innocent treble of a sweet and intelligent little ten-year-old who has just discovered the pleasures of being informative. She might have weighed seventy pounds, a freshly eloquent prepubescent, home helping her mother bake a cake, so unjaded was the voice with which she'd warmed to all this attention. She might have been chattering away while helping her father wash the car on a Sunday afternoon. I supposed I was hearing the voice of the abundantly breasted hippie at the grammar school desk who'd found Jesus.

"Why guilt?" I asked her.

"Because I wasn't being as in love with God as He deserved. My guilt was that I was interested in things of this world. Especially as I got older."

I saw the two of us drying the dishes in Youngstown, Ohio. Was she my daughter or my wife? This was now the nonsensical background to the ambiguous foreground. My mind, at this stage, was an uncontrollable thing, but then it was a marvel to me that I could continue to remain awake and that she and I—and he—could still be at it at four a.m. the next day—a marvel too that, listening to this lengthy story that couldn't make a scrap of difference, I was only plunging further under their spell.

"Which things?" I asked her. "Which things of this world?"

"My appearance. Trivial things. My friends. Entertainment. Vanity. Myself. I was not supposed to be interested in myself. That's how I decided to go into nursing. I didn't want to go into nursing, but nursing was selfless, something I could do for other people and forget about what I looked like. I could serve Christ through being a nurse. This way I would still be in good with God. I moved back to the Midwest and I joined a new church in Chicago. A New Testament church. All of us attempting to follow Christ's recommendations for living on earth. Love one another and be involved in one another's lives. Take care of your brothers and sisters. It was total bullshit. None of it actually happened, it was just a lot of talk. Some people tried. But they never succeeded."

"So what brought the Christianity to an end?"

"Well, I was working in a hospital and I started getting more involved with people I was working with. I loved people to take an interest in me because I was a waif. But twenty-five! I was getting old to be a waif. And then a guy I got involved with, a guy named Walter Sweeney, he died. He was thirty-four years old. Very young. Very passionate. Always that. And he decided that God wanted him to go on a fast. Suffering is very big, you see, a certain brand of Christian believes that God allows us to suffer to make us better servants of Him. Getting rid of the dross they call it. Well, Walter Sweeney got rid of the dross, all right. Went on a fast to purify himself. So that he could be closer to God. And he died. I found him in his apartment on his knees. And that always stayed with me, and that became the whole experience for me. Dying on his knees. Fuck that."

"You slept with Walter Sweeney."

"Yep. First one. I was chaste from about fifteen to twenty-five. I wasn't a virgin at fifteen, but from fifteen to twenty-five, I didn't even have a date. I got involved with Sweeney, then he died, and I got involved with another guy, a married man in the church. That had a lot to do with it too. Especially because his wife was a good friend of mine. I couldn't live with that. I couldn't face God anymore, so I stopped praying. It wasn't long, maybe a couple of months, but long enough to lose fifteen pounds. I tortured myself about it. I liked the idea of sex. I never could figure out the prohibition on sex. I still can't figure it out. What's the big deal? Who cares? It was senseless to me. I went to a therapist. Because I was suicidal. But he was no good. Christian Interpersonal Therapy Workshop. Guy named Rodney."

"What's Christian Interpersonal Therapy?"

"Oh, it's just Rodney talking to people. More bullshit. But then I met a guy who wasn't a Christian and I got involved with him. And it was gradual. I don't know how to make it any more clear. I grew out of it. In every sense."

"So it's sex that got you out of the church. Men."

"It's probably what got me in and, yeah, probably it helped to get me out."

"You left the world of men and then you came back to the world of men. That's the story you tell, anyway."

"Well, that was certainly part of the world I left. I also left the world of my dismal family and the world of living chaotically. And then when I was strong enough, I was able to do things on my own. I went to nursing school. That was a big move for me away from Christianity. Part of what Christianity was about for me was about not thinking. About being able to go to the elders and ask them what I should do. And going to God. In my twenties I realized that God doesn't answer. And that the elders are no smarter than I am. That I could think for myself. Still, Christianity saved me from a lot of craziness. It got me back to school, stopped me from doing drugs, from being promiscuous. Who knows where I could have ended up?"

"Here," I said. "Here is where you could have ended up—where you ended up. With him. Living chaotically with him."

You are not here to help her understand herself. Go no further. You are not the Jewish Interpersonal Therapy Workshop. It only looks that way tonight. One patient shows up, spends his hour telling you his favorite lies, then he exits, after exposing himself, and another materializes, takes possession of the pillow, and begins telling *her* favorite lies. The storification of everyday life, the poetry you hear on the Phil Donahue show, stuff *she* probably hears on the Donahue show, and I sit here as if I hadn't heard the fucked-up-shiksa story from the Scheherazade of fucked-up shiksas; as if I hadn't got myself morbidly enfolded in its pathos over thirty years ago, I sit and I listen as though to do so is my fate. In the face of a story, any story, I sit captivated. Either I am listening to them or I am telling them. Everything originates there.

"Christianity saved me from a lot of craziness," she said, "but not from anti-Semitism. I think I really got into hating Jews when I was a Christian. Before, it was just my family's stupid thing. Know why I started hating Jews? Because they didn't have to put up with any of this Christian nonsense. Death to self, you have to kill yourself, suffering makes you a better servant of Him—and they *laughed* at all our suffering. Only allow God to live through you so that you become nothing more than a vessel. So I became nothing more than a vessel while the Jews became doctors and lawyers and rich. They laughed at our suffering, they laughed at *His* suffering. Look, don't get me wrong, I loved being nothing. I mean I loved it and I hated it. I could be what I believed I was, a piece of shit, and get *praised* for it. I wore little plaid skirts, wore my hair in a ponytail, didn't fuck, and meanwhile the Jews were all smart, they were middle class, they were fucking, they were educated, they were down in the Caribbean at Christmastime, and I hated them. That started when I was a Christian, and it just kept growing at the hospital. Now, from A-S.A., I understand why else I hated them. Their cohesiveness, I hated that. Their superiority, what the Gentiles call greed, I hated that. Their paranoia and their defensiveness, always being strategic and careful, always clever—the Jews drove me crazy just by being Jews. Anyway, that was my legacy from Jesus. Until Philip."

"From Jesus to Philip."

"Yeah, looks that way. Done it all over again, haven't I? With him."
She sounded amazed. An amazing experience and it was hers.

And mine? From Jesus to Philip—to Philip. From Jesus to Walter
Sweeney to Rodney to Philip to Philip. I am the next apocalyptic
solution.

"And it's only just dawning on you here," I asked, "that he might
constitute a bit of a relapse?"

"I was coasting along, you see, winging along there, being a nurse,
seven years—I told you about all that, I told you about killing somebody—"

"Yes, you did."

"But with him I didn't know how to get *out.* I *never* know how to
get out. One guy is battier than the other and I don't know how to
get out. My trouble is I get very passionate and ecstatic. It takes me a
long time to get disillusioned with the whole unreality of everything.
I guess I was still loving people taking an interest in me the way he
took an interest in my anti-Semitism. Yeah, he *did* take over from
Jesus. He was going to purify me like the church. I need it black and
white, I guess. There's really very little that is black and white, and I
realize that the whole world is nothing but gray areas, but these mad
dogmatic people, they're kind of protection, you know?"

"Who is he? Who is this mad dogmatic person?"

"He's not a crook, he's not a fake, you're all wrong thinking that.
His whole *life* is the Jews."

"Who is he, Wanda Jane?"

"Yeah, Wanda Jane. That's me. Perfect little Wanda Jane, who has
to be invisible and a servant. Jinx the Battler, Jinx the Amazon, Jinx
who thinks for herself, who answers for herself, who makes decisions
for herself and stands up for herself, Jinx who holds the dying in her
arms and watches every kind of suffering a human being can suffer,
Jinx Possesski who's afraid of nothing and is like an Earth Mother to
her dying people, and Wanda Jane who is nothing and is afraid of
everything. Don't call me Wanda Jane. It's not funny. It reminds me
of those people I once lived with in Ohio. You know who I always
hated more than the Jews? Want to know my secret? I hated the

fucking Christians. I ran and ran and ran until all I did was circle back.
Is that what everybody does or just me? Catholicism goes very deep.
And the craziness and the stupidity goes very deep. God! Jesus! Judaism makes my third great religion and I'm still not even thirty-five. I
got a ways to go yet with God. I ought to sashay over tomorrow to
the Muhammadans and sign on with them. They sound like they got
it all together. Great on women. The *Bible*. I didn't *read* the Bible—I
would *open* the Bible and *point*, and whatever phrase I was pointing
at would give me an answer. An answer! It was *games*. The whole
thing is lunatic games. Yet I freed myself. I did it. I got better. I got
born again as an atheist. Hallelujah. So life isn't perfect and I was an
anti-Semite. If that was the worst that I wound up, given where I
began, that was a *victory*, for God's sake. Who doesn't have something
they hate? Who was I harming? A nurse who shot off her mouth about
Jews. So what. Live with it. But, no, still couldn't bear being their
offspring, still couldn't stand anything if it came from Ohio, and this
is how I got involved with Philip and A-S.A. I've just spent a year with
a lunatic Jew. *And didn't know it.* Wanda Jane didn't know it until he
got on the phone one hour ago and put in a call to Meir Kahane, to
the absolute king of religious nuts, to the Jewish Avenger himself. I'm
sitting in Jerusalem, in a hotel room, with three crazy bastards in
skullcaps screaming all at once for Philip to write down Demjanjuk's
confession, screaming where they are going to take Demjanjuk's son
and how they are going to cut him up into little pieces and mail him
back to his dad, and *still* I don't understand. Not until he puts in that
call to Kahane's number does it dawn on me that I am living an anti-
Semite's nightmare. Everything I learned at A-S.A., right down the
tube. A roomful of screaming Jews plotting to murder a Gentile child
—my Polish grandfather who drove the tractor used to tell me that
that's what they did all the *time* back in Poland! Maybe you intellec-
tuals can turn your noses up at this stuff and think that it's all beneath
you, but all this crazy stuff you think is trashy lies is just more life to
me. Crazy stuff's what most people I've known live with every *day*.
It's Walter Sweeney all over again. Dying on his knees—and I found
him there. Imagine what *that* was like. You know what my Philip said

when I told him about finding Walter Sweeney praying on his knees and dead of starvation? 'Christianity,' he said, *'goyische nachis,'* and he spat. I just go from one to the next. Rodney. Want to know what it was, Rodney's Christian Interpersonal Therapy? A guy who hadn't even graduated high school, and Wanda Jane goes to *him* for therapy. Well, I got therapy, all right. Yeah, you guessed it. Don't talk to me about that penile implant. Don't make me talk about *that.*"

When she said "implant," I thought of the way an explorer, concluding his epochal voyage, claims all the land he sees for the crown by implanting the royal flag—before they send him back in chains and he is beheaded for treason. "You might as well tell me everything," I said.

"But you think everything is *lies* when it's true, so terribly, terribly, terribly *true.*"

"Tell me about the implant."

"He got it for me."

"That I can believe."

She was crying now. Rolling down her cheeks were plump tears that had all the fullness of her own beautifully upholstered frame, an embattled child's enormous outpouring of pent-up tears, attesting to a tender nature that was simply indisputable now even to me. This raving madman had somehow got himself a wonderful woman, an out-and-out saint with a wonderful heart whose selfless life had gone monstrously wrong.

"He was afraid," she said. "He wept and wept. It was so awful. He was going to lose me to some other man, a man who could still do it. He was going to lose me, he said. I would leave him all alone to die in agony with the cancer—and how could I say no? How can Wanda Jane say no when someone is suffering like that? How can a nurse who has seen all I've seen say no to a penile implant if that is going to give him the strength to fight on? Sometimes I think that I am the only one who follows the teachings of our Lord. That's what I sometimes think when I feel him pushing that thing inside me."

"And who is he? Tell me who he is."

"Another fucked-up Jewish boy. The fucked-up shiksa's fucked-up

Jewish boyfriend, a wild, hysterical animal, that's who he is. That's who I am. That's who we are. Everything's about his mother."

"Not really."

"His mother didn't love him enough."

"But that's out of my book, isn't it?"

"I wouldn't know."

"I wrote a book, a hundred years ago."

"I know *that.* But I don't read. He gave it to me but I didn't read it. I have to hear the words. That was the hardest part of school, the reading. I have a lot of trouble with my *d*'s and *b*'s."

"As in 'double.' "

"I'm dyslexic."

"You've had a lot to overcome, haven't you?"

"You can say that again."

"Tell me about his mother."

"She used to lock him out of the house. On the landing outside their apartment. He was all of five years old. 'You don't live here anymore.' That's what she would tell him. 'You are not our little boy. You belong to somebody else.' "

"Where was this? In what city? Where was the father in all this?"

"Don't know, he doesn't say anything about the father. All he ever says is that he was always locked out by the mother."

"But what had he done?"

"Who knows? Assault. Armed robbery. Murder. Crimes beyond description. I guess the mother knew. He used to set his jaw and wait on the landing for her to open up. But she was as stubborn as he was and wouldn't give in. A little five-year-old boy was not going to be in charge of *her.* A sad story, isn't it? Then it got dark. That's when he folded. He'd start to whimper like a dog and beg for his dinner. She'd say, 'Get dinner from the people you belong to.' Then he'd beg to be forgiven six or seven times more and she would figure he was broken enough and open up the door. Philip's whole childhood is about that door."

"So this is what made the outlaw."

"Is it? I thought it's what made the detective."

"Might be what made both. The angry boy outside the door, overcome by helplessness. Unjust persecution. What a rage must have
boiled up in that five-year-old child. What defiance must have been
born in him out there on that landing. The thing excluded. Cast out.
Banished. The family monster. I am alone and despicable. No, that's
not my book, I don't go anywhere like that far. I believe he got that
from another book. The infant put out by his parents to perish. Ever
hear of *Oedipus Rex?*"

Can I help it if I felt tickled with adoration for this beguiling woman
on my bed when she said to me, gaily, with the Mae West slyness in
her voice of the woman rich with amorous surprises, "Honey, even
us dyslexics know about *Oedipus Rex.*"

"I don't know what to make of you," I said, truthfully.

"It's not easy to know what to make of you, either."

A pause followed, filled with fantasies of our future together. A
long, long pause and a long, long look, from the chair to the bed and
back.

"So. How did he settle on me?" I asked.

"How?" She laughed. "You're joking."

"Yes, how?" I was laughing now too.

"Look in the mirror someday. Who else was he going to settle on,
Michael Jackson? I can't *believe* you two. I see you guys coming and
going. Look, don't think this has been easy for me. It's totally weird. I
think I'm dreaming."

"Well, not totally. It took *some* doing on his part."

"Well, not much." And that's when I got that particular smile again,
that slow curling upward at the corner of the mouth that was to me
the epitome of sexual magic, as I've said. It has to be clear even to a
small child reading this confession that from the moment I'd pushed
back the bureau and let her slip into my room in that dress, I had
been struggling to neutralize her erotic attraction and to eradicate
the carnal thoughts aroused in me by the desperate, disheveled look
of her recumbent on my bed. Don't think it'd been easy for me,
honey, when she'd moaned in a whisper, "Put me in your bag and
take me with you." But while drinking in the roman-fleuve of her

baffled quest for guardianship (among the Protestants, the Catholics, and the Jews), I had maintained as best I could the maximum skepticism. Charm there was, admittedly, but her verbal authority was really not great, and I told myself that, in any circumstance less drastic than this (if, say, I'd sidled up to her at one of those Chicago singles bars when she was a nurse hanging out), after five minutes of listening I would have been hard put not to try my luck with someone who wasn't being endlessly reborn. Yet, all this said, the effect of her smile was to make me tumescent.

I *didn't* know what to make of her. A woman forged by the commonplace at its most cruelly ridiculous smiles up from a hotel bed at a man who has every reason in the world to be nowhere near her, a man to whom she is the mate in no way whatsoever, and the man is underground with Persephone. You are in awe of eros's mythological depths when something like that happens to you. What Jung calls "the uncontrollability of real things," what a registered nurse just calls "life."

"We aren't indistinguishable, you know."

"That word. That's the word. He uses it a hundred times a day. 'We're indistinguishable.' He's looking in the mirror and that's what he says—'We're indistinguishable.' "

"Well, we're not," I informed her, "not by a long shot."

"No? What is it then, you've got a different Life line? I do palmistry. I learned it once, hitchhiking. I read palms instead of books."

And I did next the stupidest thing I'd yet done in Jerusalem and perhaps in my entire life. I got up from the chair by the window and stepped across to the bed and took hold of the hand that she was extending. I placed my hand in hers, in the nurse's hand that had been everywhere, the nurse's tabooless, transgressive hand, and she ran her thumb lightly along my palm and then palpated in turn each of its cushioned corners. For at least a full minute she said only, "Ummm...ummm...," all the while carefully studying my hand. "It's not surprising," she finally told me very, very quietly, as though not to awaken a third person in the bed, "that the Head line is surprisingly long and deep. Your Head line is the strongest line in the hand. It's a Head line dominated by imagination rather than by money or heart or reason or intellect. There's a strong warlike component to your Fate line. Your Fate line sort of rises in the Mount of Mars. You actually have three Fate lines. Which is very unusual. Most people don't have any."

"How many does your boyfriend have?"

"Only one."

And I was thinking, If you want to get killed, if you are determined to die on your knees like Walter Sweeney, then this is the way to get the job done. This palm reader is his treasure. This recovering anti-Semite fingering your Fate line is that madman's prize!

"All of these lines from the Mount of Venus into your Life line indicate how deeply you're ruled by your passions. The deep, deep clear lines on this part of the hand—see?—intersect with the Life line. They actually aren't crossed, which means that rather than passion bringing you misfortune, it doesn't. If they were crossed, I'd say that in you sexual appetite leads to decadence and corruption. But that's not true. Your sexual appetite is quite pure."

"What do you know," I replied, thinking, Do this and he will hunt you down to the ends of the earth and kill you. You should have fled. You didn't need her answers to all your questions. Her answers are as useless to you if they are true as they are if they are false. This is his trap, I thought, just as she looked up into my face with that smile that was *her* Fate line and said, "It's all such complete bullshit but it's sort of fun—you know?" Stop. Breathe. Think. She believes you are in possession of Smilesburger's million and is simply changing sides. Anything could be happening and you'd be the last to know.

"It's sort of the hand of a . . . I mean if I didn't know anything about you, if I were reading the hands of a stranger and didn't know who you were, I would say it's sort of the hand of a . . . of a great leader."

I should have fled. Instead I implanted myself and then I fled. I penetrated her and I ran. Both. Talk about the commonplace at its most ridiculous.

8

The Uncontrollability of Real Things

Here is the Pipik plot so far.

A middle-aged American Jew settles into a suite at Jerusalem's King David Hotel and proposes publicly that Israeli Jews of Ashkenazi descent, who make up the more influential half of the country's population and who constituted the original cadre that settled the state, return to their countries of origin to resurrect the European Jewish life that Hitler all but annihilated between 1939 and 1945. He argues that this post-Zionist political program, which he has called "Diasporism," is the only means by which to avert a "second Holocaust," in which either the three million Jews of Israel will be massacred by their Arab enemies or the enemies will be decimated by Israeli nuclear weapons, a victory that, like a defeat, would destroy the moral foundations of Jewish life for good. He believes that, with assistance from traditional Jewish philanthropic sources, he can raise the money and marshal the political will of influential Jews everywhere to institute and realize this program by the year 2000. He justifies his hopefulness by alluding to the history of Zionism and comparing his supposedly unattainable dream to the Herzlian plan for a Jewish state, which, in its own time, struck Herzl's numerous Jewish critics as contemptibly ludicrous, if not insane. He concedes the troubling persistence of a substantial anti-Semitic European population but proposes to implement a massive recovery program that will rehabilitate those several tens of millions still powerless before the temptations of traditional anti-Semitism and enable them to learn to control their antipathy to their Jewish compatriots once the Jews have been rerooted in Europe. He calls the organization that will implement this program Anti-Semites Anonymous and is accompanied on his proselytizing fund-raising travels by a member of the charter chapter of A-S.A., an American nurse of Polish and Irish Catholic extraction, who identifies herself as a "recovering anti-Semite" and who came to be influenced by his ideology when he was her cancer patient in the Chicago hospital where she worked.

The champion of Diasporism and founder of A-S.A. turns out to have had a prior career as a private detective, running his own small agency in Chicago, which specialized in missing-persons cases. His involvement with political ideas and his concern for the survival of the Jews and of Jewish ideals seems to date from the cancer battle, when he felt himself summoned to dedicate to a higher calling whatever life remained to him. (In addition, the conviction of the American Jew Jonathan Pollard as an Israeli spy sensitively positioned within the U.S. defense establishment—and Pollard's coldhearted abandonment by his Israeli Secret Service handlers the moment his operation was compromised—seems to have had a strong effect on the formulation of his ideas, consolidating his fears for Diaspora Jewry so long as they are an expendable, exploitable resource to a Jewish state that, as he sees it, Machiavellianly exacts from them unquestioning loyalty.) Little is known of his earlier life other than that, as a young man, he conscientiously set out to disassociate himself from any social or vocational role that might mark him as a Jew. His acolyte mistress has spoken of a mother who disciplined him pitilessly as a small child, but otherwise his biography is a blank and, even in its sketchy outline, seems a story patched together by the same unhis-

torical imagination that dreamed up the improbabilities and exagger-
ations of Diasporism.

Now it so happens that this man bears a decided physical resemblance to the American writer Philip Roth, claims that Philip Roth is
his name as well, and is not averse to playing upon this unaccountable, if not utterly fantastical, coincidence to foster the belief that he
is the author and thus to advance the cause of Diasporism. Through
this subterfuge he is able to convince Louis B. Smilesburger, an elderly, disabled Holocaust victim who has retired unhappily to Jerusalem after having made his fortune as a New York jeweler, to
contribute to him one million dollars. But, when Smilesburger sets
out to deliver the check personally to the Diasporist Philip Roth, who
should he come upon but the writer Philip Roth, who had arrived in
Jerusalem just two days earlier to interview the Israeli novelist
Aharon Appelfeld. The writer is having lunch with Appelfeld at a
Jerusalem café when Smilesburger locates him there and, mistakenly
imagining that the writer and the Diasporist are one, approaches the
wrong man with the check.

By this time the paths of the two look-alikes have already crossed
not far from the Jerusalem courtroom where John Demjanjuk, a
Ukrainian American autoworker extradited to Israel from Cleveland
by the U.S. Department of Justice, is on trial, accused of being the
sadistic Treblinka guard and mass murderer of Jews known to his
victims as Ivan the Terrible. This trial and the uprising against the
Israeli government by the Arabs in the Occupied Territories—both
events the subject of worldwide media coverage—constitute the turbulent backdrop against which the pair enact their hostile encounters, the first of which results in the writer Roth warning the
Diasporist Roth that unless the impostor immediately repudiates his
false identity he will be brought before the authorities on criminal
charges.

The writer, still smarting from the inflammatory meeting with the
Diasporist when Mr. Smilesburger appears at the café, impulsively
pretends to be who he has been taken to be (himself!) and accepts
Mr. Smilesburger's envelope without, of course, realizing when he

does so the improbable size of the donation. Later that day, following a perturbing visit, with a Palestinian friend from his graduate school days, to an Israeli court in occupied Ramallah (where the writer is again mistaken for the Diasporist and, to his own astonished dismay, not only allows the error to go unnoted for a second time but, afterward, at his friend's home, fortifies it with an implausible lecture *extolling* Diasporism), he, the writer, loses the Smilesburger check (or it is confiscated) when a platoon of Israeli soldiers conducts a frightening search of the writer and his Arab driver as they are headed erratically back in a taxicab along the road from Ramallah to Jerusalem early that evening.

The writer, who some seven months earlier had suffered a frightening nervous breakdown presumably generated by a hazardous sleeping medication prescribed in the aftermath of a botched-up minor surgical procedure, is so perplexed by all these events and by his own incongruously self-subverting behavior in response to them that he begins to fear that he is headed for a relapse. The implausibility of so much that is happening even causes him, in an extreme moment of disorientation, to ask himself if any of it *is* happening and if he is not in his rural Connecticut home living through one of those hallucinatory episodes whose unimpeachable persuasiveness had brought him close to committing suicide the summer before. His control over himself begins to seem nearly as tenuous to him as his influence over the other Philip Roth, whom, in fact, he refuses to think of as "the other Philip Roth" or the "impostor" or his "double" but instead takes to calling Moishe Pipik, a benignly deflating Yiddish nickname out of the daily comedy of his humble childhood world that translates literally to Moses Bellybutton and that he hopes will at least serve to curb his own perhaps paranoid assessment of the other one's dangerousness and power.

On the road from Ramallah, the writer is rescued from the soldiers' hair-raising ambush by a young officer in charge of the platoon, who has recognized him as the author of a book he happened to have been reading that very day. To make amends to the writer for the unwarranted assault, Gal, the lieutenant, personally drives him by jeep back to his hotel in the Arab quarter of East Jerusalem, voluntarily confessing along the way—to one he clearly holds in high esteem—his own grave qualms about his unconscionable position as an instrument of Israeli military policy. In response, the writer launches into a renewed exposition of Diasporism, which strikes him as no less ludicrous than the lecture he gave in Ramallah but which he delivers in the jeep with undiminished fervor.

At the hotel the writer discovers that Moishe Pipik, having easily misled the desk clerk into thinking that he is Philip Roth, has gained access to his room and is waiting there for him on his bed. Pipik demands that Roth hand over to him the Smilesburger check. An agitated exchange follows; there is a calm, deceptively friendly, even intimate, interlude, during which Pipik discloses his adventures as a Chicago private detective, but Pipik's anger erupts once again when the writer reiterates that the Smilesburger check is lost, and the episode concludes with Pipik, seething with rage and overcome by hysteria, exposing his erection to the writer as he is pushed and pummeled out of the room and into the hotel corridor.

So overwrought is the writer by this burgeoning chaos that he decides to flee Israel on the morning plane to London and, after barricading his door as much against his ineptitude in the face of Pipik's provocations as against Pipik's return, he sits down at the desk by the window of his room to compose a few final questions for the Appelfeld interview, which he plans to leave with Appelfeld when he departs at dawn for the airport. From the window he is able to observe several hundred Israeli soldiers, in a nearby cul-de-sac, boarding buses that will transport them to the rioting West Bank towns. Directly below the hotel, he sees half a dozen masked Arab men stealthily racing back and forth, moving rocks from one end of the street to the other; after completing his questions for Appelfeld, he decides that he must report this rock running to the Israeli authorities.

However, no sooner does he attempt, without success, to place a call to the police than he hears Pipik's consort whispering tearfully to him from the other side of his barricaded door, explaining that Pipik, whom she gallingly persists in calling Philip, is back at the King

David Hotel plotting with Orthodox Jewish militants to kidnap
Demjanjuk's son and to hold him and mutilate him until Demjanjuk
confesses to being Ivan the Terrible. She slides beneath the door a
cloth star of the kind European Jews were forced to wear for identification during the war years, and when she tells the writer that
Moishe Pipik has worn the star beneath his clothes ever since it was
given to him as a present by Lech Walesa in Gdansk, the writer is so
affronted that he loses emotional control and once again finds himself
swallowed up in the very madness from which he had determined to
disengage himself by running away.

On the condition that she disclose to him Moishe Pipik's true identity, he unbarricades the door and lets her slip into the room. It turns
out that she is herself in flight from Pipik and has crossed Jerusalem
to call on the writer not so much in the expectation of recovering
Smilesburger's check, although she at first makes a feeble attempt at
just that, or of persuading the writer to prevent the kidnapping of
young Demjanjuk but in the hope of finding asylum from the "anti-
Semite's nightmare" in which, paradoxically, she has been ensnared
by the zealot she cannot stop nursing. Tantalizingly stretched (outstretched, stretched out, sprawled, surrendered) across the writer's
hotel bed—hers now the second unlikely head to seek restitution on
his pillow that night—and wearing a low-fashion dress that makes the
writer as uncertain of her motives as of his own, she spins a tale of
lifelong servitude and serial transformations: from the unloved Catholic child of bigoted ignoramuses into the mindless promiscuous
hippie waif, from the mindless promiscuous hippie waif into the
chaste fundamentalist stupefyingly subjugated to Jesus, from the
chaste fundamentalist stupefyingly subjugated to Jesus into a death-
poisoned Jew-hating oncology nurse, from a death-poisoned Jew-
hating oncology nurse into an obedient recovering anti-Semite . . .
and from this last way station on the journey out of Ohio, from this
to what new self-mortification? What metamorphosis next for Wanda
Jane "Jinx" Possesski and, too, for the mentally woozy, emotionally
depleted, nutrient-deprived, erotically bedazzled writer who, having
most rashly implanted himself inside her, discovers himself, even
more perilously, half in love with her?

This is the plot up to the moment when the writer leaves the woman still dolefully enmeshed in it, and, suitcase in hand, tiptoeing so as not to disturb her postcoital rest, he himself slips silently out of the plot on the grounds of its general implausibility, a total lack of gravity, reliance at too many key points on unlikely coincidence, an absence of inner coherence, and not even the most tenuous evidence of anything resembling a serious meaning or purpose. The story so far is frivolously plotted, overplotted, for his taste altogether too freakishly plotted, with outlandish events so wildly careening around every corner that there is nowhere for intelligence to establish a foothold and develop a perspective. As if the look-alike at the story's storm center isn't farfetched enough, there is the capricious loss of the Smilesburger check (there is the fortuitous appearance of the Smilesburger check; there is Louis B. Smilesburger himself, Borscht Belt deus ex machina), which sets the action on its unconvincing course and serves to reinforce the writer's sense that the story has been intentionally conceived as a prank, and a nasty prank at that, considering the struggles of Jewish existence that are said to be at issue by his antagonist.

And what, if anything, is there of consequence about the antagonist who has conceived it? What in his self-presentation warrants his consideration as a figure of depth or dimension? The macho livelihood. The penile implant. The ridiculously transparent impersonation. The grandiose rationale. The labile personality. The hysterical monomania. The chicanery, the anguish, the nurse, the creepy pride in being "indistinguishable"—all of it adding up to someone *trying* to be real without any idea of how to go about it, someone who knows neither how to be fictitious—and persuasively pass himself off as someone he is not—nor how to actualize himself in life as he is. He can no more portray himself as a whole, harmonious character or establish himself as a perplexing, indecipherable puzzle or even simply exist as an unpredictable satiric force than he can generate a plot of sequential integrity that an adult reader can contemplate seriously. His being as an antagonist, his being *altogether,* is wholly dependent on the writer, from whom he parasitically pirates what meager selfhood he is able to make even faintly credible.

But why, in exchange, does the writer pirate from *him?* This is the question plaguing the writer as his taxi carries him safely through Jerusalem's western hills and onto the highway for the airport. It would be comforting for him to believe that his impersonation of his impersonator springs from an aesthetic impulse to intensify the being of this hollow antagonist and apprehend him imaginatively, to make the objective subjective and the subjective objective, which is, after all, no more than what writers are paid to do. It would be comforting to understand his performances in Ramallah with George and in the jeep with Gal—as well as the passionate session locked up with the nurse, culminating in that wordless vocal obbligato with which she'd flung herself upon the floodtide of her pleasure, the streaming throaty rising and falling, at once husky and murmurous, somewhere between the trilling of a tree toad and the purring of a cat, that luxuriantly articulated the blissful climax and that still sounded sirenishly in his ears all those hours later—as the triumph of a plucky, spontaneous, audacious vitality over paranoia and fear, as a heartening manifestation of an artist's inexhaustible playfulness and of an irrepressibly comic fitness for life. It would be comforting to think that those episodes encapsulate whatever true freedom of spirit is his, that embodied in the impersonation is the distinctively personal form that his fortitude takes and that he has no reason at this stage of life to be bewildered by or ashamed of. It would be comforting to think that, far from having pathologically toyed with an explosive situation (with George, Gal, or Jinx) or having been polluted by an infusion of the very extremism by which he feels so menaced and from which he is now in flight, he has answered the challenge of Moishe Pipik with exactly the parodic defiance it warrants. It would be comforting to think that, within the confines of a plot over which he's had no authorial control, he has not demeaned or disgraced himself unduly and that his serious blunders and miscalculations have resulted largely from a sentimental excess of compassion for his enemy's ailments rather than from a mind (his own) too unhinged by the paranoid threat to be able to think out an effective counterplot in which to subsume the Pipikesque imbecility. It would be comforting, it would be only natural, to assume that in a narrative contest (in the realistic mode) with this impostor, the real writer would easily emerge as inventive champion, scoring overwhelming victories in Sophistication of Means, Subtlety of Effects, Cunningness of Structure, Ironic Complexity, Intellectual Interest, Psychological Credibility, Verbal Precision, and Overall Verisimilitude; but instead the Jerusalem Gold Medal for Vivid Realism has gone to a narrative klutz who takes the cake for wholesale indifference to the traditional criteria for judgment in every category of the competition. His artifice is phony to the core, a hysterical caricature of the art of illusion, hyperbole fueled by perversity (and perhaps even insanity), exaggeration as the principle of invention, everything progressively overdrawn, super-simplified, divorced from the concrete evidence of the mind and the senses—and yet he wins! Well, let him. See him not as a terrifying incubus insufficiently existent who manufactures his being cannibal-istically, not as a demoniacal amnesiac who is hiding from himself in you and can only experience himself if he experiences himself as someone else, not as something half-born or half-dead or half-crazed or half-charlatan/half-psychopath—see this bisected thing as the achievement that he is and grant him the victory graciously. The plot that prevails is Pipik's. He wins, you lose, go home—better to relin-quish the Medal for Vivid Realism, however unjustly, to fifty percent of a man than to be defeated in the struggle for recovery of your own stability and to wind up again fifty percent of yourself. Demjanjuk's son will or will not be kidnapped and tortured through Pipik's plot-ting whether you remain in Jerusalem or are back in London. Should it happen while you're here, the newspaper stories will bear not only your name as the perpetrator but your picture and your bio in a sidebar; if you are not here, however, if you are there, then there will be a minimum of confusion all around when he is tracked to his Dead Sea cave and caught with the captive and with his bearded accom-plices. That he is determined to actualize a thought that merely passed through your mind when you first saw young Demjanjuk un-protected cannot possibly impute culpability to you, however stren-uously *he* attributes to you the prize-winning plot and claims, once

his interrogation begins, merely to be the Chicago hired gun, the
private detective engaged for a fee to enact, as stand-in, as stuntman,
your drastic self-intoxicated melodrama of justice and revenge. Of
course, there will be those who will be only too thrilled to believe
him. It won't be hard for them either: they'll blame it (compassion-
ately, no doubt) on your Halcion madness the way Jekyll blamed
Hyde on his drugs; they'll say, "He never recovered from that breakdown and this was the result. It had to be the breakdown—not even
he was that dreadful a novelist."

———

But I never did escape from this plot-driven world into a more congenial, subtly probable, innerly propelled narrative of my own devising—didn't make it to the airport, didn't even get as far as Aharon's
house—and that was because in the taxi I remembered a political
cartoon I'd seen in the British papers when I was living in London
during the Lebanon war, a detestable cartoon of a big-nosed Jew, his
hands meekly opened out in front of him and his shoulders raised in
a shrug as though to disavow responsibility, standing atop a pyramid
of dead Arab bodies. Purportedly a caricature of Menachem Begin,
then prime minister of Israel, the drawing was, in fact, a perfectly
realistic, unequivocal depiction of a kike as classically represented in
the Nazi press. This cartoon was what turned me around. Barely ten
minutes out of Jerusalem I told the driver to take me back to the King
David Hotel. I thought, When he starts slicing off the boy's toes and
mailing them one at a time to Demjanjuk's cell, the *Guardian* will
have a field day. Demjanjuk's lawyers had already challenged the
integrity of the proceedings publicly, daring to announce to three
Jewish judges in a Jewish courtroom that the prosecution of John
Demjanjuk for crimes committed at Treblinka had the characteristics
of nothing less than the Dreyfus trial. Wouldn't the kidnapping dra-
matically underscore this claim as it was even less delicately made by
Demjanjuk's Ukrainian supporters in America and Canada and by his
defenders, left- and right-wing, in the Western press—namely that it
was impossible for anyone with a name suffixed *juk* to receive justice

from Jews, that Demjanjuk was the Jews' scapegoat, that the Jewish
state was a lawless state, that the "show trial" convened in Jerusalem
was intended to perpetuate the self-justifying Jewish myth of victimization, that revenge alone was the Jews' objective? To drum up world
sympathy for their client and to bolster their allegations of bias and
prejudgment, Demjanjuk's supporters could not themselves have hit
on a publicity stunt more brilliant than the one that Moishe Pipik was
planning to perform in order to vent his rage with me.

If it hadn't been so infuriatingly clear that it was I who was the
challenge he meant to defy, that this crazy kidnapping, potentially
damaging to a cause perhaps even more poignant than his own, originated in his single-minded fixation on me, I might have told the
driver to take me not to the King David Hotel but directly to the
Jerusalem police. If it hadn't seemed to me that I had been humiliat-
ingly outfoxed at every turn by an adversary who was in no way my
equal and that I had compounded my ineptness by unthinkingly accepting Smilesburger's check—and subsequently elaborated on that
error by failing to grasp the scale of the West Bank conflict and
getting myself caught after dark on the Ramallah road by an Israeli
patrol in no mood to observe the niceties of a legal search—I might
not have felt that it was now incumbent on me, and on me alone, to
face down this bastard once and for all. This is as far as his pathology
goes. As far as *mine* goes. I'd overmagnified the menace of him from
the start. You don't have to call out the Israeli marines, I told myself,
to put an end to Moishe Pipik. He's got a foot in the grave already. All
he needs is a little push. It's simple: crush him.

Crush him. I was indignant enough to think that I could. I certainly
knew that I should. Our moment had arrived, the face-to-face show-
down between just the two of us: the genuine versus the fake, the
responsible versus the reckless, the serious versus the superficial, the
resilient versus the ravaged, the multiform versus the monomaniacal,
the accomplished versus the unfulfilled, the imaginative versus the
escapist, the literate versus the unschooled, the judicious versus the
fanatic, the essential versus the superfluous, the constructive versus
the useless. . . .

The taxi waited for me in the circular drive outside the King David Hotel while, at this early hour, the armed security guard at the hotel door accompanied me to the front desk. I repeated to the desk clerk what I'd told the guard: Mr. Roth was expecting me.

The clerk smiled. "Your brother."

I nodded.

"Twin."

I nodded again. Why not?

"He is gone. No longer with us." He looked at the clock on the wall. "Your brother left half an hour ago."

Meema Gitcha's words exactly!

"They all left?" I asked. "Our Orthodox cousins, too?"

"He was alone, sir."

"No. Couldn't be. I was to meet him here with our cousins. Three bearded men in yarmulkes."

"Not tonight, Mr. Roth."

"They didn't show up," I said.

"I don't believe so, sir."

"And he's gone. At four-thirty. And not coming back. No message for me."

"Nothing, sir."

"Did he say where he was going?"

"I believe to Romania."

"At four-thirty in the morning. Of course. And did Meir Kahane visit my brother tonight, by any chance? You know who I mean? Rabbi Meir Kahane?"

"I know who Rabbi Kahane is, sir. Rabbi Kahane was not in the hotel."

I asked if I might use the pay phone across the lobby. I dialed the American Colony and asked for my old room. I had told the clerk there, after paying the bill, that my wife was asleep and would be leaving in the morning. But it turned out that she had left already.

"You're sure?" I asked him.

"Mister and Missus. They're both gone."

I hung up, waited a minute, and phoned the hotel again.

"Mr. Demjanjuk's room," I said.

"Who is calling, please?"

"This is the jail calling."

A moment later I heard an anxious, sharp "Hello?"

"You all right?" I asked.

"Hello? Who is this? Who *is* this?"

He was there, I was here, they were gone. I hung up. They were gone, he was safe. They'd fled their *own* plot!

And that plot's purpose? Only larceny? Or was the whole hoax merely that, a hoax, two crazy X's off on a lark?

Standing at the phone and thinking that this entire mishap might just have come to a sudden end, I was more mystified than ever, wondering if these were two X's who were themselves escaping the world or two X's whom the world itself was escaping or two X's who'd only been falsifying everything so as to befuddle me . . . though why that should be a goal of anyone's was the most mystifying question of all. And it looked now as though I'd probably never know the answer—and as though what had enthralled me from the start was the question! Had they wanted only me to think that all their falseness was real, or had they themselves imagined it to be real, or was their excitement in creating the Pirandellian effect by derealizing everything and everyone, beginning with themselves? Some hoax *that* was!

I returned to the front desk. "I'll take my brother's room."

"Let me give you a room that has not been occupied, sir."

I pulled a fifty-dollar bill from my wallet. "His will be just fine."

"Your passport, please, Mr. Roth."

"Our parents liked the name so much," I explained, passing it across the counter with the fifty, "that they gave it to both of us."

I waited while he examined my photograph and recorded the passport number in the registration book. He handed the passport back to me without any comment. I then filled out the registration card and received the key to suite 511. The security guard had meanwhile returned to the front door of the hotel. I gave him twenty dollars to pay the taxi driver and told him to keep the change for himself.

For the next half hour, until it was dawn, I searched Pipik's room and found nothing in any of the drawers, nothing on the desk, no notes on the notepad, no magazines or newspapers left behind, nothing beneath the bed, nothing behind the cushions of the armchair, nothing hanging in the closet or lying on the closet floor. When I peeled back the bedspread and the blanket, the sheets and pillowcases were freshly ironed and smelled still of the laundry. No one had slept there since housekeeping had made up the room the previous morning. The towels in the bathroom were also fresh. Only when I lifted the toilet seat did I find a trace of his occupancy. A kinked spiral of dark pubic hair about the size of a fourteen-point ampersand adhered to the enamel rim of the bowl. I tweezed it loose between two fingernails and deposited it into a hotel envelope from the stationery drawer of the desk. I searched the bathroom floor for a strand of her hair, an eyelash, a snippet of toenail, but the tiles had been swept spotlessly clean—nothing there either. I got up off my knees to wash my hands in the sink, and it was there that I discovered along the lip of the basin, just beneath the hot-water tap, the minute filings of a man's beard. I blotted them carefully into a square of toilet tissue—a scattering of maybe ten filings in all—folded the tissue in quarters, and put it into a second envelope. The filings could, of course, have been anyone's—they could even have been my own; he could have found them when *he* was snooping around *my* hotel bathroom and, to *seal* our oneness, transferred them here to his. Having done everything else he'd done, why not that too? Perhaps even the pubic hair was mine. It certainly could have passed for mine, but then, with coils of stray pubic hair, it's difficult often, using just the naked eye, to distinguish exactly whose is whose. Still, I took it—if he could disguise himself as the writer, I could pretend to be the detective.

These two envelopes, along with the cloth star and his handwritten "Ten Tenets of A-S.A.," are beside me on the desk as I write, here to attest to the tangibility of a visitation that even I must be continually reassured was only cloaked in the appearance of a nonsensical, crude, phantasmagorical farce. These envelopes and their contents remind me that the spectral, half-demented *appearance* was, in fact, the very earmark of its indisputable lifelike realness and that, when life looks least like what it's supposed to look like, it may then be most like whatever it is.

I also have here the audiotape cassette that, to my astonishment, I found when I went to play one of Aharon Appelfeld's taped conversations with me on my return to London. It had been inserted in the very tape recorder that I'd locked away in the hotel closet at the American Colony and that I hadn't opened or used since I'd stolen with my bag out of that room, leaving Jinx asleep in the bed. There is no way for me to explain how the cassette had got placed into my machine before I'd returned to the room other than to think that Pipik had picked the closet lock using the skills he had acquired as a tracer of missing persons. The handwriting on the label that looks so like mine is, of course, his; so is the voice babbling the toxic babble of the people who destroyed almost everything, the maddening, diseased, murderous arraignment that only *sounds* unreal. The label reads: "A-S.A. Workout Tape #2. 'Did the Six Million Really Die?' Copyright Anti-Semites Anonymous, 1988. All rights reserved."

I leave it to readers of this confession to conjecture about his purpose and, in this way perhaps, to share something of the confusion of that week in Jerusalem, the extravagant confusion aroused in me by this "Philip Roth" by whom I was beset, someone about whom (as this recording confirms) it was impossible ever to say just how much of a charlatan he really was.

Here he is, the ritual impersonator, the mask modeled with my features and conveying the general idea of me—here he is, once again, exulting in being somebody else. Within that mouth, how many tongues? Within the man, how many men? How many wounds? How many unendurable wounds!

Did six million really die? Come off it. The Jews pulled a fast one on us again, keeping alive their new religion, Holocausto-mania. Read the revisionists. What it really comes down to is *there were no gas chambers*. Jews love numbers. They love to manipulate numbers. Six million. They're not talking about the six million anymore, are they? Auschwitz was mainly a plant to produce synthetic rubber. And that's why it was so evil-smelling. They didn't send them to the gas chamber, they sent them there to work. Because there were no gas chambers, as we now found out. From chemistry. Which is hard science. Freud. That was soft science. Masson over at Berkeley has now proved that Freud's basic research was false because he did not believe these women when they talked about how they were abused. Sexually abused. Because he said society wouldn't accept it. So he changed it to child sexuality. That Siggy. The whole basis of psychoanalysis is false. You can forget that. Einstein, of course, he's been called the bomb father. He and Oppenheimer. Now they're ranting and raving against them—why did you create *that?* So you can forget about Einstein. Marx [*chuckle*], well, you know what happened to Marx. Elie Wiesel. Another Jewish genius. Only no one likes Elie Wiesel. Just like they don't like Saul Bellow. I'll give you five thousand dollars if you find someone around here, in the Chicago area, who likes Saul Bellow. Something wrong with that guy. They know he made a lot of money in real estate. Chicago has the biggest Polish population outside of Warsaw. The Poles are united by three things. The Roman Catholic Church. Fear of Russia. And hatred of the Jews. Why do they hate Jews? The Russian czars constantly sent their bad-ass Jews into Poland and they were money changers, ghetto dwellers. Jews are very ugly people. The nose doctors, etc. Notice the Jew, notice the Jew from the hips down, especially below the knees, they're all fucked up, big, long flat feet, and they have twisted feet and are bowlegged—that's a lot the part of inbreeding. The Jews don't have any friends at all. Even niggers hate Jews. The blacks growing up in the projects see five white people in their life. The Irish or Italian cop—that's changing—they see the Jewish landlord, the Jewish grocer, the Jewish schoolteacher, and the Jewish social worker. Well, of course, their landlord now is the federal government. But they feel the Jews have made a great deal of money from the blacks, but they've never given them anything but a lot of hot air. The niggers turn against Jews, *everyone* turns against Jews. Jews suffer from something called Paget's disease. People don't know about that. Look at Ted Koppel. Look at the other ones. Woody Allen, little dork asshole. Mike Wallace. The bone thickens and their legs get bowed. The women get what is called the Hebrew hump. Their nails get very hard. Hard as rocks. They have a slack in their lower jaw. You notice the Jewesses who are older, they have that slack look in the jaws as if they're a dimwit. That's why they hate us, because we don't have that. Because we remain firm. We might get a little fat. But we remain firm. You know what a Jew is. A Jew's an Arab who was born in Poland. They get heavy. Kissinger. He's got that heavy look. Heavy nose. Heavy features. And that's why they dislike us. Look at Philip Roth, for God's sake. A real ugly buggy. A real asshole. I stopped reading him when he talked about that thing in *My Life as a Man,* when he was just a neurotic fucked-up graduate student at the U. of C.—oh, Jesus, are they ever! Dirty, oh Christ, you see them. He was so hot for shiksas that he grabbed a waitress, a mental case, a divorcée with a couple of kids, he thought this was great. Nitwit. Now he's coming back into the Jewish fold again because he wants to win the Nobel Prize. Jews obviously know how to get it, they got it for Wiesel, Singer, and Bellow. Graham Greene, of course, never got it. Isaac Stern—Mozart, Schubert, Stern just can't cut it. Doesn't understand it. Well, anyway . . . where were we? Hitler had no plan to exterminate the Jews. The Wannsee conference. A. J. P. Taylor's done a lot of work on this, the British historian. He says that the documents don't exist. Hilberg, who is a real Jewish creep, says I can read documents and I know code words—oh, go fuck yourself. [*Chuckle.*] Of course, they're great for code words, symbolisms, numerology—Jewish girls are into numerology, stars, all this other stuff, futurology, they're all screwed up. By the way, the Germans do have the capacity to exterminate people. They didn't have to. They wanted to work the Jews. I would say the Germans do have a cruel streak, but so do we. We exterminated the Indians. But what happened was, they worked them—there were no gas chambers. Six million didn't die. There weren't six million Jews *in* Europe. That's one of the reasons people attack the six million figure. Now it's down to a hundred and fifty to three hundred thousand, and the reason they died was because of the breakdown of the German supply system at the end of the war and because scurvy, typhus just rampaged through the camps. You and I know the State Department didn't want them *here.* No one wanted them *anywhere.* They would appear at the Dutch border, at the Swiss border, they were turned away. No one wanted Jews in their country. Why? The Jew has a tendency —as I say, even niggers hate Jews—the Jew has a tendency to alienate every other group within society. Then when he gets in trouble, he asks people for help. Why should they give it? The Jew came out of the ghetto in eastern Europe during Napoleon's time, he was liberated, and, Christ, he ran rampant. Once they get a lock on things, they keep it. The Jews got a lock on music with Schoenberg. They haven't produced any fuckin' music worth a shit. Hollywood. It's a piece of shit. Why is it? They got a lock on it. We hear about how the Jews created Hollywood. Jews aren't creative. What have they created? Nothing. Painting. Pissarro. Did you ever read Richard Wagner on the Jews? Superficiality. That's why all their art fails. They will not assimilate with the culture in the nation in which they reside. They have superficial popularity, someone like Herman Wouk or that other guy who writes dirty books, that dopey-looking jerk, Mailer, but it doesn't last, because it's not tied to the cultural roots of the society. Saul Bellow is their nominee. Jesus Christ, he's a sad sack, right? [*Chuckle.*] He was wearing his hat—covering his bald head and also to show the world he was a kike [*chuckle*]— when he had the press conference when he won the Nobel Prize. Roth. Roth is just a fuckin' masturbator, a wanker, man, in the john, whackin' off. Arthur Miller. Doesn't he look like a fuckin' junkman, like a fuckin' junkyard owner? Their fuckin' looks go, man, they really look bad. He always had that big, long look, goofy-lookin' jerk, you know, he'll *defend your right,* whatever the fuck that means. The cultural output from the Jews has been very, very low. Very low and very poor. Well, and of course Wall Street. You know, the arrest of Boesky and the rest of them is a goy plot to discredit the wonderful Jew who has given us our prosperity. It's bullshit. They haven't given us our prosperity. They only exist in a society that's on the brink of having inflation. All their deals are predicated on inflation coming about. If you don't have inflation, if you have deflation, they are fucked. Cultural? Bullshit. They might *own* the cultural institutions but they can't produce anything. Take a look at the shit. Anything vulgar on TV, a Jewish name is on it. Norman Lear, he's one. Hides behind a Gentile name, but there's another one with the bowed legs and the whole gig. Guy I know at the NIH did a study on a whole group of rabbis. About twenty, twenty-five years ago. Said they had specific Jewish diseases. Inbreeding caused these diseases, they've been inbred too much. Nine specific Jewish diseases that hit children—Down's syndrome is one of them. They always hide people like that. Because, you know, Jews are all geniuses. They're all violin players. Nuclear physicists. And of course Wall Street geniuses like Ivan Boesky. [*Snicker, chuckle.*] You know, you never hear about the idiots, which is really because of inbreeding. They're *all* nuts. They continually have children among themselves. But of course Kissinger and so many others, they get married, have two kids, then get rid of her, then they go after their ugly shiksa bookkeeper. [*Sneering chuckle.*] Poor fuckin' sad assholes. Right? Jesus Christ, all the big dough they pay hookers. Well, let's just jump on. First of all, there's a Jewish Mafia. Try to explain to people Jacob Rubinstein, you know him as Jack Ruby, the guy who offed Oswald—well, he was a member of the Jewish Mafia, on the West Side of Chicago. Arthur Miller. He made money off of Marilyn Monroe, he and Billy Wilder, and, who's that other one, Tony Curtis, dragged her into that movie, *Some Like It Hot,* I believe when she was pregnant, and she lost the baby. Watch that movie, she's frankly pregnant. But, of course, Miller had a piece of the film—a real fuckin' scumbag *defending your right.* Really a sea-dwelling slug. The Jews who marry Gentiles are always telling them they're stupid. Had a girlfriend who was married to a Jew. The most anti-Semitic people I've ever met are people who have been married to Jews. They tell you they're fuckin' neurotic, man. I know a broad who lived with a Jew for eight or nine years. She said only ten or fifteen times did

he relax and we had good sex. He was so aware of his Jewishness and he's fuckin' a shiksa. You should see the way his parents
treated her, just like she was dogshit. Jesus, these Jews, they
have all kinds of trouble. All they fuckin' do is whine. Jonathan
Pollard. I knew a guy who went to high school with the fucking
guy. Pollard says that when he went to high school in South
Bend, Indiana—his father was a professor at Notre Dame, Notre
Dame Medical School—the gangs used to lay in wait and beat
him up. It's all bullshit, man. His old man had lots of dough and
he got him a scholarship at Stanford—typical Jew shit, you
know, probably said he had no money. Went down to Stanford,
went to Washington, he was *crazy*. The Israelis thought he was
crazy, he was a fuckin' walk-in. They treated him well, this guy's
giving us some information, but the guy's a fuckin' nut case. But,
anyway, where were we? The Jew always whines, he always
brings up anti-Semitism. I've never seen an article about a Jew,
a Hollywood star, a politician, or anyone, for Christ's sake, he
could sell hot dogs, where he doesn't talk about how, in high
school, when he was going for his violin lesson, the gangs laid
in wait to beat him up. And how he experienced anti-Semitism
when he went to the hot-dog college and he got summa cum
laude in hot-dogology and he couldn't get a job at the hot-dog
place, and all the bullshit, of course. And, of course, now we
found out about those SAT tests, that the rabbis who run schools
in Brooklyn and in other Jewish communities are selling the
SAT things, that's why these Jews are such fucking geniuses and
getting into Harvard, Yale, and Princeton and all these schools.
I've worked with them, you know. Christ, you never get any
fuckin' work out of them, always around the phone, they know
about networking, man, they *never* do any fucking work.
[*Chuckle.*] Christ, they're neurotic. They have millions and millions of dollars to fight anti-Semitism. So anti-Semitism has gone
underground. Most of these screwball KKK, Nazis, etc., are
plants. They're Jewish plants, they're set up. Friend of mine
attended one of these things at the temple. They get 'em in and
show them pictures of the Holocaust, you know, the bodies,
then they see a picture [*laughing*] of some guy down South,

screaming, with his Nazi uniform—he's a Jewish stooge. Yeah, it's for the temple. If I got in a Nazi uniform and started to yell, they would come around with pictures and photographs and all the other stuff, and then they would run it in every temple and make the old pitch for the money. Jesus Christ, you ever talk to a Farrakhan guy? What they say about the Jews is beyond belief. That we're controlled by the Jews. We're not *that* controlled by the Jews. We're controlled by their publicity, but when the numbers come out, you'd rather have the money made by Kenny Rogers and Willie Nelson than by Streisand. Streisand. *She's* got the look. Friend of mine in California is very close to the film industry [*cackle*], he's not so happy with the Jews. You know, there is a little Gentile remnant there. Disney used to be their home. But it's all been taken over. They'll tell you that any business the Jew is in is filled with kickbacks, payoffs, trading off, networking, but networking fucks you. They got to hire the nitwit brother-in-law. Why? Because the father-in-law has invested in the business, and, Jesus, they shake their head, but of course you can't fire him. So he just sits at a desk or takes long lunches, you hope. But if he gets actively involved, he fucks up everything. Jews don't put trust in the bank, they have private trusts. I know from my business experience. Jesus Christ, I dealt with so many Jews in my time. All of them have Jewish attorneys, all of them sharp dealers, all of them this, all of them that, right? My boss knows how to treat 'em, he says this is the price, fuck you. He treats them like *shit.* [*Laughter.*] He treats them like shit right away, when they come in. I wondered why he did it. He says, I used to be nice to these fucking people but you can't be nice to them. He makes them write letters, which they don't like. They *love* that fuckin' telephone. Because if they bid on something, well, I'll pay three hundred and forty thousand for it, then they come in and say, well, you know I told you three twenty on the phone, they like to fuck over your head, and with their sharp business practices they create enemies. They know they're disliked. Why? It's because of *what* they *do!* But still you can't say anything against Ivan Boesky or any of these other people. If you say anything about them you are therefore [*whispering*] *an anti-Semite.* No wonder anti-Semitism has gone underground—it *has* to. Man, how can you *not* be anti-Semitic? When you see them they're all on the fucking telephone, manipulating. For better jobs. Or helping their friends. Jesus Christ, they're born with the PR gene. Born with this aggressive gene. It's just amazing. Of course, if you fire *them*—especially if you make a Jew fire a Jew. Jesus Christ, I guess there's no such thing. Very weird and strange people. See, one of the things about Jews that I really dislike is that they don't understand the Gentile mind. You can say to the Gentile, "We suffered," and we agree, the German did push you around. Then you come out with the six million, then you extract money from the Bonn government based on six million, then you talk about this and that, then people start chipping away at that six million. Bring the six million even down to eight hundred thousand, let's say. They don't understand the goy mind. Have you ever seen any publicity about a Jew who hasn't suffered because of his faith? The "survivors." Everyone survived. There are so many Auschwitz "survivors." No one, of course, asks the question if maybe you survived by turning in your friend. The "survivors" all wrote books. You ever notice they're all the same books? *Because they're all copying from another book.* They're all the same because Jewish Control Central said, Here's the line on Auschwitz, *write it!* Oh, sly fucking devils. *Sly!*

When my phone rang at almost eight a.m. I had been asleep in the chair beside it since I'd last checked on Demjanjuk's son at about five-thirty. I had dreamed that I owed $128 million on my water bill. That was what my mind came up with after all I'd just been through.

On awakening I smelled something enormous putrefying. I smelled must and feces. I smelled the walls of a damp old chimney. I smelled the fermenting smell of sperm. I smelled her asleep in my trousers—she was that heavy, clinging, muttony stench and she was also that pleasingly unpleasing brackishness on the middle fingers of the hand that picked up the receiver of the ringing phone. My unwashed face was rank with her. Dipped in her. In everyone. I smelled of them all. The shitting driver. The fat lawyer. Pipik. He was the smell of incense and old, dried blood. I smelled of every second of every minute of my last twenty-four hours, smelled like the container of something forgotten in the refrigerator whose lid you pop open after three weeks. Not until I decompose in my coffin will I ever be so immensely pungent again.

The phone was ringing in a hotel room where nobody I knew knew that I was.

A man said, "Roth?" Again a man with an accent. *"Roth?* You there?"

"Who . . . ?"

"The office of Rabbi Meir Kahane."

"Wants *Roth?"*

"This Roth? I am the press secretary. Why do you call the rabbi?"

"Pipik!" I cried.

"Hello? This is *the* Roth, the self-hating Jewish assimilationist?"

"Pipik, where are you?"

"And fuck you too."

I bathe.

Two words.

I dress in clean clothes.

Five words.

I no longer smell.

Four words.

Eleven words, and I no longer know if I ever *did* smell like my corpse.

And this, I thought, my mind already, first thing, careening around its densely overstocked little store of concerns, this is how Demjanjuk does it. Everything putrid in the past just snaps off and falls away. Only America happened. Only the children and the friends and the church and the garden and the job have happened. The accusations? Well, they might as well charge him with owing $128 million on the water bill. Even if they had his signature on the water bill, even if they had his photograph on the water bill, how could it possibly be his water bill? How could anyone use that much water? Admittedly he bathed, sprinkled the lawn, wet down the garden, washed the car, there was a washer-dryer, an automatic dishwasher, there was water for cooking, there were houseplants to water, there were floors to wash every week, they were a family of five, and five people use water —but does that add up to $128 million worth of water? You sent me the bill for the city of Cleveland. You sent me the bill for the state of Ohio. You sent me the bill for the whole fucking world! Look at me in this courtroom, under all this, and still at the end of the day all I have sipped from my glass is maybe three or four ounces of water. I'm not saying that I don't take a drink of water when I'm thirsty, of course I do, and in the summertime I drink my fill after going out and weeding the garden. But do I look to you like somebody who could be wasteful of water to the tune of $128 *million?* Do I strike you as somebody who, twenty-four hours a day, thirty days a month, twelve months a year, year in and year out, is thinking about water and nothing else? Is water running out of my nose and my mouth? Are my clothes sopping wet? Is there a puddle where I walk, is there water under the chair where I sit? Pardon me, but you've got the wrong man. Some Jew, if I may say so, stuck six zeros on my bill just because I am Ukrainian and supposed to be stupid. But I am not so stupid that I don't know my own water bill. My bill is *one hundred and twenty-eight dollars*—one—two—eight! There has been a mistake. I am just an average suburban consumer of water and I should not be on trial for this gigantic bill!

———

As I was leaving the room on my way to get something to eat before racing off to the trial, I suddenly remembered Apter, and the thought of him wondering if I had abandoned him, the thought of his vulnerability, of his lonely, fear-ridden, fragile existence, sent me back into the room to phone him, at least to assure him that he hadn't been forgotten and that as soon as I possibly could, I would come to see him ... but it turned out that I *had* seen him. It turned out that I'd had lunch with him just the day before: while Aharon and I had been eating together at the Ticho House, Apter and I had been eating together only a few blocks away at a vegetarian restaurant off Ethiopia

Street where we'd always gone in the past for our meal together. It turned out that while Smilesburger was presenting me with his staggering contribution, Apter had been telling me again that he was afraid to go to his stall in the Old City for fear that the Arabs there would kill him with their knives. He was afraid now even to leave his room. And even in his bed, he lay awake, watchful all night long, afraid that if he were to so much as blink his eyes, they would steal through his window and devour him. He had cried and begged me to take him back with me to America, he had lost control of himself completely, bawling and shrieking that he was powerless and that only I could save him.

And I had acceded. At lunch with him I had agreed. He was to come to live in my barn in Connecticut. I had told him that I would build a big new room for him in the unused barn, fix up a room with a skylight and a bed and whitewashed walls, where he could live securely and paint his landscapes and never again have to worry about being eaten alive while he slept.

On the phone he wept with gratitude even as he reminded me of all that I had promised the day before . . . and so how could I tell him that it hadn't been me? And was I even certain that it had been Pipik? It couldn't be! It had to be Apter dreaming aloud, under the pressure of the Arab uprising; it had to be the eruption of the hysteria of a resourceless, deformed, infolded spirit on whom the grip of a horrible past was never relaxed, someone who, even without an insurrection in progress, hourly awaited his execution. It had to be Apter pining for that restful safety he could never possibly know, longing for the lost family and the stolen life; it had to be the unreality of the hysteria of this little blank-faced man shut off and in dread of everything, whose whole existence was shrinking; it had to be withdrawal and longing and fear—because if it wasn't that and had indeed been Pipik conscientiously back at work pretending he was me, if it wasn't either Apter cut loose from his tiny anchor to life and fantastically deluded or Apter openly lying, Apter simulating Apter so as to alarm me into understanding how fantastically deluded existing as Apter required him to be, if Pipik had really made it his business to hunt him down and take him to lunch and toy like this with Apter's ruined life, then I'd been exaggerating nothing, then I was up against a purpose that was as diabolical as it was intangible, I was up against someone wearing my mask who wasn't human at all, someone who could get up to anything in order to make things into what they were not. Which does Pipik despise more, reality or me?

"I won't be a small boy—don't worry, Cousin Philip. I'll just be in the barn, that's all."

"Yes," I said, "yes," and this was the only thing I was able to say.

"I'll be no bother. I won't bother anyone. I need nothing at all," Apter assured me. "I'll paint. I'll paint the American countryside. I'll paint the stone walls you told me about. I'll paint the big maple trees. I'll paint pictures of the barns and of the banks of the river."

On he went, the whole load of his life falling away as he gave free rein, at fifty-four, to his naked need and the fairy tale it engendered of the perfect refuge. I wanted to ask, "Did this happen, Apter? Did he take you to lunch and tell you about the stone walls? Or has the violence so filled you with terror that, whether you know it or not, you are making all this up?" But even as Apter fell deeper and deeper under the spell of the dream of the unhaunted life, I heard myself asking Pipik, "Did you really do this to him? Did you really excite in this banished being who can barely maintain his equilibrium this beautiful vision of an American *Gan Eden* where he will be saved from the blight and din of his past? Answer me, Pipik!" Whereupon Pipik replied, "I couldn't resist, I couldn't do otherwise, neither as a Diasporist nor as a human being. Every word he spoke was filled with his fears. How could I deny him what he's craved all his life? Why are you so outraged? What have I done that's so awful? No more than any Jew would do for a frightened Jewish relative in trouble." "And now you are my conscience, too?" I cried. "You, *you* are going to instruct me in matters of decency, responsibility, and ethical obligation? Is there nothing that you will not pollute with your mouth? I want a serious answer! Is there nothing that you will not befoul? Is there anyone you will not mislead? What joy do you take in raising false hopes and sowing all this confusion?"

I want a serious answer. From Moishe Pipik. And after that, how about peace on earth and goodwill among men? *I want a serious answer*—as who doesn't?

"Apter," I wanted to say, "you are out of contact with reality. I did not take you to lunch yesterday. I had lunch with Aharon Appelfeld, I took *him* to lunch. If you had this conversation at lunch yesterday, it was not with me. Either it was with that man who is in Jerusalem pretending to be me or it was perhaps a conversation with yourself —is it possibly an exchange you imagined?"

But every word he spoke *was* so filled with fear that I did not have the heart to do anything other than repeat "Yes" to it all. I would leave him to awaken by himself from this delusion . . . and if it was no delusion? I imagined myself ripping the tongue out of Pipik's mouth with my own two hands. I imagined myself . . . but I could not give any more thought to the possibility that this was other than a delusion of Apter's for the simple reason that I would have exploded.

———————

That morning's *Jerusalem Post* was outside my door when I left the room, and I picked it up and quickly scanned the front page. The first lead story was about the 1988 Israeli budget—"Worry over Exports Casts Shadow on New State Budget." The second lead story concerned three judges who were to be put on trial and three others who were facing disciplinary action on charges of corruption. Situated between these stories was a photograph of the defense minister visiting the wall that George had tried to take me to see the day before, and beneath that were three stories about the West Bank violence, one datelined Ramallah and headed, "Rabin Inspects Wall of Bloody Beatings." On the lower half of the page I spotted the words "PLO" and "Hezbollah" and "Mubarak" and "Washington" but nowhere the name "Demjanjuk." Nor did I find my name. I ran quickly over the paper's remaining nine pages while going down in the elevator. The only mention of the trial I could find was under the television listings. "Israel Channel 2. 8.30 Demjanjuk trial—live broadcast." And further on, "20.00 Demjanjuk trial roundup." That was all. Nothing calamitous was reported to have happened to any Demjanjuk in the night.

Nonetheless, I decided to skip breakfast at the hotel and to proceed immediately to the courtroom to be sure that Pipik was not there. I'd had no food at all since lunch with Aharon the previous noon, but I could pick up something at the coffee bar just off the entrance hall to the courtroom, and that would replenish me for now. I realized from the TV listings that the trial began much earlier in the day than I had thought, and I had to be there from the very first moment—I was bent on ousting him today, on supplanting him and taking charge completely; if necessary, I would sit in that courtroom through both the morning and the afternoon sessions so as to avert, before it could even get going, anything that he might still be plotting. Today Moishe Pipik was to be obliterated (if, by any chance, he hadn't already been the night before). Today was the end of it: Wednesday, January 27, 1988 • Shevat 8, 5748 • Jomada Tani 9, 1408.

Those were the dates printed in a row beneath the logo of the *Post.* 1988. 5748. 1408. Agreement on nothing but the last digit, dissension over everything, beginning with where to begin. It's no wonder "Rabin Inspects Wall of Bloody Beatings" when the discrepancy between 5478 and 1408 is a matter not of decades or even of a few little centuries but of four thousand three hundred and forty years. The father is superseded by the rivalrous, triumphant firstborn—rejected, suppressed, persecuted, expelled, shunned, terrorized by the firstborn and reviled as the enemy—and then, having barely escaped extinction for the crime of being the father, resuscitates himself, revives and rises up to struggle bloodily over property rights with the second-born, who is raging with envy and the grievances of usurpation, neglect, and ravaged pride. 1988. 5748. 1408. The tragic story's all in the numbers, the successor monotheists' implacable feud with the ancient progenitor whose crime it is, whose *sin* it is, to have endured the most unspeakable devastation and still, somehow, to be *in the way.*

The Jews are in the way.

The moment I stepped out of the elevator, two teenagers, a boy and a girl, jumped up from where they were sitting in the lobby and came toward me, calling my name. The girl was redheaded, freckled, on the dumpy side, and she smiled shyly as she approached; the boy was my height, a skinny, very serious, oldish-seeming boy, cavern-faced and scholarly-looking, who, in his awkwardness, seemed to be climbing over a series of low fences to reach me. "Mr. Roth!" He spoke out in a strong voice a little loud for the lobby. "Mr. Roth! We are two students in the eleventh grade of Liyad Ha-nahar High School in the Jordan Valley. I am Tal.° This is Deborah.°"

"Yes?"

Deborah then stepped forward to greet me, speaking as though she were beginning a public address. "We are a group of high school students that has found your stories very provocative in our English class. We read 'Eli, the Fanatic' and 'Defender of the Faith.' Both created question marks about the state of the American Jew. We wonder if it would be possible for you to visit us. Here is a letter to you from our teacher."

"I'm in a hurry right now," I said, accepting the envelope she handed me, which I saw was addressed in Hebrew. "I'll read this and answer it as soon as I can."

"Our class sent you last week, all the students, each one, a letter to the hotel," Deborah said. "When we received no answer the class voted to send Tal and me on the bus to make our offer directly. We'll be delighted if you accept our class's offer."

"I never got your class's letters." Because *he* had gotten them. Of course! I wondered what could possibly have constrained him from going out to their school and answering questions about his provocative stories. Too busy elsewhere? It horrified me to think about the invitations to speak he had received and accepted here if this was one he considered too inconsequential even to bother to decline. Schoolkids weren't his style. No headlines in schoolkids. And no money. The schoolkids he left to me. I could hear him calming me down. "I wouldn't dare to interfere in literary matters. I respect you too much as a writer for that." And I needed calming down when I thought about him getting and opening the mail people thought they were addressing to me.

"First of all," Tal was saying to me, "we would like to know how *you* live as a Jew in America, and how you have solved the conflicts you brought up in your stories. What's with the 'American dream'?

From the story 'Eli, the Fanatic' it seems like the only way of being a Jew in America is being a fanatic. *Is* it the only way? What about making aliyah? In Israel, in our society, the religious fanatics are seen in a negative way. You talk about suffering—"

Deborah saw my impatience with Tal's on-the-spot inquiry and interrupted to tell me, softly now, quite charmingly in that very faintly off-ish English, "We have a beautiful school, near the Kinneret Lake, with a lot of trees, grass, and flowers. It's a very beautiful place, under the Golan mountains. It is so beautiful it is considered to be Paradise. I think you would enjoy it."

"We were impressed," Tal continued, "by the beautiful style of literature you write, but still not all of the problems were solved in our mind. The conflict between the Jewish identity and being a part of another nation, the situation in the West Bank and Gaza, and the problem of double loyalty as in the Pollard case and its influence on the American Jewish community—"

I put a hand up to stop him. "I appreciate your interest. Right now I've got to be somewhere else. I'll write your teacher."

But the boy had come from the Jordan Valley on a very early bus to Jerusalem and had waited nervously in the lobby for me to wake up and get started, and he wasn't prepared, having gotten up his head of steam, to back off yet. "What comes first," he asked me, "nationality or Jewish identity? Tell us about your identity crisis."

"Not right now."

"In Israel," he said, "many youngsters have an identity crisis and make *hozer b'tshuva* without knowing what they are getting into—"

A rather stern-looking, unsmiling man, very decorously—and, in this country, uncharacteristically—dressed in a dark double-breasted suit and tie, had been watching from a sofa only a few feet away as I tried to extricate myself and be on my way. He was seated with a briefcase in his lap, and now he came to his feet and, as he approached, addressed a few words to Deborah and Tal. I was surprised that he spoke Hebrew. From his looks as well as his dress I would have taken him for a northern European, a German, a Dutchman, a Dane. He spoke quietly but very authoritatively to the two teenagers, and when Tal responded, intemperately, in Hebrew, he listened without flinching until the boy was finished and only then did he turn his cast-iron face to me, to say, in English, and in an English accent, "Please, forgive their audacity and accept them and their questions as a token of the tremendous esteem in which you are held here. I am David Supposnik,° an antiquarian. My office is in Tel Aviv. I too have come to bother you." He handed me a card that identified him as a dealer in old and rare books, German, English, Hebrew, and Yiddish.

"The annual teaching of your story 'Eli, the Fanatic' is always an experience for the high school students," Supposnik said. "Our pupils are mesmerized by Eli's plight and identify wholly with his dilemma despite their innate contempt for all things fanatically religious."

"Yes," agreed Deborah while Tal, resentful, remained silent.

"Nothing would give the students greater pleasure than a visit from you. But they know it is unlikely and that is why this young man has seized the opportunity to interrogate you here and now."

"It's not been the worst interrogation of my life," I replied, "but I'm in a rush this morning."

"I'm sure that, if you could see your way, in response to his questions, to sending a collective reply to all the students in the class, that would be sufficient and they would be extremely flattered and grateful."

Deborah spoke up, obviously feeling as bullied as Tal did by the outsider's unsought intervention. "But," she said to me, pleadingly, "they would still prefer if you *came.*"

"He has explained to you," said Supposnik, no less brusque now with the girl than he'd been with the boy, "that he has business in Jerusalem. That is quite enough. A man cannot be in two places at one time."

"Goodbye," I said, extending my hand, and it was shaken first by Deborah, then reluctantly by Tal before, finally, they turned and left.

Who can't be in two places at one time? Me? And who is this Supposnik and why has he forced those youngsters out of my life if not to force himself in?

What I saw was a man with a long head, deep-set, smallish light-colored eyes, and a strongly molded forehead from which his light brown hair was combed straight back close to the skull—an officer type, a colonial officer who might have trained at Sandhurst and served here with the British during the Mandate. I would never have had him pegged as a dealer in rare Yiddish books.

Crisply, reading my mind, Supposnik said, "Who I am and what I want."

"Quickly, yes, if you don't mind."

"In just fifteen minutes I can make everything clear."

"I don't have fifteen minutes."

"Mr. Roth, I wish to enlist your talent in the struggle against anti-Semitism, a struggle to which I know you are not indifferent. The Demjanjuk trial is not irrelevant to my purpose. Is that not where you are hurrying off to?"

"Is it?"

"Sir, everybody in Israel knows what you are doing here."

Just then I saw George Ziad walk into the hotel and approach the front desk.

"Please," I said to Supposnik, "one moment."

At the desk, where George embraced me, I found he was at the same pitch of emotion as when I'd left him the evening before.

"You're all right," he whispered. "I thought the worst."

"I'm fine."

He would not let me free myself. "They detained you? They questioned you? Did they beat you?"

"They never detained me. Beat me? Of course not. It was all a big mistake. George, *relax,"* I told him but was only able to secure my release by pressing my fists against his shoulders until we were finally an arm's length apart.

The desk clerk, a young man who hadn't been on duty when I'd checked in, said to me, "Good morning, Mr. Roth. How are things this morning?" Very jovially, he said to George, "This is no longer the lobby of the King David Hotel, it's the rabbinical court of Rabbi Roth. All his fans won't leave him alone. Every morning, they are lining up, the schoolchildren, the journalists, the politicians—we have had nothing like it," he said, with a laugh, "since Sammy Davis, Jr., came to pray at the Wailing Wall."

"The comparison is too flattering," I said. "You exaggerate my importance."

"Everyone in Israel wants to meet Mr. Roth," the clerk said.

Hooking my arm in his, I led George away from the desk and the desk clerk. "Is this the best place for you to be, this hotel?"

"I had to come. The phone is no use here. Everything is tapped and taped and will turn up either at my trial or at yours."

"George, come off it. Nobody's putting me on trial. Nobody beat me. That's all ridiculous."

"This is a military state, established by force, maintained by force, committed to force and repression."

"Please, I don't see it that way. Stop. Not now. No slogans. I'm your friend."

"Slogans? They didn't demonstrate to you last night that this is a police state? They could have shot you, Philip, then and there, and blamed the Arab driver. These are the great specialists in assassination. That is no slogan, that is the truth. They train assassins for fascist governments all over the world. They have no compunctions about whom they murder. Opposition from a Jew is intolerable to them. They can murder a Jew they don't like as easily as they murder one of us. They can and they *do.*"

"Zee, Zee, you're way over the top, man. The trouble last night was the driver, stopping and starting his car, flashing his light—it was a comedy of errors. The guy had to take a shit. He aroused the suspicion of this patrol. It all meant nothing, means nothing, was nothing."

"In Prague it means something to you, in Warsaw it means something to you—only here you, even you, fail to understand what it means. They are out to frighten you, Philip. They are out to scare you to death. What you are preaching here is anathema to them—you are challenging them at the very heart of their Zionist lie. You are the opposition. And the opposition they 'neutralize.'"

"Look," I said, "talk coherently to me. This is not making sense. Let me get rid of this guy and then you and I will have to have a talk."

"Which guy? Who is he?"

"An antiquarian from Tel Aviv. A rare-book dealer."

"You know him?"

"No. He came here to see me."

All the while I explained, George looked boldly across the lobby to where Supposnik had taken a seat on the sofa, waiting for me to return.

"He's the police. He's Shin Bet."

"George, you're in a bad way. You're overwrought and you're going to explode. This is not the police."

"Philip, you are an innocent! I won't have them brutalizing you, not you too!"

"But I'm *fine*. Stop this, please. Look, this is the texture of things over here. I don't have to tell you that. There is rough stuff on the roads. I was in the wrong place at the wrong time. There is a mix-up, all right, but that's between you and me, I'm afraid. You are not responsible. If anyone is responsible, I am responsible. You and I have to have a talk. You're confused about why I'm here. Something most unusual has been happening and I haven't been at all clever dealing with it. I confused you and Anna yesterday—I acted very stupidly at your house. Unforgivably so. Let's not talk now. You'll come with me —I have to be at the Demjanjuk trial, you'll come with me and in the taxi I'll explain everything. This has all gotten out of hand and the fault is largely mine."

"Philip, while this court for Demjanjuk is carefully weighing evidence for the benefit of the world press, scrutinizing meticulously, with all kinds of experts, the handwriting and the photograph and the imprint of the paper clip and the age of the ink and the paper stock, while this charade of Israeli justice is being played out on the radio and the television and in the world press, the death penalty is being enacted all over the West Bank. Without experts. Without trials. Without justice. With live bullets. Against innocent people. Philip," he said, speaking very quietly now, "there is somebody for you to talk to in Athens. There is somebody in Athens who believes in what you believe in and what you want to do. Somebody with money who believes in Diasporism for the Jews and justice for the Palestinians. There are people who can help you in Athens. They are Jews but they are our friends. We can arrange a meeting."

I am being recruited, I thought, recruited by George Ziad for the PLO.

"Wait. Wait here," I said. "We have to talk. Is it better for you to wait here or outside?"

"No, here," he said, smiling ruefully, "here it is positively ideal for me. They wouldn't dare to beat an Arab in the lobby of the King David Hotel, not in front of all the liberal American Jews whose money props up their fascist regime. No, here I'm much safer than in my house in Ramallah."

I made the mistake then of returning to explain politely to Supposnik that he and I would not be able to continue our conversation. He did not give me a chance, however, to say even one word, but for ten minutes stood barely half a foot from my chest delivering his lecture entitled "Who I Am." Each time I retreated an inch, preparatory to ducking away, he drew an inch closer to me, and I realized that short of shouting at him or striking him or streaking out of the lobby as fast as I could, I would have to hear him out. There was a commanding incongruousness about this Teutonically handsome Tel Aviv Jew who'd taught himself to speak English in the impeccable accent of the educated English upper class, and something also touchingly absurd about the bookish erudition of his hotel-lobby lecture and the pedantic donnish air with which it was so beautifully articulated. If I hadn't felt that I was needed urgently elsewhere, I might have been more entertained than I was; in the circumstances, I was, in fact, far more entertained than I should have been, but this is a professional weakness and accounts for any number of my mistakes. I am a relentless collector of scripts. I stand around half-amazed by these audacious perspectives, I stand there excited, almost erotically, by these stories so unlike my own, I stand listening like a five-year-old to some stranger's most fantastic tale as though it were the news of the week in review, stupidly I stand there enjoying all the pleasures of gullibility while I ought instead to be either wielding my great skepticism or running for my life. Half-amazed with Pipik, half-amazed with Jinx, and now this Shylock specialist whom half-amazing George Ziad had identified for me as a member of the Israeli secret police.

"Who I am. I am one of the children, like your friend Appelfeld,"

Supposnik told me. "We were one hundred thousand Jewish children
in Europe, wandering. Who would take us in? Nobody. America? England? No one. After the Holocaust and the wandering, I decided to
become a Jew. The ones who harmed me were the non-Jews, and the
ones who helped me were the Jews. After this I loved the Jew and
developed a hatred for the non-Jew. Who I am. Someone who has
collected books in four languages for three decades now and who has
read all his life the greatest of all English writers. Particularly when I
was a young student at the Hebrew University, I studied the Shakespeare play that is second only to *Hamlet* in the number of times it
has been performed on the London stage in the first half of the twentieth century. And in the very first line, the opening line of the third
scene of the very first act, I came with a shock upon the three words
with which Shylock introduced himself onto the world stage nearly
four hundred years ago. Yes, for four hundred years now, Jewish
people have lived in the shadow of this Shylock. In the modern world,
the Jew has been perpetually on trial; still *today* the Jew is on trial, in
the person of the Israeli—and this modern trial of the Jew, this trial
which never ends, begins with the trial of Shylock. To the audiences
of the world Shylock is the embodiment of the Jew in the way that
Uncle Sam embodies for them the spirit of the United States. Only, in
Shylock's case, there is an overwhelming Shakespearean reality, a
terrifying Shakespearean aliveness that your pasteboard Uncle Sam
cannot begin to possess. I studied those three words by which the
savage, repellent, and villainous Jew, deformed by hatred and revenge, entered as our doppelgänger into the consciousness of the
enlightened West. Three words encompassing all that is hateful in the
Jew, three words that have stigmatized the Jew through two Christian
millennia and that determine the Jewish fate until this very day, and
that only the greatest English writer of them all could have had the
prescience to isolate and dramatize as he did. You remember Shylock's opening line? You remember the three words? What Jew can
forget them? What Christian can forgive them? '*Three thousand ducats.*' Five blunt, unbeautiful English syllables and the stage Jew is
elevated to its apogee by a genius, catapulted into eternal notoriety
by 'Three thousand ducats.' The English actor who performed as

Shylock for fifty years during the eighteenth century, the Shylock of his day, was a Mr. Charles Macklin. We are told that Mr. Macklin would mouth the two *th*'s and the two *s*'s in 'Three thousand ducats' with such oiliness that he instantaneously aroused, with just those three words, all of the audience's hatred of Shylock's race. 'Th-th-th-three th-th-th-thous-s-s-sand ducats-s-s.' When Mr. Macklin whetted his knife to carve from Antonio's chest his pound of flesh, people in the pit fell unconscious—and this at the zenith of the Age of Reason. Admirable Macklin! The Victorian conception of Shylock, however—Shylock as a wronged Jew rightfully vengeful—the portrayal that descends through the Keans to Irving and into our century, is a vulgar sentimental offense not only against the genuine abhorrence of the Jew that animated Shakespeare and his era but to the long illustrious chronicle of European Jew-baiting. The hateful, hateable Jew whose artistic roots extend back to the Crucifixion pageants at York, whose endurance as the villain of history no less than of drama is unparalleled, the hook-nosed moneylender, the miserly, money-maddened, egotistical degenerate, the Jew who goes to *synagogue* to plan the murder of the virtuous Christian—*this* is Europe's Jew, the Jew expelled in 1290 by the English, the Jew banished in 1492 by the Spanish, the Jew terrorized by Poles, butchered by Russians, incinerated by Germans, spurned by the British and the Americans while the furnaces roared at Treblinka. The vile Victorian varnish that sought to humanize the Jew, to dignify the Jew, has never deceived the enlightened European mind about the three thousand ducats, never has and never will. Who I am, Mr. Roth, is an antiquarian bookseller dwelling in the Mediterranean's tiniest country—still considered too large by all the world—a bookish shopkeeper, a retiring bibliophile, nobody from nowhere, really, who has dreamed nonetheless, since his student days, an impresario's dreams, at night in his bed envisioning himself impresario, producer, director, leading actor of Supposnik's Anti-Semitic Theater Company. I dream of full houses and standing ovations, and of myself, hungry, dirty little Supposnik, one of the hundred thousand wandering children, enacting, in the unsentimental manner of Macklin, in the true spirit of Shakespeare, that chilling and ferocious Jew whose villainy flows inexorably from the innate corruption of his religion. Every winter touring the capitals of the civilized world with his Anti-Semitic Drama Festival, performing in repertory the great Jew-hating dramas of Europe, night after night the Austrian plays, the German plays, Marlowe and the other Elizabethans, and concluding always as star of the masterpiece that was to prophesy, in the expulsion of the unregenerate Jew Shylock from the harmonious universe of the angelic Christian Portia, the Hitlerian dream of a *Judenrein* Europe. Today a Shylockless Venice, tomorrow a Shylockless world. As the stage direction so succinctly puts it after Shylock has been robbed of his daughter, stripped of his wealth, and compelled to convert by his Christian betters: *Exit Jew.* This is who I am. Now for what I want. Here."

I took from him what he handed me, two notebooks bound in imitation leather, each about the size of a billfold. One was red, and impressed on its cover, in white cursive script, were the words "My Trip." The other, whose brown cover was a bit scratched and mildewed, was identified as "Travels Abroad" in gold letters that were stylized to look exotically non-Occidental. Engraved in a semicircular constellation around those words were postage-stamp-sized representations of the varied forms of locomotion that the intrepid wayfarer would encounter on his journey—a ship sailing along on the wavy waves, an airliner, a rickshaw pulled by a pigtailed coolie, bearing a woman with a parasol, an elephant with a driver perched atop his head and a passenger seated in an awninged cabinet on his back, a camel ridden by a robed Arabian, and, at the bottom edge of the cover, the most elaborately detailed of the six engraved images: a full moon, a starry sky, a serene lagoon, a gondola, a gondolier. . . .

"Nothing like this," said Supposnik, "has turned up since the discovery at the end of the war of the diary of Anne Frank."

"Whose are they?" I asked.

"Open them," he said. "Read."

I opened the red book. At the top of the entry I'd turned to, where there were lines provided for "Date," "Place," and "Weather," I read "2-2-76," "Mexico," and "Good." The entry itself, in legible largish handwriting inscribed with a fountain pen in blue ink, began, "Beautiful flight. A little rough. Arrived on time. Mexico City has a population of 5,000,000 people. Our guide took us through some sections of the city. We went to a residential section that was built on lava. The homes ranged from $30,000 to $160,000. They were very modern and beautiful. The flowers were very colorful." I skipped ahead. "Wed. 2-14-76. San Huso De Puria. We had an early lunch and then went into the pool. There are 4 of them here. Each is supposed to have curative waters. Then we went to the Spa building. The girls had a mud pack on their faces and then we went into the mikva or baths. Marilyn and I shared one. It is called a family bath. It was the most delightful experience. All my friends should visit this place. Even some of my enemies. It is great."

"Well," I said to Supposnik, "they're not André Gide's."

"It's written whose they are—at the beginning."

I turned to the beginning. There was a page titled "Time Keeping at Sea," a page about "Changing the Clock," information about "Latitude and Longitude," "Miles and Knots," "The Barometer," "The Tides," "Ocean Lanes and Distances," "Port and Starboard," a full page explaining "Conversion from US-$ into Foreign Currencies," and then the page headed "Identification," where all but a few of the blanks had been filled in by the same diarist with the same fountain pen.

My Name.	Leon Klinghoffer
My Residence.	70 E. 10th St. NY, NY 10003
My Occupation.	Appliance manufacturer (Queens)

| *Ht.* | 5-7½ | *Wgt.* | 170 | *Born* | 1916 |
| *Color* | W. | *Hair* | Brown | *Eyes* | Brown |

I AM KNOWN TO HAVE THE FOLLOWING

Diagnosis _____

Social Security No. _____

Religion _____ Hebrew _____

IN CASE OF ACCIDENT NOTIFY

Name _____ Marilyn Klinghoffer _____

"Now you see," said Supposnik gravely.

"I do," I said, "yes," and opened the brown diary he'd given me. "9-3-79. Naples. Weather cloudy. Breakfast. Took tour to Pompeii again. Very interesting. Hot. Back to ship. Wrote cards. Had drink. Met 2 nice young people from London. Barbara and Lawrence. Safety drill. Weather turned nice. Going to Captain's cocktail party in the swank [illegible] Room."

"This is *the* Klinghoffer?" I asked. "From the *Achille Lauro* hijacking?"

"The Klinghoffer they killed, yes. The defenseless Jew crippled in a wheelchair that the brave Palestinian freedom fighters shot in the head and threw into the Mediterranean Sea. These are his travel diaries."

"From that trip?"

"No, from happier trips. The diary from that trip has disappeared. Perhaps it was in his pocket when they tossed him overboard. Perhaps the brave freedom fighters used it for paper to cleanse their heroic Palestinian behinds. No, these are from the pleasant trips he made with his wife and his friends in the years before. They've come to me through the Klinghoffer daughters. I heard about the diaries. I contacted the daughters. I flew to New York to meet with them. Two specialists here in Israel, one of them associated with the forensic investigation unit of the attorney general's office, have assured me that the handwriting is Klinghoffer's. I brought back with me documents and letters from his business office files—the handwriting there corresponds to the diary handwriting in every last particular. The pen, the ink, the manufacturing date of the diaries themselves—I have expert documentation for their authenticity. The daughters have asked me to act as their representative to help them find an Israeli publisher for their late father's diaries. They want to publish them here as a memorial to him and as a token of the devotion that he felt to Israel. They have asked for the proceeds to be donated to the Hadassah Hospital in Jerusalem, a favorite charity of their father's. I told these two young women that when Otto Frank returned to Amsterdam from the camps after the war and found the diary kept by his little daughter while the Frank family hid from the Nazis in their attic, he too wanted it only to be published privately, as a memorial to her for a small group of Dutch friends. And as you well know, having yourself made Anne Frank into the heroine of a literary work, that was the modest, unassuming way in which the Anne Frank diary first appeared. I of course will follow the wishes of the Klinghoffer daughters. But I happen also to know that, like the diary of little Anne Frank, *The Travel Diaries of Leon Klinghoffer* are destined to reach a far wider audience, a worldwide audience—if, that is, I can secure the assistance of Philip Roth. Mr. Roth, the introduction to the first American publication of *The Diary of Anne Frank* was written by Eleanor Roosevelt, the much-esteemed widow of your wartime president. A few hundred words from Mrs. Roosevelt and Anne Frank's words became a moving entry in the history of Jewish suffering and Jewish survival. Philip Roth can do the same for the martyred Klinghoffer."

"I'm sorry, I can't." However, when I made to hand back the two volumes, he wouldn't accept them.

"Read them through," Supposnik said. "I'll leave them for you to read through."

"Don't be ridiculous. I can't be responsible. Here."

But again he refused to take them. "Leon Klinghoffer," he said, "could very easily have been a man out of one of your books. He's no stranger to you. Neither is the idiom in which he expresses here, simply, awkwardly, sincerely, his delight in living, his love for his wife, his pride in his children, his devotion to his fellow Jews, his love for Israel. I know the feeling you have for the achievement that these men, burdened by all the limitations of their immigrant family backgrounds, nonetheless made of their American lives. They are the fathers of your heroes. You know them, you understand them; without sentimentalizing them, you respect them. Only you can bring to these two little travel diaries the compassionate knowledge that will reveal to the world exactly who it was and what it was that was murdered on the cruise ship *Achille Lauro* on October 8, 1985. No other writer writes about these Jewish men in the way that you do. I'll return tomorrow morning."

"It's not likely I'll be here tomorrow morning. Look," I said angrily, "you cannot leave these things with me."

"I cannot think of anyone more reliable to entrust them to." And with that he turned and left me there holding the two diaries.

The Smilesburger million-dollar check. The Lech Walesa six-pointed star. Now the Leon Klinghoffer travel diaries. What next, the false nose worn by the admirable Macklin? Whatever Jewish treasure isn't nailed down comes flying straight into my face! I went immediately to the front desk and asked for an envelope large enough to hold the two diaries and wrote Supposnik's name across it and my own in the upper left-hand corner. "When the gentleman returns," I said to the clerk, "give him this package, will you?"

He nodded to assure me that he would, but no sooner had he turned to place the envelope in my room's pigeonhole than I imagined Pipik popping up to claim the package for his own the moment after I'd departed for the courtroom. However much evidence there was that I had finally prevailed and that the two of them had abandoned the hoax and taken flight, I still couldn't convince myself that he wasn't lurking nearby, fully aware of everything that had just transpired, any more than I could be one hundred percent certain that he wasn't already at the courtroom with his Orthodox coconspirators, poised to undertake the folly of kidnapping Demjanjuk's son. If Pipik returns to steal these ... well, that's Supposnik's hard luck, not mine!

Nonetheless I turned back to the desk from which I'd turned away and asked the clerk to hand me the package that I had only just deposited with him. While he watched with a barely discernible smirk suggesting that he, rather like me, saw in this scene great untapped comic potential, I tore it open, put the red diary ("My Trip") into one of my jacket pockets and the brown diary ("Travels Abroad") into the other, and then quickly left the hotel with George, who all this while, submerged in his malice, racked by God only knew what unendurable fantasies of restitution and revenge, had sat in a chair close by the door smoking cigarette after cigarette, observing the brisk stirrings of another busy day in the sedate, attractive lobby of a four-star Jewish hotel whose prosperous guests and resourceful staff were, of course, utterly indifferent to the misery caused him by their matter-of-factly manageable existence.

As we stepped into the bright sunlight, I surveyed the cars parked along the street to see if Pipik might be in one of them, hiding the way he'd hidden in his "vehicle" as a Chicago detective. I saw a figure standing on the roof of the YMCA building across the street from the hotel. It could be him, he could be anywhere—and for a moment I *saw* him everywhere. Now that she's told him how I seduced her, I thought, he's my terrorist for life. I'll be sighting him on rooftops for years to come, just as he'll be seeing me, sighted in the cross hairs of his rage.

9

Forgery, Paranoia, Disinformation, Lies

Before stepping into the taxi I quickly checked out the driver, a tiny Turkish-looking Jew a foot and a half shorter than Pipik or me and crowned with ten times more wiry black hair than the two of us possessed together. His English was less than rudimentary, and once we were in the cab George had to repeat our destination to him in Hebrew. We were as good as alone in that cab, and so between the hotel and the courtroom, I told George Ziad everything that I should have told him the day before. He listened silently and, to my astonishment, did not seem startled or at all incredulous to learn that there had been another "me" in Jerusalem all the while he'd assumed that there was only the one with whom he had been to graduate school three decades earlier. He wasn't even ruffled (he who enjoyed so few moments without his veins and arteries visibly vibrating) when I tried to diagnose for him the perverse impulse that had led me to masquerade before his wife and his son as the Diasporist fanatic tendering manic homage to Irving Berlin.

"No apologies necessary," he replied in a calmly cutting voice.

"You are still who you were. Always on the stage. How could I have failed to remember? You're an actor, an amusing actor performing endlessly for the admiration of his friends. You're a satirist, always looking for the laugh, and how can a satirist be expected to suppress himself with a raving, ranting, slobbering Arab?"

"I don't know these days what I am," I said. "What I did was stupid —stupid and inexplicable—and I'm sorry. It was the last thing Anna and Michael needed."

"But what about what *you* needed? Your comic fix. What do an oppressed people's problems matter to a great comic artist like you? The show must go on. Say no more. You're a very amusing performer —and a moral idiot!"

So no more was said by either of us during the remaining few minutes before we reached the courtroom, and whether George was a deluded madman or a cunning liar—or a great comic artist in his own right—or whether the network of intrigue he claimed to represent existed (and whether a man so out of control and continually at the breaking point could be its representative) I had no way now of finding out. *There is somebody for you to talk to in Athens. There are people who can help you there. They are Jews but they are also our friends.* ... Jews bankrolling the PLO? Is *that* what he'd been telling me?

At the courthouse, when George hopped out of his side of the taxi before I even had a chance to pay the driver, I believed I'd never see him again. Yet there he was, already at the back of the courtroom, when I slipped inside a minute or two later. Quickly catching hold of my hand, he whispered, "You're the Dostoyevsky of disinformation," and only then proceeded past me to look for a seat by himself.

The courtroom that morning was less than half full. According to *The Jerusalem Post,* all the witnesses had been heard and this was to be the third day of the summing up. I could see clearly down to where Demjanjuk's son was sitting in the second row, just to the left of the center of the hall and directly in line with the chair on the stage where his father was seated between his two guards and back of the defense counsel's table. When I saw that in the row behind

Demjanjuk junior nearly all the chairs were unoccupied, I made my way there and quickly sat down, as the court was already in session.

I'd got a set of earphones at the desk by the entrance door and, slipping them over my head, turned the dial to the channel for the English translation of the proceedings. It was a minute or two, however, before I could take in what one of the judges—the chief judge, Israeli Supreme Court Justice Levin—was saying to the witness on the stand. He was the first witness of the day, a compactly built, sturdy-looking Jewish man in his late sixties, whose substantial head —a weighty boulder onto which a pair of thick spectacles had incongruously been set—was stacked squarely atop a torso of cement building blocks. He wore slacks and a surprisingly sporty red and black pullover sweater, something in which a clean-cut young athlete might show up for a date, and his hands, a laborer's hands, a dockworker's hands, hands that looked hard as nails, were fastened to the lip of the lectern with the impassioned, bottled-up nervous ferocity of a heavyweight bursting to catapult into battle at the sound of the bell.

His name was Eliahu Rosenberg and this was not his first round in court with Demjanjuk, as I knew from a startling photograph in the Demjanjuk clipping file that had caught my attention the day I'd arrived, one in which a friendly, grinning Demjanjuk is warmly offering Rosenberg his hand to shake. The photograph had been taken about a year before, on the seventh day of the trial, when Rosenberg was asked by the prosecution to leave the witness stand and step up to the defendant's chair, some twenty feet away, to make his identification. Rosenberg had been called to testify as one of seven prosecution witnesses who claimed to recognize John Demjanjuk of Cleveland, Ohio, as the Ivan the Terrible they had known while they were prisoners at Treblinka. According to Rosenberg, he and Ivan, both men then in their early twenties, had worked in close proximity every day for nearly a year, Ivan as the guard who operated the gas chamber and supervised the detail of Jewish prisoners, the "death commandos," whose job was to empty the gas chamber of corpses, to clean it of urine and excrement so as to make it ready for the gassing of the next shipment of Jews, and to whitewash the walls, outside as well as inside, so as to cover over the bloodstains (for Ivan and the other guards oftentimes drew blood while driving the Jews into the gas with knives and clubs and iron pipes). Twenty-one-year-old Eliahu Rosenberg, recently of Warsaw, was one of the death commandos, those thirty or so living Jews whose other job, after each gassing, was carrying on stretchers—running all the while at top speed—the naked corpses of the freshly killed Jews to the open-air "roast" where, after their gold teeth were extracted for the German state treasury by the prisoner "dentist," the bodies were skillfully piled to be incinerated, children and women at the bottom for kindling, and men at the top, where they ignited more easily.

Now, eleven months later, Rosenberg had been surprisingly recalled, this time by the defense, in the midst of its summing up. The judge was telling Rosenberg, "You will listen carefully to the questions put to you and you will reply and confine yourself to the questions put to you. You will not enter into polemics nor will you lose your self-control as, unfortunately, happened more than once in the course of your testimony—"

But, as I have said, during my first few minutes inside the courtroom, I could not focus on the English translation coming through my headphones, not with young Demjanjuk in the row before me, mine to maintain surveillance over, mine to sit by and protect—if protection was indeed warranted—from the machinating Moishe Pipik, and not with these two diaries filling my pockets. *Were* they the diaries of Leon Klinghoffer? Unobtrusively as I could, I lifted them out of either pocket and turned them over and over in my hands; I even put them up to my nose, quickly one and then the other, to sniff their papery odor, that pleasant moldering smell that faintly perfumes old library stacks. Holding the red diary open in my lap, I read for a moment from a page midway through. "Thurs. 9/23/78. On way to Yugoslavia. Du Brovnik. Went past Messina and Straits. Reminded us of 1969 trip to city of Messina. New crowd got aboard at Genoa. Show tonight was great. Everyone has coughing spells. I don't know why, weather is perfect."

That comma setting off "why" from "weather"—is it likely, I asked myself, that a man in the appliance business in Queens would have deftly dropped a comma in there? In jottings as rudimentary as these should I be finding any punctuation at all? And no spelling errors anywhere other than in the writing of an unfamiliar place name? *New crowd got aboard at Genoa.* Deliberately planted there, that item? There perhaps to presage what would happen seven years hence, when, in the new crowd that boarded the *Achille Lauro* at some Italian port or other—maybe it was even at Genoa—were hidden the three Palestinian terrorists who would kill this very same diarist? Or was that simply a report of what had happened on their cruise of September 1978—a new crowd had boarded at Genoa and, for the Klinghoffers, nothing horrible ensued.

But distracted as I was from following the judge's opening remarks by the presence, in the seat before me, of young Demjanjuk, not yet kidnapped and still unharmed; distracted as I was by the diaries that had been forced on me by Supposnik—wondering whether they were forged, wondering whether Supposnik was a charlatan who was a party to the forgery or a passionate Jewish survivor who was its unsuspecting victim, wondering whether the diaries were exactly what he'd said they were, and, if so, wondering whether it really was somehow my Jewish duty to write the introduction that might then elicit publishing interest in them other than just in Israel—I was still further disconcerted by trying to puzzle out why everything I'd truthfully told George Ziad in the taxi could have been assumed by him to be, of all things, "disinformation."

It must be because he assumed, first off, that, like the antiquarian bookseller Supposnik, our tiny taxi driver was another of those Israeli secret police men that he'd been directing my attention to everywhere we met; it must be that he assumed not only that we two were under close surveillance but that I had surmised this upon getting into the cab and had then, ingeniously, come up with the story of the second Philip Roth in order to jam the interloper's circuits with so much cuckoo nonsense. Otherwise I didn't know what to make of this word "disinformation" or of the affectionate grip in which he'd taken my hand only minutes after angrily informing me that I was a moral idiot.

Admittedly, the story of my double was difficult to accept at face value. The story of anyone's double would be. It was my own difficulty accepting it that largely accounted for why I had so mismanaged just about everything having to do with Pipik and was probably mismanaging it still. But however hard it was to swallow the existence of a character as audaciously fraudulent as Moishe Pipik or to imagine him meeting with any success whatsoever, I'd have thought it still easier for George to accept this double's unlikely existence than to believe that (1) I could seriously be the proponent of a political scheme as antihistorically harebrained as Diasporism or that (2) Diasporism could possibly constitute a source of hope for the Palestinian national movement, especially one worthy of financial backing. No, only the insane desperation of a zealot who knew himself to be powerless and who had lived too long in behalf of a cause on the brink of total failure could lead someone as intelligent as George Ziad to seize with such reckless enthusiasm on an idea so spurious. And yet if George were that blinded, that defeated by suffering, that disfigured by impotent rage, then surely he would have disqualified himself long ago from anything like the position of influence that he claimed enabled him to come to see me, as he had this morning, to make arrangements for the secret Athens meeting. On the other hand, perhaps by now the mind of my old Chicago friend was so savagely unhinged by despair that he had taken to living in a dream of his own devising, "Athens" his Palestinian Xanadu and those rich Jewish backers of the PLO no more real than the imaginary friends of a lonely child.

It was not for me, after these last seventy-two hours, to reject as too outlandish the possibility that the situation for him here had driven George crazy. Yet I did reject it. It was just too insipid a conclusion. Not everybody was crazy. Resolute is not crazy. Deluded is not crazy. To be thwarted, vengeful, terrified, treacherous—this is not to be crazy. Not even fanatically held illusions are crazy, and deceit certainly isn't crazy—deceit, deviousness, cunning, cynicism, all of that is far from crazy . . . and there, that, *deceit,* there was the key to my confusion! Of course! It wasn't I who'd been deceiving George, it was George who was deceiving me! I had been suckered by the tragic melodrama of the pitiful victim who is driven nearly insane by injustice and exile. George's madness was Hamlet's—*an act.*

Yes, here's an explanation to it all! Eminent Jewish writer shows up in Jerusalem espousing a massive transfer of Israel's Ashkenazi population back to their European countries of origin. The idea may appear as grossly unrealistic to a Palestinian militant as to Menachem Begin, but that an eminent writer should come up with such an idea might not seem unrealistic to either; no, nothing peculiar to them about an eminent writer who imagines there is some correlation between his own feverish, ignorant apocalyptic fantasies and the way that struggles between contending political forces are won and lost in actuality. Of course, politically speaking, the eminent writer is a joke; of course nothing the man thinks moves anyone in Israel or anywhere else to act one way or another, but he's a cultural celebrity, he commands column inches all over the world, and consequently the eminent writer who thinks that the Jews should get the hell out of Palestine is not to be ignored or ridiculed but to be encouraged and exploited. George knows him. He's an old American buddy of George's. Seduce him, George, with our suffering. Between books all these eminent writers love five or six days in a good hotel, enmeshed in the turbulent tragedies of the heroically oppressed. Track him down. Find him. Tell him how they torture us—it's the ones who stay in the best hotels who are, understandably, particularly sensitized to the horrors of injustice. If a dirty fork on the breakfast tray elicits an angry protest to room service, imagine their outrage over the cattle prod. Rant, rave, display your wounds, give him the Celebrity Tour—the military courtrooms, the bloodstained walls—tell him that you'll take him to talk with Father Arafat himself. Let's see what kind of coverage George can whip up for Mr. Roth's little publicity stunt. Let's put this megalomaniac Jew on the cover of *Time!*

But what then of the other Jew, the megalomaniac double? All these suppositions might explain why George Ziad had damned me in the taxicab as a moral idiot and then, only minutes later, in a whispered aside at the rear of the courtroom, lauded me as the Dostoyevsky of disinformation. This spy story I'd been spinning out could indeed provide the key to George's ostensibly haywire behavior, to his so fortuitously stumbling on me in the marketplace, to his following me and pursuing me and taking me dead seriously no matter how bizarre my own performance, except for one formidable impediment to its logic: the ubiquitous Moishe Pipik. Everything that George had appeared to discount as concocted by me to confound the Israeli intelligence agent driving our cab, local Palestinian intelligence—had it taken the slightest interest in me—would already have known to be the truth through its contacts at the two hotels where Pipik and I were each openly registered in my name. And if the higher-ups in Palestinian intelligence were well aware that the Diasporist and the novelist were different people, that the King David P.R. was an impostor and the American Colony P.R. the real thing, why then would they—more precisely, why then would their agent, George Ziad—pretend to me to think that the two were identical? Particularly when they knew that I knew as well as they did of the existence of the other one!

No, Moishe Pipik's existence argued too powerfully against the plausibility of the story with which I was trying to convince myself that George Ziad was something other than insane and that there was a meaning more humanly interesting than that lurking beneath all this confusion. Unless, of course, they'd planted Pipik in the first place—unless, as I'd all but doped out the very first time I made contact with Pipik and interviewed him from London as Pierre Roget, *unless Pipik had been working for them from the start.* Of course! That's what intelligence agencies do all the time. They'd stumbled accidentally on my look-alike, who might actually be, for all I knew, in the seedy end of the detective business, and, for a fee, they had put him up to some propagandistic mischief—to spouting to whoever would listen all this thinly camouflaged anti-Zionist crap that called itself Diasporism. He was being run by my old friend George Ziad, George his coach, his contact, his brains. The last thing they'd expected was that, in the midst of it all, *I* would turn up in Jerusalem too. Or maybe that was what they'd *planned.* They had set Pipik out as the bait. But to lure me into doing what?

Why, exactly what I was doing. Exactly what I had done! *Exactly what I was going to do.* They're not just running him, they're running *me* without my knowing it! They have been since I got here!

I stopped myself right there. Everything I had been thinking—and, what's worse, eagerly believing—shocked me and frightened me. What I was elaborating so thoroughly as a rational explanation of reality was infused with just the sort of rationality that the psychiatrists regularly hear from the most far-gone paranoid on the schizophrenic ward. I stopped myself and stepped back in alarm from the hole where I was blindly headed, realizing that in order to make George Ziad "more humanly interesting" than someone simply nuts and out of control, I was making *myself* nuts. Better for real things to be uncontrollable, better for one's life to be indecipherable and intellectually impenetrable than to attempt to make causal sense of what is unknown with a fantasy that is mad. Better, I thought, that the events of these three days should remain incomprehensible to me forever than to posit, as I had just been doing, a conspiracy of foreign intelligence agents who are determined to control my mind. We've all heard that one before.

———

Mr. Rosenberg had been recalled to be questioned about a sixty-eight-page document that only now, in the closing hours of the year-long trial, had been discovered by the defense at a Warsaw historical institute. It was a 1945 report about Treblinka and the fate of the Jews there, written in Eliahu Rosenberg's own hand and in Yiddish, his first language, nearly thirty months after his escape from Treblinka, while he was a soldier in the Polish army. Encouraged to recount the story of the death camp by some Poles in Cracow, where he was then billeted, Rosenberg had spent two days writing down his memories and then gave the manuscript to a Cracow landlady, a Mrs.

Wasser, to pass on to the appropriate institution for whatever historical usefulness it might have. He had not seen his Treblinka memoir
again until on that morning a photocopy of the original was handed
to him on the witness stand and he was asked by defense counsel
Chumak to examine the signature and to tell the court if it was his
own.

Rosenberg said it was, and when there was no objection from the
prosecution, the 1945 memoir was admitted into evidence "for the
purposes," said Justice Levin, "of questioning the witness in conjunc-
tion with what it states in same on the events of the uprising at
Treblinka on the second of August, 1943. And specifically," Levin
continued, "on the subject of the death of Ivan as written down in
said statement."

The death of Ivan? At the sound of those four words coming
through the earphones in English translation, young Demjanjuk,
seated directly in front of me, began to nod his head vigorously, but
otherwise there wasn't a movement to be discerned in the courtroom, not a sound was to be heard until Chumak, with his confident
matter-of-factness, set out in his Canadian-accented English to review
with Rosenberg the relevant pages of this memoir, in which, apparently just months after the end of the European war, Rosenberg had
written of the death of the very man into whose "murderous eyes"
he had gazed with such horror and revulsion back on the seventh day
of the trial, or so he had sworn.

"I would like to go directly to the relevant portion with Mr. Rosenberg, where you wrote, 'After a few days, the date for the uprising
was set for the second day of the eighth month with no excuse'—can
you find that on page sixty-six of the document?"

Chumak then took him through his description of the heat in the
middle of the day of August 2, 1943, a heat so fierce that the "boys,"
as Rosenberg had described his fellow death commandos, who had
been working since four a.m., sobbed from pain and fell down with
the stretchers while transferring exhumed corpses to be incinerated.
The revolt had been set for four p.m., but fifteen minutes before,
there was a hand-grenade explosion and several shots rang out, sig-

naling that the uprising had begun. Rosenberg read aloud the Yiddish text and then translated into Hebrew a description of how one of the boys, Shmuel, was the first to run out of the barracks, loudly shouting the uprising's passwords, "Revolution in Berlin! There is a revolt in Berlin!" and how Mendel and Chaim, two other boys, then jumped the Ukrainian barracks guard and took the rifle from his hands.

"Now you wrote these lines, sir, and they are correct," said Chumak. "That's what happened at the time, is that correct?"

"If it pleases the court," said Rosenberg, "I think I have to explain. Because what I say here, I had heard. I hadn't seen it. There's a big difference between the two."

"But what you just read to us, sir, that Shmuel was the first to leave the barracks. Did you see him leave the barracks?"

Rosenberg said that no, he hadn't seen it himself, and that in much of what he'd written he had been reporting what others had seen and what they had told one another once they had gotten over all the fences and safely escaped into the forest.

"So," said Chumak, who was not about to let him be on this subject, "you don't write in your document that they told us about it in the forest later, you are writing it as it is happening in the document, which you have admitted your memory was better in '45 than it is today. And I put it to you that if you wrote this, you must have seen it."

Again Rosenberg set out to clarify that what he'd written was based, of necessity, on what he had been able to observe as a participant in the uprising and on what all the others had told him afterward, in the forest, about their involvement and what they had seen and done.

Zvi Tal, the bearded judge in the skullcap, stereotypically judicious-looking with his glasses set halfway down his nose, finally interrupted the repetitious duologue between Chumak and Rosenberg and asked the witness, "Why didn't you point out later, in the forest, I saw, I heard such and such—why did you write it as though you saw it yourself?"

"Perhaps it was a mistake on my part," replied Rosenberg. "Perhaps I should have noted it, but the fact of the matter is that I did hear all of this, and I have always said that in the course of the uprising, I didn't see what was happening all around me because the bullets were shrieking all around us and I just wanted to get away as quickly as possible from that inferno."

"Naturally," said Chumak, "everyone would want to get away as quickly as possible from that inferno, but if I could proceed, did you see this guard being strangled by everybody and thrown into the well —did you see that?"

"No," said Rosenberg, "it was told to me in the forest, not just to me, everyone heard about it, and there were many versions, not only that one. . . ."

Justice Levin asked the witness, "You were inclined to believe what people told you, people who had escaped as you did, to freedom from the camp?"

"Yes, Your Honor," said Rosenberg. "It was a symbol of our great success, the very fact that we heard what had been done to those *Vachmanns*, for us it was a wish come true. Of course I believed that they had been killed and that they had been strangled—it was a success for us. Can you imagine, sir, such a success, this wish come true, where people succeeded in killing their assassins, their killers? Did I have to doubt it? I believed it with my whole heart. And would that it had been true. I hoped it was true."

All of this having been explained yet again, Chumak nonetheless resumed questioning Rosenberg along the very same lines—"Didn't you see all of these events, sir, that I have read out to you?"—until finally the chief prosecutor rose to object.

"I believe," the prosecutor said, "that the witness has already replied to this question several times."

The bench, however, allowed Chumak to continue and even Judge Tal intervened again, more or less along the line of what *he* had asked Rosenberg only minutes before. "Do you agree," he said to the witness, "that it emerges from what you wrote down, if one just reads what you wrote down—that one simply cannot tell what you actually saw for yourself and what you heard about later? In other words, anyone reading this would be inclined to think that you saw everything. Do you agree?"

While the questioning dragged on about the method by which

Rosenberg had composed his memoir, I thought, Why is his technique so hard to understand? The man is not a skilled verbalist, he was never a historian, a reporter, or a writer of any kind, nor was he, in 1945, a university student who knew from studying the critical prefaces of Henry James all there is to know about the dramatization of conflicting points of view and the ironic uses of contradictory testimony. He was a meagerly educated twenty-three-year-old Polish Jewish survivor of a Nazi death camp who had been given paper and a pen and then placed for some fifteen or twenty hours at a table in a Cracow rooming house, where he had written not the story, strictly told, of his own singular experience at Treblinka but rather what he had been asked to write: a memoir of Treblinka life, a *collective* memoir in which he simply, probably without giving the matter a moment's thought, subsumed the experiences of the others and became the choral voice for them all, moving throughout from the first-person plural to the third-person plural, sometimes from one to the other within the very same sentence. That such a person's handwritten memoir, written straight out in a couple of sittings, should lack the thoughtful discriminations of self-conscious narration did not strike me, for one, as surprising.

"Now," Chumak was saying, "now this is really the heart of the whole exercise, Mr. Rosenberg—the next line of what you wrote in December of 1945." He asked Rosenberg to read aloud what came next.

" 'We then went into the engine room, to Ivan, he—who was sleeping there—' " Rosenberg slowly translated from the Yiddish in a forceful voice, " 'and Gustav hit him with a shovel on the head. And he remained lying down for keeps.' "

"In other words, he was dead?" Chumak asked.

"Yes, correct."

"Sir, on December 20, 1945, in your handwriting?"

"Correct."

"And I suppose this would be one very important piece of information in your document, sir, would it not be?"

"Of course it would be a very important piece of information," Rosenberg replied, "if it were the truth."

"Well, when I asked you about the whole document, sir, the sixty-eight pages—I asked you whether you made an accurate and correct version or recital of what occurred at Treblinka. You said, at the very beginning of my cross-examination—"

"I say again yes. But there are things which I heard."

In front of me young Demjanjuk was shaking his head in disbelief at Rosenberg's contention that eyewitness testimony recorded in 1945 could be based on unreliable evidence. Rosenberg was lying and, thought the son of the accused, lying because of his own unappeasable guilt. Because of how he had managed to live while all the others died. Because of what the Nazis had ordered him to do with the bodies of his fellow Jews and what he obediently had done, loathsome as it was for him to do it. Because to survive not only was it necessary to steal, which he did, which of course they all did all the time—from the dead, from the dying, from the living, from the ill, from one another and everyone—but also it was necessary to bribe their torturers, to betray their friends, to lie to everyone, to take every humiliation in silence, like a whipped and broken animal. He was lying because he was worse than an animal, because he'd become a monster who had burned the little bodies of Jewish children, thousands upon thousands of them burned by him for kindling, and the only means he has to justify becoming a monster is to lay his sins on my father's head. My innocent father is the scapegoat not merely for those millions who died but for all the Rosenbergs who did the monstrous things they did to survive and now cannot live with their monstrous guilt. The other one is the monster, says Rosenberg, Demjanjuk is the monster. I am the one who catches the monster, who identifies the monster and sees that he is slain. There, in the flesh, is the criminal monster, John Demjanjuk of Cleveland, Ohio, and I, Eliahu Rosenberg of Treblinka, am cleansed.

Or were these not at all like young Demjanjuk's thoughts? Why is Rosenberg lying? Because he is a Jew who hates Ukrainians. Because the Jews are out to get the Ukrainians. Because this is a plot, a conspiracy by all these Jews to put all Ukrainians on trial and vilify them before the world.

Or were *these* nothing like John junior's thoughts either? Why is this Rosenberg lying about my father? Because he is a publicity hound, a crazy egomaniac who wants to see his picture in the paper and to be their great Jewish hero. Rosenberg thinks, When I finish with this stupid Ukrainian, they'll put my picture on a postage stamp.

Why does Rosenberg lie about my father? Because he is a liar. The man in the dock is my father, so he must be truthful, and the man in the witness box is somebody else's father, so he must be lying. Perhaps it was as simple for the son as that: John Demjanjuk is my father, any father of mine is innocent, therefore John Demjanjuk is innocent —maybe nothing more need be thought beyond the childish pathos of this filial logic.

And in a row somewhere behind me, what was George Ziad thinking? Two words: public relations. Rosenberg is their Holocaust PR man. The smoke from the incinerators of Treblinka ... behind the darkness of that darkness they still contrive to hide from the world their dark and evil deeds. The cynicism of it! To exploit with shameless flamboyance the smoke from the burning bodies of their own martyred dead!

Why is he lying? Because that's what public relations is—for a weekly paycheck they lie. They call it image making: whatever works, whatever suits the need of the client, whatever serves the propaganda machine. Marlboro has the Marlboro Man, Israel has its Holocaust Man. Why does he say what he says? Ask why the ad agencies say what they say. FOR THE SMOKESCREEN THAT HIDES EVERYTHING, SMOKE HOLOCAUST.

Or was George thinking about me and my usefulness, about making me into *his* PR man? Maybe without me to intimidate with all that righteous rage, he was taking a quiet philosophical break and thinking to himself only this: Yes, it's all a battle for TV time and column inches. Who controls the Nielsen ratings controls the world. It's all publicity, a matter of which of us comes up with the more spectacular drama to popularize his claim. Treblinka is theirs, the uprising is ours —may the best propaganda machine win.

Or maybe he was thinking, wistfully, sinisterly, utterly realistically, If only *we* had the corpses. Yes, I thought, maybe it's a pathologically desperate desire for bloody mayhem that lies behind this uprising, their need for a massacre, for piles of slaughtered corpses that will dramatize conclusively for worldwide TV just who are the victims this time round. Maybe that's why the children are in the first wave, why, instead of fighting against the enemy with grown men, they are dispatching children, armed only with stones, to provoke the firepower of the Israeli army. Yes, to make the networks forget their Holocaust we will stage *our* Holocaust. On the bodies of our children the Jews will perpetrate a Holocaust, and at last the TV audience will understand our plight. Send in the children and then summon the networks—we'll beat the Holocaust-mongers at their own game!

And what was *I* thinking? I was thinking, What are they thinking? I was thinking about Moishe Pipik and what *he* was thinking. And wondering every second where he was. Even as I continued to follow the courtroom proceedings I looked around me for some sign of his presence. I remembered the balcony. What if he was up with the journalists and the TV crews, sighting down on me from there?

I turned but from my seat could see nothing beyond the balcony railing. If he's up there, I thought, he is thinking, What is Roth thinking? What is Roth doing? How do we kidnap the monster's son if Roth is in the way?

There were uniformed policemen in the four corners of the courtroom and plainclothesmen, with walkie-talkies, standing at the back of the courtroom and regularly moving up and down the aisles—shouldn't I get hold of one and take him with me up to the balcony to apprehend Moishe Pipik? But Pipik's gone, I thought, it's over....

This is what I was thinking when I was not thinking the opposite and everything else.

As to what the accused was thinking while Rosenberg explained to the court why the Treblinka memoir was erroneous, the person who best knew that sat at the defense table, the Israeli lawyer, Sheftel, to whom Demjanjuk had been passing note after note throughout Chumak's examination of Rosenberg, notes written, I supposed, in the defendant's weak English. Demjanjuk scribbled feverishly away, but after he'd passed each note to Sheftel over the lawyer's shoulder, it

did not look to me as though Sheftel gave more than a cursory glance
to it before setting it down atop the others on the table.* In the
Ukrainian American community, I was thinking, these notes, if they
were ever to be collected and published, would have an impact on
Demjanjuk's *landsmen* something like that of those famous prison
letters written in immigrantese by Sacco and Vanzetti. Or the impact
on the conscience of the civilized world that Supposnik immoder-
ately posits for Klinghoffer's travel diaries should they ever be graced
by an introduction by me.

All this writing by nonwriters, I thought, all these diaries, memoirs,
and notes written clumsily with the most minimal skill, employing
one one-thousandth of the resources of a written language, and yet
the testimony they bear is no less persuasive for that, is in fact that
much more searing precisely because the expressive powers are so
blunt and primitive.

* It was Sheftel, by the way, who would have benefited from a bodyguard to
protect him against attack. Perhaps my most unthinking mistake of all in Jerusalem was to have allowed myself to become convinced that at the culmination of
this inflammatory trial, the violent rage of a wild Jewish avenger, if and when it
should erupt, would be directed at a Gentile and not, as I initially thought, and
as happened—and as even the least cynical of Jewish ironists could have foreseen—at another Jew.

On December 1, 1988, during the funeral for Demjanjuk's auxiliary Israeli
lawyer—one who'd joined Sheftel, after Demjanjuk's conviction, to help prepare
the Supreme Court appeal and who mysteriously committed suicide only weeks
later—Sheftel was approached by Yisroel Yehezkeli, a seventy-year-old Holocaust survivor and a frequent spectator at the Demjanjuk trial, who shouted at
him, "Everything's because of you," and threw hydrochloric acid in the lawyer's
face. The acid completely destroyed the protective cover over the cornea of his
left eye and Sheftel was virtually blind in that eye until he came to Boston some
eight weeks later, where he underwent a cell transplant, a four-hour operation
by a Harvard surgeon, that restored his sight. During Sheftel's Boston sojourn
and subsequent recovery, he was accompanied by John Demjanjuk, Jr., who
acted as his nurse and chauffeur.

As for Yisroel Yehezkeli, he was convicted of aggravated assault. He was sentenced by a Jerusalem judge, who found him "unrepentant," and served three
years in jail. The court psychiatrist's report described the assailant as "not psychotic, although slightly paranoid." Most of Yehezkeli's family had been killed at
Treblinka.

Chumak was now asking Rosenberg, "So how can you possibly come to this court and point your finger at this gentleman when you wrote in 1945 that Ivan was killed by Gustav?"

"Mr. Chumak," he quickly replied, "did I say that I saw him kill him?"

"Don't answer with another question," Justice Levin cautioned Rosenberg.

"He didn't come back from the dead, Mr. Rosenberg," Chumak continued.

"I did not say so. I did not say so. I personally did not say that I saw him being killed," said Rosenberg. "But, Mr. Chumak, I would like to see him—I did not—but I did not see him. It was my fondest wish. I was in Paradise when I heard—not only Gustav but also others told me—I wanted, I wanted to believe, Mr. Chumak. I wanted to believe that this creature does not exist. Is not alive any longer. But, unfortunately, to my great sorrow, I would have liked to see him torn apart as he had torn apart our people. And I believed with all my heart that he had been liquidated. Can you understand, Mr. Chumak? It was their fondest wish. It was our dream to finish him off, together with others. But he had managed to get out, get away, survive—what luck he had!"

"Sir, you wrote in your handwriting, in Yiddish—not in German, not in Polish, not in English, but in your own language—you wrote that he was hit on the head by Gustav with a spade, leaving him lying there for keeps. You wrote that. And you told us that you wrote the truth when you made these statements in 1945. Are you saying that's not true?"

"No, it is true, this is the truth what it says here—but what the boys told us was not the truth. They wanted to boast. They were lending expression to their dream. They aspired to, their fondest wish was, to kill this person—but they hadn't."

"Why didn't you write then," Chumak asked him, "it was the boys' fondest wish to kill this man and I heard later in the forest that he was killed in such and such a way—or in another way. Why didn't you write it all down, all these versions?"

Rosenberg replied, "I preferred to write this particular version."

"Who was present with you when this version was given, this version about the boys wanting to kill him, and everyone wanting to be a hero, and killing this awful man?"

"In the forest, when they told this version there were a great many around, and we sat around for some hours before we went our own way. And there, sir, they were sitting down and each was telling his version and I took it in. And this is what I remember, I took this in and I really wanted to believe firmly that this is what had happened. But it had not come about."

When I looked at Demjanjuk I saw him smiling directly back, not at me, of course, but at his loyal son, seated in the chair in front of me. Demjanjuk was amused by the absurdity of the testimony, tremendously amused by it, even triumphant-looking because of it, as though Rosenberg's claim that he had reported accurately in 1945 what his sources, unbeknownst to him, had themselves reported inaccurately was all the exculpation necessary and he was as good as free. Was he dim-witted enough to believe that? Why *was* he smiling? To raise the spirits of his son and supporters? To register for the audience his contempt? The smile was eerie and mystifying and, to Rosenberg, as anyone could see, as odious as the hand of friendship and the warm "Shalom" that had been tendered him by Demjanjuk the year before. Had Rosenberg's hatred been combustible and had a match been struck anywhere near the witness stand, the entire courtroom would have gone up in flames. Rosenberg's dockworker's fingers bit into the lectern and his jaw was locked as though to suppress a roar.

"Now," Chumak continued, "based on the 'version' as you now call it, this version of Ivan being killed, he was struck in the head with a spade. Would you therefore expect, sir, the man who was struck with the spade to have a scar or a fractured skull or some serious injury to his head? If that happened to Ivan in the engine room?"

"Of course," replied Rosenberg, "if I were sure he had been hit and in accordance with the version I wrote down, he was then dead—where is the scar? But he wasn't there. And he wasn't there—because

he wasn't there." Rosenberg looked beyond Chumak now and, pointing at Demjanjuk, addressed him directly. "And if he had been there,
he would not be sitting across from me. This hero is grinning!" Rosenberg cried in disgust.

But Demjanjuk was no longer merely grinning, he was laughing,
laughing aloud at Rosenberg's words, at Rosenberg's rage, laughing at
the court, laughing at the trial, laughing at the absurdity of these
monstrous charges, at the outrageousness of a family man from a
Cleveland suburb, a Ford factory employee, a church member, prized
by his friends, trusted by his neighbors, adored by his family, of such
a man as this being mistaken for the psychotic ghoul who prowled
the Polish forests forty-five years ago as Ivan the Terrible, the vicious,
sadistic murderer of innocent Jews. Either he was laughing because a
man wholly innocent of any such crimes had no choice but to laugh
after a year of these nightmarish courtroom shenanigans and all that
the judiciary of the state of Israel had put him and his poor family
through or he was laughing because he was guilty of these crimes,
because he *was* Ivan the Terrible, and Ivan the Terrible was not
simply a psychotic ghoul but the devil himself. Because, if Demjanjuk
was not innocent, who but the devil could have laughed aloud like
that at Rosenberg?

Still laughing, Demjanjuk rose suddenly from his chair, and, speaking toward the open microphone on the defense lawyers' table, he
shouted at Rosenberg, *"Atah shakran!"* and laughed even louder.

Demjanjuk had spoken in Hebrew—for the second time the man
accused of being Ivan the Terrible had addressed this Treblinka Jew
who claimed to be his victim in the language of the Jews.

Justice Levin spoke next, also in Hebrew. On my headphones I
heard the translation. "The accused's words," Justice Levin noted,
"which have been placed on record—which were, 'You are a liar!'—
have been—have gone on record."

Only minutes later, Chumak concluded his examination of Rosenberg, and Justice Levin declared a recess until eleven. I left the court-

room as quickly as I could, feeling bereft and spent and uncompre-
hending, as numb as though I were walking away from the funeral of
someone I dearly loved. Never before had I witnessed an encounter
so charged with pain and savagery as that frightful face-off between
Demjanjuk and Rosenberg, a collision of two lives as immensely inimical as any two substances could be even on this rift-ravaged planet.
Perhaps because of everything abominable in all I'd just seen or simply because of the unintended fast I'd been on now for almost twenty-
four hours, as I tried to hold my place amid the spectators pushing
toward the coffee machine in the snack bar off the lobby, there was a
ragged overlay of words and pictures disturbingly adhering together
in my mind, a grating collage consisting of what Rosenberg should
have said to clarify himself and of the gold teeth being pulled from
the gassed Jews' mouths for the German treasury and of a Hebrew-
English primer, the book from which Demjanjuk had studiously
taught himself, in his cell, to say correctly, "You're a liar." Interlaced
with *You're a liar* were the words *Three thousand ducats.* I could
hear distinctly the admirable Macklin oleaginously enunciating
"Three thousand ducats" as I handed across my shekels to the old
man taking the money at the snack bar, who, to my astonishment,
was the crippled old survivor, Smilesburger, the man whose million-
dollar check I'd "stolen" from Pipik and then lost. The crowd was
so tightly packed behind me that no sooner had I paid for coffee and
a bun than I was forced aside and had all I could do to keep the
coffee in the container as I pressed toward the open lobby facing
outdoors.

So now I was seeing things too. Working the cash register from
atop a stool in the snack bar was just another old man with a bald
head and a scaling skull, who could not possibly have been the retired
New York jeweler disenchanted with Israel. I'm seeing double, I
thought, doubles, I thought, but because of not eating, because of
barely getting any sleep, or because I'm coming apart again for the
second time in a year? How could I have convinced myself that I
alone am personally responsible for overseeing the safety of Demjanjuk's son if I *weren't* coming apart? In the aftermath of that testimony,

in the aftermath of Demjanjuk's laughter and Rosenberg's rage, how could the asinine clowning of that nonsensical Pipik continue to make a claim on my life?

But just then I heard shouting outside the building and, through the glass doors, saw two soldiers armed with rifles running at full speed toward the parking lot. I ran out of the lobby after them, toward where some twenty or thirty people had now gathered to encircle whatever disturbance was transpiring. And when I heard from within that circle a voice loudly shouting in English, I knew for sure that he was here and the worst had happened. The all-out paranoid who I had by now become was asserting his panicked confidence in the unstoppable unraveling of the disaster; our mutual outrage with each other had been churned into a real catastrophe by that octopus of paranoia that, interlinked, the *two* of us had become.

But the man who was shouting looked to be nearly seven feet tall, taller by far than either Pipik or me, a treelike person, a gigantic redheaded creature with an amazing chin the shape of a boxing glove. His big bowl of a forehead was flushed with his fury, and the hands he waved about high in the air looked to be as large as cymbals—you wouldn't want your two little ears caught between the clanging of those two huge hands.

In either hand he clutched a white pamphlet, which he fluttered violently over the heads of the onlookers. Although a few in the crowd held copies of the pamphlet and were flipping through its pages, mostly the pamphlets were strewn on the pavement underfoot. The Jewish giant's English was limited, but his voice was a large, cascading thing, every inch of him in that swelling voice, and when he spoke the effect was of someone sounding an organ. He was the biggest and the loudest Jew that I had ever seen and he was booming down at a priest, an elderly, round-faced Catholic priest, who, though of medium height and rather stoutly built, looked, by comparison, like a little, shatterable statuette of a Catholic priest. He stood very rigidly, holding his ground, doing his best not to be intimidated by this gigantic Jew.

I stooped to pick up one of the pamphlets. In the center of the white cover was a blue trident whose middle prong was in the shape of the Cross; the pamphlet, a dozen or so pages long, bore the English title "Millennium of Christianity in Ukraine." The priest must have been distributing the pamphlets to those who'd left the courtroom and come outside for air. I read the first sentence of the pamphlet's first page. "1988 is a significant year for Ukrainian Christians throughout the world—it is the 1,000th anniversary of the introduction of Christianity to the land called Ukraine."

The crowd, mostly Israelis, seemed to understand neither the pamphlet's contents nor what the dispute was about, and because his English was so poor, it was a moment before what the Jewish giant was shouting was intelligible even to me and I understood that he was assaulting the priest with the names of Ukrainians whom he identified as the instigators of violent pogroms. The one name I recognized was Chmielnicki, who I seemed to recall was a national hero on the order of Jan Hus or Garibaldi. I had lived among working-class Ukrainians on the Lower East Side when I'd first come to New York in the mid-fifties and remembered vaguely the annual block parties where dozens of little children danced around the streets dressed in folk costumes. There were speeches from an outdoor stage denouncing Communism and the Soviet Union, and the names Chmielnicki and Saint Volodymyr showed up on the crayoned signs in the local shop windows and outside the Orthodox Ukrainian church just around the corner from my basement apartment.

"Where murderer Chmielnicki in book!" were the words that I finally understood the giant Jew to be shouting. "Where murderer Bandera in book! Where murderer Petlura son of bitch! Killer! Murderer! All Ukrainian anti-Semite!"

Defiantly cocking his head, the priest snapped back, "Petlura, if you knew anything, was himself murdered. Martyred. In Paris. By Soviet agents." He was an American, as it turned out, a Ukrainian Orthodox priest who, from the sound of his voice, was more than likely a New Yorker and who seemed to have come to Jerusalem all the way from New York, perhaps even from Second Avenue and Eighth Street, specifically to distribute his pamphlets celebrating the thousand years of

Ukrainian Christianity to the Jews attending the Demjanjuk trial.
Wasn't he in his right mind, either?

And then I realized that I was the one who had to be out of his
mind to be taking him for a priest and that this was more of the
masquerade, a performance designed to create a disturbance, to distract the police and soldiers, to draw away the crowd ... I could no
more free myself of the thought that Pipik was behind it all than Pipik
could free himself of the thought that I was perpetually behind him.
This priest is Pipik's decoy and part of Pipik's plot.

"No!" the Jewish giant was shouting. "Petlura murdered, yes—by
Jew! For killing Jew! By brave Jew!"

"Please," said the priest, "you have had your say, you have spoken.
Everybody can hear you from here to Canarsie—allow me, will you,
please, to address those good people here who might like to listen to
somebody else for a change." And turning away from the Jewish giant,
he resumed the lecture he'd apparently been delivering before their
ruckus had begun. As he spoke, the crowd grew larger, *just as Pipik
had anticipated.* "Around the year 860," the priest was telling them,
"two blood brothers, Cyril and Methodius, left their monastery in
Greece to preach Christianity among the Slavic people. Our forefa-
thers had no alphabet and no written language. These brothers created for us an alphabet called the Cyrillic alphabet, after the name of
one of the brothers—"

But again the Jewish giant interposed himself between the onlookers and the priest, and again he began to shout at him in that astound-
ingly large voice. "Hitler and Ukrainian! Two brother! One thing! Kill
Jew! I know! Mother! Sister! Everybody! Ukrainian kill!"

"Listen, bud," said the priest, his fingers whitening around the thick
stack of pamphlets that he was still clutching to his chest, "Hitler, for
your information, was no friend of the Ukrainian people. Hitler gave
away half of my country to Nazified Poland, in case you haven't heard.
Hitler gave Bukovina to Fascist Romania, Hitler gave Bessarabia—"

"No! Shut up! Hitler give you big present! Hitler give you big, big
present! Hitler," he boomed, "give you Jew to kill!"

"Cyril and Methodius," the priest resumed, again bravely turning his back on the giant to address the crowd, "translated the Bible and the Holy Mass into Slavonic, as the language was called. They set out to Rome, to obtain permission from Pope Adrian II to say Mass in the language they had translated. Pope Adrian approved it and our Slavonic Mass, or Ukrainian liturgy, was celebrated—"

That was as much about the brothers Cyril and Methodius as the giant Jew could bear to hear. He reached out for the priest with his two giant's hands and I saw him suddenly as created not by a malfunctioning pituitary gland but by a thousand years of Jewish dreaming. Our final solution to the Ukrainian Christianity problem. Not Zionism, not Diasporism, but Gigantism—Golemism! The five soldiers looking on with their rifles from the edge of the crowd surged forward to intervene and protect the priest, but what happened happened so quickly that before the soldiers could stop anything, everything was over and everyone was laughing and already walking away —laughing not because the priest from New York City had been lifted into the air and smashed to the ground and dispatched from this life into the next by the enormous muddy boots on the giant's two feet but because a couple of hundred pamphlets went sailing up over our heads and that was the end of that. The giant had yanked from the priest's hands all of his pamphlets, hurled them as high as he could, and with that the incident was over.

As the crowd dispersed to return to the courtroom, I stood there watching the priest set out to recover his pamphlets, some of which were scattered as far as fifty feet away. And I saw the giant, still shouting, moving off alone toward the street, where buses were running and traffic was flowing as though it was what indeed it was, in Jerusalem as everywhere else: just another day. A sunny, pleasant day at that. The priest, of course, had nothing at all to do with Pipik, and the plot that I had resolved to foil existed nowhere other than in my head. Whatever I thought or did was wrong and for the simple reason that there was, I now realized, no *right thing* for someone whose double in this world was Mr. Moishe Pipik—so long as he and I both lived, this mental chaos would prevail. I'll never again know what's really going on or whether my thoughts are nonsense or not; everything I can't immediately understand will have for me a bizarre significance and, even if I have no idea where he is and never hear tell of him again, so long as he goes about, as he does, giving my life its shallowest meaning, I'll never be free of exaggerated thoughts or these insufferable sieges of confusion. Even worse than never being free of him, I'll never again be free of myself; and nobody can know any better than I do that this is a punishment without limits. Pipik will follow me all the days of my life, and I will dwell in the house of Ambiguity forever.

The priest continued to gather up the pamphlets one by one, and because he was much older than I'd realized when he was defiantly standing up to the giant, the effort was not easy for him. He was a very weak, very stout old man, and although the encounter had not ended violently, it seemed to have left him as enfeebled as if he had in fact received a terrible blow. Maybe bending over picking up the pamphlets was making him dizzy, because he didn't look at all well. He was terrifyingly ashen, whereas facing down the giant, he had been a pluckier, much more vivid shade.

"Why," I said to him, "why, in all of this world, do you come here with those pamphlets on a day like this one?"

He'd fallen to his knees to gather together the pamphlets more easily, and from his knees he answered me. "To save Jews." A little of his strength seemed to return when he repeated to me, "To save you Jews."

"You might do better to worry about yourself." Although this had not been my intention, I stepped forward to offer him my hand; I didn't see how else he could get back on his feet. Two bystanders, two young men in jeans, two very tough customers indeed, young and lithe and scornful, were watching us from only a few feet away. The rest of the crowd had all moved off.

"If they convict an innocent man," the priest said as I tried to remember where I'd seen these two in jeans before, "this will have the same result as the Crucifixion of Jesus."

"Oh, for God's sake, not that old chestnut, Father. Not the Crucifixion of Christ *again!*" I said, steadying him now that he was standing erect.

His voice shook when he replied, not because he was winded but because my angry response had left him incensed. "Through two thousand years, Jewish people paid for that—rightly or wrongly, they paid for the Crucifixion. I don't want the conviction of Johnny to have similar results!"

And it was just here that I felt myself leaving the ground. I was being removed from where I was to somewhere else. I did not know what was happening but I felt as though a pipe were digging into either side of me and on these pipes I was being hoisted and carried away. My feet were cycling in the air, and then they met the ground and I saw that the two pipes were arms belonging to the two men in jeans.

"Don't shout," one of them said.

"Don't struggle," the other said.

"Do nothing," the first one said.

"But—" I began.

"Don't speak."

"You speak too much."

"You speak to everyone."

"You speak speak speak."

"Speak speak speak speak speak speak—"

They put me into a car, and someone drove us away. Roughly the two men patted me all over to see if I was carrying a weapon.

"You have the wrong man," I said.

The driver laughed loudly. "Good. We want the wrong man."

"Oh," I heard myself asking through a great fog of terror, "is this going to be a humorous experience?"

"For us," replied the driver, "or for you?"

"Who are you?" I cried. "Palestinians? Jews?"

"Why," said the driver, "that's the very question we want to ask you."

I thought it best to say no more, though "thought" does not describe in any way the process by which my mind was now operating. I began to vomit, which did not endear me to my captors.

I was driven to a stone building in a decaying neighborhood just back of the central market, not far from where I'd run into George the day before and somewhere very near where Apter lived. There were some six or seven tiny Orthodox children, their skulls crystalline, playing a game in the street, strikingly transparent little things, whose youngish mothers, most of them pregnant, stood not far away, holding bags of groceries from their shopping expeditions and animatedly gossiping together. Huddling close to the women were three pigtailed little girls wearing long white stockings and they alone blandly looked my way as I was propelled past them into a narrow alleyway and back through to where freshly washed undergarments were strung up on lines crisscrossing a small courtyard. We turned into a stone stairway, a door was unlocked, and we entered the rear foyer of what looked to me to be a very shabby dentist's or doctor's office. I saw a table littered with Hebrew magazines, there was a woman receptionist speaking on the phone, and then I was through another door and into a tiny bathroom, where a light was flipped on and I was told to wash.

I was a long time soaking my face and my clothes and repeatedly rinsing out my mouth. That they allowed me to be alone like this, that apparently they didn't want me to be left disgustingly smelly, that I had not been gagged or blindfolded, that nobody was banging on the door of the cubicle with the butt of a pistol telling me to hurry up—all this provided my first tinge of hope and suggested to me that these were not Palestinians but Pipik's Jews, the Orthodox co-conspirators whom he had double-crossed by ducking out and who now had me confused with him.

Once I was clean I was led, and now without too much force from behind, out of the washroom and down the corridor to a narrow staircase whose twenty-three shallow steps took us to a second story, where four classrooms angled off of a central landing. Overhead there was a skylight, opaque with soot, and the floorboards beneath my shoes were badly scuffed and worn. The place reeked of stale cigarette smoke, a smell that carried me back some forty-five years, to the little Talmud Torah, one flight above our local synagogue, where I went unenthusiastically with my friends to study Hebrew for an hour in the late afternoons three days a week in the early 1940s. The rabbi who ran the show there had been a heavy smoker and, as best I could remember it, that second floor of the synagogue back in Newark, aside from smelling exactly the same, hadn't looked too unlike this place either—shabby, dreary, just a little disagreeably slummy.

They put me in one of the classrooms and closed the door. I was alone again. Nobody had kicked me or slapped me or tied my hands or shackled my legs. On the blackboard I saw something written in Hebrew. Nine words. I couldn't read one of them. Four decades after those three years of afternoon classes at the Hebrew school, I could no longer even identify the letters of the alphabet. There was a nondescript wooden table at the front of the classroom, and in back of it a slatted chair for the teacher. On the table was a TV set. *That* we did not have in 1943, nor did we sit on these movable molded-plastic student chairs but on long benches nailed to the floor before sloped wooden desks on which we wrote our lessons from right to left. For one hour a day, three days a week, fresh from six and a half hours of public school, we sat there and learned to write backwards, to write as though the sun rose in the west and the leaves fell in the spring, as though Canada lay to the south, Mexico to the north, and we put our shoes on before our socks; then we escaped back into our cozy American world, aligned just the other way around, where all that was plausible, recognizable, predictable, reasonable, intelligible, and useful unfolded its meaning to us from left to right, and the only place we proceeded in reverse, where it was natural, logical, in the very nature of things, the singular and unchallengeable exception, was on the sandlot diamond. In the early 1940s, reading and writing from right to left made about as much sense to me as belting the ball over the outfielder's head and expecting to be credited with a triple for running from third to second to first.

I hadn't heard a bolt turn in the door, and when I hurried over to the windows I found not only that they were unlocked but that one was open at the bottom. I had merely to push it up all the way to be able to crawl out, hang full length from the sill, and then drop from the window the ten or twelve feet to the courtyard below. I could then race the twenty yards down the alleyway and, once out into the street, start shouting for help—or make directly for Apter's. Only what if they opened fire? What if I hurt myself jumping and they caught me and dragged me back inside? Because I still didn't know who my captors were, I couldn't decide which was the bigger risk: to escape or not to try to escape. That they hadn't chained me to the wall of a windowless dungeon didn't necessarily mean that they were nice fellows or that they would take lightly any failure to cooperate. But to cooperate with *what?* Hang around, I thought, and you'll find out.

I soundlessly opened the window all the way, but when I peered out to gauge the drop, a pain went jaggedly crackling through the left hemisphere of my head and whatever can pulsate in a man began to pulsate in me. I wasn't a man, I was now an engine being revved up by something beyond my control. I pulled the window down as soundlessly as I'd pulled it open, leaving it ajar at the bottom precisely as I'd found it, and, crossing to the center of the room, like the eager student who arrives first in the class, I took a seat in front of the blackboard, two rows from the teacher's table and the TV set, convinced that I had no need to jump, because I had nothing to fear from Jews, and simultaneously stunned by my childish ingenuousness. Jews couldn't beat me, starve me, torture me? No Jew could kill me?

Again I went over to the window, although this time all I did was look out into the courtyard, hoping that someone looking in would see me and understand from whatever I was able silently to signal that I was here against my will. And I was thinking that whatever it was that was happening to me and had been happening now for three days, it had all begun back when I'd first taken my seat in that small, ill-ventilated classroom that was the Newark original of this makeshift Jerusalem replica, during those darkening hours when I could barely bring myself to pay attention after a full day in the school where my heart was somehow always light, the public school from which I understood clearly, every day in a thousand ways, my real future was to arise. But how could anything come of going to Hebrew school? The teachers were lonely foreigners, poorly paid refugees, and the students—the best among us along with the worst—were bored, restless American kids, ten, eleven, twelve years old, resentful of being cooped up like this year after year, through the fall, winter, and spring, when everything seasonal was exciting the senses and beckoning us to partake freely of all our American delights. Hebrew school wasn't school at all but a part of the deal that our parents had cut with *their* parents, the sop to pacify the old generation—who wanted the grandchildren to be Jews the way that they were Jews, bound as they were to the old millennial ways—and, at the same time, the leash to restrain the breakaway young, who had it in their heads to be Jews in a way no one had ever dared to be a Jew in our three-thousand-year history: speaking and thinking American English, *only* American English, with all the apostasy that was bound to beget. Our put-upon parents were simply middlemen in the classic American squeeze, negotiating between the shtetl-born and the Newark-born and taking blows from either side, telling the old ones, "Listen, it's a new world—the kids have to make their way here," while sternly rebuking the young ones, "You must, you have to, you cannot turn your back on everything!" What a compromise! What could possibly come of those three or four hundred hours of the worst possible teaching in the worst possible atmosphere for learning? Why, everything—what came of it was *everything!* That cryptography whose signification I could no longer decode had marked me indelibly four decades ago; out of the inscrutable words written on this blackboard had evolved every English word I had ever written. Yes, all and everything had originated there, including Moishe Pipik.

I began to make a plan. I would tell them the story of Moishe Pipik. I would differentiate for them between what he was up to and what I was up to. I would answer any questions they had about George Ziad —I had nothing to hide about our meetings and conversations or even about my own Diaspora diatribes. I would tell them about Jinx, describe every last thing that they wanted to know. "I am guilty of nothing," I would tell them, "except perhaps failing to notify the police about Pipik's threat to kidnap young Demjanjuk, and even that

I can explain. I can explain everything. I came only to interview
Aharon Appelfeld." But if the people holding me here are indeed
Pipik's coconspirators, and if they have gotten me out of the way like
this precisely now to go ahead and abduct young Demjanjuk, then
that is the *last* thing I should say!

Exactly what justification should I offer—and who will swallow it
anyway? Who that comes to interrogate me will believe that there is
no conspiracy to which I am a party, no plot in which I have had a
hand, that there is no collusion here, no secret machinations between
Moishe Pipik and me or between George Ziad and me, that I have not
put anyone up to anything for any personal, political, or propagandistic reason whatsoever, that I have devised no strategy to assist Palestinians or to compromise Jews or to intervene in this struggle in any
way? How can I convince them that there is nothing artful here, no
subtle aim or hidden plan undergirding everything, that these events
are nonsensical and empty of meaning, that there is no pattern or
sequence arising from some dark or sinister motive of mine or any
motive of *mine* at all, that this is in no way an imaginative creation
accessible to an interpretive critique but simply a muddle, a mix-up,
and a silly fucking mess!

I remembered how, in the mid-sixties, a Professor Popkin had
come forward with a carefully argued theory that there was not just
a single Lee Harvey Oswald involved in killing Kennedy on November
22, 1963, but a second Oswald, a double of Oswald, who had been
deliberately conspicuous around Dallas during the weeks before the
assassination. The Warren Commission had dismissed these sightings
of a second Oswald—at times when Oswald himself could be proved
to have been elsewhere—as a case of mistaken identification, but
Popkin argued that the instances of duplication were too frequent
and the reports too well founded to be discounted, especially the
reports of those episodes in which the look-alike had been seen shopping in a gun store and flamboyantly firing weapons at a local rifle
range. The second Oswald was a real person, Popkin concluded, one
of the assassins in a conspiracy in which the first Oswald played the
role of a decoy or perhaps, unwittingly, of a patsy.

And it's this, I thought, that I'm about to go up against, some con-spiracy genius for whom it's unimaginable that anyone like me or Lee Harvey Oswald could be out there plotless and on his own. My Pipik will father my Popkin, and the patsy this time will be me.

I spent nearly three hours alone in that classroom. Instead of jump-ing from the window into the courtyard and making a run for it, instead of opening the room's unlocked door to see if it was possible simply to walk out the way I'd come in, I finally went back to my seat in the second row and sat there doing what I've done throughout my professional life: I tried to think, first, how to make credible a some-what extreme, if not outright ridiculous, story and, next, how, after telling it, to fortify and defend myself from the affronted who read into the story an intention having perhaps to do less with the author's perversity than with their own. Fellow writers will understand when I say that, excepting the difference in what might be at stake here and the dreadful imaginings that this fomented, preparing myself in that room to tell my story to my interrogator struck me as being not unlike waiting to see the review of your new book by the dumbest, clumsiest, shallowest, most thick-witted, wrongheaded, tone-deaf, tin-eared, insensate, and cliché-recycling book-reviewing dolt in the business. There's not much hope of getting through. Who wouldn't consider jumping out the window instead?

About midway through my second hour, when no one had as yet appeared to tie me up or beat me up or put a pistol to my head and begin to ask me my opinions, I began to wonder if I might not be the victim of a practical joke and nothing more perilous than that. Three thugs and their car had been hired by Pipik to scare the life out of me—it could have cost him as little as two hundred bucks and, who knows, maybe not even half that much. They'd swept me up, dumped me off, and then gone on their merry way, nothing worse to show for their half hour's work than my vomit on the tips of their shoes. It was pure Pipik, a brainstorm bearing all the earmarks of the putative private eye whose capacity for ostentatious provocation appeared to me inexhaustible. For all I knew, there was a peephole somewhere in this very room from behind which he was now watching me disgracefully being held prisoner by no one but myself. His revenge for my stealing his million dollars. His mockery for my stealing his Wanda Jane. The payoff for my breaking his glasses. Maybe she's with him, pantyless on his lap, heroically planted on his implant and conscientiously feeding his excitement by peeping at me too. I am their peep show. I have been all along. The inventiveness of this nemesis is abysmal and bottomless.

But I drove this possibility out of my mind by studying the nine words on the blackboard, focusing on each character as though if I looked long and hard enough I might unexpectedly regain possession of my lost tongue and a secret message would be revealed to me. But no foreign language could have been any more foreign. The only feature of Hebrew that I could remember was that the lower dots and dashes were vowels and the upper markings generally consonants. Otherwise all memory of it had been extinguished.

Obeying an impulse nearly as old as I was, I took out my pen, and, on the back of my bill from the American Colony, I slowly copied down the words written on the blackboard. Perhaps they weren't even words. I would have been no less stupid copying Chinese. All those hundreds of hours spent drawing these letters had disappeared without a trace, those hours might just as well have been a dream, and yet a dream in which I discovered everything that was forever thereafter to obsess my consciousness however much I might wish it otherwise.

This is what I painstakingly copied down, thinking that afterward, if there was an afterward, these markings might provide the clue to exactly where I'd been held captive and by whom.

וַיִּוָּתֵר יַעֲקֹב לְבַדּוֹ וַיֵּאָבֵק

אִישׁ עִמּוֹ עַד עֲלוֹת הַשָּׁחַר

I startled myself then by speaking out loud. I had been trying to convince myself that not everything sensible in me had as yet been stultified by fear, that I had strength enough left in me to sit tight and wait to see who and what I was truly up against, but instead I heard myself saying to an empty classroom, "Pipik, I know you are there," the first words I'd uttered since in the car I'd asked my captors if they were Palestinians or Jews. "Abduction on top of identity theft. Pipik, the case against you gets worse by the hour. It's still possible, if you want it, to negotiate a truce. I don't press charges and you leave me alone. Speak and tell me that you are there."

But no one spoke other than me.

I approached him next more practically. "How much would it take for you to leave me alone? Name a figure."

Although an all but irrefutable argument could have been made at that moment—and was, by me—that he did not answer because he had nothing to do with my abduction, was nowhere nearby, and more than likely had left Jerusalem the night before, the long silence that once again followed my calling out to him simultaneously intensified my belief that he *was* there and that he did not respond either because I had not as yet found the formula that would provoke a response or because he was enjoying this spectacle far too much to intervene or interrupt and intended to hide the face that he went around Jerusalem advertising as my own until I had reached the uttermost limits of mortification and was contritely begging on my knees for mercy. Of course I knew how pathetically ridiculous I must appear if the abduction that bore all the clownish signs of Pipik's authorship was the handiwork of someone else entirely, someone not at all clownish who constituted an even more drastic threat to me than he did and who was in fact monitoring me now, someone who far from conniving a singularly intimate, uncanny affiliation with me, one that might make him at least a little susceptible to my tender supplications, was beyond the reach of any appeal or offer or entreaty I might make. Because I feared that scrutinizing me in my molded-plastic student chair there might well be a surveillant even more alien than Pipik, lethally indifferent to my every need, to whom my name

and my face could not have meant less, I discovered myself desperate
to hear the voice of Moishe Pipik echoing mine. The plot that I had
set out to flee at dawn on the grounds of its general implausibility, its
total lack of gravity, its reliance on unlikely coincidence, the absence
of inner coherence and of anything resembling a serious meaning or
purpose, that outlandish plot of Pipik's that had disgusted me as much
by its puerility as by its treachery and deceitfulness, now seemed to
be my only hope. Would that I were still a ludicrous character in his
lousy book!

"Pipik, are you with me, are you here? Is this or is this not your
stinking idea? If it is, tell me so. Speak. I never was your enemy. Think
back on what's happened, review all the details, will you, please? Have
I no right to claim that I have been provoked? Are you blameless
entirely? Whatever pain my public standing may have caused you in
those years before we met—well, how can I be responsible for that?
And was it that injurious? Was the resemblance to me ever really
much more than what most people would think of as a nuisance? It's
not I who told you to come to Jerusalem and pretend that we two
were one—I cannot, in all fairness, be saddled with that. Do you hear
me? Yes, you hear me—you don't answer because that's not what
you hold against me. My offense is that I did not treat you with
respect. I was not willing to entertain your proposal that we set up
shop as partners. I was rude and caustic. I was dismissive and contemptuous. I was furious and threatening from the moment I saw you
and, even before that, when I laid a trap on the phone as Pierre Roget.
Look, that there is room for improvement I admit. Next time I will
try harder to see your side of things before I take aim and fire. 'Stop,
breathe, think,' instead of 'Ready, aim, fire'—I'm trying hard to learn.
Perhaps I *was* too antagonistic—perhaps. I don't really know. I am
not out to bullshit you, Pipik. You would despise me even more than
you do already if, because you have the upper hand, I started kow-
towing and kissing your ass. I am simply trying to explain that my
response on meeting you, however offensive, was well within the
range of what you might have expected from anyone in my position.
But your grievance is deeper even than that. The million bucks. That's

a lot of money. Never mind that you extorted it by passing yourself
off as me. Maybe you're right and that's not my business. Why should
I care? Especially if it's money in behalf of a good cause—and if you
see it that way and say that it is, who am I to say it isn't? I'm willing
to believe that that was all between Smilesburger and you. Caveat
emptor, Mr. Smilesburger. Though that's not my crime either, is it?
My crime is that it was I posing as you rather than you posing as me
who extorted the money under false pretenses—by pretending to be
you, I took what was not mine. In your eyes this amounts to grand
larceny. You make the deal, I reap the harvest. Well, if it makes you
feel better, I haven't come away with a red cent. I haven't got the
check. I'm in your custody here, the boys who picked me up are your
boys—you're in charge in every way, and so I'm not about to lie to
you. The check was lost. I lost it. You may or may not know this but
I haven't been contending here solely with you. The story is too long
to tell, and you wouldn't believe it anyway, so suffice it to say that
the check disappeared in a situation where I was utterly powerless.
Can't we now go together to Mr. Smilesburger and explain to him his
confusion? Get him to stop the old check and issue a new one? I
would bet another million that the first check isn't in anyone's pocket
but either got blown away by the wind or was trampled into the
ground when some soldiers roughed me up on the road from Ramallah. That's the story you won't believe, though you ought to, really—
it's not a lot stranger than yours. I got caught in the crossfire of the
fight being fought here, and that's when your check disappeared.
We'll get you another one. I'll help you get it. I'll do everything I can
in your behalf. Isn't that what you've been asking from the start? My
cooperation? Well, you've got it. This does it. I'm on your side. We'll
get you your million bucks back."

I waited in vain for him to speak, but either he believed that I was
lying and holding out on him, that his million was already in my
account, or he wanted even more, or he wasn't there.

"And I apologize," I said, "about Jinx. Wanda Jane. For a man who's
gone through and survived the physical anguish that you've suffered,
of course that's bitterly infuriating. This probably has incensed you

even more than the money. I don't expect that you would believe me if I were to tell you that to pierce your heart was not my motive or intention. You think otherwise, of course. You think I meant to punish and humiliate you. You think I mean to steal what you prize most. You think I mean to strike a blow where you are most vulnerable. It won't do me any good to try to tell you that you're wrong. Particularly as you could be partially right. Human psychology being what it is, you could even be entirely right. But since the truth is the truth, let me add insult to insult and injury to injury—I did not do what I did without some feeling. For her, I mean. I mean that muzzling a virile response to her kind of magnetism has turned out to be no easier for me than it is for you. There's yet another resemblance between us. I realize this was never the kind of partnership you had in mind but . . . But nothing. Enough. Wrong tack. I did it. I did it and in similar circumstances I would probably try to do it again. But there will be no such circumstances, that I promise you. The incident will never be repeated. I only ask you now to accept that by having been abducted and detained like this, by tasting all the terror that goes with sitting in this room not knowing what's in store for me, I have been sufficiently disciplined for trespassing against you as I have."

I waited for an answer. *This was never the kind of partnership you had in mind.* I needn't have said *that*, but otherwise, I thought, in a predicament as ambiguously menacing as this, no one could have spoken much more adroitly. Nor had I been craven. I had said more or less what he wanted me to say while still saying what was more or less true.

But when still no answer was forthcoming, I all at once lost whatever adroitness I may have had and announced in a voice no longer calm and steady, "Pipik, if you cannot forgive me, give me a sign that you're there, that you're here, that you hear me, that I am not talking to a wall!" Or, I thought, to someone even less forgiving than you and capable of a rebuke sterner even than your silence. "What do you require, burnt offerings? I will never again go near your girl, we'll get you back your goddamn money—now say something! Speak!"

And only then did I understand what he *did* require of me, not to mention understanding finally just how very maladroit I was with him and had been from the start, how unforgivably self-damaging a miscalculation it had been to deny this impostor the thing that any impostor covets and can least do without and that only I could meaningfully anoint him with. Only when I spoke my name as though I believed it was his name as well, only then would Pipik reveal himself and negotiations commence to propitiate his rage.

"Philip," I said.

He did not answer.

"Philip," I said again, "I am not your enemy. I don't want to be your enemy. I would like to establish cordial relations. I am nearly overcome by how this has turned out and, if it's not too late, I'd like to be your friend."

Nothing. No one.

"I was sardonic and unfeeling and I'm chastened," I said. "It was not right to exalt myself and denigrate you by addressing you as I have. I should have called you by your name as you called me by mine. And from now on I will. I will. I am Philip Roth and you are Philip Roth, I am like you and you are like me, in name and not only in name. . . ."

But he wasn't buying it or else he wasn't there.

He *wasn't* there. An hour later the door opened and into the classroom hobbled Smilesburger.

"Good of you to wait," he said. "Terribly sorry, but I was detained."

10

You Shall Not
Hate Your Brother
in Your Heart

I was reading when he came in. To make it appear to whoever might be observing me that I was not yet incapacitated by fear or running wild with hallucination, that I was waiting as though for nothing more than my turn in the dental chair or at the barbershop, to force my attention to something other than the timorousness that kept me nailed warily to my seat—even more urgently, to focus on something other than the overbold boldness insistently charging me now to jump out the window—I had removed from my pockets the purported diaries of Leon Klinghoffer and shunted myself, with a huge mental effort, onto the verbal track.

How pleased my teachers would be, I thought—reading, even here! But then this was not the first time, or the last, when, powerless before the uncertainty at hand, I looked to print to subjugate my fears and keep the world from coming apart. In 1960, not a hundred yards from the Vatican walls, I had sat one evening in the empty waiting room of an unknown Italian doctor's office reading a novel of Edith Wharton's, while on the far side of the doctor's door, my then wife underwent an illegal abortion. Once on a plane with a badly smoking engine, I had heard the pilot's horrifyingly calm announcement as to how and where he planned to set down and had quickly told myself, "You just concentrate on Conrad," and continued my reading of *Nostromo,* mordantly keeping at the back of my mind the thought that at least I would die as I'd lived. And two years after escaping Jerusalem unharmed, when I wound up one night an emergency patient in the coronary unit of New York Hospi⁺al, an oxygen tube in my nose and an array of doctors and nurses fastidiously monitoring my vital signs, I waited for a decision to be made about operating on my obstructed arteries while reading, not without some pleasure, the jokes in Bellow's *The Bellarosa Connection.* The book you clutch while awaiting the worst is a book you may never be capable of summarizing coherently but whose clutching you never forget.

When I was a small boy in my first classroom—I remembered this, sitting obediently as a middle-aged man in what I could not help thinking might be my last classroom—I had been transfixed by the alphabet as it appeared in white on a black frieze some six inches high that extended horizontally atop the blackboard, "Aa Bb Cc Dd Ee," each letter exhibited there twice, in cursive script, parent and child, object and shadow, sound and echo, etc., etc. The twenty-six asymmetrical pairings suggested to an intelligent five-year-old every duality and correspondence a little mind could possibly conceive. Each was so variously interlocked and at odds, any two taken together so tantalizing in their faintly unharmonious apposition that, even if viewed as I, for one, first apprehended the alphabet frieze—as figures in profile, the way Nineveh's low-relief sculptors depicted the royal lion hunt in 1000 B.C.—the procession marching immobilely toward the classroom door constituted an associative grab bag of inexhaustible proportions. And when it registered on me that the couples in this configuration—whose pictorial properties alone furnished such pure Rorschachish delight—each had a name of its own, mental delirium of the sweetest sort set in, as it might in anyone of any age. It only remained for me to be instructed in the secret of how these letters could be inveigled to become words for the ecstasy to

be complete. There had been no pleasure so fortifying and none that
so dynamically expanded the scope of consciousness since I'd
learned to walk some fifteen hundred days before; and there would
be nothing as remotely inspirational again until a stimulant no less
potent than the force of language—the hazardous allurements of the
flesh and the pecker's irrepressible urge to squirt—overturned angelic childhood.

So this explains why I happened to be reading when Smilesburger
appeared. The alphabet is all there is to protect me; it's what I was
given instead of a gun.

In September 1979, six years before he was thrown in his wheelchair over the side of the *Achille Lauro* by Palestinian terrorists,
Klinghoffer and his wife were on a cruise ship bound for Israel. This
is what I read of what he'd written in the leather-bound diary with
the rickshaw, the elephant, the camel, the gondola, the airliner, and
the passenger ship engraved in gold on its cover.

> *9/5*
> *Weather clear*
> *Friday. Sunny*

Took tour through Greek port of Piraeus and city of Athens.
Guide was excellent. The city of Athens is a modern bustling
city. Lots of traffic. Went up to the Acropolis and saw all the
ancient ruins. It was a well-guided and interesting tour. Got
home about 2.30. Quarter of 4 on way to Haifa, Israel. A very
interesting afternoon. Tonight was the night. After dinner there
was a singer from Israel. Gave a performance. I was one of the
judges for queen of the ship. It was all hilarious. What a night.
To bed at 12.30.

> *9/6 Sea calm*
> *Weather good*

Another pleasant day. Young Dr. and his wife going to Israel to
look into opening a hospital with a group of French Jewish

doctors in a large town in the south of Israel. In case something happens in France they will have a foot in Israel and an investment. Met many people, made a lot of friends in 7 days. They all loved Marilyn. She never looked so rested and pretty. Bed late. Up early. Ship to dock at Haifa tomorrow.

9/7
Haifa

What excitement. Young and old alike. Many away on tours for as long as 40 days. Some longer. Ziv and wife for 3 months singing in America. Others just cruising. What expressions of joy to be home in their country. How they love Israel. Hotel Dan a beautiful place. Accommodations good.

9/8
Haifa to Tel Aviv

The trip from Haifa to Tel Aviv over 1½ hours. The roads modern. Traffic some parts heavy. Building going on all over. Houses. Factories. It is astonishing for a country born of war and living a war to be so vibrant. The soldiers all over the place with their full packs and rifles. Girls and boys alike. Booked for tours all over the place. We are tired. Worth the tiredness. Listening to radio in lovely room looking over the blue Mediterranean.

9/8 W. sunny
Tel Aviv

Up at 7. Started to tour. Tel Aviv. Yaffo. Rehovoth. Ashdod. 50 kilometers around Tel Aviv. The activity. The building. The reclaiming of sand dunes and making towns and cities grow is astonishing. The old Arab city of Yaffo is being torn down and instead of slums that have existed for years a new city has been planned and is being erected.

The Agricultural College, the Chaim Weizmann Institute is a garden spot in Rehovoth. Its beautiful buildings, its hall of learning, its surroundings are something to see. A busy delightful educational day and a new respect for the land born of war and still plagued.

9/9 Sunny
Tel Aviv

Up at 5.45 to go to the Dead Sea. Sodom. Beersheba. Over the steep hills and down to the lowest spot on earth. What a day. 12 hours again. Terrific what is going on in this small country. Building. Roads. Irrigation. Planning and fighting. It was a very hard day but a rewarding one. Visited kibbutz at the end of the earth where young married families live in complete loneliness and unfriendly neighbors to build a land. Guts. Plain guts.

9/10
Jerusalem

What a city. What activity. New roads. New factories. New housing. Thousands of tourists from all over. Jew and Gentile alike. Got here at 11 and went on tour. The shrine of the Holocaust. And my Marilyn broke down. I had tears in my eyes also. The city is a series of hills. New and old. The garden where Billy Rose's art exhibit is. Also the museum is in the most beautiful setting. The museum is large, roomy, and full of art objects. Looking over the city from this site is grand. Supper. Walked the streets. To bed at 10.

9/11 Thursday

Looking at the hills of Jerusalem in the year 1979. It is a beautiful view. The geography is the same but with modern living, good roads, trucks, busses, cars, air conditioning to make life better.

The climate here is cool at night, warm during the day except when the wind blows from the desert.

9/12
Sunny

Went to the Old City of Jerusalem. Wailing Wall. Jesus tomb. David's. Walked through narrow streets of the Arab quarter. Full of stores which are small stalls. Smells and dirt predominant. Our hotel was the border line between Israel and Jordan. The goings on in front of the W.W. were interesting. The constant praying. Bar Mitzvahs. Weddings. Etc. Got home at 1. Again tired after all touring. 2½ hour tour, all walking. No cars in the Old City. Next Hadassah Hospital. The women of America should be proud of what their efforts have done. On the grounds there is a building that is used as a research center and houses pictures of Jews killed in Germany. Horrifying between resentment and tears that well up in your eyes. You wonder how a civilized Christian nation could allow a little pimp to lead them to such atrocities. Then on to where Herzl the founder of Zionism and his family were buried. Also a cemetery built on the hills of men who died in all the wars. Ages ranging from 13 to 79. All sol-' diers. Then to the Knesset, college, and other important centers of government and learning.
This city is just beautiful. Full of history and wonders. All roads lead to Jerusalem not Rome. I am glad to have the opportunity to get here.

9/13
Shabbas and
Rosh Hoshana

It is 6 o'clock A.M. And from our room in the King David Hotel we have the most beautiful view, looking over the hills of Jerusalem. Just 500 yards away from our hotel was the Jordanian border where snipers stood in the ruins of the Old City and shot into the New City. There were 39 houses of worship there and

the Arabs blew them all up in the last War. These people de-
serve all the help and praise of all of the Diaspora. The defenders
of this country are 18 to 25. There are soldiers all over the city
but inconspicuous. It is a modern city with all of the old ruins
preserved. This is our final day in the city the Jews prayed to
come back to for 2000 years and I can now understand why. I
hope they never have to leave.

I was reading when Smilesburger came in, and I was also writing,
making notes—while I went probingly through each plodding page
of the diaries—for the introduction that Supposnik claimed would
expedite Klinghoffer's American and European publication. What else
was I to do? What else do I know *how* to do? It was not even in my
hands. The thoughts began to drift in a bit at a time and I began
groping both to disentangle them and to piece them together—an
inherent activity, a perpetual need, especially under the pressure of
strong emotions like fear. I wrote not on the back of the American
Colony bill, where I'd already recorded the mysterious Hebrew
words chalked up on the blackboard, but in the dozen or so unused
pages at the tail end of the red diary. I had nothing else on which to
record anything of any length, and gradually, when the old habituated
state of mind firmly took root and, as a protest perhaps against this
inscrutable semicaptivity, I found myself working step by step into
the familiar abyss, the initial shock of appending one's own profane
handwriting to the handwriting of a murdered martyr—the transgressive feelings of a good citizen vandalizing, if not exactly a sacred
work, certainly a not insignificant archival curio—gave way before
an absurdly schoolboyish assessment of my situation: I had been bru-
tally abducted and carted off to this classroom specifically for this
purpose and would not be freed until a serious introduction, with the
correct Jewish outlook, was satisfactorily composed and handed in.
  Here are the impressions I had begun to elaborate when Smilesburger made his wily appearance and loquaciously announced why in
fact I was there. As I would learn by the time he was done with me,
two thousand words countenancing Klinghoffer's humanity was the
least the situation demanded.

The terrific ordinariness of these entries. The very reasonable ordinariness of K. A wife he's proud of. Friends he loves to be with. A little money in his pocket to take a cruise. To do what he wants to do in his own artless way. The very embodiment, these diaries, of Jewish "normalization."

An ordinary person who purely by accident gets caught in the historical struggle. A life annotated by history in the last place you expect history to intervene. On a cruise, which is out of history in every way.

The cruise. Nothing could be safer. The floating lockup. You go nowhere. It's a circle. A lot of movement but no progress. Life suspended. A ritual of in-betweenness. All the time in the world. Insulated, like a moon shot. Travel within their own environment. With old friends. Don't have to learn any languages. Don't have to worry about new foods. In neutral territory, the protected trip. *But there is no neutral territory.* "You, Klinghoffer, of the Diaspora," crows the militant Zionist, "even at the point where you thought you were most safe, you weren't. You were a Jew: not even on a cruise is a Jew on a cruise." The Zionist preys on the Jewish urge for normalcy anywhere but in Fortress Israel.

The shrewdness of the PLO: they will always figure out the way to worm their way into the tranquilizing fantasy of the Jew. The PLO too denies the plausibility of Jewish safety other than armed to the teeth.

You read K.'s diaries with the whole design in mind, as you read the diary of A.F. You know he's going to die and how, and so you read it through the ending back. You know he's going to be pushed over the side, so all these boring thoughts he has— which are the sum total of everybody's existence—take on a brutal eloquence and K. is suddenly a living soul whose subject is the bliss of life.

Would Jews without enemies be just as boring as everybody else? These diaries suggest as much. What makes extraordinary all the harmless banality is the bullet in the head.

Without the Gestapo and the PLO, these two Jewish writers (A.F. and L.K.) would be unpublished and unknown; without the Gestapo and the PLO any number of Jewish writers would be, if not necessarily unknown, completely unlike the writers they are.

In idiom, interests, mental rhythms, diaries like K.'s and A.F.'s confirm the same glaring pathos: one, that Jews are ordinary; two, that they are denied ordinary lives. Ordinariness, blessed, humdrum, dazzling ordinariness, it's there in every observation, every sentiment, every thought. The center of the Jewish dream, what feeds the fervor both of Zionism and Diasporism: the way Jews would be people if they could forget they were Jews. Ordinariness. Blandness. Uneventful monotony. Unembattled existence. The repetitious security of one's own little cruise. But this is not to be. The incredible drama of being a Jew.

Although I'd only met Smilesburger the day before at lunch, my shock at the sight of him advancing on his crutches through the classroom door was akin to the astonishment of catching sight on the street, after thirty or forty years, of a school friend or a roommate or a lover, a famously unimpaired ingenue whom time has obviously reveled in recasting in the most unbefitting of character roles. Smilesburger might even have been some intimate whom I had thought long dead, so agitatingly eerie was the impact of discovering that it was he and not Pipik into whose custody I had been forcibly taken.

Unless, because of the "stolen" million, he had joined forces with Pipik . . . unless it was he who had engaged Pipik to entrap me in the first place . . . unless *I* had somehow ensnared *them*, unless there was something I was doing that I was not aware of doing, that I could not stop doing, that was the very opposite of what I wanted to be doing, and that was making everything that was happening to me seem to be happening to me without my doing anything. But assigning myself a leading role when I couldn't have felt more like everyone's puppet was the most debilitating mental development yet, and I fought off the idea with what little rationality I retained after almost three hours of waiting alone in that room. Blaming myself was only another way of not thinking, the most primitive adaptation imaginable to a chain of unlikely events, a platitudinous, catchall fantasy that told me nothing about what my relations were to whatever was going on here. I had not summoned forth, by some subterranean magic, this cripple who called himself Smilesburger just because I'd imagined that I'd seen him in the refreshment area adjacent to the courtroom when, in fact, taking the cash was an elderly man who, I now realized, bore little resemblance to him at all. I had blundered idiotically and even been half-demented, but I had not myself summoned up *any* of this: it wasn't my imagination calling the shots but my imagination that was being shattered by theirs, whoever "they" might be.

He was dressed just as he'd been at lunchtime the day before, in the neat blue businessman's suit, the bow tie, and the cardigan sweater over his starched white shirt, the attire of the fastidious jewelry-store owner; and his strangely grooved skull and scaling skin still suggested that, in handing him problems, life had not settled for half-measures and restricted his experience of loss merely to the use of his legs. His torso swung like a partially filled sandbag between the crutches whose horseshoe-shaped supports cupped his forearms, the burden of ambulation as torturous for him today as it had been yesterday and, more than likely, ever since he'd been impeded by the handicap that gave his face the wasted, worn-down look of someone sentenced to perpetually struggle uphill even when he feels the need of nothing more than a glass of water. And his English was still spoken with the immigrant accent of the tradesmen who sold cotton goods from a pushcart and herring from a barrel in the slum where my grandparents had settled and my father had grown up. What was new since yesterday, when there had appeared to be penned into this body nothing but the most unspeakable experience of life, was the mood of gracious warmth, the keen peal of exhilaration in the raw, rumbling voice, as though he were not ponderously poling himself forward on two sticks but slaloming the slopes at Gstaad. The demonstration of dynamism by this wreck struck me as either self-satire at its most savage or a sign that encaged in this overabundantly beleaguered human frame was nothing but resistance.

"Good of you to wait," he said, swinging to within inches of my chair. "Terribly sorry, but I was detained. At least you brought something to read. Why didn't you turn on the television? Mr. Shaked is summing up." Spinning himself about with three little hops, virtually pirouetting on his crutches, he advanced to the teacher's table at the front of the classroom and pressed the button that brought the trial to life on the screen. There, indeed, was Michael Shaked, addressing the three judges in Hebrew. "This has made him a sex symbol—all the women in Israel are now in love with the prosecutor. They didn't open a window? So stuffy here! Have you eaten? Nothing to eat? No lunch? Soup? Some salads? Broiled chicken? To drink—a beer? A soda? Tell me what you like. Uri!°" he called. Into the open doorway stepped one of that pair of bejeaned abductors who had looked vaguely familiar to me out in the parking lot where my last act as a free man was to lend a helping hand to an anti-Semitic priest. "Why no lunch, Uri? Why are the windows shut? No one turns on television for him? Nobody does anything! Smell it! They play cards and they smoke cigarettes. Occasionally they kill someone—and they think this is the whole job. Lunch for Mr. Roth!"

Uri laughed and left the room, pulling the classroom door shut behind him.

Lunch for Mr. Roth? Meaning what? The improbable fluency of that heavily accented English, the gracious amiability, the edge of paternal tenderness in that deeply masculine voice . . . all of it meaning what?

"He would have torn to pieces anyone who came within an inch of you," Smilesburger said. "A more ferocious watchdog than Uri I could not have found for you. What is the book?"

But it was not for me to explain anything, even what I was reading. I didn't know what to say, didn't even know what to ask—all I could think to do was to start shouting, and I was too frightened for that.

Maneuvering his carcass into the chair, Smilesburger said, "No one told you? They told you nothing? Inexcusable. No one told you I was coming? No one told you you could go? No one came to explain that I would be late?"

No reply necessary to sadistic baiting. Don't tell them again that they've got the wrong man. Nothing you say can make anything better; all you've said so far in Jerusalem has only made things worse.

"Why are Jews so thoughtless with one another? To keep you sitting here in the dark like this," said Smilesburger ruefully, "without even offering a cup of coffee. It persists and persists and I do not understand. Why are the Jews so lacking in the fundamental courtesies of social intercourse even between themselves? Why must every affront be magnified? Why must every provocation initiate a feud?"

I had affronted no one. I had provoked no one. I could explain that million dollars. But to his satisfaction? Without Uri reappearing *to feed me my lunch?* I didn't answer.

"The Jew's lack of love for his fellow Jew," Smilesburger said, "is the cause of much suffering among our people. The animosity, the ridicule, the sheer hatred of one Jew for another—why? Where is our forbearance and forgiveness of our neighbor? Why is there such divisiveness among Jews? It isn't only in Jerusalem in 1988 that there is suddenly this discord—it was in the ghetto, God knows, a hundred years ago; it was at the destruction of the Second Temple two thousand years ago. Why was the Second Temple destroyed? Because of this hatred of one Jew for another. Why has the Messiah not come? Because of the angry hatred of one Jew for another. We not only need Anti-Semites Anonymous for the goy—we need it for the Jew himself. Angry disputes, verbal abuse, malicious backbiting, mocking gossip, scoffing, faultfinding, complaining, condemning, insulting—the blackest mark against our people is not the eating of pork, it is not even marrying with the non-Jew: worse than both is the sin of Jewish speech. We talk too much, we say too much, and we do not know when to stop. Part of the Jewish problem is that they never know what voice to speak in. Refined? Rabbinical? Hysterical? Ironical? Part of the Jewish problem is that the voice is too loud. Too insistent. Too aggressive. No matter what he says or how he says it, it's inappropriate. *Inappropriateness* is the Jewish style. Awful. 'For each and every moment that a person remains silent, he earns a reward too great to be conceived of by any created being.' This is the Vilna Gaon quoting from the Midrash. 'What should a person's job be in this world? To make himself like a mute.' This is from the Sages. As one of our most revered rabbinical scholars has beautifully expressed it in an admirably simple sentence not ten syllables long, 'Words generally only spoil things.' You do not wish to speak? Good. When a Jew is as angry as you are, there is almost nothing harder for him than to control his speech. You are a heroic Jew. On the day of reckoning, the account of Philip Roth will be credited with merits for the restraint he has displayed here by remaining silent. Where did the Jew get it in his head that he has always to be talking, to be shouting, to be telling jokes at somebody's expense, to be analyzing over the telephone for a whole evening the terrible faults of his dearest friend? 'You shall not go about as a tale bearer among your people.' This is what is written. You shall not! It is forbidden! This is law! 'Grant me that I should say nothing that is unnecessary. . . .' This is from the prayer of the Chofetz Chaim. I am a disciple of the Chofetz Chaim. No Jew had more love for his fellow Jews than the Chofetz Chaim. You don't know the teachings of the Chofetz Chaim? A great man, a humble scholar, a revered rabbi from Radin, in Poland, he devoted his long life to trying to get Jews to shut up. He died at ninety-three in Poland the year that you were born in America. It is he who formulated the detailed laws of speech for our people and tried to cure them of the bad habits of centuries. The Chofetz Chaim formulated the laws of evil speech, or *loshon hora*, the laws that forbid Jews' making derogatory or damaging remarks about their fellow Jews, even if they are true. If they are false, of course it's worse. It is forbidden to speak *loshon hora* and it is forbidden to listen to *loshon hora*, even if you don't believe it. In his old age, the Chofetz Chaim extolled his deafness because it prevented him from hearing *loshon hora*. You can imagine how bad it had to have been for a great conversationalist like the Chofetz Chaim to say a thing like that. There is nothing about *loshon hora* that the Chofetz Chaim did not clarify and regulate: *loshon hora* said in jest, *loshon hora* without mentioning names, *loshon hora* that is common knowledge, *loshon hora* about relatives, about in-laws, about children, about the dead, about heretics and ignoramuses and known transgressors, even about merchandise—all forbidden. Even if someone has spoken *loshon hora* about you, you cannot speak *loshon hora* about him. Even if you are falsely accused of having committed a *crime,* you are forbidden to say who did do the crime. You cannot say 'He did it,' because that is *loshon hora.* You can only say 'I didn't do it.' Does it give you an idea of what the Chofetz Chaim was up against if he had to go that far to stop Jewish people's blaming and accusing their neighbors of everything and anything? Can you imagine the animosity he witnessed? Everyone feeling wronged, being hurt, bristling at insults and slights; everything everybody says taken as a personal affront and a deliberate attack; everyone saying something derogatory about everyone else. Anti-Semitism on the one side, *loshon hora* on the other, and in between, being squeezed to death, the beautiful soul of the Jewish people! The poor Chofetz Chaim was an Anti-Defamation League unto himself—only to get Jews to stop defaming *one another.* Someone else with his sensitivity to *loshon hora* would have become a murderer. But he loved his people and could not bear to see them brought low by their chattering mouths. He could not stand their quarreling, and so he set himself the impossible task of promoting Jewish harmony and Jewish unity instead of bitter Jewish divisiveness. Why couldn't the Jews be one people? Why must Jews be in conflict with one another? Why must they be in conflict with themselves? Because the divisiveness is not just between Jew and Jew—it is within the individual Jew. Is there a more manifold personality in all the world? I don't say divided. Divided is nothing. Even the goyim are divided. But inside every Jew there is a *mob* of Jews. The good Jew, the bad Jew. The new Jew, the old Jew. The lover of Jews, the hater of Jews. The friend of the goy, the enemy of the goy. The arrogant Jew, the wounded Jew. The pious Jew, the rascal Jew. The coarse Jew, the gentle Jew. The defiant Jew, the appeasing Jew. The Jewish Jew, the de-Jewed Jew. Shall I go on? Do I have to expound upon the Jew as a three-thousand-year amassment of mirrored fragments to one who has made his fortune as a leading Jewologist of international literature? Is it any wonder that the Jew is always disputing? He *is* a dispute, incarnate! Is it any wonder that he is always talking, that he talks imprudently and impulsively and thoughtlessly and embarrassingly and clownishly and that he cannot purify his speech of ridicule and insult and accusation and anger? Our poor Chofetz Chaim! He prayed to God, 'Grant me that I should say nothing that is unnecessary and that all my speech should be for the sake of Heaven,' and meanwhile his Jews were speaking everywhere simply for the sake of *speaking*. All the time! Couldn't stop! Why? Because inside each Jew were *so many speakers*. Shut up one and the other talks. Shut him up, and there is a third, a fourth, a fifth Jew with something more to say. The Chofetz Chaim prayed, 'I will be careful not to speak about individuals,' and meanwhile individuals were all his beloved Jews could talk about day and night. For Freud in Vienna life was simpler, believe me, than it was for the Chofetz Chaim in Radin. They came to Freud, the talking Jews, and what did Freud tell them? Keep talking. Say everything. No word is forbidden. The more *loshon hora* the better. To Freud a silent Jew was the worst thing imaginable—to him a silent Jew was bad for the Jew and bad for business. A Jew who will not speak evil? A Jew who will not get enraged? A Jew with no ill word for anyone? A Jew who will not feud with his neighbor, his boss, his wife, his child, his parents? A Jew who refuses to make any remark that could possibly hurt someone else? A Jew who says only what is strictly permissible? A world of such Jews as the Chofetz Chaim dreamed of, and Sigmund Freud will starve to death and take all the other psychoanalysts with him. But Freud was no fool and he knew his Jews, knew them better, I am sad to say, than his Jewish contemporary, the Jewish heads to his Jewish tails, our beloved Chofetz Chaim. To Freud they flocked, the Jews who couldn't stop talking, and to Freud they spoke such *loshon hora* as was never heard from the mouths of Jews since the destruction of the Second Temple. The result? Freud became Freud because he let them say everything, and the Chofetz Chaim, who told them to refrain from saying practically everything they wanted to say, who told them they must spit the *loshon hora* out of their mouths the way they would spit out of their mouths a piece of pork that they had inadvertently begun to eat, with the same disgust and nausea and contempt, who told them that unless they were one hundred percent certain that a remark was NOT *loshon hora*, they must suppose that it was and shut up—the Chofetz Chaim did not become popular among the Jewish people like Dr. Sigmund Freud. Now, it can be argued, cynically, that speaking *loshon hora* is what makes Jews Jews and that there was nothing more Jewishly Jewish to be conceived of than what Freud prescribed in his office for his Jewish patients. Take away from the Jews their *loshon hora*, and what do you have left? You have nice goyim. But this statement is itself *loshon hora*, the worst *loshon hora* there is, because to speak *loshon hora* about the Jewish people *as a whole* is the gravest sin of all. To berate the Jewish people for speaking *loshon hora*, as I do, is itself to commit *loshon hora*. Yet I not only speak the worst *loshon hora* but compound my sin by forcing you to sit here and listen to it. I am the very Jew I am berating. I am *worse* than that Jew. That Jew is too stupid to know what he is doing, while I am a disciple of the Chofetz Chaim, who knows that, so long as there is all this *loshon hora*, the Messiah will never come to save us—and still I speak *loshon hora* as I just this moment did when I called this other Jew stupid. What hope is there then for the dream of the Chofetz Chaim? Perhaps if all the pious Jews who do not eat on Yom Kippur were instead to give up for one day speaking *loshon hora* . . . if, for one moment in time, there were not a single word of *loshon hora* spoken by a single Jew . . . if together all the Jews on the face of the earth would simply shut up for *one second*. . . . But as even a *second* of Jewish silence is an impossibility, what hope can there be for our people? I personally believe that why the Jews left those villages in Galicia like Radin and ran to America and came to Palestine was, as much as anything, to escape their own *loshon hora*. If it drove crazy a saint of forbearance and great conversationalist like the Chofetz Chaim, who was even glad to go *deaf* so as to hear no more of it, one can only imagine what it did to the mind of the average nervous Jew. The early Zionists never said so, but privately more than one of them had to have been thinking, I will even go to Palestine, where there is typhoid, yellow fever, malaria, where there are temperatures of over a hundred degrees, so as never again to have to hear this terrible *loshon bora!* Yes, in the Land of Israel, away from the goyim, who hate us and thwart us and mock us, away from their persecution and all the chaos this causes within us, away from their loathing and all the anxiety and uncertainty and frustration and anger this engenders in every last Jewish soul, away from the indignity of being locked up by them and shut out by them, we will make a country of our own, where we are free and where we belong, where we will not insult one another and maliciously speak behind one another's backs, where the Jew, no longer awash with all his inner turmoil, will not defame and derogate his fellow Jews. Well, I can testify to it—I am, unfortunately, an example of it—the *loshon bora* in Eretz Yisroel is a hundred times worse, a thousand times worse, than it ever was in Poland in the lifetime of the Chofetz Chaim. Here there is *nothing* we will not say. Here there is such divisiveness that there is no restraint whatsoever. In Poland there was the anti-Semitism, which at least made you silent about the faults of your fellow Jews in the presence of the goyim. But here, with no goyim to worry about, the sky is the limit; here no one has the least idea that, even without goyim to be ashamed in front of, there are still things you cannot and you must not say and that maybe a Jewish person should think twice before he opens wide a Jewish mouth and announces proudly, as Sigmund Freud urged him to, the worst thoughts about people he has in his head. A statement that will cause hatred—they say it. A statement that will cause resentment—they make it. A malicious joke at somebody's expense—they tell it, they print it, they broadcast it over the nightly news. Read the Israeli press and you will read worse things said about us there than a hundred George Ziads are able to say. When it comes to defaming Jews, the Palestinians are *pisherkebs* next to *Ha'aretz.* Even at *that* we are better than they are! Now, once again it can be cynically argued that in this phenomenon lies the very triumph and glory of Zionism, that what we have achieved in the Land of Israel that we could never hope to attain with the goyim listening is the full flowering of the Jewish *genius* for *loshon bora.* Delivered at last from our long subjugation to the Gentiles' ears, we have been able to evolve and bring to perfection *in less than half a century* what the Chofetz Chaim most dreaded to behold: a shameless Jew who will say anything."

And what, I was frantically asking myself, is this overelaborated outpouring leading us on to? I could not fathom the subject here. Was this some shadowy bill of attainder condemning me for *my* language sins? What's any of it got to do with the missing money? His extravagant lamentation for this Chofetz Chaim was merely self-entertainment, brutishly spun out to pass the time until Uri arrived with *my lunch* and the real sadistic fun began—this was my best and most horrifying guess. Assaulted and battered by yet another tyrannical talker whose weapon of revenge is his unloosened mouth, somebody whose purposes lurk hidden, ready to spring, behind the foliage of tens of thousands of words—another unbridled performer, another coldly calculating actor, who, for all I knew, wasn't even crippled but only crashed about on a couple of crutches the better to enact his bitterness. This is the hater who *invented loshon hora*, the unshockable one, the unillusioned one, pretending to be shocked by the human disgrace, the misanthrope whose misanthropic delight is to claim loudly and tearfully that it's hatred he most hates. I am in the custody of a mocker who despises everything.

"It's said," Smilesburger resumed, "that only one law of *loshon hora* remained unclear to the Chofetz Chaim. Yes, a Jew could not, under any circumstances, defame and denigrate a fellow Jew, but was it also forbidden to say something damaging about, to denigrate and to belittle, oneself? About this the Chofetz Chaim remained uncertain for years. Only in his very old age did something happen that made up his mind for him on this troublesome point. Traveling away from Radin in a coach one day, he found himself seated beside another Jew, whom he soon engaged in a friendly conversation. He asked the Jew who he was and where he was going. With excitement the Jew told the old man that he was going to hear the Chofetz Chaim. The Jew did not know that the old man he was addressing happened to be the Chofetz Chaim himself and began to heap praise on the sage he was on his way to hear give a speech. The Chofetz Chaim listened quietly to this glorification of himself. Then he said to the Jew, 'He's really not such hot stuff, you know.' The Jew was stunned at what the old man had dared to say to him. 'Do you know who you are talking about? Do you realize what you are saying?' 'Yes,' replied the Chofetz Chaim, 'I realize very well what I am saying. I happen to know the Chofetz Chaim, and he really isn't all he's cracked up to be.' Back and forth went the conversation, the Chofetz Chaim repeating and elaborating his reservations about himself and the Jew growing angrier by the moment. At last the Jew couldn't stand this scandalous talk any longer and he slapped the old man's face. The coach by then had rolled up to its stop in the next town. The streets all around were jammed with followers of the Chofetz Chaim excitedly awaiting his arrival. He disembarked, a roar went up, and only then did the Jew in the coach understand whom he had slapped. Imagine the poor man's mortification. And imagine the impression that his mortification made on as loving and gentle a soul as the Chofetz Chaim. From that moment onward, the Chofetz Chaim decreed that a person must not utter *loshon hora* even about himself."

He had charmingly recounted the story, expertly, wittily, so very graceful in his speech despite his heavy accent, his tone mellifluous and quite spellbinding, as though with a treasured folktale he were coaxing a little grandchild to sleep. I wanted to say, "Why do you entertain me, in preparation for what? Why am I here? Who exactly are you? Who are these others? What is Pipik's place in all of this?" I suddenly wanted *so much* to speak—to shout for help, to cry out in distress, to demand from him some explanation—that I felt ready to jump not from the window but from my own skin. Yet by this time the wordlessness that had begun as something closely resembling hysterical aphonia had become the bedrock on which I was building my self-defense. Silence had settled in now like a tactic, albeit a tactic that even I recognized he—Uri—they—whoever—wouldn't have much trouble negating.

"Where is Uri now?" Smilesburger asked, looking down at his watch. "The man is half a man and half a panther. If on the way to the restaurant there is a pretty soldier girl . . . But this is the price you pay for a specimen like Uri. Again I apologize. It's days since you've eaten a nutritious meal. Someone else might not be so gracious about this terrible situation. Another man of your eminence reeling with hunger might not be so civil and restrained. Henry Kissinger would be screaming at the top of his lungs had he been made to wait alone in a stuffy room like this for the likes of a crippled old nobody like me. A Henry Kissinger would have got up and stormed out of here hours ago, would have hit the ceiling, and I wouldn't blame him. But you, your even temper, your self-possession, your cool head . . ." Hoisting himself up on his feet, he hobbled to the blackboard, where, with a stump of chalk he wrote in English, "YOU SHALL NOT HATE YOUR BROTHER IN YOUR HEART." Beneath that he wrote, "YOU SHALL NOT TAKE VENGEANCE OR BEAR ANY GRUDGE AGAINST THE CHILDREN OF YOUR PEOPLE." "But then maybe secretly," he said while he wrote, "you are amused and this explains your patient composure. You have one of those Jewish intellects that seize naturally on the comical side of things. Maybe everything is a joke to you. Is it? Is *he* a joke?" Having finished at the blackboard, he was gesturing to the TV screen, where the camera had momentarily focused on Demjanjuk as he scribbled a note for his defense attorney. "In the beginning he used to nudge Sheftel all the time. Sheftel must have told him, 'John, don't nudge me, write me notes,' so now he writes notes that Sheftel doesn't read. And why is his alibi so hopeless? Doesn't that surprise you? Why such a contradictory jumble of places and dates that any first-year law student could discredit? Demjanjuk's not intelligent but I thought at least he was cunning. You would think he would have got someone long ago at least to help him with the alibi. But then this would entail telling someone the truth, and that he *has* been too cunning for. I doubt if even the wife knows. The friends don't. The poor son doesn't. Your friend Mr. Ziad calls it a 'show trial.' Ten years of hearings in America by American immigration and the American courts. A trial in Jerusalem before three distinguished judges and under the scrutiny of the entire world press already going on for over a year. A trial where nearly two days are taken up with arguing over the paper clip on the identity card to establish if the paper clip is authentic or not. Mr. Ziad must be making a joke. So many jokes. Too many jokes. Do you know what it amuses some people to say? That it's a Jew who runs the PLO. That surrounded by a circle of henchmen as inept as he is, Arafat could not himself, without at least *some* Jewish assistance, administer a multinational racket with ten billion dollars in assets. People say that, if there is not a Jew to whom Arafat reports, there must be a Jew in charge of the money. Who but a Jew could rescue this organization from all the mismanagement and corruption? When the bottom fell out of the Lebanese pound, who but a Jew prevented the PLO from taking a bath at the Beirut banks? Who now manages the capital outlay for this rebellion that is their latest futile public-relations stunt? Look, *look* at Sheftel," he said, drawing my attention once again to the TV set. Demjanjuk's Israeli lawyer had just risen to raise an objection to some remark of the prosecutors. "When he was in law school here and the government had canceled Meyer Lansky's entry visa, Sheftel became chairman of Students for Meyer Lansky. Later he became Lansky's lawyer and *got* Lansky a visa to come. Sheftel calls this American Jewish gangster the most brilliant man he ever met. 'If Lansky had been in Treblinka,' Sheftel says, 'the Ukrainians and the Nazis wouldn't have lasted three months.' Does Sheftel believe Demjanjuk? That isn't the point. It's more that Sheftel can never believe the state. He would rather defend the accused war criminal and the renowned gangster than side with the Israeli establishment. But even this is still a very long way from a Jew who manages the PLO portfolio, let alone a Jew who makes them charitable contributions. Do you know what Demjanjuk said to Sheftel after the Jews had fired the Irishman O'Connor and put Sheftel in charge of the case? Demjanjuk told Sheftel, 'If I'd had a Jewish lawyer to begin with, I'd never be in this trouble now.' A joke? Apparently not. The man who sits accused of being Ivan the Terrible is reported to have said it: 'If only I'd had a Jewish lawyer. . . .' So I ask once again, is it necessarily a joke, and only a joke, that the sound investments in stocks, in bonds, in real estate, in motels and currency and radio stations that have given the PLO some financial independence from their Arab brothers are said to have been made for them by Jewish advisers? But just who *are* these Jews, if they really exist? What is their motive, if they really exist? Is this only stupid Arab propaganda, designed to try to embarrass the Jews, or is it true and truly embarrassing? I can more readily sympathize with the motives of a traitorous Jew like Mr. Vanunu, who gives to the British press our nuclear secrets, than the motives of a rich Jew who gives his money to the PLO. I wonder if even the Chofetz Chaim could find it in his heart to forgive a Jew so defiant of the Torah prohibition that tells us we must not take vengeance against the children of our people. What is the worst *loshon hora* compared to putting Jewish money in the pockets of Arab terrorists who machine-gun our youngsters while they play on the beaches? True, it is told to us by the Chofetz Chaim that the only money you can take with you when you die is what you spent here in charity— but charity to the PLO? That is surely not the way to amass treasures in Heaven. You shall not hate your brother in your heart, you shall not follow a multitude to do evil, and you shall not write checks to terrorists who kill Jews. I would like to know the names that are signed on those checks. I would like to have a chance to talk to these people and to ask what they think they are doing. But first I must find out if they truly exist other than in the hate-filled imagination of this mischievous friend of yours, so bursting with troublemaking tricks and lies. I never know whether George Ziad is completely crazy, completely devious, or completely both. But then this is the problem we have with the people in this region. Are there really in Athens rich Jews waiting to meet you who support our worst enemy, Jews ready to put their wealth at the disposal of those who have wished to destroy us from the moment that this country first drew breath? Suppose for the sake of argument that there are five of them. Suppose there are *ten* of them. How much can they contribute—a million apiece? Inconsequential beside what's given to Arafat every year by a single corrupt little Arabian sheikh. Is it worth tracking them down for a measly ten million? Can you just go around killing rich Jews because you don't like the people they give their money to? On the other hand, can you reason with them instead, people so poisoned with perversity to begin with? Probably it is best to forget about them and leave them to their everlasting shame. And yet I can't. I am obsessed by them, these seemingly responsible members of the community, these two-faced fifth-column Jews. All I want to do is to converse with one of them, if such a one exists, the way I am conversing with you. Am I misguided in my Jewish zeal? Am I being made a fool of by an Arab liar? The Chofetz Chaim reminds us, and I believe it, that 'the world rests on those who silence themselves during an argument.' But perhaps the world will not cave in immediately if you should dare now to say a few words. *Should* such Jews prey on my mind like this? What is your opinion? With all the work still to be done for the Jews of the Soviet Union, with all the problems of security that beset our tiny state, why devote one's precious energy to hunting down a few self-hating Jews in order to discover what makes them tick? About these Jews who defame the Jewish people, the Chofetz Chaim has told us everything anyway. They are driven by *loshon hora*, and like all who are driven by *loshon hora*, they will be punished in the world to come. And so why, in our world, should I pursue them? That is the first question I have for you. The second is this: If I do, can I count on Philip Roth to assist me?"

As though at last the cue had been uttered for which he'd been waiting, Uri entered the classroom.

"Lunch," said Smilesburger, smiling warmly.

The dishes were crammed onto a cafeteria tray. Uri set the tray beside the TV set, and Smilesburger invited me to pull up my chair and begin to eat.

The soup wasn't plastic, the bread was not cardboard, the potato was a potato and not a rock. Everything was what it was supposed to be. Nothing as clear as this lunch had happened to me in days.

It was only with the food passing into my gullet that I remembered I'd first seen Uri the day before. Two young men in jeans and sweatshirts who had looked to me to be produce workers had been identified by George Ziad as Israeli secret police. Uri was one of them. The other, I now realized, was the guy at the hotel who'd offered to blow me and Pipik. As for this classroom, I thought, they'd just borrowed it, maybe because they figured, not so stupidly, that it would be a particularly effective place to lock me in. They'd gone to the principal and said, "You were in the army, we know about you, we've read your file, you're a patriotic guy. Get everybody the fuck out of your school after one this afternoon. This afternoon the kids are off." And probably he never complained. In this country, the secret police get everything they want.

At the conclusion of my lunch, Smilesburger handed me, for the second time, the envelope with the million-dollar check. "You dropped this last night," he said, "on your way back from Ramallah."

———

Of the questions I asked Smilesburger that afternoon, the ones to which I could least believe I was being given a straight answer had to do with Moishe Pipik. Smilesburger claimed that they had no better idea than I did of where this double of mine had emerged from, of who he was or whom he might be working for—he certainly wasn't working for them. "The God of Chance delivered him," Smilesburger explained to me. "It is with intelligence agencies as it is with novelists —the God of Chance creates in us. First the fake one came along. Then the real one came along. Last the enterprising Ziad came along. From this we improvise."

"You're telling me that he's nothing but a crackpot con man."

"To you there must be more, to you this must be a singular occurrence rich with paranoidal meaning. But charlatans like him? The airlines offer them special rates. They spend their lives crisscrossing the globe. Yours took the morning flight to New York. He is back in America."

"You made no effort to stop him."

"To the contrary. Every effort was made to help him on his way."

"And the woman?"

"I know nothing about the woman. After last night, I would think that you know more than anyone does. The woman, I suppose, is one of those women for whom adventure with a crook is irresistible. Phallika, the Goddess of Male Desire. Am I mistaken?"

"They are both gone."

"Yes. We are down to just one of you, the one not a crackpot, not a charlatan, not a fool or a weakling either, the one who knows how to be silent, to be patient, to be cautious, how to remain unprovoked in the most unsettling circumstances. You have received high grades. All instincts excellent. Never mind how you quaked inside or even that you vomited—you did not shit yourself or take a wrong step. The God of Chance could not have presented a better Jew for the job."

But I was not taking the job. I had not been extricated from one implausible plot of someone else's devising to be intimidated into being an actor in yet another. The more Smilesburger explained about the intelligence operation for which he bore the code name "Smilesburger" and for which he proposed I volunteer, the more infuriated I became, not merely because his overbearing playfulness was no longer a bewildering puzzle that kept me stunned and on my guard, but because, once I had finally eaten something and begun to calm down, it registered on me just how cruelly misused I had been by these phenomenally high-handed Israelis playing an espionage game that seemed to me to have at the heart of it a fantasy forged in the misguided brain of no less a talent than Oliver North. My initial gratitude toward the putative captors who had been kind enough to feed me a piece of cold chicken after having forcibly abducted me and then held me prisoner here against my will so as to see how well I might hold up on a mission for *them*—the gratitude gave way, now that I felt liberated, to outrage. The magnitude of my indignation alarmed even me, yet I could do nothing to control the eruption once it had begun. And Uri's brutish, contemptuous stare—he'd returned with a Silex to pour me a fresh cup of coffee—enraged me still more, especially after Smilesburger told me that this subordinate of his who'd fetched my lunch had been following me everywhere. "The ambush out on the Ramallah road?" Uri, I learned, had been there for that, too. They had been running me like a rat through a maze without my knowledge or consent and, from everything I could gather, with no precise idea of what, if any, the payoff for them might be. Smilesburger had been operating on no more than a hunch, inspired by the presence in Jerusalem of Pipik—whom an informant had identified as an impostor only hours after he'd been ushered through immigration with the phony passport identifying him as me —and then by my arrival a week later. How could Smilesburger call himself professional if a coincidence so fraught with the potential for creative subterfuge had failed to ignite his curiosity? Surely a novelist could understand what it meant to be confronted with a situation so evocative. Yes, he was like a writer, a very lucky writer, he explained, warming sardonically to the comparison, who had fallen upon his own true subject in all its complex purity. That his art was aesthetically impure, a decidedly lesser form of contrivance owing to its gross utilitarian function, Smilesburger was willing to grant—but still the puzzle presented to him was exactly the writer's: there is the dense kernel, the compacted core, and how to set loose the chain reaction is the question that tantalizes, how to produce the illuminating explosion without, in the process, mutilating oneself. You do as the writer does, Smilesburger told me: you begin to speculate, and to speculate with any scope requires a principled disregard for the confining conventions, a gambler's taste for running a risk, a daring to tamper with the taboo, which, he added flatteringly, had always marked my own best work. His work too was guesswork, morally speaking. You try your luck, he told me. You make mistakes. You overdo and underdo and doggedly follow an imaginative line that yields nothing. Then something creeps in, an arguably stupid detail, a ridiculous gag, an embarrassingly bald ploy, and this opens out into the significant action that makes the mess an *operation,* rounded, pointed, structured, yet projecting the illusion of having been as spontaneously generated, as coincidental, untidy, and improbably probable, as life. "Who knows where Athens might lead? Go, for George Ziad, to Athens, and if you convincingly play your role there, then this meeting he dangled before you, the introduction, in Tunis, to Arafat, could well come to pass. Such things do happen. For you this would be a great adventure, and for us, of course, having you in Tunis would be no small achievement. I myself once spent a week with Arafat. Yasir is good for a laugh. He has a wonderful twinkle. He's a showman. Very, very demonstrative. In his outward behavior, he's a terrific charmer. You'd enjoy him."

In response I shook in his face the embarrassingly bald ploy itself, the ridiculous gag, the stupid detail that was his million-dollar check. "I am an American citizen," I said. "I am here on a journalistic assignment for an American newspaper. I am not a Jewish soldier of fortune. I am not a Jewish undercover agent. I am not a Jonathan Pollard, nor do I wish to assassinate Yasir Arafat. I am here to interview another writer. I am here to talk to him about his books. You have followed me and bugged me and baited me, you have physically manhandled me, psychologically abused me, maneuvered me about like your toy for whatever reason suited you, and now you have the audacity—"

Uri had taken a seat on the windowsill and was grinning at me while I unleashed all my contempt for these unforgivable excesses and the wanton indecency with which I had been so misused.

"You are free to leave," said Smilesburger.

"I am also free to bring an action. This is actionable," I told him, remembering all the good it had done me to make the same claim to Pipik at our first face-to-face encounter. "You have held me here for hours on end without giving me any idea of where I was or who you were or what might be going to happen to me. And all in behalf of some trivial scheme so ridiculous that I can hardly believe my ears when you associate it with the word 'intelligence.' These absurdities you concoct without the slightest regard for my rights or my privacy or my safety—this is intelligence?"

"Perhaps we were also protecting you."

"Who asked you to? On the Ramallah road you were protecting me? I could have been beaten to death out there. I could have been shot."

"Yet you were not even bruised."

"The experience was nonetheless most unpleasant."

"Uri will chauffeur you to the American Embassy, where you can lodge a complaint with your ambassador."

"Just call a taxi. I've had enough Uri."

"Do as he says," Smilesburger told Uri.

"And where am I? Where exactly?" I asked, after Uri had left the room. "What is this place?"

"It's not a prison, clearly. You haven't been chained to a pipe in a windowless room with a blindfold around your eyes and a gag in your mouth."

"Don't tell me how lucky I am that this isn't Beirut. Tell me something useful—tell me who this impostor is."

"You might do better to ask George Ziad. Perhaps you have been even more misused by your Palestinian friends than by me."

"Is this so? This is something you *know?*"

"Would you believe me if I said yes? I think you will have to gather your information from someone more trustworthy as I will have to gather mine with the assistance of someone a little less easily affronted. Ambassador Pickering will contact whom he sees fit to about my conduct, and, whatever the consequences, I will live with them as best I can. I cannot believe, however, that this has been an ordeal that will scar you forever. You may even be grateful someday for whatever my contribution may have been to the book that emerges. It may not be all that such a book might be if you chose to proceed a bit further with us, but then you know just how little adventure a talent like yours requires. And in the end no intelligence agency, however reckless, can rival a novelist's fantastical creations. You can get on now, without interference from all this crude reality, creating for yourself characters more meaningful than a simple thug like Uri or a tryingly facetious thug like me. Who is the impostor? Your novelist's imagination will come up with something far more seductive than whatever may be the ridiculous and trivial truth. Who is George Ziad, what is *his* game? He too will become a problem more complexly resonant than whatever the puerile truth may be. Reality. So banal, so foolish, so *incoherent*—such a baffling and disappointing nuisance. Not like being in that study in Connecticut, where the only thing that's real is you."

Uri poked his head into the room. "Taxi!"

"Good," said Smilesburger, flipping off the TV set. "Here begins your journey back to everything that is self-willed."

But could I be sure this taxi was going to turn out to be a taxi, when I was increasingly uncertain that these people had any affiliation whatsoever with Israeli intelligence? What proof *was* there? The profound illogic of it all—was *that* the proof? At the thought of that "taxi," I suddenly felt endangered more by leaving than by staying and listening for as long as it took to figure out the safest possible means of extricating myself.

"Who are you?" I asked. "Who assigned you to me?"

"Don't worry about that. Represent me in your book however you like. Do you prefer to romanticize me or to demonize me? Do you wish to heroize me or do you want instead to make jokes? Suit yourself."

"Suppose there *are* ten rich Jews who give their money to the Palestinians. Tell me why that is your business."

"Do you want to take the taxi to the American Embassy to lodge your complaint or do you want to continue to listen to someone you cannot believe? The taxi will not wait. For waiting you need a limousine."

"A limousine then."

"Do as he says," Smilesburger said to Uri.

"Cash or credit card?" Uri replied in perfect English, laughing loudly as he went off.

"Why does he stupidly laugh all the time?"

"This is how he pretends not to have a sense of humor. It's meant to frighten you. But you have held up admirably. You are doing wonderfully. Continue."

"These Jews who may or may not be contributing money to the PLO, why haven't they a perfect right to do with their money whatever they wish without interference from the likes of you?"

"Not only do they have a right as Jews, they have an inescapable moral duty as Jews, to make reparations to the Palestinians in whatever form they choose. What we have done to the Palestinians is wicked. We have displaced them and we have oppressed them. We have expelled them, beaten them, tortured them, and murdered them. The Jewish state, from the day of its inception, has been dedi-

cated to eliminating a Palestinian presence in historical Palestine and
expropriating the land of an indigenous people. The Palestinians have
been driven out, dispersed, and conquered by the Jews. To make a
Jewish state we have betrayed our history—we have done unto the
Palestinians what the Christians have done unto us: systematically
transformed them into the despised and subjugated Other, thereby
depriving them of their human status. Irrespective of terrorism or
terrorists or the political stupidity of Yasir Arafat, the fact is this: as a
people the Palestinians are totally innocent and as a people the Jews
are totally guilty. To me the horror is not that a handful of rich Jews
make large financial contributions to the PLO but that every last Jew
in the world does not have it in his heart to contribute as well."

"The line two minutes ago was somewhat at variance with this
one."

"You think I say these things cynically."

"You say everything cynically."

"I speak sincerely. They are innocent, we are guilty; they are right,
we are wrong; they are the violated, we the violators. I am a ruthless
man working in a ruthless job for a ruthless country and I am ruthless
knowingly and voluntarily. If someday there is a Palestinian victory
and if there is then a war-crimes trial here in Jerusalem, held, say, in
the very hall where they now try Mr. Demjanjuk, and if at this trial
there are not just big shots in the dock but minor functionaries like
me as well, I will have no defense to make for myself in the face of
the Palestinian accusation. Indeed, those Jews who contributed freely
to the PLO will be held up to me as people of conscience, as people
of *Jewish* conscience, who, despite every Jewish pressure to collabo-
rate in the oppression of the Palestinians, chose instead to remain at
one with the spiritual and moral heritage of their own long-suffering
people. My brutality will be measured against their righteousness and
I shall hang by my neck until I am dead. And what will I say to the
court, after I have been judged and found guilty by my enemy? Will I
invoke as my justification the millennial history of degrading, humiliating, terrifying, savage, murderous anti-Semitism? Will I repeat the
story of our claim on this land, the millennial history of Jewish settle-

ment here? Will I invoke the horrors of the Holocaust? Absolutely not. I don't justify myself in this way now and I will not stoop to doing it then. I will not plead the simple truth: 'I am a tribesman who stood with his tribe,' nor will I plead the complex truth: 'Born as a Jew where and when I was, I am, I always have been, whichever way I turn, condemned.' I will offer no stirring rhetoric when I am asked by the court to speak my last words but will tell my judges only this: 'I did what I did to you because I did what I did to you.' And if that is not the truth, it's as close as I know how to come to it. 'I do what I do because I do what I do.' And your last words to the judges? You will hide behind Aharon Appelfeld. You do it now and you will do it then. You will say, 'I did not approve of Sharon, I did not approve of Shamir, and my conscience was confused and troubled when I saw the suffering of my friend George Ziad and how this injustice had made him crazy with hatred.' You will say, 'I did not approve of Gush Emunim and I did not approve of the West Bank settlements, and the bombing of Beirut filled me with horror.' You will demonstrate in a thousand ways what a humane, compassionate fellow you are, and then they will ask you, 'But did you approve of Israel and the existence of Israel, did you approve of the imperialist, colonialist theft that *was* the state of Israel?' And that's when you will hide behind Appelfeld. And the Palestinians will hang you, too, as indeed they should. For what justification is Mr. Appelfeld from Csernowitz, Bukovina, for the theft from them of Haifa and Jaffa? They will hang you right alongside me, unless, of course, they mistake you for the other Philip Roth. If they take you for him, you will at least have a chance. For that Philip Roth, who campaigned for Europe's Jews to vacate the property they had stolen, to return to Europe and to the European Diaspora where they belonged, *that* Philip Roth was their friend, their ally, their Jewish hero. And that Philip Roth is your only hope. This man, your monster, is, in fact, your salvation—*the impostor is your innocence.* Pretend at your trial to be him and not yourself, trick them with all your wiles into believing you two are one and the same. Otherwise you will be judged a Jew just as hateful as Smilesburger. *More* hateful, for hiding from the truth the way you do."

"Limousine!" It was Uri back at the door of the classroom, the smiling muscleman, mockingly unantagonistic, a creature who clearly didn't share my rationalized conception of life. His was a presence I couldn't seem to adapt to, one of those powerfully packaged little five-footers who have organized just a bit too skillfully everything that's disparate and fluctuating in the rest of us. The eloquence of all that sinewy tissue unimpaired by intellect made me feel, despite the considerable advantage of my height, like a very small and helpless boy. Back when the battlers settled everything and anything that was in dispute, the whole male half of the human species must have looked more or less like Uri, beasts of prey camouflaged as men, men who didn't need to be drafted into armies and put through specialized training in order to learn how to kill.

"Go," said Smilesburger. "Go to Appelfeld. Go to New York. Go to Ramallah. Go to the American Embassy. You are free to indulge your virtue freely. Go to wherever you feel most blissfully unblamable. That is the delightful luxury of the utterly transformed American Jew. Enjoy it. You are that marvelous, unlikely, most magnificent phenomenon, the truly liberated Jew. The Jew who is not accountable. The Jew who finds the world perfectly to his liking. The *comfortable* Jew. The *happy* Jew. Go. Choose. Take. Have. You are the blessed Jew condemned to nothing, least of all to our historical struggle."

"No," I said, "not a hundred percent true. I am a happy Jew condemned to nothing who is condemned, however, from time to time to listen to superior Jewish windbags reveling in how they are condemned to everything. Is this show finally over? All rhetorical strategies exhausted? No means of persuasion left? What about turning loose your panther now that nothing else has shattered my nerves? He can tear open my throat, for a start!"

I was shouting.

Here the old cripple swung up onto his crutches and poled himself to the blackboard, where he half effaced with his open palm the scriptural admonitions he'd written there in English, while the Hebrew words that someone else had written he let stand untouched. "Class dismissed," he informed Uri and then, turning back to me, said, disappointedly, "Outraged *still* at having been 'abducted'?"—and at that moment he resembled almost exactly the sickly and vanquished old man, speaking a rather more meager and circumscribed English, whom he had impersonated at lunch the day before, blasted-looking suddenly, like someone bested by life long ago. But *I* hadn't bested him, that was for sure. Perhaps it had just been a very long day of thinking up ways of trapping rich Jews who weren't giving money to the UJA. "Mr. Roth Number One—use your good Jewish brain. How better to mislead your Palestinian admirers than to let them observe us forcibly abducting their treasured anti-Zionist celebrity Jew?"

With that, even I had heard enough, and after close to five hours as Smilesburger's captive I finally worked up the courage to leave through the door. I might be risking my life but I simply could not listen any longer to how nicely it fit in with their phantasmagoria to do with me whatever they liked.

And nobody did anything to stop me. Uri, happy-go-lucky Uri, pushed the door open all the way and then, clownishly standing at rigid attention like the lackey he was not, pressed himself against the wall to allow maximum passageway for my exit.

I was out in the foyer at the top of the landing when I heard Smilesburger call out, "You forgot something."

"Oh no I didn't," I called back, but Uri was already beside me, holding the little red book that I had been reading earlier to try to concentrate my forces.

"Beside your chair," Smilesburger answered, "you left one of Kling-hoffer's diaries."

I took the diary from Uri just as Smilesburger appeared in the classroom door. "We are lucky, for an embattled little country. There are many talented Jews like yourself out in our far-flung Diaspora. I myself happened to have had the privilege of recruiting the distinguished colleague of yours who created these diaries for us. It was a task that he came to enjoy. At first he declined—he said, 'Why not Roth? It's right up his alley.' But I told him, 'We have something else in mind for Mr. Roth.'"

EPILOGUE

Words
Generally
Only Spoil Things

I have elected to delete my final chapter, twelve thousand words describing the people I convened with in Athens, the circumstances that brought us together, and the subsequent expedition, to a second European capital, that developed out of that educational Athens weekend. Of this entir book, whose completed manuscript Smilesburger had asked to inspect, only the contents of chapter 11, "Operation Shylock," were deemed by him to contain information too seriously detrimental to his agency's interests and to the Israeli government to be published in English, let alone in some fifteen other languages. I was, of course, no more obliged to him, his agency, or the state of Israel to suppress those forty-odd pages than I was to submit the entire manuscript or any part of it for a prepublication reading. I had signed no statement beforehand promising to refrain from publishing anything about my mission or to seek clearance for publication from them, nor had this subject been discussed during the briefings that took place in Tel Aviv on the two days after my abduction. This was a potentially disruptive issue which neither party

had wished to raise, at least for the time being, my handlers because
they must have believed that it was not so much the good Jew in me
as the ambitious writer in me consenting, finally, to gather intelligence for them about "Jewish anti-Zionist elements threatening the
security of Israel" and I because I had concluded that the best way to
serve my professional interest was to act as though it were nothing
but the good Jew, rising to the call of duty, who was signing on as an
Israeli operative.

But why *did* I do it—given all the risks and uncertainties that
exceeded by far the dangers of the unknown that adhere to writing
—and enter into that reality where the brutal forces were in combat
and something serious was at stake? Under the enchantment of these
alluringly effervescent characters with their deluge of dangerous talk,
spinning inside the whirlpool of their contradictory views—and
without the least control over this narrative Ping-Pong in which I
appear as the little white ball—was I simply susceptible as never
before to a new intensification of the excitement? Had my arresting
walk through the wilderness of this world—the one that began with
Halcion, that Slough of Despond, and after the battle with Pipik, King
of the Bottomless Pit, concluded in the dungeon of the Giant Mossad
—germinated a new logic for my Jewish pilgrimage? Or, rather than
betraying my old nature, was I succumbing at long last to a basic law
of my existence, to the instinct for impersonation by which I had so
far enacted and energized my contradictions solely within the realm
of fiction? I really couldn't see what was behind what I was doing,
and that too may have accounted for why I was doing it: I was en-
livened by its imbecilic side—maybe *nothing* was behind it. To do
something *without* clarity, an inexplicable act, something unknow-
able even to oneself, to step outside responsibility and give way fully
to a very great curiosity, to be appropriated unresistingly by the
strangeness, by the dislocation of the unforeseen . . . No, I could not
name for myself what it was that drew me in or understand whether
what was impinging on this decision was absolutely everything or
absolutely nothing, and yet, lacking the professional's ideology to fire
my fanaticism—or fueled perhaps by the ideology of the profession-

ally unideological like myself—I undertook to give the most extreme performance of my life and seriously to mislead others in something more drastic than a mere book.

Smilesburger's private request that he have the opportunity, before publication, to read about whatever aspect of the operation I might "see fit to exploit someday for a best-selling book" was made some two and a half years before I even decided to embark on this nonfictional treatment rather than to plumb the idea in the context, say, of a Zuckerman sequel to *The Counterlife*. Since, once the job for him was completed, I never heard from Smilesburger again, it shouldn't have been difficult by the time I got around to finishing the eleventh chapter of *Operation Shylock* nearly five years later to pretend to have forgotten his request—irritatingly tendered, at our parting, with that trademark taunting facetiousness—or to simply disregard it and proceed, for good or bad, to publish the whole of this book as I had its predecessors: as an unconstrained writer independent of any interference from apprehensive outside parties eager to encroach on the text.

But when I'd come to the end of the manuscript, I found I had reasons of my own for wanting Smilesburger to take a look at it. For one thing, now that all those years had passed since I'd been of service to him, he might possibly be more forthcoming about the several key factors still mystifying me, particularly the question of Pipik's identity and his role in all of this, which I remained convinced was more fully documented in Smilesburger's files than in mine. He could also, if he was willing, correct whatever errors had crept into my depiction of the operation, and, if I could persuade him, he might even tell me a little something about his own history before he'd become Smilesburger for me. But mostly, I wanted him to confirm that what I was reporting as having happened had, in fact, taken place. I had extensive journal notes made at the time to authenticate my story; I had memories that had remained all but indelible; yet, odd as it may strike those who haven't spent a lifetime writing fiction, when I finished chapter 11 and sat down to reread the entire manuscript, I discovered myself strangely uncertain about the book's verisimilitude. It wasn't that, after the fact, I could no longer believe that the unlikely had befallen me as easily as it does anyone else; it was that three decades as a novelist had so accustomed me to *imagining* whatever obstructed my impeded protagonists—even where raw reality had provided the stimulus—that I began to half believe that even if I had not invented *Operation Shylock* outright, a novelist's instincts had grossly overdramatized it. I wanted Smilesburger to dispel my own vague dubiousness by corroborating that I was neither imperfectly remembering what had happened nor taking liberties that falsified the reality.

There was no one other than Smilesburger I could look to for this certification. Aharon had been there at lunch when a semidisguised Smilesburger dropped off his check, but he had otherwise witnessed nothing at first hand. A bit exuberantly, I had recounted to Aharon the details of my first meetings in Jerusalem with Pipik and Jinx, but I'd never told him anything more, and afterward I asked him as a friend to treat confidentially what I'd said and to repeat the stories to no one. I even wondered if, when Aharon came to read *Operation Shylock*, he might not be tempted to think that what he'd actually seen was all there was and that the rest was only a tale, an elaborately rounded out and coherent scenario I had invented as the setting for a tantalizingly suggestive experience that had amounted, in reality, to absolutely nothing, certainly to nothing coherent. I could easily imagine him believing this, because, as I've said, on first reading through the finished manuscript even I had begun to wonder if Pipik in Jerusalem could have been any more slippery than I was being in this book about him—a queer, destabilizing thought for anyone other than a novelist to have, a thought of the kind that, when carried far enough, gives rise to a very tenuous and even tortured moral existence.

Soon enough I found myself wondering if it might be *best* to present the book not as an autobiographical confession that any number of readers, both hostile *and* sympathetic, might feel impelled to challenge on the grounds of credibility, not as a story whose very *point* was its improbable reality, but—claiming myself to have imagined what had been munificently provided, free of charge, by superinventive actuality—as fiction, as a conscious dream contrivance, one whose latent content the author had devised as deliberately as he had the baldly manifest. I could even envision *Operation Shylock,* misleadingly presented as a novel, being understood by an ingenious few as a chronicle of the Halcion hallucination that, momentarily, even I, during one of the more astounding episodes in Jerusalem, almost supposed it might be.

Why not *forget* Smilesburger? Inasmuch, I told myself, as his existence is now, by my sovereign decree, no more real than is anything else earnestly attested to here, corroboration by him of the book's factual basis is no longer possible anyway. Publish the manuscript uncut, uncensored, as it stands, only inserting at the front of the book the standard disclaimer, and you will more than likely have neutralized whatever objections Smilesburger might have wished to raise had he been given access to the manuscript. You will also be sidestepping a confrontation with the Mossad that might not have been to your liking. And, best, you will have spontaneously performed on the body of your book the sacrosanct prank of artistic transubstantiation, the changed elements retaining the appearance of autobiography while acquiring the potentialities of the novel. Less than fifty familiar words is all it takes for all your problems to be solved.

This book is a work of fiction. Names, characters, places, and incidents either are products of the author's imagination or are used fictitiously. Any resemblance to actual events or locales or persons, living or dead, is entirely coincidental.

Yes, those three formulaic sentences placed at the front of the book and I'd not only satisfy Smilesburger but give it to Pipik once and for all. Just wait till that thief opens this book to find that I've stolen his act! No revenge could possibly be more sadistically apt! Providing, of course, that Pipik was alive and able to savor sufficiently—and to suffer painfully—how I had swallowed him whole. . . .

I had no idea what had become of Pipik, and my never having

heard from or about him again after those few days in Jerusalem made
me wonder if perhaps he had even died. Intermittently I tried to
convince myself, on the basis of no evidence other than his absence,
that he had indeed been felled by the cancer. I even developed a
scenario of the circumstances in which his life had ended that was
intended to parallel the flagrantly pathological course of what I surmised about how it had been lived. I pointedly set myself to working
up the kind of veiled homicidal daydream that occurs often enough
in angry people but that's generally too blatantly suffused by wishful
thinking to afford the assurance that I was groping for. I needed a
demise for him neither more nor less incredible than everything else
about the lie that he was, needed it so as to proceed *as if* I had been
delivered from his interference for good and it was safe to write
truthfully of what had happened, without my having to fear that
publishing my book would provoke a visitation a lot more terrible for
me than his aborted Jerusalem debut.

I came up with this. I imagined a letter from Jinx turning up in my
mailbox, written in a hand so minuscule that I could only decipher it
with the aid of the magnifying lens from my two-volume set of the
OED. The letter, some seven pages long, had the look of a document
smuggled out of a prison, while the calligraphy itself suggested the
art of the lacemaker or the microsurgeon. At first glance I found it
impossible to attribute this letter to a woman as robustly formed and
sensuously supple as Pipik's buxom Wanda Jane, who had claimed,
moreover, to be on such bad terms with the alphabet. How could this
exquisite stitching be her handiwork? It wasn't until I remembered
the hippie waif who'd found Jesus, the servile believer whose comfort
had come from telling herself, "I'm worthless, I'm nothing, God is
everything," that I could even begin to move beyond my initial incre-
dulity to query the likelihood of the narrative so peepingly revealed
there.

As it happened, there was nothing I read in that letter, extreme
though it was, that I couldn't bring myself to believe about *him.*
However, what made me more suspicious than even the handwriting
was the alarming confession, halfway through, that Wanda Jane made

about herself. It was simply too shocking to believe that the woman whom Smilesburger labeled "Phallika" in deference to her natural juiciness had performed the act of necrophilia that she reported almost as blithely as if she were remembering her first French kiss at the age of thirteen. His maniacal power over her couldn't possibly have been so grotesque as that. Surely what I was reading was a description not of something she had done but of something that he wanted me to think she had done, a fantasy specifically devised to inform his eternal rival of just how dazzlingly unbreakable a hammerlock he had on her life—intended, moreover, to so contaminate her memory for me as to render her eternally taboo. It was malicious pornography and could not have happened. What she had inscribed here, as though with the point of a pin, attesting to his hold on her and to her worshipful, ghoulish adoration of him, was what her dictator had dictated in the hope of keeping her and me from ever coupling again, not merely after his death but during his life, which —as I was forced to deduce from this quintessentially Pipikish ploy —had by no means come to its sorry end.

So he lived—he was back. Far from assuring me that he was gone, never again to return to plague me, this letter—admittedly, as perhaps only I would interpret it—proclaimed with his usual sadistic ingenuity the resurgence of Pipik's powers and the resumption of his role as my succubus. He and no one else had written this letter to plunge me back into that paranoiac no-man's-land where there is no demarcation between improbability and certainty and where the reality of what menaces you is all the more portentous for being inestimable and obscure. He had imagined her here as he would have her be: a ministering instrument serving him in extremis and, after his death, worshiping his virility in a most unimaginable way. I could even explain the unvarnished self-portrait he presented of a dying man perpetually on the verge of all-out insanity as the most conclusive evidence he could think to offer of the miraculous devotion he could inspire in her regardless of how fiendishly he might behave. No, it didn't surprise me that he would make not the slightest effort to conceal the depths of his untruthfulness or to disguise or soften in any way the vulgar, terrifying charlatan to whom she was enslaved. To the contrary, why should he not *exaggerate* his awfulness, misrepresent himself as even more monstrous than he was, if his intention was to frighten me off her forever?

And I *was* frightened. I had almost forgotten how readily I could be undone by the bold audacity of his lies until that letter arrived, ostensibly from Wanda Jane, asking me to believe that my all too indestructible nemesis was no more. What better measure of my dread of his reappearing than the masochistic perversity with which I quickly transformed the welcome news of his death into the confirmation of his continued existence? Why not take a cue instead from what had happened in Jerusalem and recognize in everything hyperbolical the most telling proof of the letter's authenticity? Of course she's telling the truth—there is nothing here at all inconsistent with what you already know of them, *least* of all what is most repugnant. And why go to the trouble even to imagine a letter like this if, instead of taking heart from the news of having outlasted him, instead of being fortified by your victory over him, you self-destructively build into the letter egregious ambiguities that you then exploit to undermine the very equanimity you are out to achieve?

Answer: Because what I have learned from what I've gone through with them—and with George, with Smilesburger, with Supposnik, with *all* of them—is that any letter less dismayingly ambiguous (or any more easily decipherable) that failed to belie itself in even the minutest way, any letter whose message inspired my wholehearted belief and purged, if only temporarily, the uncertainties most bedeviling to me, wouldn't convince me of anything other than the power over my imagination of that altogether human desire to be convinced by lies.

So here then is the substance of the letter I came up with to spur me on to tell the whole of this story, as I have, without the fear of being impeded by his reprisal. Someone else might have found a more effective way to quiet his own anxiety. But, Moishe Pipik's dissent notwithstanding, I am not someone else.

When it became apparent that Philip had probably less than a year to live, they had moved up from Mexico—where, in desperation, he had imprudently put his faith in a last-ditch course of drug therapy outlawed in the United States—and sublet a furnished little house in Hackensack, New Jersey, half an hour north of my hometown of Newark. That was another catastrophe, and six months later they had moved on to the Berkshires, only some forty miles north of where I have been living for the last twenty years. In a small farmhouse they rented on a remote dirt road halfway up a wooded mountainside, he set about, with his waning strength, to dictate into a tape recorder what was to have been his grand treatise on Diasporism, while Wanda Jane got work as an emergency-room nurse in a nearby hospital. And it was here that they found some respite at last from the melodrama that had forged their indissoluble union. Life became calm. Harmony was restored. Love was rekindled. A miracle.

Death came suddenly four months later, on Thursday, January 17, 1991, just hours after the first Iraqi Scud missiles exploded in residential Tel Aviv. Ever since he'd been working with the tapes, his physical degeneration had become all but imperceptible, and to Wanda it had seemed as though the cancer might once again have gone into remission, perhaps even as a consequence of the progress that he made each day on the book and that he talked about so hopefully each evening when she came home from the hospital to bathe him and make dinner. But when the pictures flashed over CNN of the wounded on stretchers being hurriedly carried from the badly damaged apartment buildings, he was beyond consoling. The shock of the bombardment made him cry like a child. It was too late now, he told her, for Diasporism to save the Jews. He could bear neither to witness the slaughter of Tel Aviv's Jews nor to contemplate the consequences of the nuclear counterattack that he was certain the Israelis would launch before dawn, and, brokenhearted, Philip died that night.

For two days, wearing her nightgown and watching CNN, Wanda remained beside the body in the bed. She comforted him with the news that no Israeli strike of any sort was going to be launched in retaliation; she told him about the Patriot missile installations, manned by American servicemen, protecting the Israelis against renewed attacks; she described to him the precautions that the Israelis were taking against the threat of Iraqi germ warfare—"They are not slaughtering Jews," she assured him, "they're going to be all right!" But no encouragement she was able to offer could bring him back to life. In the hope that it might resuscitate the rest of him, she made love to his penile implant. Oddly enough, it was the one bodily part, she wrote to me, "that looked alive and felt like him." She confessed without so much as a trace of shame that the erection that had out-lived him had given her solace for two days and two nights. "We fucked and we talked and we watched TV. It was like the good old days." And then she added, "Anybody who thinks that was wrong doesn't know what real love is. I was far nuttier as a little Catholic taking Communion than having sex with my dead Jew."

Her sole regret was having failed to relinquish him to the Jews to bury like a Jew within twenty-four hours of his death. *That* was wrong, sinfully wrong, particularly for him. But caring for Philip as if for her own sick little boy in the isolation of that quiet little moun-tainside house, she had fallen more deeply in love with him than ever before and as a result had been unable to let him go without reenact-ing, in that posthumous honeymoon, the passion and the intimacy of their "good old days." In her defense she could only say that once she understood—and she was herself so far gone that the realization had been awfully slow in coming—that no amount of sexual excite-ment could ever resurrect his corpse, she had acted with dispatch and had had him promptly buried, with traditional Jewish rites, in a local cemetery dating back to pre-Revolutionary Massachusetts. He had chosen the plot there himself. To be surrounded in death by all these old Yankee families, with their prototypical Yankee names, had seemed to him exactly as it should be for the man whose gravestone was to bear beneath *his* name the just, if forlorn, epithet "The Father of Diasporism."

His aversion to me—or was it to my shadow?—had apparently reached its maniacal crescendo some months earlier, when they were living in New Jersey. After Mexico, she wrote, he had decided they would make their home there while he set to work on *His Way,* the scandalous exposé of me whose writing had taken possession of him and whose publication as a full-length book was to reveal me to the public as a sham and a charlatan. They took pointless drives around blighted Newark, where he was determined to unearth "documentation" that would disclose how I was not at all the person I pretended to be. Sitting with him in their car across the street from the hospital where I was born, and where drug-dealers now congregated not two minutes away, she wept and begged him to come to his senses while he fulminated for hours about my lies. One morning, as they ate breakfast in the kitchen of their Hackensack house, he explained that he had restrained himself long enough and that, against the opponent I had revealed myself to be in Jerusalem, he could be bridled no longer by the rules of fair play. He had made up his mind to confront my aged father that very day with "the truth about his fraudulent son." "*What* truth?" she had cried. "*The* truth! That everything about him is a lie! That his success in life is based on a lie! That the role he plays in life is a lie! That misleading people about who he is is the only talent the little shit has! *He's* the fake, *that's* the irony—*he's the fucking double,* a dishonest impostor and fucking hypocritical fake, and I intend to tell the world, starting today with his stupid old man!" And when she then refused to drive him to my father's Elizabeth address (which he'd written on a piece of paper he'd kept in his wallet since their return from Mexico), he lunged at her with his fork, sharply stabbing the back of the hand that, just in the nick of time, she had thrown out to protect her eyes.

Now, not a day had passed since they'd moved to New Jersey—some days, not even an hour—when she had not plotted running away from him. But even when she looked down at the holes punched into her skin by the tines of his fork and at her blood seeping out of them, even then she could find neither the strength nor the weakness to abandon him to his illness and run for her life. Instead she began to scream at him that what was enraging him was the failure of the Mexican cure—the charlatan was the phony doctor in Mexico, all of whose claims had been filthy lies. At the root of his rage was the *cancer.* And that was when he told her that it was the writer who had *given* him the cancer—contending for three decades with the treachery of that writer was what had brought him, at only fifty-eight, face-to-face with death. And that was when even the self-sacrificing devotion of Nurse Possesski gave way and she announced that she could no longer live with someone who was out of his mind —she was leaving!

"For him!" he exclaimed in a triumphant voice, as though it were the cure for his cancer that she had finally revealed. "Leaving the one who loves you for that lying son of a bitch who fucks you every which way and then disappears!"

She said no, but of course it was true—the dream of being rescued was of being rescued by me; it was the very dream she'd enacted on the night she'd pushed Walesa's six-pointed star beneath the door of my hotel room in Arab Jerusalem and pleaded to be given refuge by the original whose existence so inflamed the duplicate.

"I'm going! I'm getting out of here, Philip, before something worse happens! I cannot live with a savage child!"

But when she rose from the breakfast table, at long last primed to break the bonds of this inexplicable martyrdom, he sobbed hysterically, "Oh, Mommy, I'm sorry," and tumbled to his knees on the kitchen floor. Pressing her bleeding hand against his mouth, he told her, "Forgive me—I promise I'll never stab you again!" And then this man who was all malaise, this unshameable, intemperate, conniving madman driven as recklessly by ungovernable compulsion as by meticulous, minute-by-minute miscalculation, this mutilated victim who was all incompleteness and deficiency, whose every scheme was a fiasco and against whose hyperbole she was, as always, undefended, began to lick the wound he had inflicted. Grunting with contrition, growling showily with remorse, he lapped thirstily away at her with his tongue as though the blood oozing out of this woman's veins were the very elixir for which he'd been searching to prolong the calamity that was his life.

Because by this time he didn't weigh much over a hundred pounds, it wasn't that difficult for someone with her strength to lift him off the floor and virtually carry him in her arms up the stairs to the bed.

And while she sat beside him there, holding his trembling hands in hers, he revealed where he really came from and who he really was, a story irreconcilable with everything he had told her before. She refused to believe him and, in her letter to me, would not repeat even one detail of the things to which he pleaded guilty. He had to have been delirious, she wrote, because, if he wasn't, then she would have had to have him either arrested or institutionalized. When, at last, there was nothing disgraceful that a man could do that was left for him to confess to, darkness had enveloped their street and it was time to feed him dinner with her throbbing bandaged hand. But first, using a sponge and a basin of warm water, she gently bathed him right there in the bed and, as she did every night, massaged his legs until he purred. What did it matter in the end who he was and what he had done, or who he thought he was and what he thought he had done or was capable of doing or was emboldened enough to have done or was ill enough to have imagined he had done or imagined he must have done to have made himself fatally ill? Pure or depraved, harmless or ruthless, would-be Jewish savior or thrill-seeking, duplicitous, perverted betrayer, he was suffering, and she was there to assuage that suffering as she had been from the start. This woman whom he had stabbed in the hand at breakfast (while aiming for her face) put him to sleep—without his even having to ask—with a sweetly milking, all-consuming blow job that blotted out all his words, or so she said, or so said whoever had told her what to say in that letter in order to warn me off ever writing a single sentence for publication about these coarse, barbaric irrationalists of mine, these two catastrophists sustained by their demonic conflict and the theatrical, maddening trivia of psychosis. Her letter's message to me was this: *Find your comedy elsewhere. You bow out, and we'll bow out. He'll be as good as dead. But dare to ridicule either one of us in a book, and we'll never leave you alone again. You have met your match in Pipik and Jinx, both of whom are alive and well.* And this message, of course, was the very antithesis of the assurance that the letter had been conceived to provide.

The morning after the reconciliation, everything that worked to drain away her courage started up once again, even though it seemed at first that the shock even to him of the savagery with that fork might have at last reined in his desperation. He addressed her, on that morning after, "in a soothing voice like yours," she wrote, a voice contained, modulated, expressive of all that she longed for and sometimes secretly dreamed of finding by taking the unthinkable revenge of fleeing to the sanctuary of me.

He informed her that they were leaving New Jersey. She was to go out to the backyard and burn in the barbecue pit the four first-draft chapters of *His Way.* That abhorrent obsession was over. They were going.

She was ecstatic—now she could stay on at her task of keeping him alive (as if, she admitted, she could ever have left him to die in agony by himself). Making a life with his namesake was a fairy tale anyway. I, as he'd reminded her, had wanted her "only for sex" while what he wanted from her, with all the scorching intensity that only the dying can feel, alone and resourceless on their island of fear, was "everything," she wrote, *"everything"* that she had in her to give to a patient.

They were leaving New Jersey to move to the Berkshires, where he would write the book on Diasporism that would be his legacy to the Jews.

Since dyslexic Wanda had never read a page I or any other novelist had written, it wasn't until they'd settled down in western Massachusetts that she learned it was where I'd located the home of the wearily heroic E. I. Lonoff, whose example of Flaubertian anchoritism confirms the highest literary ideals of writer-worshiping Nathan Zuckerman, the young novice of *The Ghost Writer.* However, if she could not understand how, having begun by stealing my identity, Pipik was now bent on further compounding the theft by turning into parody (*his* way) the self-obliterating dedication of the selfless Lonoff, she did know that I made my home less than an hour south, in Connecticut's northwestern hills. And the provocation my proximity was bound to be was enough to reawaken her dread, and with that, of course, the inextinguishable fantasies of breaking free that the edifying encounter with me had inspired. (I should never have found her irresistible, I thought. It didn't take a genius to foresee this.)

"Oh, darling," she cried, "forget him, I beg you. We'll burn *His Way* and forget he ever existed! You can't leave where he was born to go to live where he's living now! You can't keep following him like this! Our time together is too precious for that! Being anywhere near this man drives you nuts! You'll only fill up with poison again! Being there will just make you crazy again!"

"Being near him now can only make me sane," he told her, as senseless on the subject as ever. "Being near him can only make me strong. Being near him is the antidote—it's how I am going to beat this thing. Being near him is *the cure."*

"As far from him as we can!" she pleaded.

"As close to him as we can," he replied.

"Tempting fate!" she cried.

"Not at all," he answered. "See him if you want to."

"I didn't mean *me* and fate—I meant *you*. First you tell me he gave you the cancer, now you tell me he's the cure! But he has nothing to do with it *either way*. Forget him! Forgive him!"

"But I do forgive him. I forgive him for who he is, I forgive myself for who I am, I even forgive you for who you are. I repeat to you— see him if you wish. See him again, seduce him again—"

"I don't want to! You're my man, Philip, my only man! I wouldn't be here otherwise!"

"Did you say—did I hear you right? Did you actually say 'You're my Manson, Philip'?"

"My man! Man! You're my M-A-N!"

"No. You said 'Manson.' Why did you say Manson?"

"I did *not* say Manson."

"You said I was your Charles Manson, and I would like to know why."

"But I *didn't!*"

"Didn't what? Say Charles or say Manson? If you didn't say Charles but only Manson, did you mean merely to say man-son, did you only mean I was your infantile, helpless creep, your 'savage child,' as you told me yesterday, did you mean only to insult me like that again first thing today, or did you mean *what you meant*—that you live with me like those zombie girls who worshiped Manson's tattooed dick? *Do* I terrorize you like Charles Manson? Do I Svengali you and enslave you and scare you into submission—is that the reason you remain loyal to a man who is already half a corpse?"

"But *that's* what's doing this to you—death!"

"It's *you* who's doing this to me. *You said I was your Charles Manson!*"

And here she screamed, "You are! Yesterday! All those horrible, horrible stories! You are! *You're worse!*"

"I see," he replied in my soothing voice, the voice that only minutes earlier had awakened so much hope in her. "So this is what comes of the fork. You haven't forgiven me at all. You ask me to forgive him for his diabolical hatred of me, *and I do,* but *you* cannot find it in your heart to forgive four little pinpricks on the back of your hand. I tell horrible stories, horrible, *horrible* stories, and *you* believe me."

"I didn't believe you! I definitely did *not* believe you."

"So, you *don't* believe me. But you never believe me. I can't win, even with you. I tell you the truth and you *don't* believe me, I tell you lies and you *do* believe me—"

"Oh, death is doing this, *death*—this isn't you!"

"Oops—not me? Who then? Shall I guess? Can't you think for one single moment about anybody but him? Is looking at me and thinking of him what gets you through our awful life? Is that what you imagine in the bed, is that how you are able, without vomiting, to satisfy my repellent desires—by pretending you're in Jerusalem satisfying his? What's the stumbling block? That his is real and mine is fake? That he is healthy and I am sick? That I will die and disappear and he will live on forever through all those wonderful books?"

Later in the morning, while he was sleeping off that tirade in their bed, she did as he had instructed and, in the barbecue pit on the back lawn, destroyed the unfinished manuscript of *His Way.* She knew that even if he awakened he was far too depleted to haul himself over to the window to watch her, and so, before dumping the contents of his briefcase straight into the flames, she quickly looked to read what she could of his exposé of me. Only there was nothing there. All the pages were blank.

And so too were the tapes on which he'd claimed to have been recording his Diasporism book while she was off working her hospital shift during those last months of his life in the Berkshires. Six weeks after his death, though she still feared that hearing his disembodied voice might unleash those paroxysms of grief that had nearly killed her in the days after she'd relinquished his body to be buried by the Jews, she found herself one night yearning so for his presence that she had sat down with the tape recorder at the kitchen table and discovered that the tapes were blank as well. Alone in that remote little mountainside house, vainly listening for his voice on one tape after another, sitting all night and into the morning playing side after side and hearing absolutely nothing—and remembering too those mystifyingly empty pages that she had burned to cinders that awful morning in New Jersey—she understood, as people will often fully perceive the suffering of their loved ones only after they are gone, that I was the barrier to everything. He had not been lying about that. I was the obstacle to the fulfillment of his most altruistic dreams, choking off the torrent of all the potential originally his. At the end of his life, despite everything that he had been ordained to tell the Jews to prevent their destruction, the thought of my implacable hostility had impeded him from telling them anything, just as the menace of his Mansonish hatred (if I understood this letter correctly) was now supposed to stifle me.

Dear Jinx [I wrote],

    You have my sympathy. I don't know how you survived intact such a harrowing experience. Your stamina, patience, endurance, tolerance, loyalty, courage, forbearance, strength, compassion, your unwavering devotion while watching him struggle helplessly in the death grip of all those deep-buried devils that were tearing to pieces the last of his life—it's all no less astonishing than the ordeal itself. You must feel that you've awakened from a colossal nightmare even as you continue to grieve over your loss.

I'll never understand the excesses he was driven to by me—or by his mystique of me—all the while pleading the highest motives. Was it enchantment, that I cast a spell? It felt the other way round to me. Was it all about death and his struggle to elude it—to elude it as me, to be born again in me, to consign dying to me? I'd like to be able someday to understand what he was saving himself from. Though maybe to understand that is not my duty.

Recently I listened again to the so-called A-S.A. workout tape that found its way into my tape recorder back in my Jerusalem hotel. What was *that* chilling thought-stream about? This time round I wondered if maybe he wasn't Jewish at all but a pathological Gentile, stuck with the Jewish look and out to exact unbridled revenge on the whole vile subspecies as represented by me. Could that possibly be true? Of his entire arsenal of stupid stunts, that sham—if such it was—remains the most sinister, demented, and, alas, compelling . . . yes, aesthetically alluring to me in its repugnant, sickish, Céline-like way. (Céline was also unhinged, a genius French novelist and clamorous anti-Semite circa World War II whom I try hard to despise—and whose reckless books I teach to my students.) But what then to conclude? All I know for sure is that the dreadful wound that never healed preceded my appearance as a writer, I'm certain of that—I'm not, I can't be, the terrible original blow. All the dizzying energy, all the chaos and the frenzy behind the pointlessness of contending with me, points to something else.

That he was immobilized as an author is not my fault, either. The deathbed tapes were blank and all those pages empty for very good reasons other than fear of my blockading publication. It's writing that closes people off from writing. The power of the paranoid to project doesn't necessarily extend to the page, bursting though he may be with ideologies to save the imperiled and with exposés to unfrock the fakes. The inexhaustible access to falsification that fortifies paranoidal rage has nothing in common with the illusion that lifts a book free of the ground.

His Way was never his to write. *His Way* was what lay in his way, the crowning impossibility to the unrealizable task of bury-ing the shame of what shamed him most. Can you tell me what was so unbearably humiliating about whoever he originally was? Could what he began as have been any more scandalous or any less legitimate than what he became in the effort to escape it by becoming somebody else? The seeming paradox is that he could go so shamelessly overboard in the guise of me while, if my guess is right, he was all but annihilated by shame as himself. In this, actually, he came closer to the experience of authorship than he ever did thinking about writing those books and en-acted, albeit back to front, a strategy for clinging to sanity that wouldn't be unfamiliar to many novelists.

But is anything I'm saying of interest to you? Maybe all you want to know is if I want to get together again now that he's finally out of the way. I could take a drive up some afternoon. You could show me his grave. I wouldn't mind seeing it, despite the oddness of reading the name on his stone. I wouldn't mind seeing you, either. Your abundant forthcomingness left a strong impression. The temptation is enormous to mine you for every last bit of information you can supply about him, though that, admittedly, isn't the enticement that comes most pictorially to mind.

Well, I'd love to get together with you—yet I can't think of a worse idea for either one of us. He may have been resonant with fragments of my inner life but, as best I can figure it out, that wasn't the charge he carried for you. Rather, there was a ma-cabre, nothing-to-lose, staring-death-in-the-face kind of man-hood there, some macabre sense of freedom he had because he was dying—willing to take all kinds of risks and do anything because there's so little time left—that appeals to a certain type of woman, a macabre manliness that makes the woman roman-tically selfless. I understand the seduction, I think: something about the way he takes that leads you to give the way you give. But it's something about the frighteningly enticing way you give that leads me to wonder about what *you* take in exchange for the crazy burden. In short, you'll have to complete the recovery from anti-Semitism without me. I'm sure you'll find that, for a woman so willing to sacrifice herself so much, for a nurse with a body and soul like yours, with your hands, your health, your illness, there will be plenty of Jewish men around who will volunteer to help you on your way to loving our people as you should. But I'm too old for heavy work like that. It's already taken up enough of my life.

The most I can offer is this: what he couldn't write I'll ghost-write for him and publish under his name. I'll do my best to be no less paranoid than he would have been and to do everything I can to make people believe that it was written by him, his way, a treatise on Diasporism that he would have been proud of. "We could be partners," he told me, "copersonalities who work in tandem rather than stupidly divided in two." Well, so we shall be. "All you do," he protested, "is resist me." That's true. While he lived and raged I couldn't do otherwise. I had to surmount him. But in death I embrace him and see him for the achievement that he was—I'd be a very foolish writer, now that he's gone, not to be my impostor's creature and, in my workshop, partake of his treasure (by which I no longer mean you). Your other P.R. assures you that the impostor's voice will not be stifled by him (meaning me).

This letter remained unanswered.

———

It was only a week after I'd sent a copy of my final manuscript to his office that Smilesburger phoned from Kennedy Airport. He had received the book and read it. Should he come to Connecticut for us to talk it over, or would I prefer to meet in Manhattan? He was staying with his son and his daughter-in-law on the Upper West Side.

The moment I heard the resonating deep rumble of that Old Country voice—or rather, heard in response the note of respectful compliance in my own, disquieted though I was by his abrupt and irritating materialization—I realized how specious were my reasons for getting myself to do as he'd asked. What with the journals I'd kept and the imprint of the experience on my memory, it was transparently ridiculous to have convinced myself that I needed Smilesburger to corroborate my facts or to confirm the accuracy of what I'd written, as ridiculous as it was to believe that I had undertaken that operation for him solely to serve my own professional interests. I had done what I'd done because he had wanted me to do it; I'd obeyed him just as any other of his subordinates would have—I might as well have been Uri, and I couldn't explain to myself why.

Never in my life had I submitted a manuscript to any inspector anywhere for this sort of scrutiny. To do so ran counter to all the inclinations of one whose independence as a writer, whose *counter-suggestiveness* as a writer, was simply second nature and had contributed as much to his limitations and his miscalculations as to his durability. To be degenerating into an acquiescent Jewish boy pleasing his law-giving elders when, whether I liked it or not, I had myself acquired all the markings of a Jewish elder was more than a little regressive. Jews who found me guilty of the crime of "informing" had been calling for me to be "responsible" from the time I began publishing in my middle twenties, but my youthful scorn had been plentiful and so were my untested artistic convictions, and, though not as untrammeled by the assault as I pretended, I had been able to hold my ground. I hadn't chosen to be a writer, I announced, only to be told by others what was permissible to write. The writer redefined the permissible. *That* was the responsibility. Nothing need hide itself in fiction. And so on.

And yet there I was, more than twice the age of the redefining young writer who'd spontaneously taken "Stand Alone!" as his defiant credo, driving the hundred miles down to New York early the next morning to learn from Smilesburger what he wanted removed from my book. Nothing need hide itself in fiction but are there no limits where there's no disguise? The Mossad was going to tell me.

Why *am* I a sucker for him? Is it just what happens between two men, one being susceptible to the manipulations of the other who feels to him more powerful? Is his that brand of authoritative manhood that is able to persuade me to do its bidding? Or is there something in my sense of his worldliness that I just don't feel I measure up to, because he's swimming in the abrasive tragedies of life and I'm only swimming in art? Is there something in that big, tough—almost romantically tough—mind at work that I am intellectually vulnerable to and that makes me trust in his judgment more than in my own, something perhaps about his moving the pieces on the chessboard the way Jews always wished their fathers could so no one would pull those emblematic beards? There's something in Smilesburger that evokes not my real father but my *fantastic* one—that takes over, *that takes charge of me.* I vanquish the bogus Philip Roth and Smilesburger vanquishes the real one! I push against him, I argue against him, and always in the end I do what he wants—in the end I give in and do everything he says!

Well, not this time. This time the terms are mine.

Smilesburger had chosen as the site for our editorial meeting a Jewish food store on Amsterdam Avenue, specializing in smoked fish, that served breakfast and lunch on a dozen Formica-topped tables in a room adjacent to the bagel and bialy counter and that looked as though, years back, when someone got the bright idea to "modernize," the attempt at redecoration had been sensibly curtailed halfway through. The place reminded me of the humble street-level living quarters of some of my boyhood friends, whose parents would hurriedly eat their meals in a closet-sized storeroom just behind the shop to keep an eye on the register and the help. In Newark, back in the forties, we used to buy, for our household's special Sunday breakfasts, silky slices of precious lox, shining fat little chubs, chunks of pale, meaty carp and paprikaed sable, all double-wrapped in heavy wax paper, at a family-run store around the corner that looked and smelled pretty much as this one did—the tiled floor sprinkled with sawdust, the shelves stacked with fish canned in sauces and oils, up by the cash register a prodigious loaf of halvah soon to be sawed into crumbly slabs, and, wafting up from behind the showcase running the length of the serving counter, the bitter fragrance of vinegar, of onions, of whitefish and red herring, of everything pickled, peppered, salted, smoked, soaked, stewed, marinated, and dried, smells with a lineage that, like these stores themselves, more than likely led straight

back through the shtetl to the medieval ghetto and the nutrients of
those who lived frugally and could not afford to dine à la mode, the
diet of sailors and common folk, for whom the flavor of the ancient
preservatives was life. And the neighborhood delicatessen restaurants
where we extravagantly ate "out" as a treat once a month bore the
same stamp of provisional homeliness, that hallmark look of something that hadn't quite been transformed out of the eyesore it used to
be into the eyesore it aspired to become. Nothing distracted the eye,
the mind, or the ear from what was sitting on the plate. Satisfying folk
cuisine eaten in simple surroundings, on tables, to be sure, and without people spitting in their plates, but otherwise earthly sustenance
partaken in an environment just about as unsumptuous as a feasting
place can get, gourmandizing at its most commonplace, the other end
of the spectrum of Jewish culinary establishments from the commo-
diously chandeliered dining salon at Miami Beach's Fontainebleau.
Barley, eggs, onions, soups of cabbage, of beets, inexpensive everyday
dishes prepared in the old style and devoured happily, without much
fuss, off of bargain-basement crockery.

By now, of course, what was once the ordinary fare of the Jewish
masses had become an exotic stimulant for Upper West Siders two
and three generations removed from the great immigration and just
getting by as professionals in Manhattan on annual salaries that, a
century earlier, would have provided daily banquets all year long for
every last Jew in Galicia. I'd see these people—among them, sometimes, lawyers, journalists, or editors I knew—taking pleasure,
mouthful by mouthful, in their kasha varnishkas and their gefilte fish
(and riveted, all the while they unstintingly ate, to the pages of one,
two, or even three daily papers) on those occasions when I came
down to Manhattan from Connecticut and took an hour off from
whatever else I was doing to satisfy my own inextinguishable appetite
for the chopped-herring salad as it was unceremoniously served up
(*that* was the ceremony) at one of those very same tables, facing
onto the trucks, taxis, and fire engines streaming north, where Smilesburger had suggested that we meet for breakfast at ten a.m. to discuss
my book.

After shaking Smilesburger's hand and sitting down directly across from him and the coatrack against which his forearm crutches were leaning, I told him how I rarely came to New York without stopping off here for either a breakfast or a lunch, and he answered that he knew all about that. "My daughter-in-law spotted you a couple of times. She lives just around the corner."

"What does she do?"

"Art historian. Tenured professor."

"And your son?"

"International entrepreneur."

"And his name?"

"Definitely not 'Smilesburger,'" he said, smiling kindly. And then, with an open, appealing, spirited warmth that I was unprepared for from this master of derisive artifice and that, despite its disarming depth of realness, couldn't possibly have been purged of all his callous shrewdness, he carried me almost to the edge of gullibility by saying, "And so how are you, Philip? You had heart surgery. Your father died. I read *Patrimony*. Warmhearted but tough. You've been through the wringer. Yet you look wonderful. Younger even than when I saw you last."

"You too," I said.

He clapped his hands together with relish. "Retired," he replied. "Eighteen months ago, freed of it all, of everything vile and sinister. Deceptions. Disinformation. Fakery. 'Our revels now are ended,... melted into air, into thin air.'"

This was strange news in the light of why we were meeting, and I wondered if he wasn't simply attempting to gain his customary inquisitorial upper hand; here at the very outset, by misleading me once again, this time, for a change, by encouraging me to believe that my situation was in *no* way threatening and that I couldn't possibly be shanghaied into anything but a game of checkers by a happy-go-lucky senior citizen like him, a pensioner wittily quoting Prospero, wandless old Prospero, bereft of magical power and casting a gentle sunset glow over a career of godlike treachery. Of course, I told myself, there's no apartment just around the corner where he's stay-

ing with a daughter-in-law who'd spotted me eating here before; and
the chocolaty tan that had led to a dramatic improvement of his skin
condition and that gave an embalmed-looking glow of life to that
heavily lined, cadaverous face stemmed, more than likely, from a
round of ultraviolet therapy administered by a dermatologist rather
than from retirement to the Negev. But the story I got was that, in a
desert development community, he and his wife were now happily
gardening together only a mile down the road from where his daughter, her husband, and their three adolescent children had been living
since the son-in-law had moved his textile business to Beersheba. The
decision to fly to America to see me, and, while here, to spend a few
days with his two American grandchildren, had been made wholly on
his own. My manuscript had been forwarded to him from his old
office, where he hadn't set foot since his retirement; as far as he could
tell, no one had opened the sealed envelope and read the manuscript,
although it wouldn't be difficult for either of us, he said, to imagine
the response there if anyone had.

"Same as yours," I offered.

"No. Not so considered as mine."

"There's nothing I can do about that. And nothing they can do
about it."

"And, on your part, no responsibility."

"Look, I've been around this track as a writer before. My failed
'responsibility' has been the leitmotif of my career with the Jews. We
signed no contract. I made no promises. I performed a service for
you—I believe I performed it adequately."

"More than adequately. Your modesty is glaring. You performed it
expertly. It's one thing to be an extremist with your mouth. And even
that is risky for writers. To then go and do what you did—there was
nothing in your life to prepare you for this, nothing. I knew you could
think. I knew you could write. I knew you could do things in your
head. I didn't know you could do something as large in reality. I don't
imagine that you knew it either. Of course you feel proud of your
accomplishment. Of course you want to broadcast your daring to the
whole world. I would too if I were you."

When I looked up at the young waiter who was pouring coffee into our cups, I saw, as did Smilesburger, that he was either Indian or Pakistani.

After he moved off, having left behind our menus, Smilesburger asked, "Who will fall captive to whom in this city? The Indian to the Jew, the Jew to the Indian, or both to the Latino? Yesterday I made my way to Seventy-second Street. All along Broadway blacks eating bagels baked by Puerto Ricans, sold by Koreans. . . . You know the old joke about a Jewish restaurant like this one?"

"Do I? Probably."

"About the Chinese waiter in the Jewish restaurant. Who speaks perfect Yiddish."

"I was sufficiently entertained in Jerusalem with the Chofetz Chaim —you don't have to tell me Jewish jokes in New York. We're talking about my book. Nothing was said beforehand, not one word, about what I might or might not write afterward. You yourself drew my attention to the professional possibilities the operation offered. As an enticement, if you recall. 'I see quite a book coming out of this,' you told me. An even better book if I went on to Athens for you than if I didn't. And that was before the book had even entered my mind."

"Hard to believe," he responded mildly, "but if you say so."

"It was what you said that put it *into* my mind. And now that I've written that book you've changed your mind and decided that what would truly make it a better book, for your purposes if not mine, would be if I were to leave Athens out entirely."

"I haven't said that or anything like it."

"Mr. Smilesburger, there's no advantage to be gained by the old-geezer act."

"Well"—shrugging his shoulders, grinning, offering it for whatever an old geezer's opinion was worth—"if you fictionalized a little, well, no, I suppose it might not hurt."

"But it's not a book of fiction. And 'a little' fictionalization isn't what you're talking about. You want me to invent another operation entirely."

"I want?" he said. "I want only what is best for you."

The Indian waiter was back and waiting to take the order.

"What do you eat here?" Smilesburger asked me. "What do you like?" So insipid a man in retirement that he wouldn't dare order without my help.

"The chopped-herring salad on a lightly toasted onion bagel," I said to the waiter. "Tomato on the side. And bring me a glass of orange juice."

"Me too," said Smilesburger. "The same exactly."

"You are here," I said to Smilesburger, "to give me a hundred other ideas, just as good and just as true to life. You can find me a story even more wonderful than this one. Together we can come up with something even more exciting and interesting for my readers than what happened to have happened that weekend in Athens. Only I don't want something else. Is that clear?"

"Of course you don't. This is the richest material you have ever gotten firsthand. You couldn't be clearer or more disagreeable."

"Good," I said. "I went where I went, did what I did, met whom I met, saw what I saw, learned what I learned—and nothing that occurred in Athens, absolutely nothing, is interchangeable with something else. The implications of these events are intrinsic to these events and to none other."

"Makes sense."

"I didn't go looking for this job. This job came looking for me, and with a vengeance. I have adhered to every condition agreed on between us, including sending a copy of the manuscript to you well before publication. In fact, you're the first person to have read it. Nothing was forcing me to do this. I am back in America. I'm no longer recovering from that Halcion madness. This is the fourth book I've written since then. I'm myself again, solidly back on my own ground. Yet I did do it: you asked to see it, and you've seen it."

"And it was a good idea to show it. Better me now than someone less well disposed to you later."

"Yes? What are you trying to tell me? Will the Mossad put a contract out on me the way the Ayatollah did with Rushdie?"

"I can only tell you that this last chapter will not go unnoticed."

"Well, if anyone should come complaining to me, I'll direct them to your garden in the Negev."

"It won't help. They'll assume that, no matter what 'enticement' I offered back then, no matter how irresistible an adventure it may be for you to write about and to crow about, you should know by now how detrimental your publishing this could be to the interests of the state. They'll maintain that confidence was placed in your loyalty and that with this chapter you have betrayed that confidence."

"I am not now, nor was I ever, an employee of yours."

"Theirs."

"I was offered no compensation, and I asked for none."

"No more or less than Jews all around the world who volunteer their services where their expertise can make a difference. Diaspora Jews constitute a pool of foreign nationals such as no other intelligence agency in the world can call on for loyal service. This is an immeasurable asset. The security demands of this tiny state are so great that, without these Jews to help, it would be in a very bad way. People who do work of the kind you did find compensation not in financial payment and not in exploiting their knowledge elsewhere for personal gain but in fostering the security and welfare of the Jewish state. They find their compensation, *all of it*, in having fulfilled a Jewish duty."

"Well, I didn't see it that way then and I don't now."

Here our food arrived, and for the next few minutes, as we began to eat, Smilesburger pedantically discussed the ingredients of his late beloved mother's chopped herring with the young Indian waiter: her proportion of herring to vinegar, vinegar to sugar, chopped egg to chopped onion, etc. "This meets the highest specifications for chopped herring," he told him. To me he said, "You didn't give me a bum steer."

"Why would I?"

"Because I don't think you've come to like me as much as I've come to like you."

"I probably have," I replied. "As much exactly."

"At what point in the life of a negative cynic does this yearning for the flavors of innocent childhood reassert itself? And may I tell the joke, now that the sugared herring is running in your blood? A man comes into a Jewish restaurant like this one. He sits at a table and picks up the menu and he looks it over and decides what he's going to eat and when he looks up again there is the waiter and he's Chinese. The waiter says, '*Vos vilt ihr essen?*' In perfect Yiddish, the Chinese waiter asks him, 'What do you want to eat?' The customer is astonished but he goes ahead and orders and, with each course that arrives, the Chinese waiter says here is your this and I hope you enjoyed that, and all of it in perfect Yiddish. When the meal's over, the customer picks up the check and goes to the cash register, where the owner is sitting, exactly as that heavyset fellow in the apron is sitting at the register over there. In a funny accent much like my own, the owner says to the customer, 'Everything was all right? Everything was okay?' And the customer is ecstatic. 'It was perfect,' he tells him, 'everything was great. And the waiter—this is the most amazing thing —the waiter is Chinese and yet he speaks *absolutely perfect Yiddish.*' '*Shah,* shhh,' says the owner, 'not so loud—he thinks he's learning English.' "

I began to laugh, and he said, smiling, "Never heard that before?"

"You would think by now I'd have heard all the jokes there are about Jews and Chinese waiters, but no, not that one."

"And it's an old one."

"I never heard it."

I wondered while we ate in silence if there could be any truth in this man at all, if anything could exist more passionately in him than did the instinct for maneuver, contrivance, and manipulation. Pipik should have studied under him. Maybe he had.

"Tell me," I suddenly said. "Who hired Moishe Pipik? It's time I was told."

"That's paranoia asking, if I may say so, and not you—the organiz-ing preconception of the shallow mind faced with chaotic phenom-ena, the unthinking man's intellectual life, and the everyday occupational hazard of our work. It's a paranoid universe but don't overdo it. Who hired Pipik? Life hired Pipik. If all the intelligence agencies in the world were abolished overnight, there would still be Pipiks aplenty to complicate and wreck people's orderly lives. Self-employed, nonessential nudniks whose purpose is simply *balagan,* meaningless mayhem, a mess, are probably rooted more deeply in reality than are those who are only dedicated, as you and I are, to coherent, essential, and lofty goals. Let's not waste any more frenzied dreaming on the mystery of irrationality. It needs no explanation. There is something frighteningly absent from life. One gets from someone like your Moishe Pipik a faint idea of all that's missing. This revelation one must learn to endure without venerating it with fantasy. Let us move on. Let us be serious. Listen to me. I am here at my own expense. I am here, on my own, as a friend. I am here because of you. You may not feel responsible to me, but I happen to feel responsible to you. I *am* responsible to you. Jonathan Pollard will never forgive his handlers for abandoning him in his hour of need. When the FBI closed in on Pollard, Mr. Yagur and Mr. Eitan left him utterly on his own to fend for himself. So did Mr. Peres and Mr. Shamir. They did not, in Pollard's words, 'take the minimum precaution with my personal security,' and now Pollard is incarcerated for life in the worst maximum-security prison in America."

"The cases are somewhat dissimilar."

"And that's what I'm pointing out. I recruited you, perhaps even with a false enticement, and now I will do *everything* to prevent your exposing yourself to the difficulties that the publication of this last chapter could cause for a very long time to come."

"Be explicit."

"I can't be explicit, because I am no longer a member of the club. I only can tell you, from past experience, that when someone causes the kind of consternation that is going to be caused by publishing this chapter as it now stands, indifference is never the result. If anyone should think that you have jeopardized the security of a single agent, a single contact—"

"In short, I am being threatened by you."

"A retired functionary like me is in no position to threaten anyone. Don't mistake a warning for a threat. I came to New York because I couldn't possibly have communicated to you on the phone or through the mail the seriousness of your indiscretion. *Please* listen to me. In the Negev now, I have begun to catch up on my reading after many years. I started out by reading all of your books. Even the book about baseball, which, you have to understand, for someone of my background was a bit like reading *Finnegans Wake.*"

"You wanted to see if I was worth saving."

"No, I wanted to have a good time. And I did. I like you, Philip, whether you believe me or not. First through our work together and then through your books, I have come to have considerable respect for you. Even, quite unprofessionally, something like familial affection. You are a fine man, and I don't wish to see you being harmed by those who will want to discredit you and to smear your name or perhaps to do even worse."

"Well, you still give a beguiling performance, retired or not. You are a highly entertaining deceiver altogether. But I don't think that it's a sense of responsibility to me that's operating here. You have come on behalf of your people to intimidate me into shutting my mouth."

"I come quite on my own, at substantial personal expense actually, to ask you, for your own good, here at the end of this book, to do nothing more than you have been doing as a writer all your life. A little imagination, please—it won't kill you. To the contrary."

"If I were to do as you ask, the whole book would be specious. Calling fiction fact would undermine everything."

"Then call it fiction instead. Append a note: 'I made this up.' Then you will be guilty of betraying no one—not yourself, your readers, or those whom, so far, you have served faultlessly."

"Not possible. Not possible in any way."

"Here's a better suggestion, then. Instead of replacing it with something imaginary, do yourself the biggest favor of your life and just lop off the chapter entirely."

"Publish the book without its ending."

"Yes, incomplete, like me. Deformed can be effectual too, in its own unsightly way."

"Don't include what I went specifically to Athens to get."

"Why do you persist in maintaining that you undertook this operation as a writer only, when in your heart you know as well as I now do, having only recently enjoyed all your books, that you undertook and carried it out as a loyal Jew? Why are you so determined to deny the Jewish patriotism, you in whom I realize, from your writings, the Jew is lodged like nothing else except, perhaps, for the male libido? Why camouflage your Jewish motives like this, when you are in fact no less ideologically committed than your fellow patriot Jonathan Pollard was? I, like you, prefer never to do the obvious thing if I can help it, but continuing to pretend that you went to Athens only for the sake of your calling—is this really less compromising to your independence than admitting that you did it because you happen to be Jewish to the core? Being as Jewish as you are is your most secret vice. Any reader of your work knows that. As a Jew you went to Athens and as a Jew you will suppress this chapter. The Jews have suppressed plenty for you. Even you'll admit that."

"Yes? Have they? Suppressed what?"

"The very strong desire to pick up a stick and knock your teeth down your throat. Yet in forty years nobody's done it. Because they are Jews and you are a writer, they give you prizes and honorary degrees instead. Not exactly how his kind have rewarded Rushdie. Just who would you be without the Jews? *What* would you be without the Jews? All your writing you owe to them, including even that book about baseball and the wandering team without a home. Jewishness is the problem they have set for you—without the Jews driving you crazy with that problem there would be no writer at all. Show some gratitude. You're almost sixty—best to give while your hand is still warm. I remind you that tithing was once a widespread custom among the Jews as well as the Christians. One tenth of their earnings to support their religion. Can you not cede to the Jews, who have given you *everything,* one eleventh of this book? A mere one fiftieth, probably, of one percent of all the pages you have ever published, *thanks to them?* Cede to them chapter 11 and then go overboard and, whether it is true or not, call what remains a work of art. When the newspapers ask, tell them, 'Smilesburger? That blabbering cripple with the comical accent an Israeli intelligence officer? Figment of my fecund imagination. Moishe Pipik? Wanda Jane? Fooled you again. Could such walking dreams as those two have possibly crossed *any-one's* path? Hallucinatory projections, pure delirium—that's the book's whole point.' Say something to them along these lines and you will save yourself a lot of *tsuras.* I leave the exact wording to you."

"Yes, Pipik too? Are you finally answering me about who hired Pipik? Are you telling me that Pipik is a product of *your* fecund imagination? Why? Why? I cannot understand why. To get me to Israel? But I was already coming to Israel to see Aharon Appelfeld. To lure me into conversation with George? But I already knew George. To get me to the Demjanjuk trial? You had to know that I'm interested in those things and would have found it on my own. Why did you need him to get me involved? Because of Jinx? You could have gotten another Jinx. What is the reason from your side for constructing this creature? From the point of view of the Mossad, which is an intelligence operation, goal-oriented, *why did you produce this Pipik?*"

"And if I had a ready answer, could I in good conscience tell it to a writer with a mouth like yours? Accept my explanation and be done with Pipik, please. Pipik is not the product of Zionism. Pipik is not even the product of Diasporism. Pipik is the product of perhaps the most powerful of all the senseless influences on human affairs and that is *Pipikism,* the antitragic force that inconsequentializes every-thing—farcicalizes everything, trivializes everything, superficializes everything—our suffering as Jews not excluded. *Enough* about Pipik. I'm suggesting to you only how to give coherence to what you tell the newspapers. Keep it simple, they're only journalists. 'No excep-tions, fellas: hypothetical book from beginning to end.'"

"George Ziad included."

"George you don't have to worry about. Didn't his wife write to you? I would have thought, since you were such friends. . . . *Don't* you know? Then I have to shock you. Your PLO handler is dead."

"Is this so? Is *this* fact?"

"A horrible fact. Murdered in Ramallah. He was with his son. Five times he was stabbed by masked men. They didn't touch the boy. About a year ago. Michael and his mother are living again in Boston."

Free at last in Boston—and now never to be free—of fealty to the father's quest. One more accursed son. All the wasted passion that will now be Michael's dilemma for life! "But *why?*" I asked. "Murdered for what reason?"

"The Israelis say murdered as a collaborator by Palestinians. They murder one another like this every day. The Palestinians say murdered by Israelis—because Israelis are murderers."

"And what do you say?"

"I say everything. I say maybe he was a collaborator who was murdered for the Israelis by Palestinians who are also collaborators —and then maybe not. To you who have written this book, I say I don't know. I say the permutations are infinite in a situation like ours, where the object is to create an atmosphere in which no Arab can feel secure as to who is his enemy and who is his friend. *Nothing is secure.* This is the message to the Arab population in the territories. Of what is going on all around them, they should know very little and get everything wrong. And they do know very little and they do get everything wrong. And if this is the case with those who live there, then it follows that for someone like you, who lives *here*, you know even less and get even more wrong. That's why to describe your book, laid in Jerusalem, as a figment of your imagination might not be as misleading as you fear. It might be altogether accurate to call the *entire* five hundred and forty-seven pages hypothetical formulation. You think I'm such a deceiver, so let me now be cruelly blunt about his book to a writer whose work I otherwise admire. I am not qualified to judge writing in English, though the writing strikes me as excellent. But as for the content—well, in all candor, I read it and I laughed, and not only when I was supposed to. This is not a report of what happened, because, very simply, you haven't the slightest idea of what happened. You grasp almost nothing of the objective reality. Its meaning evades you completely. I cannot imagine a more inno-cent version of what was going on and what it signified. I won't go so far as to say that this is the reality as a ten-year-old might understand it. I prefer to think of it as subjectivism at its most extreme, a vision of things so specific to the mind of the observer that to publish it as anything *other* than fiction would be the biggest lie of all. Call it an artistic creation and you will only be calling it what it more or less is anyway."

We had finished eating a good twenty minutes earlier and the waiter had removed all the dishes except our coffee cups, which he'd already been back to refill several times. I had till then been oblivious to everything but the conversation and only now saw that customers were beginning to drift in for lunch and that among them were my friend Ted Solotaroff and his son Ivan, who were at a table up by the window and hadn't yet noticed me. Of course I'd known that I wasn't meeting Smilesburger in the subterranean parking garage where Woodward and Bernstein used to go to commune with Deep Throat, but still, at the sudden sight of someone here I knew, my heart thumped and I felt like a married man who, spotted at a restaurant in ardent conversation with an illicit lover, quickly begins to calculate how best to introduce her.

"Your contradictions," I said softly to Smilesburger, "don't add up to a convincing argument, but then, with me, you don't believe you need any argument. You're counting on my secret vice to prevail. The rest is an entertainment, amusing rhetoric, words as bamboozle-ment, your technique here as it was there. Do you even bother to keep track of your barrage? On the one hand, with this book—the whole of it now, not merely the final chapter—I am, in your certifi-ably *un*paranoid view, serving up to the enemy information that could jeopardize the security of your agents and their contacts, infor-mation that, from the sound of it, could lay the state of Israel open to God only knows what kind of disaster and compromise the welfare and security of the Jewish people for centuries to come. On the other hand, the book presents such a warped and ignorant misrepresenta-tion of objective reality that to save my literary reputation and pro-tect myself against the ridicule of all the clear-eyed empiricists, or from punishments that you intimate might be far, far worse, I ought to recognize this thing for what it is and publish *Operation Shylock* as—as what? Subtitled 'A Fable'?"

"Excellent idea. A subjectivist fable. That solves everything."

"Except the problem of accuracy."

"But how could you know that?"

"You mean chained to the wall of my subjectivity and seeing only my shadow? Look, this is all nonsense." I raised my arm to signal to the waiter for our check and unintentionally caught Ivan Solotaroff's eye as well. I'd known Ivan since he was an infant back in Chicago in the mid-fifties, when the late George Ziad was there studying Dostoyevsky and Kierkegaard and Ivan's father and I were bristling graduate students teaching freshman composition together at the university. Ivan waved back, pointed out to Ted where I was sitting, and Ted turned and gave a shrug that indicated there could be no place on earth more appropriate than here for us to have run into each other after all our months of trying in vain to arrange to get together for a meal. I realized then the unequivocal way in which to introduce Smilesburger, and this made my heart thump again, only now in triumph.

"Let's cut it short," I said to Smilesburger when the check was placed on the table. "I cannot know things-in-themselves, but you can. I cannot transcend myself, but you can. I cannot exist apart from myself, but you can. I know nothing beyond my own existence and my own ideas, my mind determines entirely how reality appears to me, but for you the mind works differently. You know the world as it really is, and I know it only as it appears. Your argument is kiddie philosophy and dime-store psychology and is too absurd even to oppose."

"You refuse absolutely."

"Of course I do."

"You'll neither describe your book as what it is not nor censor out what they're sure not to like."

"How could I?"

"And if I were to rise above kiddie philosophy and dime-store psychology and invoke the wisdom of the Chofetz Chaim? 'Grant me that I should say nothing unnecessary. . . .' Would I be wasting my breath if, as a final plea, I reminded you of the laws of *loshon hora?*"

"It would not even help to quote Scripture."

"Everything must be undertaken alone, out of personal conviction. You're that sure of yourself. You're that convinced that only you are right."

"On this matter? Why not?"

"And the consequences of proceeding uncompromisingly, independent of every judgment but your own—to these consequences you are indifferent?"

"Don't I have to be?"

"Well," he said, while I snapped up the check before he could take it and compromisingly charge breakfast to the Mossad, "then that's that. Too bad."

Here he turned to the crutches that were balanced behind him on the coatrack. I came around to assist him to his feet, but he was already standing. The disappointment in his face, when his eyes engaged mine, looked as though it couldn't possibly have been manufactured to deceive. And must there not be a point, even in him, where manipulation stops? It caused a soundless but not inconsiderable emotional upheaval in me to think that he might actually have shed his disguises and come here out of a genuine concern for my welfare, determined to spare me any further misfortune. But even if that was so, was it any reason to cave in and voluntarily give them a pound of my flesh?

"You've come a long way from that broken man whom you describe as yourself in the first chapter of this book." He had somehow gathered up his attaché case along with the crutches and clutched the handle round with what I noticed, for the very first time, were the powerful, tiny, tufted fingers of a primate somewhat down the scale from man, something that could swing through a jungle by its prehensile tail in the time that it would take Smilesburger to get from our table to the street. I assumed that in the attaché case was my manuscript. "All that uncertainty, all that fear and discomposure—it all seems safely behind you now. You are impermeable," he said. "Mazel tov."

"For now," I replied, "for now. Nothing is secure. Man the pillar of instability. Isn't that the message? The unsureness of everything."

"The message of your book? I wouldn't say so. It's a happy book, as I read it. Happiness radiates from it. There are all kinds of ordeals and trials but it's about someone who is recovering. There's so much élan and energy in his encounters with the people he meets along the way that anytime he feels his recovery is slipping and that thing is coming over him again, why, he rights himself and comes through unscathed. It's a comedy in the classic sense. He comes through it *all* unscathed."

"Only up to this point, however."

"That too is true," said Smilesburger, nodding sadly.

"But what I meant by 'the unsureness of everything' was the message of *your* work. I meant the inculcation of pervasive uncertainty."

"That? But that's a permanent, irrevocable crisis that comes with living, wouldn't you say?"

This is the Jewish handler who handles me. I could have done worse, I thought. Pollard did. Yes, Smilesburger is my kind of Jew, he is what "Jew" *is* to me, the best of it to me. Worldly negativity. Seductive verbosity. Intellectual venery. The hatred. The lying. The distrust. The this-worldliness. The truthfulness. The intelligence. The malice. The comedy. The endurance. The acting. The injury. The impairment.

I followed behind him until I saw Ted rise to say hello. "Mr. Smilesburger," I said, "one minute. I want you to meet Mr. Solotaroff, the editor and writer. And this is Ivan Solotaroff. Ivan's a journalist. Mr. Smilesburger pretends to be a gardener in the desert these days, fulfilling the commandments of our Lord. In fact, he's an Israeli spymaster, the very handler who handles me. If there is an inmost room in Israel where somebody is able to say, 'Here lies our advantage,' then it's the joy of the Smilesburgers to obtain it. Israel's enemies would tell you that he is, institutionally, simply the sharp end of national and patriotic and ethnic psychosis. I would say, from my experience, that if there is such a thing in that frenetic state as a central will, it appears to me to be invested in him. He is, to be sure, as befits his occupation, also an enigma. Is he, for instance, assing around on these crutches? Is he actually a great athlete? This too

could be. At any rate, he has treated me to some wonderfully confusing adventures, which you will soon be reading about in my book."

Smiling almost sheepishly, Smilesburger shook hands first with the
father and then with the son.

"Spying for Jews?" Ivan asked me, amused. "I thought you made a
living spying *on* them."

"A distinction, in this case, without a difference—and a source of
contention between Mr. Smilesburger and me."

"Your friend," said Smilesburger to Ted, "is impatient to construct
his own disaster. Has he always been in this hurry to overdo things?"

"Ted, I'll call you," I said, even while Ted stood towering above
Smilesburger, puzzling over what sort of connection we might have
other than the one I had so deliberately and loquaciously delineated.
"Ivan, good to see you. So long!"

Softly Ted said to Smilesburger, "Take care now," and together my
handler and I made our way to the register, where I paid the bill, and
then we were out of the store and into the street.

On the corner of West Eighty-sixth Street, only a few feet from the
steps of a church where a destitute black couple slept beneath a filthy
blanket as the midday traffic rolled noisily by, Smilesburger offered
me his attaché case and asked me to open it for him. I found inside
the photocopied pages of the original eleven chapters of this book,
still in the large manila envelope in which I'd initially mailed them to
him, and beneath that, a second, smaller envelope, thick and oblong,
just about the size and shape of a brick, my name written boldly
across the face of it.

"What's this?" I asked. But I had only to heft the envelope in my
hand to realize what it contained. "Whose idea is this?"

"Not mine."

"How much is in here?"

"I don't know. I would think quite a lot."

I had a violent urge to heave the envelope as far as I could out into
the street, but then I saw the shopping cart crammed with all the
worldly goods belonging to the black couple on the steps of the
church and thought to just go over and drop it in there. "Three

thousand ducats," I said to Smilesburger, repeating aloud for the first time since Athens the identifying code words that I'd been given to use by him before leaving on the mission purportedly for George.

"However much it is," he said, "it's yours."

"For what? For services already rendered or for what I'm now being advised to do?"

"I found it in my briefcase when I got off the plane. Nobody has told me anything. I opened the briefcase on the way in from Kennedy. There it was."

"Oh, for Christ's sake!" I shouted at him. "This is what they did to Pollard—shtupped the poor schnuk with money until he was compromised up to his ears!"

"Philip, I don't want what doesn't belong to me. I don't wish to be accused of stealing what isn't mine. I ask you please to take this off my hands before I am the one who is compromised in the middle of an affair where I no longer play any role. Look, you never put in for your Athens expenses. You charged the hotel to American Express and even got stuck with a big restaurant bill. Here. To cover the costs you incurred spying at the fountainhead of Western civilization."

"I was thinking, just before, that I could have done much worse than you," I said. "Now it's hard to imagine how." I held the envelope containing my manuscript under my arm while placing the envelope full of money back in the attaché case. "Here," I said, snapping the case shut and offering it to Smilesburger, but he held tightly to his crutches, refusing to accept it back. "All right," I said and, seeing that the woman who'd been sleeping beside her companion on the church steps was awake now and cautiously watching the two of us, I set the case down on the pavement before Smilesburger's feet. "The Mossad Fund for Homeless Non-Jews."

"No jokes, please—pick up the case," he said, "and take it. You don't know what could be in store for you otherwise. Take the money and do what they want. Ruining reputations is no less serious an intelligence operation than destroying nuclear reactors. When they are out to silence a voice they don't like, they know how to accomplish it without the blundering of our Islamic brothers. They don't issue a stupid, barbaric *fatwa* that makes a martyred hero out of the author of a book that nobody can read—they quietly go to work on the reputation instead. And I don't mean halfheartedly, as they did in the past with you, turning loose the intellectual stooges at their magazine. I mean hardball—*loshon hora*: the whispering campaign that cannot be stopped, rumors that it's impossible to quash, besmirchment from which you will never be cleansed, slanderous stories to belittle your professional qualifications, derisive reports of your business deceptions and your perverse aberrations, outraged polemics denouncing your moral failings, misdeeds, and faulty character traits —your shallowness, your vulgarity, your cowardice, your avarice, your indecency, your falseness, your selfishness, your treachery. Derogatory information. Defamatory statements. Insulting witticisms. Disparaging anecdotes. Idle mockery. Bitchy chatter. Malicious absurdities. Galling wisecracks. Fantastic lies. *Loshon hora* of such spectacular dimensions that it is guaranteed not only to bring on fear, distress, disease, spiritual isolation, and financial loss but to significantly shorten a life. They will make a shambles of the position that you have worked nearly sixty years to achieve. No area of your life will go uncontaminated. And if you think this is an exaggeration you really *are* deficient in a sense of reality. Nobody can ever say of a secret service, 'That's something they don't do.' Knowledge is too dispersed for that conclusion to be drawn. They can only say, 'Within my experience, it wasn't done. And beyond that again, there's always a first time.' Philip, remember what happened to your friend Kosinski! The Chofetz Chaim wasn't just whistling Dixie: there is no verbal excess, no angry word, no evil speech that is unutterable to a Jew with an unguarded tongue. You are *not* Jonathan Pollard—you are being neither abandoned nor disowned. Instead you are being given the benefit of a lifetime's experience by someone who has developed the highest regard for you and cannot sit by and watch you destroyed. The consequences of what you've written are simply beyond calculation. I fear for you. Name a raw nerve and you recruit it. It is not a quiet book you've written—it is a *suicidal* book, even within the extremely Jewish stance you assume. Take the money, please. I beg you. I beg you. Otherwise the misery you suffered from Moishe Pipik will seem like a drop in the bucket of humiliation and shame. They will turn you into a walking joke beside which Moishe Pipik will look like Elie Wiesel, speaking words that are only holy and pure. You'll *yearn* for the indignities of a double like Pipik; when they get done desecrating you and your name, Pipik will seem the personification of modesty, dignity, and the passion for truth. Lead them not into temptation, because their creativity knows no bounds when the job is to assassinate the character even of a *tzaddik* like you. A righteous person, a man of moral rectitude, that is what I have come to understand you to be—and against the disgrace of such a person it is my human obligation to cry out! Philip, pick up the attaché case, take it home, and put the money in your mattress. Nobody will ever know."

"And in return?"

"Let your Jewish conscience be your guide."

Note to the Reader

This book is a work of fiction. The formal conversational exchange with Aharon Appelfeld quoted in chapters 3 and 4 first appeared in *The New York Times* on March 11, 1988; the verbatim minutes of the January 27, 1988, morning session of the trial of John Demjanjuk in Jerusalem District Court provided the courtroom exchanges quoted in chapter 9. Otherwise the names, characters, places, and incidents either are products of the author's imagination or are used fictitiously. Any resemblance to actual events or locales or persons, living or dead, is entirely coincidental. This confession is false.

penguin.co.uk/vintage